The Unthinkable Triangle

Joana Starnes

BY THE SAME AUTHOR:

FROM THIS DAY FORWARD
~ *The Darcys of Pemberley* ~

THE SUBSEQUENT PROPOSAL
~ *A Tale of Pride, Prejudice & Persuasion* ~

THE SECOND CHANCE
~ *A 'Pride & Prejudice' ~ 'Sense & Sensibility' Variation* ~

THE FALMOUTH CONNECTION
~ *A 'Pride & Prejudice' Variation* ~

MISS DARCY'S COMPANION
~ *A 'Pride & Prejudice' Variation*

MR BENNET'S DUTIFUL DAUGHTER
~ *A 'Pride & Prejudice' Variation*

Copyright © 2015 by Joana Starnes

Cover design: © 2015 Joana Starnes
Insets: public domain artwork
Ornamental vectors designed by Freepik

ISBN: 978-1514337554
ISBN-10: 151433755X

⁕

What greater torment is there
for a steadfast heart
than being torn
between
Loyalty and Love?

⁕

New Characters

*In addition to well-known and much-loved characters, there are a few others.
Most of them are incidental to the story and are listed below only as a memory aid.*

Earl of Langthorne, Lady Langthorne: *Colonel Fitzwilliam's parents*

Lord Morton: *Colonel Fitzwilliam's eldest brother*

Harriet, Lady Lytham: *Colonel Fitzwilliam's married sister*

Mr Henry Fitzwilliam: *Colonel Fitzwilliam's youngest brother*

Lady Emily Fitzwilliam: *Colonel Fitzwilliam's youngest sister*

Mr Weston: *Mr Darcy's valet*

Peter, Thomas, Simon: *Mr Darcy's footmen*

Dr Graham: *Mr Darcy's physician*

Miss Wyatt, Miss Grantley, Miss Hewitt, Miss Morley:
Miss Darcy's acquaintances in town

Captain Wilson, Captain Henshaw, Major Sir Henry Vernon-Rees:
Some of Colonel Fitzwilliam's fellow officers

Doña Teresa Patricia de Mendoza y Aguilar:
Major Sir Henry Vernon-Rees's most particular acquaintance

Mr Thomas Metcalfe: *A gentleman with connections in Kent*

Monsieur Dupont: *Miss Darcy's dancing master*

⁓⊙⊙⁓

Note: All historical references to the Peninsular Campaign are from
Sir Arthur Bryant's *'Years of Victory 1802-1812'* and *'The Age of Elegance 1812-1822'*

Chapter 1

The playful staccato of the piece dripped from her nimble fingers, as joyous and lively as her delightful person, and Darcy settled into the showy yet uncomfortable sofa to enjoy it better.

He was not allowed to. His aunt's decisive tones broke the magic, just as they always did.

"Miss Bennet plays tolerably well, but her taste does not equal Anne's. Anne would have performed delightfully, if her health had allowed her to apply."

Darcy pursed his lips, lest an ill-advised comment escape him, little as he cared for the untoward pronouncement.

"And so would I," Lady Catherine continued. "If I had ever learnt, I should have been a great proficient. There are few people in England, I suppose, who have more true enjoyment of music than myself, or a better natural taste."

'*And if I had ever learnt, I would have surpassed Mozart,*' Darcy inwardly scoffed and, out of patience with his aunt and her farfetched, arrogant assertions, he left his seat and made his way towards the pianoforte, where *she* sat, still doing full justice to the most uplifting piece he had ever been privileged to hear.

Fitzwilliam was at her side, timely turning the pages – no mean feat, for such a fast-paced tune. His cousin said something that Darcy could not catch, but he wished Fitzwilliam had more sense than to distract her and expose her to Lady Catherine's snide comments if she faltered.

She did not. With uncommon skill, comparable only to Georgiana's, she drifted from the lively piece into another, which she could seemingly play without the benefit of music sheets. A milder, slower one she must have known quite well and which allowed her to engage in conversation, without the need to follow demanding scores full of fast-flowing notes.

Fitzwilliam replied — some other comment delivered *sotto voce*. Knowing him, it must have been some thinly-veiled reflection on present circumstances and overbearing company. She appeared to take it in good cheer but would not allow herself to be dragged further into it, by all accounts more attuned than his cousin to what was civil and proper and due their host, regardless of how ill the host chose to deport herself. And then Fitzwilliam said something else, a passing comment on her skill, it sounded like, now that Darcy had slowly ambled closer. More suitable, that, and he heard her thank his cousin, then elaborate on the fact that she and any of her sisters who had showed an inclination were encouraged to learn and were provided with all the masters they required.

Fitzwilliam laughingly observed that any such kindness was thoroughly wasted on himself and most of his siblings.

For the first time in living memory, Darcy found himself wishing for his cousin's ease in company or, dash it, even Bingley's. Fitzwilliam was chatting to her now, as unperturbed as he would be with his own sisters or with Georgiana — a feat which, to his frustration, Darcy could not equal.

And yet, despite his cousin's natural advantages, it was *him* she glanced towards when she raised her eyes from the skilled work of her fingers, and the arch, flirtatious look was for him and him alone.

"You mean to frighten me, Mr Darcy, by coming in all this state to hear me? But I will not be alarmed. There is a stubbornness about me that never can bear to be frightened at the will of others. My courage always rises with every attempt to intimidate me."

Involuntarily, his lips twitched at her teasing comment and, throwing caution to the wind, Darcy felt emboldened to respond in kind.

"I shall not say that you are mistaken," he replied, "because you could not really believe me to entertain any design of alarming you; and I have had the pleasure of your acquaintance long enough to know that you find great enjoyment in occasionally professing opinions which in fact are not your own."

She flashed him another glance and laughed heartily, before turning to her other companion.

"Your cousin will give you a very pretty notion of me, and teach you not to believe a word I say. I am particularly unlucky in meeting with a person so well able to expose my real character in a part of the world where I had hoped to pass myself off with some degree of credit. I think it very ungenerous of him— ”

“Indeed it is, Darcy!” Fitzwilliam grinned and leaned back in his winged chair to see him, and presumably goad him, better.

Darcy spared no glance at his cousin. His eyes stayed fixed on her as she resumed, her fingers still skilfully trailing the soft tune along the keys.

“Impolitic too, for he is provoking me to retaliate, and such things may come out as will shock his relations to hear.”

How very like her, to archly hint at settling old scores!

So much the better.

He knew full well that some things *should* be aired. Perhaps he could go as far as offering a veiled apology for one particular offence, one unguarded comment he had long regretted. He could think of no better way to do so than in the present comfortable company so, matching the jesting manner she had so kindly chosen, Darcy retorted lightly:

“I am not afraid of you.”

“Pray let me hear what you have to accuse him of,” Fitzwilliam urged, his grin growing even wider. “I should like to know how he behaves among strangers.”

She smilingly obliged. She gave no hints of his ungentlemanly remark to Bingley – which hopefully she had not heard – but archly recounted how, little as she wished to pain his relations, she felt compelled to tell the truth. And the truth was that at the Meryton assembly he had only danced *four* dances.

What was there to say? What veiled words could he use to convey the apology meant for her alone? Why was it that, at this crucial moment, he found himself tongue-tied and unable to string the right words together?

“At that time, I had not the honour of knowing any lady in the assembly beyond my own party,” was all that he could offer.

The excuse was paltry, and well he knew it.

By all accounts she knew it too, for she airily retorted:

“True. And nobody can ever be introduced in a ballroom.”

Was that an indication that she had heard him so uncivilly refuse Bingley’s offer of an introduction? If so, he could not let this pass. He ought to say something. But what the deuce was he to say, and how?

She was not disposed to wait much longer. She played another chord, then she dismissed him in a neat, blithe fashion that raised his ire, much as he knew that *she* was not at fault.

"Well, Colonel Fitzwilliam, what do I play next? My fingers await your orders."

Inwardly, Darcy rebelled. He could not leave it thus.

"I have not the talent which some people possess, of conversing easily with those I have never seen before. I cannot catch their tone of conversation or appear interested in their concerns, as I often see done," he said, in a stern attempt to justify himself to her, though why he should feel driven to such extremes he would not address, not now.

Admittedly, his actions were not above reproach. But to feel obliged to justify his inborn reluctance to pander to the common, the dreary and the trite? Had it come to *this*? Had she come to rule him to so great an extent that his very nature should require justification? Then surely this was an even stronger reason why she should be forsaken, over and above all the other eminently valid ones.

And yet the sweetness of her arch reproof easily quelled his instinctive rebellion, when she gently observed that she never thought her skill at the pianoforte inferior to other women's through lack of talent – merely lack of practice.

Thus, he did not rebel against her power over him. Instead, his tone and mien softened as he spoke in earnest, and perhaps more openly than in the entire course of their acquaintance:

"You are perfectly right. You have employed your time much better. No one admitted to the privilege of hearing you can think anything wanting," he declared frankly. "And yet, Miss Bennet, we neither of us perform to strangers."

ೞಲಿ ಲಿೞ

The conversation stayed with him late into the night as he nursed his brandy wondering what she had made of it, and indeed what *he* was to make of this encounter.

There she was, in his path again, just when he thought he had distanced himself from this unsuitable fascination, when he had grown to hope that he had put the past behind him at last.

He drained his glass and scoffed. So now he had begun to deal in falsehoods even to himself. Put the past behind him? Ha! The very notion! What of the weeks – months – when the past had been as vividly alive as her? As sparkling, as vibrant, as terribly attractive, surpassing everything that his tame existence had to offer. His tame, bland existence suffused in little more than duty and, worse still, in the triteness he could no longer abide.

Forsake her? And do what? Succumb to the sameness? Marry some dull Miss who would have nothing going for her but a portion and the right connections? Forget the sparkle that made his life worth living?

Would he not do his duty better towards everyone that mattered if he was also happy? And not just he, but everybody entrusted to his care? Would any of the Miss Bingleys of the *ton* be a better sister than her to Georgiana? A better trustee for the welfare of his people and his tenants, of all that was Pemberley? A better mother for his children?

He reined in the thoughts, for they were leading in the wrong direction. Yes, he desired her. More than he had ever desired any woman. But, for better or for worse, he was a Darcy, and he knew full well that his decisions must be guided by a great deal more than the misleading stirrings of desire.

And she *had* more to offer. Yes, she was enticing. But she was also wise and kind and good. And full of life and cheerful. Would she not do a world of good to Georgiana, cajole her out of her misplaced guilt and the lowest of spirits, and teach her to enjoy the world around her to the full, just as she did? Would she not bring fair kindness into the lives of his people – and sheer bliss to his?

What did they matter, her unsavoury connections? They would be hundreds of miles away and as far removed from their sphere as he could wish them. He could grit his teeth and bear them for a visit once a year, maybe less. For most of the time he could forget about Mrs Bennet, consign her to the godforsaken place where she belonged and bask in the joy that Elizabeth was his – his other half, his helpmeet, his very own treasure and delight.

They would work to tarnish his joy, and well he knew it.

Most of his relations, most of his acquaintances.

Well, hang them! Let them try!

Of course, they would be in the right to think that the Darcy name should have been aligned with a vast deal better than third-rate attorneys and Cheapside shopkeepers, but few would dare say so, and they *could* go hang.

His nearest and dearest would learn to appreciate her and see her sterling worth, unblemished by unfortunate connections. They would understand that he must have his heart's desire – must have *her* – and even if they should harbour reservations, they at least would want him to be happy.

Happiness. With her. A heady thought – a heady promise. His at last, after all this time of self-denial. A just reward for a valiant effort. His at last!

He would speak up, by Jove! Speak up and secure her. Once his sojourn with Lady Catherine reached its end. Not before, naturally. No need to provoke that self-willed relation into acrimony towards either himself or her. Soon. Not long now. Three days, four at the utmost. He would say his piece, secure her hand and then dash off to town to petition for a special licence, so that they could be married as soon as it was issued. A fortnight after his proposal – and not one day more!

Hopefully the loud matron, Elizabeth's mother, would not delay matters with talk of frippery and wedding clothes. Surely she must see that Elizabeth would want for nothing and they might as well forgo such preparations, for there was little doubt that their meagre means could not furnish her with the sort of apparel that the Mistress of Pemberley would have it in her power to command.

He frowned as it suddenly occurred to him that the first journey from Rosings ought not be to Berkeley Square and the Archbishop's palace at Lambeth, but to a secluded spot in Hertfordshire, to address the issue of Mr Bennet's blessing.

Elizabeth would want him to do so – for all he knew, she might not even be of age and parental consent might be required. Presumably Mr Bennet would be ready to take a leaf out of his wife's book and see promptly enough that the union was in his daughter's interest, and thus not cause any untoward delay.

Just above a fortnight, and he would be wed to the one woman who fulfilled his heart's desire!

That night, he found it very hard indeed to fall asleep.

❦

Three days passed and the only balm against his mounting impatience was her soothing presence, secured every day by determined efforts to encounter her in her forest ambles.

It had been a challenge to find her the first time, as the people at the parsonage could offer poor guidance, but once he had been able to locate her, she had sweetly informed him at some point during their stroll together that this happened to be her favourite walk.

Why she should be surprised to come upon him in the very same spot the following day he truly could not fathom, for after all she had supplied the information and she should have guessed that he would follow. Perhaps – and it did not speak well of her if she was willing to stoop to such devious tactics – perhaps she was feigning ignorance as to his feelings to urge him to declare himself.

The time would come.

On the same shaded walk, at midday, on the morrow.

The time would come. And it could not come soon enough!

❦

The excessively ornate *or moulu* clock on the mantelpiece in the library struck ten, and Darcy arched a brow as he refilled his glass. Had he not known his cousin to be a strong man, frequently exposed to danger and able to withstand it, he might have grown concerned. Fitzwilliam had vanished shortly after four, having announced in passing that he was of a mind to call at the parsonage.

Announced to him, that is to say, not Lady Catherine, which was just as well, for later on, when he failed to show up for dinner, her ladyship's ire remained directed at her thoughtless nephew and did not extend to involve all the occupants of the aforementioned place.

Sternly declaring that she was not about to keep dinner waiting for an inconsiderate young man who did not deign to observe the hour, Lady Catherine sat down to the repast in predictably high dudgeon and remained so for the rest of the evening. If anything, her disposition steadily worsened as time wore on and her wayward nephew still did not appear, not even to pay due homage in the drawing room.

Darcy found it impossible to guess where his cousin might have taken himself to, for surely he could not have extended his call at the parsonage for such an uncivilly long time.

Presumably he had gone for a lengthy ride over the meadows and then taken refuge in some alehouse or other. For Fitzwilliam's sake, Darcy could only hope that tales of his exploits would not reach Lady Catherine until after their removal from these parts. She would not take kindly to her relation showing to all and sundry that he favoured alehouse fare and alehouse company so far above her own.

Mercifully ignorant of Fitzwilliam's whereabouts, but still incensed at his continued absence, the lady of the house finally lost her appetite for holding court in the drawing room and withdrew to her chambers, with a stern comment regarding ill-mannered young men who had lost the habit of gentlemanly conduct after too many years spent in the officers' mess.

Rather pleased that he was spared the onerous task of enduring his aunt's ill-humour, Darcy gratefully retired to the library to nurse a drink or two while he settled within himself how to go about the significant business of the morrow.

In some ways, he was rather glad of his cousin's absence. Richard knew him well, better than anybody, and he would have seen that something was amiss. Nay, not amiss. He would have seen that something was preying on his thoughts and that he was as unable to sit still as a cat on hotplates. He would have seen it and pestered him for the reason, and Darcy would much rather he did not. Richard was his best friend, the brother he had never had – but still, some things ought not be revealed to one's relations first.

Tomorrow – aye, tomorrow he would be happy to share his best news with Richard. But now he would rather keep his thoughts and plans strictly for *her*.

The door opened noisily to admit the very man whose absence Darcy had rejoiced in but, rather than slamming it shut with equal force, Fitzwilliam pressed it softly in its lock with all the skill of a well-trained footman.

"Damn. I quite forgot," he muttered.

"What did you forget, Cousin?"

"That I was supposed to lie low in my tracks if I did not wish to be summoned for a grilling before our esteemed aunt."

"Fear not, she has retired an hour ago, with imprecations on ungrateful wretches," Darcy said with a smile as he refilled his glass and then filled one for his cousin.

"Has she?"

"Voiced imprecations? Not as such. I was merely teasing— "

"I could not care less for imprecations," Fitzwilliam cut in, inordinately cheerful. "I was keen to know if she has retired."

"She has."

"Thank goodness. I have been lying low in my bedchamber – bless that man, Omerod. Our aunt's butler is worth his weight in gold, Darcy, have you noticed? He uttered not a word about my having gone into hiding and sent a tray up as well, bless his heart. Not that I could touch it but still, I was most grateful for the kindness."

"Why could you not touch it? Moreover, why on earth would you go into hiding?"

"Come now, Darcy! Have you not been tempted, at least once in a while, to evade our dearest aunt's presence?" Fitzwilliam laughed and his inordinately gleeful manner gave Darcy pause in offering the brandy he had poured. "Her talents are well and truly wasted," Fitzwilliam chortled. "If only she could be in command of the Royal Dragoons. I could well imagine my hardened companions quaking in their boots before her. Even that old stick, Wilson, who has seen some action on countless battlefields," he added with an immoderate guffaw.

Having heard as much, Darcy carried his own glass to his lips, but left the other on the marble-topped sideboard. He set his own drink down and cast a smiling glance at his relation.

"Have you been drinking, Fitzwilliam?"

"Aye. The nectar of the gods. Aphrodite's own witching brew," his companion retorted with another chuckle.

"Honestly, Cousin! I know Lady Catherine is a trial on one's patience, but drowning yourself at the local watering-hole is not an adequate solution. And so immoderately too. I have never seen you quite so foxed."

A diverted smile was his first answer. Then Fitzwilliam spoke up.

"I am not foxed, Cousin."

"Is that so? You could have fooled me," Darcy retorted and, unseemly as it was, he brought himself to advance a step or two, until he was close enough to sniff. He sniffed, then declared in some surprise, "I daresay you are not. So what ails you?"

"Nothing ails me," the other replied promptly. "Quite the opposite, in fact," he added as he picked up one of Lady Catherine's mantelshelf ornaments to gaze at it for an uncommonly long time, then set it back only to pick another, inspect it with a gleeful snort and set it down again.

"Well, if you are determined to play the fool, then pray proceed at leisure. I shall leave you to it. I should get some sleep. I have things on my mind, something to do tomorrow," Darcy blurted out without thinking, only to instantly curse himself for his loose tongue.

Thankfully, Fitzwilliam did not ask him what it was, but instead chuckled.

"Sleep, eh? I cannot imagine falling asleep anytime soon, myself."

"Cousin, you are in fine fettle. You flit about, you fiddle with Lady Catherine's porcelain, you talk in riddles. If there is anything I can do to help, pray let me know. If not, then you should seek your berth. I assume you are not in trouble, judging by your spirits, but— "

Fitzwilliam laughed.

"Trouble? You might be surprised to hear that I find myself in more trouble than ever. But so be it."

Darcy gave up inquiring into his cousin's meaning and poured himself another brandy. Seemingly Fitzwilliam was not about to seek his berth and whatever he might wish to say would be said in his own good time or not at all, but clearly the prodding and the questioning had no effect whatever.

"I trust you remember me laughing at— Nay, mercilessly mocking all the poor fools who would declare themselves in love," Fitzwilliam jovially observed. "Well, I find myself reaping the rewards. Captain Henshaw would laugh himself into a fit to hear it, after all the raillery he got from me over his infatuation."

That was new, Darcy thought.

And perhaps a touch too close for comfort.

"Are you in love, Cousin?" he soberly asked.

"Worse, Darcy, worse!" the other replied, but his mien and his words were puzzlingly incongruous.

Baffled, Darcy stood aside watching his cousin pour himself a drink, then down it in one draught and turn towards him without warning.

"Can you keep a secret, Darcy? Of course you can, you were born poker-faced. I mean keeping a secret from Lady Catherine, who can be more unpleasant than the devil if she chooses, and I would rather she does not get the chance. Not to me, and particularly not to *her.*"

Before Darcy could ask again what or rather whom he was speaking of, Fitzwilliam burst out, clearly unable to contain himself.

"Darcy, I am engaged to be married! I proposed today and Miss Bennet had the kindness to say yes! Now, I can see that you are stunned. Before you say anything, aye, I know that in some respects this is sheer madness, since we both have precious little to live on. She is far from wealthy and so am I, but somehow things will come together. Thank goodness for Old Boney. At least my soldier's pay will see us through for as long as the war lasts, and then I shall find a way to keep us afloat. Damme, I would even go into trade if I have to, and if this does not send my esteemed father into a fit of apoplexy, then I do not know what would. You say nothing... What, no congratulations? I am that sorry, Darcy! I was hoping to have *you* on my side at least. I know how wild it seems and bordering on the irresponsible. Believe you me, I did try very hard indeed to keep a clear head and tell myself this is not a prudent choice. Pater will rant and rave and others will follow, but I say hang them! I had not known her a se'nnight before I felt we were perfectly matched. I could not leave her, Darcy, and go my own way. I cannot lose her. I love her. And I was hoping that even you might come to see why. I know she does not meet with your approval in more than one regard but, for my sake, I was hoping you could overlook it and wish us joy," Fitzwilliam concluded at last, his open countenance reflecting genuine emotion, and he stepped forward, his right hand outstretched.

From the moment that the thunder had struck, Darcy had heard less than one word in twenty. All the while, three other words screamed in his head, over and over.

'This cannot be! This cannot be! This cannot be!'

What mockery was this – what nightmare?

If it was a nightmare, then good Lord, pray let him awaken!

And yet the heavens remained silent, and the nightmare raged on.

His cousin was not silent, but his words held no meaning, as though they were spoken in a foreign tongue. At long last, he stopped talking and offered him his hand.

Through nothing but numb force of habit, Darcy took it and clasped it, then abruptly excused himself, his steps carrying him faster and faster through the silent house.

'Dead man walking – how dreadfully fitting.'

The thought flitted through his shock-struck mind, soon to be followed by disjointed, lightning-like flashes, as he walked out of the house into the pitch-dark garden. Elizabeth married to Fitzwilliam – his closest relation, in spirit if not blood. And he would see them together constantly. In town. At Ashford. And at Pemberley. Married to his cousin. He would be expected to attend the wedding. See her at the altar pledging herself to his closest friend. See them walk away to be man and wife together!

He gasped for breath, as though punched in the stomach – or as though he was about to be violently sick.

⚘⚘⚘

At dawn, the Darcy carriage thundered away from Rosings.

When they finally awoke at a much more reasonable hour, short notes were handed to the Colonel and Lady Catherine to excuse – but not explain – his abrupt departure.

Several months later Fitzwilliam determined that, upon reflection, *this* should have been his first hint that something was terribly wrong.

Chapter 2

The house in Berkeley Square was very quiet.

Georgiana was at Pemberley, thank goodness, so he would not have to face the superhuman effort of hiding his anguish from her yet. Most of his people were at Pemberley as well – he was supposed to travel there soon after leaving Rosings and no provisions had been made for a lengthy stay in town. Thus, of a household of fifty-odd people, it was just the housekeeper, a handful of maids, his valet and a footman who attended him now. And still there were too many. He wanted to see no one. He had no wish for food and no need to be helped in and out of elegant apparel.

His servants' attempts to fall into established patterns were brusquely rebuffed. Unasked-for trays of food were sent away and Weston, his valet, was told in no uncertain terms to come when he was summoned, and not a moment sooner.

After a few unprecedented outbursts of uncommon ire, they learned to keep out of his way as he roamed from his chambers to his study in a futile struggle to grasp the enormity of what had come to pass.

It was impossible to do so, and no amount of effort was making any difference.

Lost to him forever. Not merely lost, but married to his cousin – firmly in his life, but never his! How in God's name was he to bear it and not become unhinged? How was he to have her at his table as Richard's wife, and not betray himself? How was he to see her, time and again, as his goddamned *cousin*, and give no sign that he wanted her more than he had ever wanted any woman? How was he to keep up the pretence, day after excruciating day?

There was no escape from the hell of his own making, and it burned like molten lead to know he could have spoken months before Fitzwilliam had even met her. He could have spoken last November, and by now they might have been already wed.

She would have been his, not Richard's. And if his cousin should have had the horrible misfortune of falling in love with his wife, then it would have been Fitzwilliam's hell, not his. Fitzwilliam's the crushing grief, the anguish. It would have been for him to be torn asunder between loyalty and a need so deep that it burned its way into his very soul.

Eyes tightly shut against the horrifying future, Darcy dug his fingers in his hair, his temples pressed hard between cold palms as though to force out thoughts that tore and slashed and hounded him into a world so dark that, by comparison, insanity seemed a generous blessing. Yet, as he knew full well, there was worse to come.

৽৹৹

Five days ago Weston, Mr Darcy's valet, had found it very hard indeed to break a longstanding habit and, instead of welcoming Colonel Fitzwilliam into the house in Berkeley Square, have Thomas the footman tell him that his master was from home, according to Mr Darcy's own express instructions.

When he had returned from Rosings looking like storm and thunder, in the fiercest tones he had told them all – the handful that were currently in town to serve him – that he was not at home for anybody. Yet, in view of the long-acknowledged closeness between the two cousins, when the Colonel had come to call, Mr Weston had valiantly broken his master's injunction to come when he was summoned and not before, and had made his way into Mr Darcy's study to ask if an exception should be made for Colonel Fitzwilliam.

"No," had been the answer.

Just that, and nothing else – so, with a countenance more inscrutable than usual, Mr Weston had instructed Thomas to return to the entrance hall and lie at his master's behest, as servants were often asked to do but, to date, not in this household.

A great many things that never used to happen in this household were happening now. Mr Darcy's uninterrupted show of temper, for one. He had always been a firm and considerate master, who expected the best but gave the best as well, in wages and in treatment. He had never taken out his personal frustrations on his servants, not even last year, after that fateful trip to Ramsgate, when the discreet Mr Weston knew he might have had reason enough.

Nor had he ever spent so many days in isolation, shunning every sort of company, even that of his nearest cousin, and disdaining sleep, sustenance, personal appearance or changes of apparel – and, deeply perturbed, the loyal valet could only wonder what might have happened to make him do so now.

To his growing concern, the following days brought no change for the better. In fact, they brought no change at all.

When change did come, a fortnight to the day from the abrupt departure from her ladyship's seat in Kent, it was markedly and shockingly for the worse. Mr Darcy had never been one for imbibing and was astute enough to see that neither joys nor answers to heartache and conundrums lay at the bottom of the brandy glass or of the port decanter.

For some reason known only unto him, today his views were different. He had taken his first glass at breakfast – or, to be precise, instead of breakfast – and several had followed in the course of the day. Wine, thank goodness, and Weston was grateful for small mercies for, had it been port or brandy on an empty stomach, he would have long collapsed by now in self-inflicted stupor, and that was one indignity the faithful servant did not wish to see his young master finally succumb to.

Surreptitious attempts to spirit away unfinished bottles had no effect. Although clearly in his cups, Mr Darcy was far from lost to his surroundings or his senses, and Weston's vain efforts were promptly arrested in their tracks.

"I would thank you to return those bottles to their place," Weston heard his master say evenly, without turning – just as he thought he had made good his escape. "Or at least one of them. The other is all but empty and you may take it with you. Just instruct Thomas to bring back the same. *Bourgogne Chambertin 1784*, the only one befitting this sort of celebration," Mr Darcy added with a snort which, were it not for the acute bitterness, might have been misconstrued as laughter.

Mr Darcy was not a man of many words. It was not in his nature, and he had spoken less than ever over the past fortnight. But today drink seemed to have made him more inclined to talk, and Weston felt it might do him good to be encouraged.

His burden would be eased perhaps, or at least he might be distracted from emptying yet another of the bottles preserved from the year of his birth for the express purpose of being opened at the celebration of his marriage.

That foolish boy, Thomas, should have known better than to touch that particular reserve without a word to higher-ranking servants, regardless of his master's instructions on the matter.

Now, come to think of it, why would Mr Darcy make such an ill-judged request in the first place?

"Celebration, Sir?" Weston cautiously spoke up. "May I ask what you are celebrating?"

"You may not. But I might tell you anyway. I am drinking to the day when all was supposed to be set right – only to blow spectacularly into pieces. An anniversary, if you will. A fortnight since the death of hope!" he toasted, raising his glass before bringing it to his lips.

"What hope would that be, Sir?"

At that, Darcy closed his eyes and, pinching the bridge of his nose between thumb and forefinger, he shook his head.

"Nay, Weston, I am not so far gone as to tell you that," he muttered.

And yet, despite the pronouncement, he suddenly swayed. Presumably closing his eyes and shaking his head at the same time was unwise under the circumstances. His eyes flashed open as he reached to steady himself.

"Now would be a good time to leave me," Mr Darcy instructed, his voice firmer than his bearing. "I am quite certain you are as unwilling to be party to my celebration as I am to share it. Be sure to leave those bottles on the sideboard though, and send Thomas up with another. Or better still, a couple."

There was little Mr Darcy's man could do when faced with a direct order, so he did as bid, at least as regards the two bottles secreted about his person, under his coat-fronts and under an arm each. With a bow, he made his exit from Mr Darcy's study, wondering how he could delay obeying, if he could not wholly disregard, the order to deplete that reserve even further.

To his vast relief, he was soon to receive an answer.

Strangely, it came in the shape of disregarding yet another order.

Well, be that as it may. Hopefully Mr Darcy would not be provoked into dismissing him for outright disobedience. But, order or no order, he had left his loyal valet with no choice, once he had seen fit to resort to the bottle.

Thus, when Thomas came to him to announce the caller, Weston blandly told him to show the Colonel up.

⋘ ⋙

The ever so familiar step and voice brought the oddest mixture of relief and horror. It was good to see him – it was sheer hell – and Darcy groaned quietly as his cousin bounded into his study and greeted him with excessively great cheer. And then Fitzwilliam caught sight of his appearance and drew up short.

"Good heavens, Darcy, what is it? You look like the very devil!"

The warm tones of affectionate concern made Darcy cringe. This was the man who had stood beside him in the direst times of trouble. Not just in the recent near-catastrophe involving Georgiana, but in almost every instance of personal anguish that he could remember. Wickham's malicious acts as children, his father's all too frequent choice to bend his ear to the tales of an unworthy favourite, or early days at school amongst indifferent and often cruel strangers. Also at the dreadful time of his mother's premature passing. And later on, during his father's protracted illness, horrible suffering and subsequent demise. Fitzwilliam had stood by him throughout all this and more. And even now, when he knew what he knew, the genuine affection in his cousin's voice stirred emotions in him, that would not serve him well.

"Come, man! Do not keep me hanging!" the other urged, his concern mounting. "Is this to do with Georgiana?"

"No. It is not," Darcy finally replied.

His cousin exhaled sharply in obvious relief.

"Thank goodness!" he exclaimed with fervour. "For a moment I thought— What with your abrupt departure, and now this," the Colonel added with an all-encompassing gesture towards his relation's attire and employment. "Then may I ask, what brought this on?"

Darcy huffed.

"Cannot a man have his private celebration without others jumping to conclusions? Georgiana is well, ensconced at Pemberley with her companion. I am safe enough here, and I should imagine you are also well. So let us leave it at that, shall we?" he added tersely and emptied his glass.

"Hm. I see I have come at a bad time," Fitzwilliam observed. "A pity. I wished to speak with you."

"Speak, then."

"The point is, will you remember?"

"Trust me, Cousin, I am finding it impossible to forget!"

"Forget what? I said nothing yet."

"No matter. What did you wish to speak of?"

"Elizabeth, of course."

Of course. Darcy swallowed hard. Elizabeth. His Elizabeth. Only she was not *his* Elizabeth any longer – if she had ever been – nor was it his right to speak of her thus.

Without further prompting, Fitzwilliam pressed on, oblivious to everything but his own thoughts, as a man in love was apt to be, and Darcy cringed again, easily recognising the emotion.

"Truth be told," his cousin smiled brightly as he settled in the seat across the desk, "your abrupt departure might have been inconvenient and damned unmannerly into the bargain, but I cannot complain. At least it gave me the excuse I needed to extend my stay until Elizabeth's own departure, without our dear aunt sniffing out the truth before it could be announced."

There it was again – the name, naturally spoken, a granted right.

And his heart lurched every time he heard it on his cousin's lips.

Darcy swallowed again and his features tightened.

"It worked out well, so I shall not inquire into your reasons, nor upbraid you for leaving me stranded. Instead, I suppose I should thank you for the opportunity to spend another week at Rosings. It would have been very hard indeed to leave mere days after our engagement. Besides, we got the chance to talk. Not that we have ever lacked it, but this time it was different. We got to talk more openly, once we had reached our understanding, and also look into closer matters, which we needed to address in any case."

We. We. We!

The oft-repeated word burned like a branding iron, as did the notion of their association.

"Glad I could be of service," Darcy said curtly, as soon as he could speak.

He might have saved himself the trouble.

The other continued, as though he had not heard.

"I never thought I would see the day when I would like to be at Rosings better than anywhere," he chortled. "And no, this is not mere infatuation speaking, but the place had its distinct advantages. Mrs Collins is a very discreet friend, and regardless of Lady Catherine's high opinion of her own prowess, neither she nor her parson got wind of what was happening under their very noses. Less self-involved characters would have made for more determined chaperones, if you know what I mean," Fitzwilliam added with another chuckle – and Darcy froze.

The horrible notion cut through the haze of deliberate intoxication and brought with it the same reaction as on the night when he had heard of the engagement: that he was about to be violently sick.

"No, I do *not* know what you mean!" he heard himself thunder. "If you are implying you have used their laxity to your advantage to anticipate your vows— "

The shock spilled from his own countenance into Fitzwilliam's in less than an instant.

"Of course not! How dare you even think it? What sort of a rogue do you think I am? What the devil has got into you of late?"

Pointless relief and acute guilt washed over him and Darcy raised his hands from the desk, palms forward, before letting them drop again with a sigh.

"I beg your pardon. That was a dreadful thing to say."

"I should bloody well think so!" the other fumed, far from mollified.

"So what did you mean?" Darcy asked, knowing that he had to.

"Before you accused me of behaving like a cad towards the woman I professed to love?" Fitzwilliam scathingly retorted, and Darcy sighed once more.

"Just so."

"Well, if you must know," Fitzwilliam resumed, the wish to speak of her clearly stronger than his lingering resentment, "what I meant was that, for the entire week, we could meet unhindered, walk through Lady Catherine's woodland, and talk, Darcy, *talk!*

Yes, of course I kissed her, not that this is any concern of yours, but to suggest that I would— "

"It was uncalled for, and I apologised," Darcy interjected, wincing at the image his cousin's angry words had conjured.

Elizabeth in his arms. Elizabeth responding to his kisses!

"What did you talk of?" he asked, in a desperate endeavour to make the dreadful image fade.

"Her family. Mine. Plans for the future," Fitzwilliam retorted curtly, then warmed up to the subject. "Bless her heart, she tried to warn me about what I should expect when I arrive at Longbourn to ask for her father's consent. An acquired taste, she called her relations, which not many could tolerate with ease. She said *you* did not, and I daresay I can see why. The mother must have grated on your sensibilities. She certainly grated on Elizabeth's, I can tell you that," he ruefully chuckled, unwittingly paining his cousin with the notion that, for once, he and Elizabeth might have thought the same, even if it was merely about her mother.

"It did not bother me as such," Fitzwilliam resumed, "but Elizabeth was visibly mortified to hear her mother's raptures about her second daughter marrying into the Earl of Langthorne's family. Little does she know that the connection brings no fortune and certainly no glory. But I might as well start from the beginning. We left Hunsford Monday last together, *chaperoned* of course," he emphasised. "Miss Lucas travelled with us, as did Mr Gardiner's manservant. I assume you are not acquainted with Mr and Mrs Gardiner. You must have had neither the wish nor the opportunity. He is a most successful London merchant and although my esteemed parents are bound to turn up their noses at the Gardiners' Cheapside residence, they have precious little else to object to. They are wonderful people, very genteel and in no way inferior to people of fashion. Indeed, they are superior to many that I know. I was asked to stay for dinner and so I got to know them better. I also made Miss Bennet's acquaintance – Elizabeth's eldest sister. In fact, I came to speak to you about her too, but firstly I should finish my account. We made no open reference to our understanding, Elizabeth and I, since Mr Bennet's consent was yet to be sought, but I should imagine that the Gardiners and Miss Bennet were too astute not to put two and two together and draw the obvious conclusion from my presence there. Besides, Elizabeth might have told them something in private conversations. Needless to say, I said nothing to *my* family on my return home. I saw no point in stirring the hornets' nest before visiting Longbourn. We set off at first light, chaperoned again," he unforgivingly added, "by both Miss Bennet and Miss Lucas, and we were warmly welcomed when we arrived at Longbourn. In my case, the welcome was almost incandescent when the two youngest sisters heard of my commission," he laughed good-naturedly, "as they seem to have a strong partiality for officers."

It was an understatement, and Darcy could picture the scene with no effort of imagination. Miss Kitty and Miss Lydia batting their eyelids in flirtatious displays – not that the notion riled him any more. It did not matter. Nothing did.

"By the bye," Fitzwilliam resumed, "have you heard that Wickham is quartered in Meryton and spreading tales about you, the disgusting worm?"

Even the name that he abhorred could barely trigger a reaction.

"What tales?" Darcy asked quietly, not really caring.

"I am digressing now, but I must tell you this. Once the youngest sisters had dropped something to that effect in conversation, I thought it best to speak to Elizabeth about it. Of course, it had to wait, the private interview with Mr Bennet was far more important, but— "

Darcy had no wish to be told of his cousin's private interview with Mr Bennet. He could not hear of it and keep an even mien. It had come to something, if he would much rather speak of his worst foe.

"So what is this of Wickham?" he woodenly prompted.

"I was getting to it, but I might as well tell you now. A long and sordid tale, this is. It seems he had no scruples in blackening your name and claimed you refused to honour your father's last wishes to grant him the living— "

"The devil he did!" Darcy burst out, outright indignation shaking him from his stupor.

"Just as I tell you. He spun this tale of woe to everyone in Meryton and, since he is such a smirking and simpering fellow, everyone believed him. Of course, I made it my business to leave Elizabeth in no misapprehension of his vile nature. I told her about the compensation Wickham received from you in lieu of the living and… hm! You might abuse me for it now, but I fear I have also disclosed his dealings with Georgiana. To nobody but her,"

Fitzwilliam hastily added, clearly determined to appease him. "You can imagine she is eminently to be trusted, and besides she will be part of the family ere long. She will not share it with all and sundry. But you must see I could not leave her sisters unprotected in the face of that rogue's wiles. For all we know, he might form a design on one of them, once the future connection between the Bennets and the Earl of Langthorne is revealed. Needless to say, before I left Longbourn I made a point of seeing Forster as well – you must have met him, he is the colonel of the regiment stationed in Meryton. Wickham's commanding officer, ever since he joined their ranks. I dropped a few words in his ear about the scoundrel's propensity to leave behind unpaid debts and broken reputations so, with any luck, he might be prevented from causing too much harm. But never mind the vermin. Let me get back to my tale. I will own it now, I had a great deal of concern regarding Mr Bennet's consent. Elizabeth told me much about him and I rightly surmised he is not the sort to be blinded by the empty glitter of my father's name. Besides, there seems to be a very strong attachment between Elizabeth and her father, and I was much concerned that he would not look with a friendly eye on her proposed engagement to a penniless soldier— "

"Penniless, Cousin?" Darcy retorted glumly, as he fought against the very foolish urge to pin his hopes on Mr Bennet withholding his consent. He was not likely to – and had he been, Fitzwilliam would not have been so cheerful.

"Very nearly so," his cousin replied, "particularly when I compare myself to you or to my dear elder brother, which I have always found to be a most unprofitable exercise," Fitzwilliam added with a laugh, then sobered. "I never used to care about such things. You may remember that I used to call them shallow trappings. But it is very different now, and it weighs on me that I cannot give her more. She deserves the world – and I could not care one jot if you laugh to hear me say so. She is the one woman who deserves the best, especially as she asks for nothing."

The words sunk in, and this time brought not burning envy but the deepest sadness. She did deserve the best. Everything a man could give her.

He could have given her so much more than Fitzwilliam, yet she had asked for nothing of him, but settled for his cousin's far more modest offerings instead.

As though compelled by some crafty devil to say the words that would inflict the utmost pain, Fitzwilliam continued.

"She asks for nothing but affection, and at least of that she will never be in want. Thank goodness, her father had the kindness to see it my way – our way," he amended, unknowingly twisting the knife deeper. "He did express concern as to my ability to change my accustomed way of life for a more frugal one, but then concluded that he was pleased to see I was of the same mind as Mr Pomfret."

"Mr Pomfret?" Darcy repeated blankly.

"Aye. You know, in his *'Lines to a friend inclined to marry'*. I daresay my future father-in-law was rather surprised that I knew enough of poetry to catch the reference. There was something in Mr Pomfret's poem about a happy union and a delightful life requiring nothing but a genteel sufficiency and love."

This cut again, so very deeply that Darcy could not bite back the sharp retort:

"If you have quite finished quoting old-fashioned poetry, pray tell me, is there anything in particular that you came here for?"

The other glanced up and raised a brow but refrained to comment until, at length, he said:

"There is, in fact. But judging from your present temper, I rather doubt that you are willing to assist me, so I shall move on to the other point— "

"What was your first?"

"No matter. My other point pertains to your friend Bingley and Miss Bennet. During our talks at Rosings, Elizabeth came to speak of her sister suffering from unrequited love. Now you and I know it was far from unrequited and Bingley only walked away from Hertfordshire at your persuasion. No, I did not tell her that," he added, before Darcy even thought to ask. "Regardless of your own reservations as to my future marriage, I am still hoping that one day my best friend and my wife will get along, and knowledge of your role in the affair would have put you in her blackest books forever. I was hoping though that you might find a way to right the wrong and bring them back together. That poor youngster, Bingley, who does as he is bid like some wretched pup, deserves better than being punished for his blind trust in your false opinion of the lady. And as for Miss Bennet, she seems made for him and I wonder how you failed to see it. The same childish trust in the goodness of others, the same willingness to see the best in people and do them good turns, even when they ill deserve them. Granted, they are both as lost as the proverbial babes in the woods in this wicked world of ours, but if they choose to be lost together, who is to tell them nay?"

But Darcy was no longer listening, as he pondered darkly on what he had just learned. So. He had been in the wrong about Miss Bennet. Far from being indifferent to Bingley, she was suffering as a result of his abrupt departure. Suffering from what she thought was unrequited love.

He would have dismissed the words as nothing but pompous exaggeration, had they come from anyone but Elizabeth, albeit indirectly – and had he not recently developed a dreadfully accurate understanding of that precise feeling.

Unrequited love.

She had never cared for him, had she? Had it all been in his imagination, the untold connection, the wordless understanding? And as for the words – the witty repartee, their sparkling exchanges – had they also meant nothing to her? Or had she despaired of him ever speaking out, and had agreed to have Fitzwilliam instead, as *something* was of course better than nothing?

He frowned at the unworthy thought – unworthy of him as well as her – but before he could delve deeper into painfully pointless speculations, Fitzwilliam resumed.

"So can I trust you to bestir yourself and address this matter in my absence?" he prompted rather sharply, but Darcy was too drained to take offence.

"You can," he tiredly assented.

So, by the looks of it, they would all have their *'happily ever after'* – except him. He bit his lip. If only he could leave the country altogether. Forget about his duties. Pemberley. Georgiana. Forget about Elizabeth. Travel the world, go and discover the source of the Nile. Or better still, go to war and with any luck leave his bones somewhere in Portugal or Spain, under some carved words or other. *Dulce et decorum est pro patria mori.*

He reached and refilled his glass.

"So are you going to tell me why you are in your cups at this hour in the morning?" Fitzwilliam drawled as he leaned back in his chair.

Yet all he got was a terse "I should imagine not."

"If memory serves, you said it was a private celebration."

"Did I say that?"

"You did."

Neither of them spoke further and, in the ensuing silence, Fitzwilliam reached for the nearest bottle and brought it closer to inspect the markings. He raised a brow and gave a smirk of appreciation.

"Not bad. So, what are you celebrating?"

"If I get you a glass, will you stop asking?"

"I might, if that old stuff is still worth drinking."

"It is," Darcy said curtly and made to stand.

"Nay, sit there," Fitzwilliam casually protested. "You will do yourself an injury. I can find a glass."

He did. He brought it back and filled it, took a sip and once more curled his lips in appreciation.

"You are right. It *is* worth drinking. So, what are we drinking to?"

"You said you would stop asking."

"I said I might. But have it your way, for a while at least."

They both fell silent yet again, each nursing his own glass.

"If you will not tell me that, then would you tell me something else?"

Darcy tensed and, inwardly cursing the wine-induced haze, he willed his scattered wits together.

"I might," he cautiously replied, involuntarily echoing his cousin's words. "What do you wish to know?"

"What have you against my marriage?"

Darcy barely suppressed a start at the quiet but blunt question – or at least he hoped he did.

"What makes you think I have anything against it?" he tried to hedge, but Fitzwilliam would have no truck with it.

"I know you think the worst of her relations. You said so all too often, and Elizabeth confirmed it. I also know that you have always thought I would marry better. True enough, she has no connections and no portion, but would you trust my judgement when I tell you she has everything else a man could hope for? You may not like her, for whatever reasons of your own that I can scarce begin to fathom, for I will not do you the injustice to suspect you of disliking her merely for not deferring to you like so many damsels of our general acquaintance. I will not probe, but I pray matters will mend between the two of you. Will you not try, for my sake, to accept her?"

From his deepest hell, Darcy wished he could beg for mercy. Plead for the agony to stop – for an end to the cruel torture. Yet he could not, for it would bring nothing but a different hell, where all the sores would be laid into the open.

His voice dreadfully ragged, all he could say was, "I shall try."

"Good. I thank you, for I need your help."

'Sweet Lord! What now?'

"What can I do?" he said aloud.

"As you can imagine, Mater and his lordship are very far from pleased. So is my nuisance of a brother, with his pompous views on suitable connections. I spoke to them on my return from Longbourn and got the reply I was expecting – but that made it not a shade more palatable, I tell you. Long story short, I was hoping you would be willing to speak well of her in my absence."

He failed to register the sudden change in his cousin's countenance and quietly continued.

"So far, they have laboured to find enough reasons why there is no time to meet her before I set sail. The devil of it is that my hands are tied, and well they know it. I cannot resign my commission and cast aside the only source of income I am assured of at present. Nor can I alter the date of my departure."

"When must you embark?"

"In eight days' time. Needless to say, I would have wished to marry before I set sail, but she deserves to have a proper wedding and not a rushed, patched-up affair. She says she sets no store by such foolish fripperies, but I have sisters, and know better. Besides, I would have wished to leave her in our home once we are wed, and not her father's. Not surprisingly, my dearest Mamma jumped at the excuse as soon as I was foolish enough to let her have it, and said that a house must be found and refurbished before a date is set, and that would take a while. I am no dunce and I know they are merely playing for time for, in the same breath, Mater suggested that nothing is announced till my return— "

"And are you planning to go along with it?" Darcy asked lamely.

"I know not. In some respects, it might serve her better if I did. Elizabeth, I mean, of course – not my mother. Which brings me to the favour I would have liked to ask— "

"Another favour, Cousin?" Darcy shot back without thinking, a brow arched in dry, sardonic query.

By the time some measure of sense returned to him it was too late, and Darcy was not surprised to see Fitzwilliam look injured. With a deep sigh, he apologised.

"Forgive me. I am not myself."

His cousin put his glass down, and at length retorted:

"Yes. That is precisely what I was afraid of. Listen, Darcy, I know I have asked a great deal of you today, and if there was anyone I could trust more— "

"Heavens above!" Darcy involuntarily groaned, then bit his lip. "I beg your pardon yet again. Pray, continue."

Fitzwilliam frowned.

"Never mind. This is not the time. I shall return on the morrow."

"With any luck, by tomorrow I shall be dead and preserved in alcohol for all eternity."

"There is hardly enough alcohol in that fancy bottle," Fitzwilliam exclaimed, exasperated. "If this is your game, you should call for brandy."

"Perhaps I shall. Now, this favour you were speaking of…?"

"This is not the time," Fitzwilliam repeated. "You would do much better to tell me why exactly you are aiming to preserve yourself in alcohol."

"So that posterity might observe me at leisure. *Ecce homo*, with all his foibles and mistaken notions."

Fitzwilliam's features contorted in vexation, then he pursed his lips. He sighed and spread a hand over his furrowed brow to rub his temples, then leaned over the desk.

"I wish you would tell me what this is all about. Forgive me, I have been engrossed in my own concerns – too engrossed perhaps. I see you are troubled, otherwise you would not be trying to drink yourself into a stupor. Come, speak up. You can talk to me. What ails you, Darcy? Can I be of assistance?"

Bitter laugh fought with a heavy sigh in his chest – and neither won. After a long silence, all that Darcy said was, "This time you cannot."

"What makes you so certain?"

The only answer was a shrug.

"At the very least I can listen," Fitzwilliam urged, but the warm insistence was met with an exhausted plea.

"Leave be, Cousin! I am in no humour to discuss it."

"Yes, I can see *that*. And I would let you take your time, but there is not a great deal left. Eight days, to be precise. So we might as well do away with the coaxing. Come now, out with it."

"Would you not leave be for once?" Darcy repeated with mounting impatience. "You are like a hound with a bone!"

"You know me well," Fitzwilliam grinned, but the affectionate raillery did not serve its purpose. Quite the contrary. Darcy's countenance darkened into a scowl.

To no avail, of course. The other merely laughed.

"Ah! There we have it. The proverbial Darcy glare. Save it for others, Cousin. Will you ever learn it does not work on me?"

With a groan of acute vexation, Darcy ran his hands over his face.

"Fitzwilliam, desist or leave, I beg you!" he burst out and at that the Colonel sighed.

"I see you are determined to be stubborn. I would dearly like to browbeat you into submission or at the very least drink you under the table till you talk. But knowing you, it might take the best part of a se'nnight. A waste of good brandy, if you ask me."

He got no reply to the friendly sally and at last Fitzwilliam was forced to concede defeat for the present.

"Have it your way then. But would you promise to write when you do find yourself in humour to discuss it?"

There seemed to be no other way of bringing the prodding to an end, so Darcy gave him what he asked for.

"Fine!" he all but growled – one more deception among many.

"A small concession, but so be it. Perhaps I should charge Bingley to pester you while I am gone. Or Georgiana."

This was beyond the pale, and Darcy glowered.

"For everybody's sake, I trust you are not in earnest!"

Fitzwilliam sobered, all teasing gone from his voice and countenance.

"You know I am not. But even so, it would do you good to speak to someone."

Darcy's jaw tightened. He could speak to no one. Not to Bingley – it seemed that before long he would marry into the same family. Not to Georgiana – of course not! Nor to any of his other relations or his so-called friends who, in truth, were little more than distant acquaintances. His closest friend, his only real friend, was the man before him. So there was no one he could unburden himself to.

"I thank you, Cousin," he said tiredly. "But never mind me now. Go ahead, ask your favour."

"Are you quite certain this is a good time?"

With another sigh, Darcy pushed the glass from him.

"It is. As good as any. So speak up."

Yet Fitzwilliam did not. He stood instead and walked to the window. Hands on his lapels, he stared outside deep in thought, for a long while. Darcy did not prompt him, and finally Fitzwilliam spoke of his own accord, his back still turned.

"Would you see that she wants for nothing if I am gone?"

The look of shock that flashed over his cousin's haggard features was too obvious for concealment. Regardless, with Fitzwilliam facing the other way, it would have gone unnoticed – but for the fact that the shock spilled into words.

"Good Lord in Heaven!" Darcy whispered.

'How much more could a man take?'

The Colonel cast a glance over his shoulder.

"I beg your pardon?"

"Nothing. Nothing," Darcy replied swiftly.

Caught in his own concerns, the other let it pass.

He turned around and words started to flow freely.

"It is just that, with my mother's deliberate procrastination and everything else, I cannot ensure that she is well protected, not to the extent I want her to be. I have changed my will of course, and everything I own will go to her if the worst should happen, but my other stipulations might be disregarded if there is malicious intent, and I would not put it past them to discount my wishes. Since we are not wed, she has no legal standing as heir to any future bequests that are to come my way, such as my share of my uncle Wentworth's property for instance, or Aunt Agatha's. It would mean a great deal to know that you are prepared to stand up to my wilful relations on my behalf and see that she gets whatever I might have been due."

The tenor of the conversation was fast becoming far too much for Darcy – but then again too many conversations had become far too much of late.

"Do not dwell on this, Fitzwilliam," he urged in a whisper.

"I would be a vast deal easier if I knew she would be protected, no matter what."

Another long sigh was his answer, before Darcy replied quietly but firmly.

"She will be. I promise."

Along with a great many things that day, his brevity went unnoticed, and the Colonel fervently said:

"I thank you, Darcy. I am, as ever, greatly in your debt."

The other shrugged.

"Do not mention it. Besides, it will not come to it. You will be safe and you will return home to everything a man could wish for," he added very softly, with no emphasis, merely a statement of truth.

"God willing," Fitzwilliam replied soberly, then his tone lightened. "You know, I have always thought *you* had everything a man could wish for," he good-naturedly observed as he walked back to the desk to retrieve his wineglass.

Aye – and so did *he*. But Darcy made no answer.

Instead, he tossed his drink down in one draught.

Chapter 3

Georgiana surreptitiously eyed her brother over the book she was holding merely as a guise, for she had not read a line, nor turned a page these ten minutes together. He did not seem to notice either the guarded glance or her blatant inattention to her book. Ever since they had retired to the parlour after dinner, he had been sitting there, staring into space for what seemed like an age. Just as he had that morning, when the post had been brought in, and he had read Mr Bingley's letter.

Why he should be thus affected Georgiana could not begin to fathom, or indeed why he had not even attended his friend's wedding. But then there was a vast deal she could not fathom lately.

Why had he not repaired to Pemberley after his return from Rosings as arranged, for one? Why had he not written anything but a blunt, curt scribble to beg her pardon for his absence, with no further indication as to its cause or his future plans? Why had he remained uniformly silent – and still absent – for weeks on end, until she had been overcome with worry and had requested that Morgan, the second coachman, convey her uninvited to Berkeley Square, along with Mrs Annesley, her companion? Why had she found him haggard and exhausted, a shadow of his former self? Why had he been displeased to see her, much as he had valiantly sought to hide it? And above all, why did he look as though life had no savour any longer and he carried all the burdens of the world?

She did not question him – she did not dare. She had never questioned him in sixteen years, and now was not the time to start. She merely asked, as gently and carefully as she could, whether there was anything she could do for him.

"No, sweetling, there is not," was his sole answer, and she did not dare ask again.

If only Richard were still here! He would know what to do, know how to help him. But Richard had returned to the battlefield six weeks ago or more, and even now he might be facing mortal peril...

Georgiana shuddered. She would not think of this now, she could not bear it. He would be safe, he must be, and return home to all who loved him. Unwittingly, her lips curled into a smile at the comforting notion her musings had just led to. A short while ago, in a very private conversation, her cousin Emily, Richard's youngest sister, had imparted news that had warmed her heart. Apparently, while he was at Rosings, Richard had formed an attachment which was returned, and now he was engaged!

The news of his engagement, Emily said, had greatly unsettled his lordship and Lady Langthorne, for the young lady was not of the standing they aspired to.

"But it matters not," Emily had cheerfully added. "They will relent. And if they do not, Richard said he would marry her regardless. He is smitten, Georgiana! A besotted man, if ever I saw one. I always thought that my sensible brother would make a prudent match and I was sorry for it, for he needs love in his life a great deal more than he needs a vast income – and I do believe he found it. She loves him too, he says, is this not charming? Oh, how I wish to meet her! But Mamma would have none of it, she privately told me she has no wish to encourage this infatuation, as she terms it, and would not call upon her, nor invite her to Langthorne House. I wish there was a way, though. Oh, I know we shall meet when Richard returns, he would not deny me, and besides he must be keen to introduce her to those of us who favour the connection. Needless to say, Morton is not best pleased, but then he had always danced to my father's tune. Well, never mind him. For my part, I am eager to make her acquaintance. How can we arrange it? Would you lend a hand? You could ask your brother. Richard said he knows her too. Are you not curious to meet her?"

She was, of course. Richard in love! Nothing could give her greater pleasure – except perhaps learning that her own dear brother had formed a similar attachment, and it was returned. For now, this seemed a rather distant prospect. But perhaps the other wish might soon be granted – Emily's and hers. With that in mind, the words unthinkingly escaped her:

"Shall we not travel into Hertfordshire then, Brother?"

To her surprise and slight remorse, he gave a violent start.

"*Hertfordshire?* No! Of course not!"

"Why not? Do you not wish to give Mr Bingley joy in person?"

To that, he replied blandly, "I do not."

Georgiana pursed her lips and suddenly determined it was time to set the book aside.

"Have you and Mr Bingley had some sort of disagreement, Brother?"

"None whatever," he replied gruffly. "Georgiana, to what these questions tend?"

She blushed furiously to find herself thus interpellated. Deviousness was something she had never mastered and she felt mortified to be caught out.

"Nothing in particular," she ventured. "'Tis only that I thought this would be the best excuse for... that is, I... Emily and I would very much like to make Miss Bennet's acquaintance, and this might be— "

"Out of the question!" her brother thundered and forcefully employed the armrests to propel himself out of his chair. He strode to the fireplace, then spun around to face her. "How do you know of this?" he inquired sternly.

Dejectedly, Georgiana lowered her eyes.

"Emily told me. It seems that Richard had revealed everything to her before he left. That Lord and Lady Langhorne disapprove of the connection, and so does Morton, but our other cousins are delighted and would like to hear more of the young lady who has captured Richard's heart. Emily learned from him that you know her too. So Fitzwilliam, pray tell me, what is she like?"

Disappointingly, her brother did not answer. He turned away to rest his fist on the mantelpiece. Silence fell, broken only by the crackling of the fire, still lit although it was June; but a cold, wet June that chilled one to the bone.

Suddenly, Georgiana shivered. The chill went deeper, for some reason, and no merry fire could dispel it, just as she could not dispel her brother's unaccountable ill-humour. And yet she persisted.

"Why is it so out of the question for me and Emily to meet her, Brother? Do you...? Do you disapprove of Richard's choice?"

Concern seeped into her voice. Surely Richard had not been taken in! Not a fortune-hunter perhaps, he had no fortune, not as such, but he had standing, good expectations and the best connections.

From the fireside the answer came at last, leaden and quiet.

"I do not."

"So there is genuine attachment on the lady's side?"

His next reply was also long in coming and, when it did come, it was curt and barely audible.

"I assume so."

"You assume – or you know?"

A moment later, Georgiana dearly wished she had refrained from probing further. To her regret and shock, her brother lost his temper.

"How is a third party to *know* in cases such as these? Georgiana, really! Your questions are uncalled for. And I would appreciate it if you kept them to yourself."

With that, he stormed out of the little parlour, leaving his sister mortified, confused and thoroughly distraught.

ഏ~ இ~

So now there was more guilt to add to all his troubles, Darcy thought as he strode out of the parlour and into his quiet, darkened study. Guilt for lashing out at Georgiana for faults that had never been her own.

"What is she like?" she had asked him.

Perfect? The best a man could hope for?

And as unattainable as the stars in the sky?

He found his way to the seat behind the desk despite the darkness, and dropped himself in it, closing his eyes. He must conquer this. Somehow. He had to. Deception had always been alien and abhorrent, but in this hell, deception was his only ally. Somehow, *somehow*, he must conquer this!

ഏ~ இ~

The well-tended gardens were shrouded in mist at that time in the morning – long, hazy fingers stretching this way and that and then withdrawing, slowly vanquished by the rising sun.

Hands behind his back, Darcy walked along the gravelled path, pebbles scrunching under his heavy footsteps.

He had given in. At last, he had given in. To the steady sense of guilt over his unfair outburst to Georgiana. To Bingley's entreaties that he come to stay. And to his own base, but unconquerable desire to see *her* again, and damn the consequences! He had given in.

Thus, he was now at Netherfield, witnessing the bliss that Bingley claimed he had been instrumental in creating. He gave a gruff, impatient snort. Bingley, bless him, in his unremitting kindness seemed to have forgotten everything about his role in delaying the very same bliss, and had only chosen to remember that, just as Fitzwilliam had requested, Darcy had indeed bestirred himself, spoken to Bingley and set the wrong to rights.

Once informed of the true state of Miss Bennet's affections, Bingley had lost no time in returning to Hertfordshire and labouring to regain her trust. Her hand was gained soon after – her heart he had never lost – and now there they were, in wedded bliss that was already a month old.

Despite his better instincts, Darcy had eschewed attending the wedding and had resisted Bingley's earnest entreaties that he stand up with him as his best man.

No claims of friendship, no lingering guilt about having persuaded Bingley down the wrong path could overcome the anguish of standing by the altar and watching Elizabeth advancing down the aisle while knowing she was lost to him forever.

So he had concocted some elaborate excuse – business in town that demanded his continued presence. Bingley was hurt, as Darcy knew full well, but had readily forgiven this transgression, just as he had forgiven all his other ones. Which, to an extent, was part of the reason why Darcy felt he owed him this at least: to call at Netherfield and pay his respects to Bingley and his new wife in person, much as the endeavour plunged him deeper into his own hell.

For he had found her there. She had come to stay for a fortnight, shortly after the newlyweds' return from Scarborough. She had stood beside her sister and new brother to greet him and his party as soon as his carriage had drawn to a halt at the porticoed entrance. And his wasted heart had lurched and twisted as soon as his eyes had alighted on her beloved countenance, as it surely would from now until forever, and there was nothing he could do to alter that.

Dinner was hell – not that he had expected otherwise – and his wretched cousin Morton, Fitzwilliam's eldest brother, did his utmost to compound the acute mortification.

Upon reflection, Morton's presence at Netherfield was as much Darcy's fault as Lord and Lady Langthorne's for, had he not given in to Emily's pleading to be allowed to join them, so that she could meet Richard's affianced, his uncle and aunt would not have felt compelled to send Morton along, as living embodiment of their distaste for the connection.

True to his own nature and clearly acting on express instructions, Morton had lost no opportunity to make his feelings known, and supercilious remarks had poured out throughout dinner, goading Darcy into exerting himself to act as antidote.

She had not seemed perturbed by Morton's remarks, although they had often crossed the line into outright malice. It was as if she was prepared for that – and presumably Fitzwilliam had prepared her. Yet, more than once, Darcy had felt her steady gaze settled upon him with something very much like disbelieving wonder whenever he had spoken up to counter his eldest cousin's comments, as though his stance surprised her. As though she had expected him to play to Morton's tune.

"Ah, there you are. I have been looking for you," the very man's voice rang out, disrupting his uncomfortable reverie.

Darcy frowned. He could have done without his cousin's presence now, just as he could have done without it the previous evening.

"Morton. I was not expecting you so early in the morning. Not quite your hour, is it?" Darcy drawled in his turn.

"Yes, well. Uncommon circumstances, you know," the other shrugged. "Myself, I would much rather have my own home comforts, but here we are. And all thanks to that old dunce, our Richard."

Darcy made no reply and, distasteful as it was, he resigned himself to seeing Morton fall into step with him. No more was said as they both made their way into the shrubbery. Mist swirled around them still, partly concealing the artfully-shaped mounds of verdure that bordered their convoluted path.

Just as he opened his lips to excuse himself, the other snorted.

"So very much like Richard to have his head turned by a pretty face. Would you believe it? A penniless country chit. With charms aplenty and a figure to unhinge a saint, I grant you, but still! Marriage, Darcy? Shackle himself to— "

Darcy's retort was crisp and prompt.

"I suggest you refrain from such remarks."

"What remarks?" the other shrugged, then sneered. "I will own, she is a fine morsel. That bosom – Lord Almighty! I can see why Richard was— "

"You are speaking of a fine lady who is soon to be your *sister !* " Darcy rasped, but the other would not heed the warning that would have given pause to better men.

"Oh, quit being such a sanctimonious old prig! You will not tell me that you would have said nay to such a delicious package. I would readily tumble her in the hay myself, but *marry* her?"

A thick curtain of boiling blood seemed to have settled over Darcy's senses, preventing him from registering anything for a few dark moments. It was only the sharp impact of gloved fist upon hard jaw that drew him from the roiling haze. Then the next image that sunk in was Morton bringing up a hand to touch his bloodied lip. Matching stains now marred his own tan gloves, but Darcy did not notice. With grim satisfaction, he saw his cousin drawing up to assume the Eton pugilistic stance.

"Have you run mad?" Morton bellowed, then spat a mouthful of blood. "I have sent my seconds for far less than this!"

"Then send your blasted seconds!" Darcy heard himself hiss. "You know where to find me. Just as you know I am a better shot than you and I have always bested you with a rapier. And if you do not send your seconds, then rest assured I *will* send mine if you ever utter such repulsive filth again, in my presence or otherwise," he enunciated darkly, his voice filled with deadly purpose and the steely resolve of one who had nothing to lose.

Somehow, it seemed to penetrate through the other's posturing anger and Morton fell back, his hands dropped by his side.

"You and Richard!" he spat with impotent fury. "Peas in a pod. Stand up for him as always then, if it pleases you. For my part, I say damn you both!" Morton viciously threw over his shoulder as a Parthian shot and, to his own good fortune and Darcy's enduring sanity, vanished down the misty path that led back to the house.

Alone once more, Darcy exhaled and unthinkingly rubbed his gloved right fist against the other hand. No regrets followed on the heels of his violent outburst. If anything, it felt good to have released at least some small part of his anger and frustration.

A fleeting grimace of vindictive pleasure twisted his features at the thought of Morton's shock, as obvious as the traces of blood at the corner of his mouth. Served him right, the vermin! And it was just as well that he had assumed it was all done on Richard's behalf, rather than in response to his own feelings.

Darcy pursed his lips and locked his hands behind his back again as he walked away from the spot of the stormy encounter. For better or for worse, he did not catch sight of the silhouette clad in pale yellow muslin that remained behind, hidden in a mist-shrouded alcove – an unwilling witness to the whole unsavoury exchange.

⋙ ⋘

Elizabeth shivered as she gathered the shawl about her shoulders. Not so much for cold, although the morning mist was uncommonly chilling. Yet far more so was the confrontation that had suddenly flared under her very eyes. The violence of it, the sheer hatred!

Aye, she had expected Richard's older brother to be against their union. Richard had warned her of it and had not minced his words any more than she had sugar-coated hers when she had sought to describe her family. Yet she had not expected remarks as vile, as base as the ones she had heard the Viscount utter – nor had she expected Mr Darcy to be so violent when he had come to her defence.

Undoubtedly any man of decency and feeling would have taken umbrage at such repulsive conduct, but raise his fists in anger? And for *her*? To defend a union he scarce condoned, as she had half-suspected and Richard had confirmed?

Of course, she knew full well that he had acted thus to champion his cousin, not herself. Richard had referred to their longstanding friendship and bond of affection.

At the time, such revelations had come as a surprise, for she had not thought Mr Darcy capable of such depth of feeling. But then at the time her view of him had been severely jaundiced due to Mr Wickham's lies, before Richard had set her to rights on that score and had disclosed the full extent of Mr Wickham's treachery and the suffering he had inflicted on Mr Darcy and his blameless sister.

And now she was proven wrong once more. He *was* capable of depth of feeling, little as he chose to advertise the matter.

She shivered again, then raised her slender shoulders. Perhaps she should become accustomed to the fact that there was more to Mr Darcy than readily met the eye…

ჲტ ჟტ

Before the day was out, Lord Morton had left Netherfield, taking his young sister with him and, of the assembled party, only two could understand his haste or have an inkling as to why his jaw was bruised and his lip swollen.

Compared to the previous night, dinnertime was devoid of acrimony, but it was also very quiet. Mr Bingley spoke, or at least he tried to, assisted by his wife on occasion, but Mr Darcy was almost uniformly silent, as was his shy sister. As for Elizabeth, she was so caught in thought that she often failed to make the right responses to her new brother's cheerful chatter.

She would have dearly liked to thank Mr Darcy for championing her on Richard's behalf, but there was no way to do so without revealing she had been party to that repulsive conversation. And, in view of his most honourable conduct, she would have liked to seek his pardon too, for having so readily believed the worst of him on account of Mr Wickham. But, yet again, she could think of no way to broach that awkward subject. Best left alone, she knew.

Yet, of their own volition, her eyes seemed determined to dart in his direction, to find him staring at his food upon the plate or mindlessly toying with it, scarcely eating, as though he was engrossed with other matters. He looked up once, suddenly alerted to her covert scrutiny, and their eyes met across the beautifully decorated table. His jaw tightened, and then he looked away as he reached for his glass of wine.

Elizabeth pursed her lips and returned to her chicken and creamed parsnips. It seemed that regardless of the events of the morning, and much as Richard hoped for a rapprochement between his future wife and his dearest cousin, it would be very long in coming.

Through no fault of her own, she suddenly resolved as she cut herself another morsel. She *would* try to effect a better understanding, for Richard's sake – and perhaps Mr Darcy's too.

✤✤✤

He should have left by now, and well he knew it. He should have taken himself away from Netherfield, and left the unthinkable temptation far behind. Not the heartache though – there was no way to rid himself of *that*.

And yet he stayed. Day after day, woefully unable to leave the place while she was still under the same roof. Without the imposition of the obnoxious members of her family, who were three miles away, at Longbourn. Without the vexation that Lord Morton had caused and… without Richard.

Although Richard was present in every wrenching thought, in every fleeting moment of stolen guilty pleasure of watching her when she was not aware that he was looking. Seeing her lips curl into a cheerful smile as she chatted to Bingley or her sister, or as she sought to cajole Georgiana out of her usual reserve.

It was another source of bitterness intermingled with wistful joy to see that his beloved sister was endeavouring to open up to her – at least as much as her temperament allowed. And every moment spent at Netherfield brought the agony of knowing just how heaven might have looked, had Elizabeth said yes to him, not Richard.

He clasped his hands behind his back again as he wandered down the same path where he had put Morton in his place.

Aye, he should leave. Take Georgiana and return to town, or entomb himself at Pemberley, rather than let dead dreams lure him even deeper into hell. But… there were only two days left until she would return to Longbourn. Two days until the achingly beautiful illusion would be shattered anyway…

"Mr Darcy. Good morning to you, Sir."

The soft voice, coming from an alcove to his right, made him start so violently, like the veriest clod, that she could not have failed to notice. She gave a little rueful laugh as she left her bench and came to join him on the path.

"Forgive me. I see I have disturbed you from your thoughts. I shall leave you to your solitary amble," she quietly offered, but before she could turn away he protested swiftly, without thinking.

"No, pray do not."

"Are you quite certain I am not intruding?"

"Your company is always welcome, Miss Bennet," he could not help replying, and offered her his arm.

She took it, and they fell into step together.

"You are very kind."

"Not at all. I— "

"Yes?"

"Nothing," he retracted – and indeed there was nothing he could safely say.

Behind his back, his free hand twitched and he suppressed a sigh as he inhaled the all too familiar sweet fragrance that drifted towards him on the early summer breeze. And then there was naught but silence as they strolled together. Naught but silence for the longest time, until at last she broke it and glanced up at him.

"To own the truth, Sir, I am very glad of this encounter," she suddenly began.

"You are?" was all that his disordered senses permitted him to say.

For a variety of reasons, he had nearly always felt tongue-tied in her presence. Even more so now, when those dark eyes settled on him in earnest, wreaking havoc through every sense and feeling.

"I am. You see, I was hoping for a private interview before either of us leave Netherfield," she straightforwardly told him, sending him deeper into troubled confusion.

He made no answer, and although his prolonged silence seemed to give her pause, nevertheless she brought herself to quietly resume, with a little wistful smile.

"You seem to harbour no curiosity, Sir, but I shall press on regardless. You see— "

"I beg your pardon," Darcy felt compelled to offer, once he had regained a measure of his senses. "I did not wish to imply disinterest. I was merely… surprised."

"I do not wonder, given the history of our acquaintance," she ruefully retorted. "But rest assured, Mr Darcy," she added on a playful note that cut through him with all the shards of futile recollections, "at least this time I have every intention to be civil."

"You have never been otherwise, Miss Bennet," he replied, his voice low and leaden.

"Oh, come now, Sir," she cheerfully chided. "I do appreciate your gallantry, but we both know that on countless occasions I have been nothing of the sort. So there is little wonder that you disapprove of me."

"Disapprove of you?" he shot back, louder than he had intended, the shock of her declaration having gained the upper hand. And then he recollected himself, and his voice regained its usual timbre. "Forgive me, I see now that you must be jesting."

"No, Mr Darcy, I am not."

Stark confusion overspread his countenance again, as he eagerly searched hers.

"Then your comment was in earnest?"

"Very much so."

His eyes clouded.

"In that case, I owe you a profuse apology for having given that impression. I have…" His voice faltered. He cleared it and resumed quietly but firmly, as he looked away: "Miss Bennet, I have never disapproved of you."

"Oh."

Her tone clearly indicated she was either disbelieving or nonplussed so, dreadfully unwise as it might have been, Darcy could not stop himself from adding:

"My manner must have been at fault, and perhaps my temper. Never has reserve served me so poorly, if it led you to believe me disapproving when in fact from the earliest hours of our acquaintance I have held you in the deepest admiration and esteem."

He knew that he had foolishly ventured into very dangerous waters as soon as the earnest words escaped him, yet she did not seem to notice any of the undertones. He might have felt a measure of relief – had her prompt retort not brought a turmoil of a very different nature.

"Even at the Meryton assembly?"

She must have recognised the look of acute mortification for what it was, for she instantly retracted.

"Forgive me. I should not have said that. Especially today, when I approached you intending to mend bridges."

"They are not in need of mending, Miss Bennet," he replied, his voice suffused in the deepest contrition. "But I do have another apology to make for my insolence on that particular occasion. I was hoping you had not heard that comment, but this is no excuse for my own conduct. I can only assure you that, time and again, I have wished those words unsaid."

"Then let them be so," she retorted warmly, then impulsively turned to him, her hand outstretched. "Shall we endeavour to be friends then, Mr Darcy, especially as we are soon to be relations?"

Her other hand dropped from the crook of his right arm, freeing it for the offered handshake – and thus he was left with no excuse for his hesitation.

Friends? Heavens above, *relations?*

His insides twisted at the very notion, yet there was nothing he could do but consent to shake on it. Anything else would have been misconstrued as a rebuff – so he reached out to take her hand in his. She wore no gloves, and neither did he this morning, they were still stained with Morton's blood. The touch of her cool skin sent a sharp shock through his fingers, and he swallowed hard.

A futile thought occurred, that this was the first time he had held her hand thus – no gloves, and not a brief, casual touch either – and the aching intimacy of the moment was heartbreaking.

His other hand came up of its own volition, to cradle her small one in both of his. And, before he could remind himself of the need for carefully guarded conduct, his back was already bending, until his lips brushed against her fingers. Another shock, another set of shards racing through his veins to break his heart anew. And sharp desire clamouring for release, demanding that he take her in his arms and claim her lips – claim her as his. His, not Richard's. His!

His back stiffened with the supreme effort of conquering the sudden attack of madness, and he swiftly straightened, letting her hand drop.

"Of course," he forced himself to say, but his voice would not obey him. The words came hoarse and ragged. He cleared it again. "Forgive me, I must leave you now," he abruptly offered, before bowing and retreating at a considerable pace.

He left for town three hours later, along with his surprised and very disappointed sister – for clearly he could not trust himself to stay another day at Netherfield!

Chapter 4

Days, weeks, months went by in a kaleidoscope of grey, although this was the brightest summer Derbyshire had seen in many years. For that at least, Darcy was grateful. A vast number of improvements were planned at Pemberley, and in the dry weather they were all happening at once, keeping him engaged in riding from one end of the vast estate to the other, to supervise the progress more closely than a master had ever seen the need to, either before or since.

A lesser man would have sought distraction at the gambling tables or found oblivion in soft arms, or in too many bottles. This was not his way. With the exception of one fateful day earlier in the spring, any such indulgence was not even considered. Such sources of illusory comfort were so alien to his nature that they were not even perceived as an indulgence, but as a great effort, too great to warrant the exertion.

His prescription of choice – his laudanum – was Pemberley, as it had always been. Yet, just as laudanum, it could only offer palliation. For some conditions, there was no proven cure.

When every planned improvement was concluded and there was nothing left to hide behind, Darcy conceded it was time to consider another of his duties: that to Georgiana.

Several letters had arrived at Pemberley from his aunt, during his self-imposed exile. From Lady Langthorne, that was to say, not Lady Catherine. She had repeatedly emphasised in her communications that he could not seclude the child at Pemberley forever. Perhaps she was not ready for her coming-out, but she should move in society more, she should be seen, she should have the benefit of masters, for she was nearing her seventeenth birthday, and something *must* be done to ease her way into her first Season.

Without a doubt, Georgiana was not ready to contemplate her coming-out, and neither was he.

But there was truth in his aunt's exhortations. It was not fair on Georgiana to keep her in seclusion any longer, with just himself and Mrs Annesley for company.

So they returned to town together – for better or for worse.

⁕⁕⁕

Bingley was in town. A chance encounter at the club several days after his own arrival apprised him of that fact. He had been in town for many weeks, established at the townhouse he had purchased – on Charles Street, of all places!

Bingley might have found the name auspicious. Darcy did not. His friend's new residence was just around the corner. Less than two hundred yards from his own front door.

Of course, old ties and plain civility required that he meet with Bingley whenever they would both find themselves in town. He was prepared for that. But not for having Elizabeth's eldest sister settled on his very doorstep.

Regardless, niceties had to be observed; so he called in Charles Street with Georgiana to pay his respects, all the while wishing – dreading – to hear anything of *her*. He did not. The only reference Mrs Bingley made to her relations during that brief morning call was to reply in the affirmative when Georgiana civilly asked if they were in good health. However, there was every chance she would have more to say later today. There was nothing to be done about it, he could not avoid inviting them to Berkeley Square for dinner any longer. A note was sent, and he expected them tonight.

Perhaps he would have been better advised to ask them in more extensive company, rather than expose himself to the risk and discomfort of a small family dinner. Even Mrs Annesley was away, visiting relations for a fortnight, so it was to be just the four of them, and at first it had seemed the wisest choice. Not so now, but what was done was done. They would come, they would drive him to distraction with their own happiness and with tidings of *her* – or perhaps lack thereof – and then they would be gone and he would have a respite before he would have to consider seeing them again.

He dressed with unusual care for the evening, although for the life of him he could not justify it, then was tempted to withdraw to his study for a while.

Yet some niggling thought advised he really ought not leave Georgiana to wait alone for their guests' arrival, so he obeyed and went to the drawing room to join her.

The sense of duty did not serve him well.

Had he been in his study when the guests were announced, he would have had the benefit of privacy and perchance subdued lighting to conceal his shock.

As it was, he did not. In the brightness of the drawing room, his shock must have been readily apparent when Peter, the first footman, opened the door to announce the arrival of Mr and Mrs Bingley – and Miss Bennet.

He blanched and stood, then belatedly bowed.

The Bingleys' greetings went woefully unheeded. His eyes were for her alone, as were his words, when at last he spoke.

"Miss Bennet! What a remarkable surprise," he incautiously stammered, and cursed himself a moment later, when a blush spread over her cheeks and deep mortification came to cloud her brow.

"Surprise, Sir? I thought my brother had sent word…"

"Dash it, Darcy, did I not?" a flustered Bingley interjected, his countenance and manner reminiscent of that of a child chastised for bounding into a china shop. "I know I wrote the note but… did I not send it? I must have been distracted with… No matter. I must beg your pardon for the inconvenience," he added, the ill-chosen words making Elizabeth's blush deepen.

"Not at all," Darcy retorted swiftly. "You are most welcome! Peter, would you see to the arrangements?"

The footman bowed and promptly withdrew to do his master's bidding and alter the setting in the dining room, although in all likelihood the well-trained butler who had greeted the party at the door must have ascertained the need and orchestrated it already.

"I must add my apologies to Mr Bingley's," Elizabeth said quietly. "I arrived yesterday morning. My father and I were eager to see Jane and he escorted me to town," she elaborated, the faltering words tumbling one after the other in a clear indication of her acute discomfort.

"Pray, do not trouble yourself. You are most welcome," Darcy earnestly repeated. "Do sit. But… is Mr Bennet not with you?"

It was a foolish question, more tumbling words – his own this time – to alleviate the tension for, unless Mr Bennet had suddenly acquired the power of making himself invisible, it was plain to see he was not of the party.

Elizabeth answered nonetheless.

"No, my father would not stay for long. He set off to Longbourn a few hours ago."

"I hope he will arrive in safety," Darcy said civilly, in lieu of a more inspired comment. "Pray, do sit. Can I offer you a glass of sherry? Or Madeira?"

The duties of a host were a good excuse for temporary employment and Darcy took his time in filling the glasses, allowing Bingley to distribute them for him, before he took his own and came to join them.

It would not do to stare, nor dwell on the pain and pleasure of having her under his roof at last. She was exquisite, the lingering traces of the earlier blush still making her cheeks glow. She did not look towards him, but to Georgiana as she made a civil inquiry into his sister's comfort and pursuits, and for a moment he allowed himself the forbidden thrill of taking in every detail of her appearance – until she closed her perfect lips on the rim of the wineglass to take a sip of her Madeira, and he was forcibly reminded of the wisdom of looking away.

He turned towards Mrs Bingley with a valiant effort at some sort of conversation and the lady smilingly obliged, with eager assistance from her garrulous husband. He took a sip of his own drink, inwardly blessing Bingley for his expansive chatter, and for bringing Elizabeth to his house in the first place.

When Peter returned to announce dinner, his friend lost no time in doing his duty and offered his arm to Georgiana, and then he gave the other to his wife, unwittingly leaving Darcy to all manner of feelings and reflections as he followed the trio with Elizabeth's small hand on his arm.

It was sheer insanity to torture himself with the notion that she might have walked with him thus, every day. That this might have been her home, her dinner table. That she might have sat across from him, entertained their guests with her peerless sparkle – then stayed with him. In his house, in his arms, in his bed, in his life.

It was insanity, painful and destructive, yet for a few brief moments he allowed himself the pernicious comfort of the exquisite poison as they walked along the corridor, not to the main dining room with its too long table, but to the bittersweet intimacy of the smaller dining parlour.

It was skilfully set up for a cosy dinner, with all the comforts and none of the formality, which only served to prolong the dangerous illusion. The only sobering reminder of their real circumstances was the fact that she did not sit across from him; that place was Georgiana's. Yet it was not sobering enough – for she sat closer, at his left, making him intensely aware of her presence throughout dinner.

He would have been attuned to it even if they had been separated by dozens of guests and elaborate serving dishes or flower arrangements. But with the distance measured in nothing more than inches, he could hear every word, every trill of laughter. He could sense any movement, without even looking. With every breath, he would inhale her distinctive fragrance, a haunting admixture of jasmine and gardenia that he could associate with no one but her.

He barely touched his food, and barely spoke. In fact, he was wholly unaware of this failing until Bingley asked, from his own seat at Georgiana's side:

"Are you well, Darcy? You are very silent, even more than usual, and that is no mean feat," he smiled at his own sally. "In fact, I would say you look positively grim. I trust there is nothing of import troubling you."

'Nothing of import! Heavens above, Bingley! If you only knew.'

His friend did not, nobody did, which was *some* form of mercy.

"I thank you, I am well," he said at last. "Pray, forgive me. I was… distracted."

"Thank goodness. I was afraid you might have had bad tidings of some sort."

"None whatever," Darcy replied, inwardly marvelling for a fleeting moment at the ease with which he was now dispensing falsehoods.

It was just as well. The skill was badly needed.

"What of the Colonel? Any recent word of him?"

"He is in Madrid," Darcy replied concisely, only to involuntarily glance towards Elizabeth when he heard her delivering the same, at almost the same time.

Their eyes met briefly, and then he looked away.

So Richard wrote to her. Of course he would.

"Already?" Bingley queried. "I thought I read in the papers about Salamanca. The first Spanish town to be liberated in three years, they said, the first great victory after Badajoz. A valiant endeavour, the storming of that fortress. Taken at great cost against all odds. Did he write you more about it?"

Darcy said nothing, leaving her room to comment if she wished, although he knew full well that, to his good fortune in more ways than one, Fitzwilliam had not faced the dangers of that particular assault. He had been at Rosings then, claiming his own victory, on a very different front...

But Elizabeth did not comment, and Darcy felt obliged to do so.

"He wrote about the victory at Salamanca in July, and that they marched into Madrid a few weeks ago, on the 12th of August. As to future plans, Lord Wellington is too wise to share them with the *Morning Chronicle* and presumably is not allowing his officers to share them with us either. May I suggest one of those rose-flavoured sweetmeats, Mrs Bingley? Miss Bennet? Or a lavender *cachou*? The latter might be an acquired taste, but they are a great favourite with Georgiana, along with most of Mr Gunter's delectable wares."

Mrs Bingley declined the offer of a sweetmeat and chose an orange-flavoured ice instead, but Elizabeth smilingly declared her full confidence in Georgiana's indirect recommendation. She sampled the *cachou*, pronounced it delicious, then moved on to an elderflower mousse and a conversation that no longer touched upon Badajoz or Madrid.

Before long, Georgiana asked if the ladies might be willing to follow her to the drawing room for coffee, and Darcy was left with Bingley in a room that still held the faintest scent of jasmine and gardenia. He stood to refill the glasses then returned to his seat, only to see Bingley shifting in his own with as much patience as a tethered pup. He suppressed a sigh. He was very fond of Bingley, but the man's excitable spirits were at times terribly hard to bear.

"Well, Darcy," his friend suddenly began, "perhaps I ought to apologise again for my distraction and the confusion I have caused with my misplaced note. I could not fail to see you were put out by the unexpected addition to our party," he said ruefully, and at that Darcy glanced up in panic.

Heavens, is that what Bingley thought – what *she* thought? That his sour temper was caused by her arrival uninvited? It was very nearly worse than the three of them guessing the real reason, and he lost no time in setting his friend to rights.

"Not so, Bingley, not at all! Pray assure Miss Bennet and your wife that nothing could be further from the truth! The fault is mine, I have... I have some concerns that preoccupy me. Not grave," he lied, "merely distracting. It is I who should apologise for giving the impression that the change of plans was anything but welcome."

"Oh. That is a relief, for me at least. But what of your concerns? Can I be of assistance?"

"I thank you, no. Just some business matters," he dissembled.

"Well! I trust you can resolve them to your satisfaction," the other said, and thankfully did not seem to expect an answer, for none was forthcoming. Instead, he carried on. "Now, as to my own distraction that had caused the problem in the first place, or shall we say, the misunderstanding. The reason is, Darcy, that I have great tidings!" he burst out, and his grin grew wider. "I trust Jane would not mind my sharing them with you. You are my closest friend and I *must* tell someone, or else I shall explode. I am to be a father, Darcy! Can you believe it? Early in the spring. The dearest girl told me yesterday, just before Mr Bennet and Elizabeth came to town to see us, and I must own I scarcely know what I did with myself that morning and frankly ever since!"

"I am delighted for you both," Darcy replied promptly, ashamed of his earlier intolerance of his friend's excitable nature.

At least this time Bingley had reasons aplenty to be cheerful, and Darcy offered his warm congratulations and best wishes. If the sentiment was tinged with sadness and more than a little envy, he did his best to keep that to himself – although chances were that Bingley would not have noticed anyway, just as he did not notice that for the remainder of the time they spent together at the dinner table, it was he who did almost all the talking.

At last, Bingley straightened in his chair.

"Forgive me Darcy, for rattling on so."

"Not at all. Of course you would wish to talk. 'Tis good to see you happy."

"Thank you," the other beamed and clapped him on the shoulder. "Yes, I am. A great deal more than I deserve. But never mind that now. Shall we rejoin the ladies?"

They did. They walked towards the drawing room but then changed course, for the sound of the pianoforte drew them towards the music room instead. Georgiana must have been persuaded to entertain their guests with song, Darcy determined.

Yet the clear voice that rose in a poignant aria was not Georgiana's – and he stood transfixed for a long moment, before quietly walking in to take a seat and listen to Elizabeth singing softly about the sweetest sorrow that nothing could dispel.

.⚬ℚ ℚ⚬.

"Can I persuade you now to take my place, Miss Darcy?" Elizabeth asked as she stood from the pianoforte.

She had played for the best part of an hour, in turns coaxing unbearably sweet or very lively tunes from the instrument – and tugging at Darcy's heartstrings in the process.

He took a deep breath, in equal measure disappointed that she would play no longer and thankful for the end of the exquisite torture. He turned to his sister to add his gentle encouragement to Elizabeth's entreaties and Georgiana allowed herself to be persuaded.

She played for them, a faithful rendition of a difficult composition to begin with, earning the delighted praise of their guests and Darcy's silent gratitude for the opportunity to regain some of his composure as he listened to the familiar piece and endeavoured not to glance too often towards the chair where Elizabeth was sitting.

Afterwards, Georgiana played again, a rondo this time, then two short quadrille pieces, and finally agreed to trade the pianoforte for the harp.

Her first choices were cheerful, light and pleasing. Another short rondo, a sprightly country dance, then Mr Bishop's *'Summer Moon'*, and in the latter her beautiful voice mingled with the exquisite harmonies of the harp, to make their guests clap with undisguised enchantment when she reached the end.

The third choice, however, was dreadfully unwise. Darcy knew as much from the very first notes, as soon as he recognised the celebrated ballad.

It was Mr Dibdin's lament for a departed hero who had lost his life in the pursuit of duty, and told of a valiant arm forever stilled, of loving hearts forever separated.

The lines would have been deeply moving even recited as a poem. Joined with the poignant sound of the harp, they were unbearable.

A surreptitious glance in Elizabeth's direction confirmed that his apprehension was well-founded. Under his very eyes, hers filled with tears. She sought to conceal her discomposure by staring at the pattern on her dress, then at the portrait on the wall beside her, but it was plain to see that her heart was breaking – and, at this further proof of her attachment to his cousin, so did his.

He swallowed hard and stood to walk to Georgiana.

"Sweetling, I must beg your pardon. I hope you will forgive the interruption, but I was so taken with the last song you played. What was it? *'Summer Moon'*? Delightful! Would you be so kind as to sing that one again?"

It was unprecedented for him to disrupt her playing and he was loath to do so, but it could not be helped. Although surprised and slightly disconcerted, Georgiana readily complied.

Once his request was granted, she thankfully did not return to the mournful ballad. Perhaps she thought that the interruption had spoilt the impact of its beauty, or perhaps she had belatedly understood his reasons.

Elizabeth certainly did.

A glance of warm gratitude conveyed as much, when he regained his seat. He knew he should acknowledge it in some way or another, but he did not know how. A brief smile might have served, had he not lost the habit. So he just bowed his head, his expression lifeless.

As lifeless as the house became an hour later, when the guests decided it was time they took their leave.

∽◌◍◌∼

When Bingley wrote to reciprocate and invite him and Georgiana to dine in Charles Street, Darcy knew what he should expect. She would be there still, Bingley had confirmed it, so this time Darcy was prepared for the encounter.

Yet he was woefully unprepared for what was to come.

The footmen had barely folded away the white tablecloth to reveal the green, then neatly arranged the dishes of the second cover in a pleasing pattern, when the door was quietly opened and Bingley's butler entered, to announce none other than Fitzwilliam.

The room erupted in cries of surprise and pleasure and there was little wonder that they all rushed to him – some quicker than others. Darcy stood as well, cast his napkin on the table and walked sedately to shake his cousin's hand.

There was no room for him to do so. Elizabeth was holding one of Richard's hands between both her own, and Bingley availed himself of his other elbow, entreating him to join them and calling to the butler to set another place. A chair was duly brought – a footman fetched one from those lined against the wall – and Bingley came to set it himself next to Elizabeth's.

She verily glowed. A brightness that hurt the eye – or at the very least hurt Darcy's. He took his seat in silence while the others settled into theirs talking all at once, even Georgiana, eager to learn by what fortunate circumstance Richard was in their midst.

Darcy did not hear the others.

He heard only *her* when she exclaimed:

"What joy! What brings you here?"

"To town? Dispatches. True enough, 'tis not common practice to employ a colonel for the purpose, but my commanding officer has a heart of gold. He knew I had to embark too soon after our engagement, so he did me a good turn."

"You must convey my thanks," Elizabeth smiled warmly, and Darcy looked away.

"I certainly shall. As to my presence here, I called in Berkeley Square to see you, Darcy – and Norwell, that sly old fox, your butler, was astute enough to give me the very best of news. He told me where you were, where you all were, and I rushed to follow. What good fortune, to find you in town," he said to Elizabeth and reached to take her hand and press it to his lips.

She blushed a most delightful shade of pink and eagerly retorted:

"Good fortune indeed. I arrived just a few days ago." She left her hand in his, and added with feeling, "I am so happy you are well. You have grown so very dark! This suntan— "

"The healthful effect of a summer campaign," Fitzwilliam laughed and most of the party joined him.

They still talked at once, requesting all manner of detail, and under the cover of their constant, cheerful chatter, Darcy's long silences went largely unheeded. He barely remembered to toy with his food upon the plate and offer the odd comment, the odd quiet question. Of all the thoughts that preyed upon him, one was worse than most: it was a vile world, this, where his cousin unexpectedly returned from the battlefield, and he was not glad.

Since he could not feel the joy, he tried to feign it. He tried very hard indeed. He struggled to talk, smile, appear cheerful. But every word, laugh, sigh or whisper of joyful reunion between the engaged couple was yet another knife twisted in his breast, and he could not bear the pain much longer.

When it became quite obvious that they were holding hands under the table, Darcy reached for his wineglass and drained it, wishing he could at least stand and leave, but Mrs Bingley had not stirred from her seat yet, so he was chained to his.

At last she stood, and Elizabeth and Georgiana moved to follow. It came as no surprise that Fitzwilliam did too. After a four-month separation, no power under heaven could have kept him at his port, when his affianced was in a nearby chamber.

No power under heaven could make Darcy join them and subject himself of his own free will to the agonies of Tantalus. Thus, when Bingley suggested they rejoin the others, Darcy begged leave to briefly explore the library instead.

"Whatever for?" Bingley exclaimed in laughing surprise. "Believe me, Darcy, I am ashamed to own it, but 'tis not worth your while. My library here is no better than the one at Netherfield."

"Nevertheless…"

"If you insist…"

Darcy insisted, so his friend let him have his way. They ambled down the corridor together, but soon parted and Bingley carried on towards the drawing room without him.

Alone at last, painfully so, Darcy pressed his eyes shut and released the groan he had withheld for above an hour. He ran his fingers through his hair and walked into the library – only to wish he had gone anywhere else. Anywhere but there!

The door moved noiselessly on its hinges to reveal a scene he had pictured often in his imagination, but so far had been spared the agony of witnessing with his own eyes.

His lungs emptied of air and he recognised the familiar sensation of a violent punch in the pit of his stomach, because the library was far from deserted. His cousin and Elizabeth were there, locked in a tight embrace. Kissing. As though starved. Deep, hungry kisses – their just reward after too long a separation.

He looked away, but it was too late. Branded in his memory, the image would not leave him. Not now. Probably never.

He dug his nails into his palms, stepped back and reached to close the door. He was too late with that as well. Alerted by some sound or movement, the couple turned towards him. Fitzwilliam released her from his arms and, supremely unabashed, he shrugged and smiled. Elizabeth's lips rounded into a silent *'Oh!'*

His throat unbearably dry, Darcy swallowed.

"Excuse me," he said quietly, stepped further back and closed the door. His fist clenched on the frame until his knuckles whitened, then he relaxed the grip, let his arm drop and straightened his shoulders.

At least one thing was certain. Now the drawing room was safe.

ഹൈ ♱ ⚬

They followed soon – although not soon enough – and came to sit on the only sofa left unoccupied. The one across from him.

He did not wish to glance that way and made every effort not to, yet his eyes seemed to have developed a will of their own and would dart in their direction until, inevitably, he caught Elizabeth's. She blushed a hint of scarlet, but met his eyes squarely. And then her chin came up and her brow arched in a look of defiance he could not fail to recognise. He had seen it once before, in another time, and it said just as clearly: *'Despise me if you dare!'*

And then she turned away and pointedly placed her hand into Fitzwilliam's who, at Bingley's request, had just begun to tell them of the march into Madrid.

Apparently the regiments had been welcomed with pealing bells, waving palm fronds, fountains flowing wine and women casting flowers and kerchiefs into their path. Dancers pirouetted ahead of the columns, householders crowded in to break the ranks with gifts and wine, soldiers were dragged into doorways and feasted and the revelries continued through the night.

"So – fiesta, flamenco and grateful señoritas for all and sundry!" Darcy heard himself scoff, in the most contemptible manner.

He was not surprised at the severe glance of censure Elizabeth cast his way. He undoubtedly deserved it. His other punishment followed soon enough. Taking no offence at his untoward comment, Fitzwilliam settled a warm look on his betrothed, only to find it was returned in full. He stroked her hand, their tender gaze unbroken even as he retorted mildly:

"For some perhaps, Cousin. But certainly not all."

The heavy sigh turned at the last moment into a reasonably convincing cough, Darcy trained his eyes onto the carpet at his feet.

The night was young. And it would be long and horrid.

෴

His expectations were confirmed. If anything, the trial was even longer than he had anticipated, for his cousin came to spend the night in Berkeley Square. It was only natural that Darcy should offer, and he wanted to do so anyway – did he not?

Inevitably, this led to a long spell in his study, over brandy. Inevitably, Elizabeth's name was mentioned again and again, along with all manner of plans for the future. Inevitably, by the time his cousin was quite finished, Darcy was thoroughly drained and weary to the bone. And when Fitzwilliam came back from the clouds at last, to ask if whatever had troubled him last time they met, in April, was resolved by now, inevitably Darcy had to resort to barefaced lies.

෴

Fitzwilliam's time in town was very short. Nine days, nothing more. During his stay he called in Charles Street daily – and Darcy did not follow. He did not call after Fitzwilliam's departure either and learned from Bingley, when they chanced to meet at their club again, that Elizabeth had returned to Longbourn. So there would be no more risks – or no more chances – of encounters in Green Park, at church or at Gunter's. So much the better, for it could not be any worse.

Then Bingley came one day to ask a question. He brought it up without preamble, soon after they were settled with refreshments in the study.

"I was wondering, Darcy, know you of a way of getting something in safety to your cousin?"

"What would that be?"

"This," Bingley said, as he produced a small velvet pouch. He tugged at the strings and, carefully for him, he let its contents slide onto Darcy's desk.

It was a small miniature, in a thin golden frame worked in a delicate leaf pattern, but the goldsmith's skill was lost on Darcy, for the ivory oval held an exquisite rendition of Elizabeth. He bent his head for a closer look, then leaned back in his chair.

From his own seat across from him, Bingley resumed.

"She had it made while she was staying with us. A pity it was not finished while Fitzwilliam was still in town, but there we have it. She was reluctant to entrust it to the mail coach and the Lisbon packet, and I cannot blame her. Before she left, I offered to ask you if there was a way to send it more securely. She was unsure of the wisdom of it, but in the end relented. So, have you any thoughts?"

He had thoughts aplenty, though none pertaining to safe couriers.

"Leave it with me," Darcy said at last. "I shall make inquiries."

"I thank you. I appreciate it. Then you might have this too, if you do not mind," he added, fumbling in his pocket to produce a neatly folded letter. "I told her I would put it in the post if there was no way to send the miniature, but otherwise they might as well go together. The letter stands a better chance of reaching him that way."

Darcy nodded, but said nothing further.

"Well, I shall not keep you. I just wanted to ask you about these and tell you that we should be leaving shortly, Jane and I. We will return to Netherfield next week. Would you care to join us? Or if not now, then perhaps later in the year? You would be most welcome. Most welcome indeed."

Of Bingley's welcome Darcy held no doubt. The wisdom of the scheme, or rather lack thereof, was a wholly different matter.

"I thank you, but I fear I must decline. Georgiana ought to be in town. We should be making preparations for her coming-out."

"Oh. Would that be in the coming Season?"

"I expect so."

"Then I wish you well, both of you. And of course the offer stands. Do come and bring her too, once the pair of you have had your fill of morning calls and dancing masters. At the very least, pray come for Christmas."

"I am much obliged, but we shall have to see about that later."

"Let me know what you decide. I should leave you to your papers now. Unless you would care to accompany me to Brooks's?"

"I thank you, not today. But I shall call upon you on the morrow to bid farewell to Mrs Bingley."

"You are most welcome, Darcy. Anytime."

And Bingley did leave him to his papers, as he said he would. But the neat stacks were destined to remain untouched from the moment the miniature was placed upon his desk.

He brought it closer, still resting on the dark red velvet.

It was masterfully done in scrupulous detail, the likeness captured to perfection. The oval of her face, the shape and exact colour of her eyes, the remarkably fine lashes. The promise of a smile in her glance and on the rosy lips, a hint of pink in the flawless cheeks. A long wavy lock trailing to one side, as though it had just ceased fluttering in the breeze.

The miniature was painted with the greatest skill, and Darcy wondered who the artist might have been. No matter. That avenue was closed. The very same artist could not be approached without a strong risk of exposure. But thankfully there must be dozens of highly skilled miniaturists in town.

Ever so carefully, he returned the delicate creation to its velvet pouch and placed it in his pocket, before walking to sharply tug the bell pull.

"Pray order the carriage, Thomas," he instructed the footman who promptly came in to attend him, "and let Miss Georgiana know I shall be gone for about an hour."

⁓ ⁕ ⁓

The pair of Argand lamps cast a good light on the table covered in thick golden velvet, and Darcy placed the miniature in the best illuminated spot.

"Is this your work, by any chance?" he cautiously asked Mr Cosway, who had been commissioned oftentimes before to capture Darcy likenesses into miniatures.

"I fear not, Sir. It is vaguely reminiscent of Mr Engleheart's style, but I cannot be certain."

"Do not concern yourself. I wish to know if it might be copied."

"Of course. Although, if I am allowed to add, it would be preferable to paint from the original. That is to say, perhaps the young lady might be induced to sit for me?"

"That will not be possible, I fear."

"Then I shall do my best to replicate it. A trifle irregular perhaps, but if this is the only option…?"

"It is."

"I see."

Silence fell after that brief exchange.

Darcy shifted in his seat, then spoke again.

"I ought to mention that time is rather of the essence. I regret having to ask for haste as well as a faithful reproduction, but there would be… hm!… shall we say, ample compensation."

The older man cast him a glance from behind the gold-rimmed spectacles and Darcy squared his shoulders, refusing to speculate whether experience and age might have helped the artist recognise the signs. For all he knew, over the years the man might have had countless strange requests from young foolish patrons who should have known better.

Whatever his opinions might have been, Mr Cosway kept them to himself and resumed the careful examination of the delicate object. Once fully satisfied, he set it down again, removed his spectacles and folded them with sparse, precise motions.

"If you can leave it with me now, Sir, the copy will be finished by the middle of next month."

⁂

And so it was; timely delivered and a perfect replica, so much so that, were it not for the pattern on the frames, Darcy would have been hard-pressed to tell the difference. There they were now, one alongside the other, on his desk. One for himself, the other for Fitzwilliam. If only it were as simple in life – that would have been the answer to everybody's problems! A bitter laugh escaped him at the unseemly thought and Darcy reached to place the original in its velvet pouch, then wrapped the copy and put it in his breast-pocket.

He leaned back in his chair and closed his eyes, steeling himself for the final task until, with a muted oath, he stirred from his inaction to open the drawer and retrieve the blasted letter he had secreted there, out of sight but in no way out of mind.

It had silently mocked him for the entire time that he had waited for Mr Cosway to give proof of his skill. Much as he sought to, he could not make himself forget that it was there. Elizabeth's letter locked in his desk drawer – her innermost thoughts, in her own hand, under a fragile seal.

He had in turns cursed it, pretended to ignore it, stared at it, held it and even gone as far as inspecting the neatly applied seal with undue insistence. A trim patch of wax, marked with a floral pattern, but without initials, presumably for the use of other ladies in the household, not just hers.

The red eye of the seal had stared right back, wickedly taunting him, daring him to act. There were ways, it seemed to hint. A sharp knife could work wonders in a steady hand. A thin film of fresh wax would easily secure an undamaged seal back in its place – and no one need know the letter had been opened.

Shamefully, he had considered it. Repeatedly.

He would have liked to think it was an ingrained sense of honour that had held him back and kept him on the honest path. Perhaps. Yet there was another, equally strong reason. Or rather a question. What did he expect to find? There was nothing good to hope for in her letter. There could be nothing worse than the evidence of his own eyes. Nothing as harrowing as their kiss in Bingley's library.

Another muted oath and then, "Enough!"

He reached for a fresh sheet of hot-pressed paper to pen a few bold lines for Fitzwilliam, that would convey good wishes and explain why it was he who sent Elizabeth's miniature and her letter.

He found brown paper and wrapped the pouch containing the delicate piece of ivory for further safety, then enveloped it in a neat parcel along with his own letter and hers. The parcel was sealed and secured with string.

A few days later, it would begin its long south-eastward journey, in the saddlebags of a young British officer bound for the Peninsula, while the twin of Fitzwilliam's *'Elizabeth'* would remain in Berkeley Square, to foster empty dreams and sleepless nights.

Chapter 5

Longbourn stood silent amid fields and meadows covered by a thin layer of snow that brightened the surroundings and tricked the eye into believing it was almost dawn, rather than a mere hour after midnight. Yet no eye was open to be taken in. The household slept at peace, knowing nothing of the carriage that was driving towards Meryton as fast as the dark, slippery roads allowed.

When a loud rumble came to herald its hurried passage through the gates of Longbourn, it only alerted the housekeeper and a very nervous maid. But the insistent rapping at the doors awakened everybody and they sprang up to light their candles, wrap themselves in whatever came to hand and hurry out into the corridor to learn the cause of the disturbance. Some were intrigued, others alarmed and a few found the novelty exciting. Mrs Bennet wailed that they were about to be murdered in their beds. Of them all, only Mr Bennet made his way downstairs in his gown, nightcap and slippers. He held out his candle and cautiously opened the front door by an inch or two. The young man liveried as a footman was unknown to him. Not so the fellow's haggard-looking master who stood beside him, and Mr Bennet opened the door wide.

"Mr Darcy! What brings you here in the middle of the night?"

The reaction was instinctive, born out of surprise. Even a man of lesser intellect would have grasped that the lateness of the hour and the visitor's countenance could not possibly bode well. Mr Bennet was not a man of lesser intellect, so he instantly sobered.

"Ill tidings, is it?" he asked quietly and, at Darcy's nod, he motioned him in. "Come, Sir. Come into my study. And your people of course, let them come in too, 'tis a cold night," he added with a shiver.

Mr Darcy turned to the young footman.

"Fetch Peter, would you, and wait for me in here. Pray let Joseph know I would much rather he stays with the horses. I shall return directly to speak to him."

And then he followed Mr Bennet into his study and closed the door behind him – to Lydia's bitter disappointment. She had crept downstairs and peeped around the corner, just in time to catch a glimpse of the visitor's grim profile as he made his way into her father's habitual refuge. She would have dearly liked to hear more, but the closed door put paid to all those hopes. But she still knew more than her sisters did, so she hastened above-stairs to boast of the extra knowledge.

"'Tis Mr Darcy and he looks like thunder," she eagerly whispered, and Elizabeth blanched.

Meanwhile, in the study, Mr Bennet did not mince his words.

"Must I prepare my daughter for the worst, Sir?" came the straightforward question, and he received a straightforward answer.

"Not yet. He is alive – but only just."

"Where is he?"

"At my house in town. I thought E— Miss Bennet ought to know. And… it might do him good to see her."

"So he is conscious."

"On occasion."

"I daresay I can wait for the details. Besides, it serves no purpose to have you give them twice. Help yourself to brandy. I shall fetch Elizabeth."

Alone in the study, Darcy did not help himself to brandy. Nor was he kept waiting long. Once Lydia had triumphantly broadcast the little she had learned, Elizabeth had hurried to her room to dress and insistently begged for Kitty's assistance. It was willingly granted. Thus, when Mr Bennet went in search of her, he found her almost ready to come down. With swift, deft motions despite unsteady hands, she braided her hair and just about finished pinning it up into a plain chignon, when she heard new commotion erupting in the hallway. Predictably, the loudest voice was her mother's.

"Mr Bennet! Mr Bennet! What news?"

"What news, Papa?"

"This is about the Colonel, is it not? My poor, poor girl – widowed before she is even wed!"

"Is he lost to us, Papa?"

"No one is lost, child, although some might have lost their senses. Go now. Pray go and dress. There has been enough flapping of nightclothes in the hallway," Elizabeth heard her father say, and her spirits were revived a little.

She carelessly pushed the last hairpin in place and rushed to let him in, but Mr Bennet would not enter. He took her hand and pressed it between both of his as he quietly delivered the modicum of comfort he knew he could safely offer.

"While there is life, there is hope, my Lizzy — and he is alive, at Darcy's house. Join us when you are ready. He will tell us the rest."

"I am ready now!"

"Then come."

They made their way together, barely squeezing past the huddled forms of Mrs Bennet and her three younger daughters, who all had something to say and showed no inclination of obeying Mr Bennet's repeated instructions to retire to their chambers and make themselves fit for company.

That being said, he failed to take his own advice, for he was still wearing his nightclothes, complete with cap and slippers, when he walked back into the study. Yet the apparel diminished nothing of his dignity, and besides no one could care less. Least of all Darcy. His eyes were for Elizabeth alone. Wrapped in her shawl, her hands clasped to her chest, she looked frail and frightened, and he loathed the ill tidings he had come to give.

"What news, Sir?" she breathlessly asked as he sprang up to greet her.

"My cousin is in Berkeley Square," Darcy began cautiously. "He was injured in the last assault on Burgos. Not severely, just a number of flesh wounds, but he caught a pernicious fever in the weeks that followed. The regiments retreated in freezing cold and foul weather and, in his weakened state, it did him no favours. He caught an infection to his chest — the physician speaks of pleurisy now, and fears something else... Peripneumony, if I remember rightly. Fitzwilliam is... not well. I thought you might wish to go to him — if you would allow it, Sir," he concluded, with a swift glance towards Mr Bennet.

They both replied at once.

"Yes, of course! I thank you."

"By all means. But you cannot go alone."

"Jane would agree to come with me, I hope. And Charles."

"The best notion," Darcy interjected. "Forgive me, I was not thinking straight. I should have stopped at Netherfield on the way, it would have gained us time."

"No matter," Mr Bennet replied, then added firmly, "Nay, leave them be. I will travel with you, Lizzy. I shall leave a note to be delivered to Mr Bingley in the morning and I trust they would be kind enough to follow us to town, or at least send word to their people in Charles Street— "

"As to that, Sir," Darcy spoke up again, "I hope you will agree to stay in Berkeley Square. It makes more sense and you are very welcome. It would be good if Mrs Bingley follows, though not to open house, just… for comfort and support."

He did not look at Elizabeth as he said that, but her sharp intake of breath compelled him to.

"Take heart," he urged, in a low but very earnest voice, striving to persuade both her and himself. "He is in good hands. Dr Graham is said to be very skilled. There is hope."

He saw her lips move, but could not hear her, as she whispered Mr Bennet's words of comfort like a prayer.

"While there is life, there is hope."

ာ၉ၜ ၆ၜ

With surprising energy for a man of his disposition, Mr Bennet rose to the occasion and took care of everything. He instructed Mrs Hill to see to a warm drink for Mr Darcy and his people, including the beleaguered coachman, temporarily relieved from his duties by the stable lads from Longbourn. He wrote the note for Mr Bingley. He got his man to pack his trunk, and a trustworthy maid to do the same for Elizabeth. He strictly forbade his wife and younger daughters from pestering their visitor with questions and laments while Mr Darcy waited in the study for Elizabeth and him to ready themselves for travel, leaving them just the meagre comfort of gathering to see them off, with fluttering kerchiefs, warm wishes and entreaties to write promptly.

After the commotion of the hasty departure, the carriage seemed very quiet. It was just the rattling of the wheels and the cries of the coachman urging the team on that broke the silence – until Darcy

64

spoke up to ask Miss Bennet if she was warm enough and offer her another travelling rug, then belatedly remembered to extend the same courtesy to the young lady's father. They both thanked him and declined, then Elizabeth added:

"Is there anything else you can tell me?"

He could barely see her face in the pale glimmer of the carriage lights, but her voice carried all the anxiety her countenance might have betrayed.

"Not a vast deal," he sighed. "Not of his condition."

In truth, Fitzwilliam's man had apprised him of the trials and tribulations that Wellington's hapless regiments had been forced to endure, but it made for a distressing tale which he saw no purpose in burdening her with.

After losing more than two thousand men in several failed assaults on the fortress of Burgos, the Commander-in-chief had been compelled to order the retreat to the bleak hills on the Portuguese frontier, but every adverse circumstance, from inclement weather to woeful human error, had conspired against them.

Unprecedented gales had turned every stream into a torrent and the roads into rivers of icy mud that rose to the men's ankles and sometimes their knees. For several days, there had been no prospect of any bivouac but the drenched ground. Moreover, through a horrific blunder on the part of a newly-appointed Quartermaster General, the supplies had gone astray far to the north.

Battered by icy winds and drenched to their skins, the troops had found themselves also deprived of rations and had been forced to make do with acorns and raw carrion. In mere days, a glorious army had been reduced to a pitiful mass of famished wretches and the field hospitals on the Agueda were now teeming with the thousands laid low by typhus, dysentery and ague.

In some ways, Fitzwilliam's progressively worsening condition had worked to his advantage, if anyone could term it such, for it had led his commanding officer to insistently request that he be one of the few hundreds sent forth to Oporto, to be embarked on ships bound for Portsmouth. Thus, he was at least returned to his home country and within reach of the best care he could possibly receive.

No, he would not tell her of adversity, Darcy determined, but speak instead of fortunate circumstances, few as they might have been.

"Thankfully he was one of those returned to Portsmouth."

"How did you learn of it?"

"His man sent word. But there was no one in residence at the Langthorne townhouse at this time of year, so the housekeeper brought the note to me."

"Thank goodness you were there! The hospitals in Portsmouth must be… "

'Grim places', Darcy silently finished the thought. The one he had hastened to fetch Fitzwilliam from certainly was. A vast receptacle of suffering humanity – the untold price of too long a war.

From the other corner of the carriage, Mr Bennet chose to speak up again.

"Should you not try to rest a little, Lizzy? I know, I know," he interjected in response to her disjointed protest. "But you have barely had a wink of sleep tonight and you will need your strength. Come, let me put this rug around you and rest your head on my shoulder. You are too old for a lullaby now, more's the pity," he tenderly added with a semblance of a chuckle, "but not too old to listen to your papa once in a while. Come, Lizzy, humour me," he earnestly entreated, making Darcy repent of any instance when he had inwardly censured Mr Bennet for being a too detached, too uncaring father.

It was not his place to offer anything. Certainly not the same sort of comfort and very likely not even an opinion, so Darcy said nothing, much as he concurred with the older gentleman. She needed all her strength to face what lay ahead.

She must have seen the wisdom of it too, for she replied with a heavy sigh:

"Thank you, Papa. I shall try."

But she did not. Not yet.

In the poor light, Darcy saw her turn to him instead.

"Your cousin owes you a great deal, Sir, and so do I. I thank you."

A silent nod would not suffice this time – it was too dark. So he cleared his voice to say, "Pray, do not mention it, Miss Bennet. I could have done no less."

It was still dark, but dawn was drawing nearer when the Tottenham Court Road turnpike came into view at last. On the opposite seat, father and daughter were still huddled together under the travelling rugs and neither stirred, leading the unobservant to assume they were asleep. Mr Darcy, who was far from unobservant, knew that this was not the case, at least where the daughter was concerned. She had been fully awake since Highgate and although her face was turned towards the window, every now and then he could see her eyes were still wide open, glittering in the darkness. Glittering with tears? Perhaps. He could not tell.

He did not speak to offer empty comfort or false assurances of sorts and, in her turn, she said nothing either. In fact, barely a word was spoken since the *Green Man* at Barnet, where they had stopped for the briefest time to bate the horses. But when the carriage carefully rounded the awkward corner into Davies Street which led into Berkeley Square, Darcy did speak up, with the only truth that he was allowed to offer:

"Miss Bennet, everything humanly possible will be done for him. I promise."

Her eyes turned to him then, and they *were* full of tears.

"I thank you, Sir. I know."

ঙৈ ঙৈ

A tired-looking footman – Simon, the youngest of all three – opened the door for them, and Darcy thanked him with a nod when he came to take Elizabeth's pelisse and bonnet, then Mr Bennet's things and his.

"Would you like me to come up with you, my child?" Mr Bennet asked, affectionate concern lining his kindly features.

"No, Papa. You should warm yourself."

"Pray see to the fire in the morning parlour, Simon," Darcy instructed, "and fetch some tea as well."

With a bow to his master and a "This way, Sir" to the elderly visitor, Simon left to do as bid. Mr Bennet squeezed his daughter's hand and followed, leaving her and Darcy in the large and silent entrance hall.

"Shall we, Miss Bennet?" Darcy gestured and, at her eager nod, he led her to the curving staircase.

They made their way up, their footsteps quiet on the marble stairs and then inaudible on the thick-carpeted corridor that led to the sick-chamber. He opened the fifth door and ushered her in. A strong scent of vinegar and lemons met them on the threshold and Elizabeth stepped into the room, her eyes instantly drawn to the wide canopied bed.

In the treacherous light of the flickering candles, the gaunt features seemed to move – but no, he was asleep, reclining partly upright on several pillows. From a chair at the bedside, an older bewigged gentleman sat up at their entrance, his finger flying to his lips in a request for silence.

They obeyed and Darcy noiselessly closed the door. The doctor stood and came to them, showing no surprise at the arrival of a young lady whom he had never seen before. Undoubtedly Darcy had informed him of his purpose before setting off to Longbourn on his mission.

This was neither the time nor the place for introductions, so only silent nods of greeting were exchanged before the doctor proceeded to inform them in very quiet tones of the patient's condition, which was all they wished to ask about in any case.

"He has just fallen asleep a quarter of an hour ago, after a very restless night. The fever is still high, 'tis not showing any sign of breaking."

"And his breathing?" Darcy asked, just as quietly.

"Laborious, as you can hear. The oppression on his lungs is too severe. Having him recline on several pillows offers some relief, but not enough."

"Shall I send for more steaming water?"

"Perhaps later. The commotion would disturb his sleep. The air is humid enough for now."

It was very humid, Elizabeth belatedly observed. Steam was rising from several open tea-urns placed about the room, as well as from a bubbling kitchen cauldron mounted in the fireplace, in an improvised arrangement.

"Why the steam?" she asked in a whisper.

"It moistens the air and eases his breathing," the doctor explained briefly. "It also helps him cough, which is what he needs to clear his chest. Unfortunately, coughing also causes him severe pain and disturbs his sleep."

As though to prove the doctor right, a loud racking cough suddenly broke the silence, and Elizabeth darted her eyes towards the bed, to see hideous agony contorting the features of the man she had pledged herself to. His hand went to press hard on the right side of his chest, as if the effort to limit its movement might help relieve the pain. It did not seem to make a great deal of difference, and he groaned.

Then his eyes opened, drifted – and settled on her. He blinked. The chapped lips curled into a disbelieving smile, before releasing a hoarse whisper:

"Elizabeth?"

With a muffled sob she rushed to him, not stopping to ask for the doctor's permission. She took and clasped the hand reaching out to her, then brought the burning fingers to her lips.

"It *is* you! When— ?"

Another racking cough cut his question short and Elizabeth urged swiftly:

"Do not speak. Shh. Do not speak now. Rest."

Belatedly, she turned to the doctor.

"I can sit with him – can I not?"

"Of course," the older man replied, moved by young love, or quick to recognise a losing battle. "But I have to insist he remain silent."

"Oh, he will! You have my word."

"Good. It is essential. Might I also advise against all manner of unrest, disturbance or… hm!… too strong emotions."

A smile reminiscent of his former self fluttered on Colonel Fitzwilliam's lips at that.

"I shall do my best," he whispered.

Yet, the doctor's injunctions notwithstanding, his countenance did show very strong emotions as his eyes returned to the young woman at his side, then moved over her shoulder to the young man standing motionless behind her.

"Thank you," he said warmly to the latter.

"No need," Darcy replied. "Excuse me. I should see to— "

He made for the door without finishing his sentence and opened it, then stopped and turned.

"Rest, Richard," he urged softly. "Try to sleep. And get well."

‧❀❁❀‧

Mr and Mrs Bingley arrived by noon on the following day, to offer every support that was in their power to give. Despite Darcy's insistence, they would not stay in Berkeley Square. They both thought it would have been an unnecessary imposition upon a household that was already burdened, when their own home was just around the corner. Besides, despite his deep concern for his new sister, his best friend and his best friend's cousin, Mr Bingley was reluctant to expose his wife to any risks, in view of her delicate condition, although of course he kept that to himself.

In truth, their constant attendance in Berkeley Square was hardly necessary. Plenty were at hand to care for the patient, and every wagging tongue that might have found fault with Elizabeth taking up residence at Darcy's house unaccompanied by her married sister would be silenced by her father's presence – for unsurprisingly Mr Bennet would not dream of returning to Longbourn and abandoning his favourite daughter to her fears, at this time of anxiety and peril.

Thus, while at hand to offer daily company and succour, Mr and Mrs Bingley would return each night to their own home, leaving Elizabeth and her father to their quarters in Berkeley Square.

Not that Elizabeth would have made much use of them, had she been left to her own devices. Georgiana's warm and sometimes tearful entreaties for her to go and rest kept falling on deaf ears, as did Darcy's.

Only Mr Bennet's quiet authority had a chance of swaying her, and even that carried little weight until supported by her betrothed's painfully breathless pleas. To appease him – or rather silence him – Elizabeth would eventually obey and leave his care to the others, although never for longer than a couple of hours at a time.

They attended him in turns, just one of them, or alongside the doctor, or in constantly changing pairings.

Beyond that first dawn, when he had felt compelled to walk out and leave them to their heartfelt reunion, Darcy had no longer sought to regulate his comings and goings, regardless of who was keeping watch over his cousin at the time.

It came as no surprise that, more often than not, it would be Elizabeth. Georgiana was too young and Mr Bennet and Mrs Annesley too old and frail to be kept by the bedside for too long.

So, time and again, and especially in the grim hours of the night, they would find themselves caring for him together. Raising him to help him drink, take nourishment or cough. Cooling his brow when the fever mounted. Cajoling him into taking the vile draughts that Dr Graham was insistently prescribing. Watching him snatch a few minutes of fitful slumber and agonising for him when his rest was disrupted by bouts of racking cough that were supposed to help, yet brought nothing but pain. Exchanging frightened glances when the horrible bouts of coughing showed no sign of abating. Rushing to bring him a warm drink when they did abate, and striving to hide their fear when the cough would recommence to torment him until he would collapse back on his pillows, exhausted and breathless.

Then they would hasten to refresh the flannels applied to his affected side, soak them in the hot decoction of camomile and elderflowers that the housekeeper had prepared at the doctor's instructions, then wring them and spread them on his chest again. And if their hands touched as they did so, this sparked no untoward emotion in Darcy. It could not, not *now*. No more than sitting there watching Elizabeth stroke Fitzwilliam's brow as she whispered tearful, disjointed words of tenderness and comfort.

It sparked no jealousy, no envy. The horrific sight of his cousin fighting for every breath – for his life, even – had drained him of all shameful jealousy, leaving just oppressive anguish.

Every past instance of begging for an answer to his heartache over Elizabeth's engagement to his cousin returned to torture him with all the sharpness of excruciating guilt.

This was not the answer he had begged for!

Not this! Merciful God, not this!

'Let him live!' was his one and only prayer, as flashing recollections of days of boyhood came unbidden to join ranks with dark thoughts from recent months and point accusing fingers, like as many ghosts of Banquo. Unlike Macbeth's, Darcy's own hands were not stained in blood, but every fibre of his being knew that his cousin's death was not the answer he had prayed for. It was not a deliverance, but the worst possible sentence.

'Good Lord in Heaven, let him live!'

⁓ঙ৹ ৹ঙ⁓

The heavens remained silent and Fitzwilliam's condition was no better. Tirelessly, Dr Graham fought to tip the balance in his favour with every remedy he knew, from the common bleeding to admixtures of camphor, sweet almonds and mint water, or decoctions of seneca, or vinegar of squills. To his partial satisfaction, the latter seemed effective, for the cough had begun to do its office and help clear his chest rather than torment him needlessly, but the fever was still mounting, with severe chills and restlessness that eventually gave way to loss of consciousness and delirium.

The crisis was drawing nearer, the old doctor knew full well, and there was little to be done now but support the patient with strengthening draughts and let nature take its course. He felt for the young man, and no less for his two regular attendants, who were not only weary to the bone, but also dreadfully alarmed to see the patient delirious or in convulsions. Urging them to rest had never served a purpose and Dr Graham was loath to waste his breath. Instead, he sought to reassure them that the alarming symptoms were merely nature's struggles to overcome the intractable disease.

He understood their anguish. Their loved one's suffering was terrible to watch. Even more so since they were powerless against it, and there was nothing they could do but pray. So they must have prayed. The old doctor knew he did. What he did not know was that for Darcy the same three words had become a mantra: '*Let him live!*'

⁓ঙ৹ ৹ঙ⁓

The mantra stayed with him that night, as he kept watch over his cousin. He was the only one awake. Elizabeth had fallen asleep in her chair by the bedside. The doctor's stern injunctions had not swayed her. Dr Graham had even gone as far as threatening to bodily remove her to her chamber, with the admonition that he could not care for more than one patient at a time and she would be of no use to her betrothed if she collapsed from lack of sleep and sheer exhaustion. To no avail, of course. The only concession she had been prepared to make was to snatch some rest in a wing chair, at Darcy's solemn promise he would wake her if there was the slightest change.

There was none. Fitzwilliam was still unconscious, the fever high. He was no longer restless after the draught the doctor had administered before returning to his own seat, where he was now slumped, overcome with fatigue. The room was quiet but for Fitzwilliam's laboured breathing and the doctor's gentle snoring in his corner.

In the oppressively still chamber, Darcy battled with his oppressive thoughts.

Striking a bargain with his Maker might have been wrong – a prideful notion, bordering on the sinful. But it was born of desperation, and he could not help himself. So this was precisely what he did, as he clasped his cousin's hand and silently prayed.

'Let him live – and I shall do my part. She will be a sister to me, just as Georgiana. Just as she should have been from the moment she said yes to Richard. I will subdue every improper wish. Just let him live!'

The creak of Elizabeth's chair made him look up with a violent start, his eyes bloodshot, red-rimmed with tiredness and clouded with tears. Instinctively, he drew a hand over his face and turned away from her.

He heard the chair creak again and then the soft patter of footsteps. He tensed as a hand was laid gently on his shoulder.

"He will be well. We must believe it," he heard her say, her tearful whisper laden with an ardent need to hope, and also with unmistakable compassion.

He did not look up this time, but reached to press her hand where it still lay on his shoulder, then let his hand drop and sat up straighter as he echoed:

"Aye. We must."

"You should try to rest a little too…"

"No. I thank you. I am well."

She did not argue the point but turned to feel Fitzwilliam's brow, then stroked his face with unsteady fingers.

"Still feverish?"

She nodded, but he had already guessed the answer from her countenance. He stood to fetch a fresh flannel and held it out to her, so that she could moisten the gaunt features. And they both settled back to wait, in the deathly quiet of the ill-lit chamber.

⚬ຄ℮ ℮ຄ⚬

The crisis came the following day, and it was dreadful. Convulsions, restless thrashing and delirious murmurs came to terrify them with the horrible notion that every shallow breath they heard would be the last. The doctor did his best as the ravaging condition did its cruellest worst and, devoid of any means to help, the other two stood watching the seemingly endless struggle, over torturous hours which neither thought to count.

It was not yet midnight when Dr Graham gave a sudden exclamation that could have signalled either relief or despair. Darcy and Elizabeth looked up, waiting for the verdict. It was not long in coming. The older man's exhausted features glowed with satisfaction, which was a mercy, for his first words were woefully misleading.

"'Tis all over now— "

They blanched and in one voice they asked in horrified confusion: "What— ?"

"The Lord be praised, it is all over!" the doctor incautiously repeated. Fatigue might have been to blame, otherwise with his experience he could have chosen his words better. Then, thankfully, he elaborated, "The worst is over. I will not say that he is wholly out of danger, but the fever is finally broken. He is drenched and his brow is as cool as I should wish it. I have great hopes that he will recover," he continued, but the two barely heard the last words as they rushed to touch Fitzwilliam's face in turn and have the proof of their own senses that at last they could bring themselves to hope.

It was indeed so. His brow was no longer burning and, for the first time since she had learned of Fitzwilliam's injury, Elizabeth broke into a violent flood of tears. On the other side of the large bed, Darcy bowed his head in fervent gratitude.

⚬ຄ℮ ℮ຄ⚬

The sickroom was quiet once again.

The doctor had superintended the cumbersome yet necessary process of changing the drenched bedclothes with fresh ones, sweetened with lavender, and likewise the patient's apparel. Then he had gone to rest at last in well-earned comfort in the bedchamber prepared for him, which he had so far made precious little use of, and urged the others to seek their beds as well, for he could vouch for the Colonel's current safety.

He was not surprised that they failed to listen. He had seen it oftentimes before. The loved ones would very rarely pay heed to his exhortations in cases such as these and, after many days and nights of fear and anguish, they would still insist on remaining at the bedside, to reassure themselves of their right to hope.

The master of the house, the young man's cousin, proved no exception, as did the young lady. As soon as the patient's nightclothes and bed linen had been changed and she had been allowed back into the sickroom, she had settled herself in her customary place and would not budge, in blatant disregard of the doctor's orders, until at last she had succumbed to heavy sleep, which was to be expected after the dreadful time she had endured.

Before leaving the room to seek his berth, the old doctor shook his head, first towards the sleeping woman and then to her equally obstinate companion.

"She should be made to get a decent rest," he told the latter, "or she might be taken ill herself. And so should you, Sir, if you do not mind me saying. Your cousin is safe for now, I can assure you. You should take yourself to bed, and so should this headstrong young woman, or someone should be summoned to convey her. Doubtlessly you will ignore me," he muttered with mild vexation, "although for both your sakes I wish you would not. But be that as it may. I shall leave you now," he added, and in due course he proved himself as good as his word, leaving Darcy to do just as he chose.

Predictably, he chose to steadfastly keep watch over his cousin. Still reclining on several pillows, Fitzwilliam seemed to be in peaceful repose and even now Darcy could scarce believe that he was indeed sleeping, rather than being rendered unconscious by the fever.

There was no doubt that Elizabeth was asleep. Her head was leaning to one side against the headrest, her breathing slow and even. Good. She needed to recover. He was loath to disturb her, but the old doctor might have had the right of it. She should get some decent rest at last. A proper night's sleep in a comfortable bed, not just a few hours of slumber in a wing chair.

Darcy stood from his own seat and came to bend down on one knee beside her.

"Eliz— Miss Bennet?" he amended.

She did not stir, which was little wonder, and he reached for the hand resting limply at her side, to cradle it in his. It was small and very cold. He brought it to his cheek and held it there, the thin fingers loosely curled around his own. And time stood still – and so did he. Only his thumb moved, in light, rhythmic strokes tracing the same recurring pattern, while his eyes kept retracing another pattern of their own. Dark auburn locks in charming disarray, wispy ringlets trailing at her temples. Closed eyelids, faintly tinged with purple, and incredibly long lashes. An adorably-shaped nose, perfect in its barely noticeable imperfection. Mouth – flawless, and ever so slightly curled up at the corners. Softly curved cheeks that would form a dimple when she smiled in earnest.

The small hand twitched in his when at last he turned his head to press it to his lips. He returned it to her side and softly urged again:

"Miss Bennet? Dr Graham said you ought to get some restful sleep," he whispered, as though she could hear him.

She did not. Her breathing still came slow and even and she gave no sign of imminent awakening. Perhaps the old doctor was in the right about this too – someone should be summoned to take her to her chambers. Yet, even as he thought it, Darcy knew that he would summon no one. Instead, he gingerly slipped one arm around her back and the other underneath her, to carefully lift her off her chair. He braced himself and stood with ease holding the light and very precious burden. He raised her closer to his chest and her head fell against his shoulder, her face upturned, achingly beautiful and almost childlike in repose.

Her cheeks were very pale and so were the full lips. So close. If he only bent his head… One indulgence – the first one and the last. Inches from his own, her lips parted, releasing a faint sigh, and his chest tightened, as did his eyes, firmly closed against the exquisite temptation.

He sighed – a heavy, tortured sound. His eyes still closed, he bent his head just enough to press his lips on the smooth brow for a long, harrowing moment. There was no added fragrance of jasmine and gardenia this time, just the scent of her warm skin and her hair – and he inhaled, shaken to his core by the deep yearning that it stirred in him. Far beyond desire. Much more than temptation. A staggering sense of belonging, of homecoming. Yearning and fulfilment, all in one.

He winced, opened his eyes and raised his head, gaining some distance from the cruel trick of chemistry and nature. This was not home – at least not for him. It was high time to accept the truth. And he *would*, by God, even if it killed him! It was time to do his part; keep his side of the bargain.

His gaze fixed on the perfect features, he swallowed hard and his voice came in a ragged whisper.

"Farewell, my love. God bless you, and be happy."

And then he turned to chastely carry her to her own bedchamber, failing to notice that in the light of the few guttering candles, a pair of very deep blue eyes were glittering under the canopy of the large bed, watching his every move in confused and disbelieving horror, and remained firmly fixed on his retreating back.

Chapter 6

As though of their own volition, his footsteps brought him back to the sick-chamber, numb and weary, to come across the only sight that could gladden his drained heart.

"Richard! You are awake!"

"Aren't I just," the other muttered, in a voice that by all accounts should have been far too weak for sarcasm, yet somehow it conveyed the sentiment nevertheless.

"Let me get the doctor."

"No. Stay. And close that blasted door," Fitzwilliam instructed, then began to cough.

Darcy did as bid and hastened to the bedside to pass him a scrap of cloth. The other took it to his mouth, but nothing came up this time, and Fitzwilliam leaned back onto his pillows.

"There is no pain now when you cough."

"So I have noticed."

"Would you like a drink?"

"Are you offering brandy?"

"You cannot be in earnest! Barley-water should suffice."

He filled a glass and, out of habit, reached to hold it to his cousin's lips, but of course there was no further need to do so.

Fitzwilliam drained the glass and returned it.

"Thank you," he sighed, and closed his eyes.

"I should let you sleep," Darcy offered and made to stand, but the other reached to hold his arm and stop him.

"Not yet."

"Is there anything else I could get you? Are you hungry?"

Fitzwilliam shook his head, his eyes fixed on the ornate canopy. And then suddenly they came to pierce into his cousin's as he drawled:

"My apologies for disobliging you."

"Nonsense. How?"

78

"By pulling through," Fitzwilliam retorted curtly, and before Darcy could even begin to put his thoughts in order and grasp the implications, he instinctively shot back:

"That is a vile thing to say!"

"Is it?"

They eyed each other squarely and neither spoke, until Fitzwilliam said evenly and crisply:

"I believe your exact words were *'Farewell, my love'*. Or was I mistaken?"

As though prodded with a hot fire iron, Darcy sprang to his feet. Yet he did not go far, but flung himself on the chair by the bedside, that had been Elizabeth's. He raked his fingers through his hair and exhaled, before turning a stricken countenance upon his cousin.

"Well?" Fitzwilliam prompted, but Darcy said nothing.

What was there to say?

"*Well?* " the other repeated.

Darcy cringed.

"Forgive me. You did not need this. Least of all now," was all that he could offer.

"I was not asking for a damned apology!" his cousin snapped, but the outburst was too much for his weakened chest and he began to cough again.

"Then what do you want from me?" Darcy pleaded, when the other had collapsed back on the pillows and the room was once more quiet.

The reply was prompt and sharp.

"The truth, for a change."

And still Darcy would not speak, and at last Fitzwilliam lost his patience.

"How long?"

"How long what?"

"Do not play the fool. How long have you been in love with her?"

Darcy gave a tired sigh.

"Does it matter?"

"Yes! How long?" the other mercilessly pressed. "A month? Six? A whole blasted year?" he lashed out, only to be cut short by another bout of coughing. "Answer me!" he ordered, as soon as he could speak.

Elbows on his knees and head in hands, Darcy complied.

"Almost for as long as I have known her," he quietly owned, and then looked up. If he was expecting clemency in response to his honesty or his prior claim, he was to be horribly disappointed. His reply only served to rile his cousin further.

"Damn you, Darcy!" he burst out with something very much like hatred. "Damn you and your abominable pride!"

Oddly free of the pestering cough this time, he poured his diatribe unhindered.

"You would not offer for her – too lowly for you, is she? So your grand plan is what? Act the romantic part of the dark silent lover? What role am I assigned, pray tell, in your preposterous charade? Do you expect me to sit back and witness you coveting my wife? *Love her* – heavens above! If you have truly loved her for as long as that, then why the devil did you not offer marriage?"

Goaded beyond endurance, Darcy sprang to his feet once more, and this time turned away from his cousin's sickbed.

"Because you offered first," he bitterly retorted without thinking, then raked his fingers through his hair again, regretting it already.

He sighed. It was done now. The truth was out so, for all that it was worth, he finally gave his cousin the full story.

"I was going to propose the following morning…"

Nothing was heard behind him but the crackling of the fire.

"I see. Well, that explains a great many things," Fitzwilliam quietly remarked after a while.

"Such as?"

"Your silences. Your strange displays of temper."

Darcy shrugged and made no answer. It was Fitzwilliam who spoke with great reluctance, yet clearly unable to restrain himself.

"Does she know?" he asked.

At that, Darcy spun around to face him.

"Of course not! What sort of a cad do you think I am?"

"What of the touching adieu I have just witnessed?"

It was Darcy's turn to have sheer hatred glinting in his eyes.

"What of it?"

"Very noble, in theory. In practice, however…"

Darcy features tightened. His position was indefensible, and well he knew it, yet his cousin had no right to mock. Presumably regretting it himself, Fitzwilliam's voice lost every trace of sarcasm.

"How do you propose to go about it? Are we to never see each other once I am married?"

Darcy sighed.

"I do not know."

His sigh was echoed from the bed.

"I suppose I should feel remorse of sorts," Fitzwilliam resumed, "for stepping in to send your schemes awry. But I cannot. You should have spoken when you had the chance. Lord knows you must have had plenty of time to do so."

"Do you think I need to be told?" Darcy retorted, stung. "It has been on my mind every blasted day since— Damn it, Richard! I know I am the only one to blame. Do you imagine I can bear it?"

"And do you imagine *I* can bear to know that you – *you*, of all goddamned people – are in love with her as well? And worse still, that she could have been the mistress of Pemberley, and everything I have to offer her is paltry in comparison?"

With great effort, Darcy forced himself to voice the ultimate truth.

"She has chosen *you*."

"It was not a choice precisely, was it?"

"What is the purpose of all this?" Darcy burst out, distress fuelling his vexation. "What are you suggesting? That we both should have offered? This is insane! She would have accepted neither, rather than knowingly come between us."

"Perhaps," Fitzwilliam conceded. "And now? Do you imagine that someone as astute as she would not guess the truth before too long?"

Darcy brought his hand up to tiredly rub his temples.

"We shall have to ensure she does not."

"Fine words! How? Am I to uproot her to the wilds of Scotland or to goodness knows what other country to put distance between us? I will not do it, Cousin! I am not asking her to leave everyone and everything she holds dear!" Fitzwilliam resumed, once more incensed, and the effort of forcing out the angry rush of words brought on another bout of coughing. "Damn," he muttered, at the sight of the soiled cloth.

"Let me have that. You should drink."

"Amen to that. Anything left of your *Bourgogne Chambertin*? Perhaps the pair of us should have another celebration."

"Oh, hold your tongue and drink your barley-water!" Darcy shot back as he reached to pour another glass, and for a moment the natural return to old patterns of quick repartee and irreverent banter brought a modicum of comfort. For that brief moment, it was as though they were back in the days when nothing stood between them; when it was the pair of them against the uncaring world.

Darcy suppressed a sigh. Perhaps they might find a way to keep this. He did not know how, but dearly hoped they could. He had lost too much already, and could not afford to lose his cousin too.

Fitzwilliam took the glass and drank, then leaned back against the pillows with a muted oath. He met Darcy's rueful stare, and no words were needed to show that their thoughts matched, as did their wishes. For too many years they had understood each other without words. Nevertheless, he spoke.

"I cannot remember if I even thanked you. For hauling my carcass all the way from Portsmouth, to begin with, and… for everything else."

"You did."

"Did I?"

"Yes. And there was no need."

"Anyway… I— "

"What?"

"I wish it were anyone but you, Darcy," Fitzwilliam said with feeling, then added, in a vain attempt at lightening the tone, "My blockhead of a brother, for example."

"Not a chance," Darcy retorted, like for like. "Morton's taste in women is appalling."

"Too true. By the bye, rumour has it that you gave him a bruised lip."

"How did you hear of it?"

"Mater wrote. She was quite shocked at your lack of manners. But she did not know any of the particulars. What was it about?"

"Nothing of import."

"Still, I would have liked to see it. Took me back to the good old days, I can tell you that."

Involuntarily, Darcy chuckled. Many were the times when they had stood shoulder to shoulder against Morton's greater bodily strength, until they had grown strong enough to fight their own battles. Just as they had sided against Lord Langthorne's blatant disinterest in his second son, or his own father's preference for

Wickham, or in every other instance when one of them had found himself in need of a helping hand.

He stood from the bed and went to put more coal on the fire, then returned to sit in the chair by the bedside and stretched his legs before him.

"Just go to bed, Darcy," his cousin grumbled. "I am not in need of a night-nurse."

"Brave words from a man who cannot stand," Darcy shot back, only to have a small cushion flung in his general direction. "*Quod erat demonstrandum*. If you had any strength at all, that cushion should have reached me. But thank you just the same, that was very thoughtful. I happened to need one," he drawled as he reached to pick it off the floor and toss it carelessly under his head.

"Just do me a favour and refrain from snoring. Or talking in your sleep."

"Have you ever known me to do either?"

"I know you used to kick. Or was that Henry?"

"Henry. I tend to fight my battles in broad daylight."

"As Morton can bear witness," the other retorted with a chuckle that turned into another cough. "So, what is the current tally?"

"I lost count. I daresay it was my turn though. The last episode of fisticuffs I can remember was between you and him."

"What of— ?"

"Will you not stop talking? You will get that cough flaring up again. How can a man get a wink of sleep?"

"Easily. Go back to your own quarters."

"In a while. Now hush."

He was not in earnest, which was just as well for, true to form, the other was not easily hushed. The boyish banter that brought comfort to both continued for a while, until at last the bedchamber was silent and both drifted into dreamless sleep.

This was how Elizabeth found them an hour before dawn, when she awoke in her own bedchamber with no recollection of how she might have got there, and walked over to the sickroom to reassure herself of Richard's safety.

To her great joy, he seemed to be sleeping peacefully, his brow cool, his breathing easier. She carefully withdrew her fingers and forbore to stroke his hair for fear of waking him, just as she forbore to hold his hand or lean to brush her lips against his cheek.

She reached to smooth his bedcover instead, as she gave silent thanks for his recovery.

The sight of the gaunt features almost brought tears to her eyes but, thank goodness, they were no longer feverish, nor contorted in pain. He looked so very different. Not just compared to the horrific days of peril, but to every instance that she could remember.

It should not have come as a surprise. People were often greatly altered in repose. They seemed vulnerable somehow, and a great deal younger. Why, even her own father... Or, for that matter, Mr Darcy who, at that precise moment, was looking like a tousled-haired boy, rather than the severe gentleman whose mere frown was apt to make weaker souls tremble.

She smiled at her own pert thoughts. Of course, she knew by now there was great warmth of feeling behind the stern *façade*. For his sister – and his cousin. She had seen tears in his eyes the other night, when she had awoken to find him clasping Richard's hand, his lips moving in mute, fervent prayer. And last night too, when they were terrified that they would lose him.

Praise be, they did not. They would not. Dr Graham said Richard would recover. With a soft glance and a brimming heart, Elizabeth rearranged the quilt and raised it to his chin then, on impulse, she tiptoed to drape another one over Mr Darcy's sleeping form as well.

Somehow, it seemed a great deal easier to give him the full affection of a sister, after the last horrible days when they had been comrades in arms, fighting side by side for Richard. That being said, it did not even cross her mind to stroke his brow. Newfound kinship aside, they were not related.

So she just ensured he was well covered, replaced two candles that were nearly burnt out, checked that Richard was still comfortable and the fire was safe then, with a warm gaze encompassing both men, she returned to her bedchamber to lie down for a little longer. And the troubled house was at peace at last.

◦๑๑ ๑๑๑◦

The sound of joyful chatter reached him in the corridor when, partially refreshed after a few hours of sleep and a welcome bath, Darcy made his way back to his cousin's chamber.

He had awoken when a maid had come to tend the fire and had repaired to his quarters, leaving Fitzwilliam to his rest.

He was awake now and receiving visitors, it seemed. By the sound of it, they were all there. He could hear Georgiana's voice mingling with Elizabeth's, and with Mr Bennet's on occasion. Good. That should make it easier. He straightened his shoulders and walked in with a valiant smile.

"Good morning."

"Morning? I should say good day," Fitzwilliam retorted from the bed, a willing ally in the charade they had to play.

Darcy rolled his eyes and took up his own part in earnest.

"And now he can speak. Praise be for the mercy."

He came to drop a kiss on the top of Georgiana's head and greeted the others with a fleeting smile and cursory nods, then fetched himself a chair.

"So, how are you?" he turned back to his cousin. "Has Dr Graham seen you yet?"

"Seen, prodded, filled me with draughts and left copious instructions. He has gone now."

"Home?"

"I should imagine so. He will return later."

"What of his instructions?"

"There is a long list somewhere. What elixirs to swallow, what I should do and not do, what I should eat and when. I call it a damned nuisance."

"Aye. You would."

"More punctilious than Lady Catherine, and that is saying something."

"Well! It would not harm you to do as you are told for once."

"Aye, like a child in leading strings. That should take some getting used to."

"Oh, leave off! You could complain for England," Darcy retorted promptly and shifted in his seat.

Last night the banter had felt natural. Not so now. They were both trying too hard. He thinned his lips and looked around, his glance settling on no one in particular as he asked everybody:

"Have you sat down for breakfast yet? If not, I can ask for some trays to be brought up."

"What, and torment me with all manner of delicacies that the good doctor has forbidden, while all I am allowed is my miserable gruel? You had much better go and indulge at leisure," Fitzwilliam urged them, and at that Elizabeth laughed lightly.

"You are showing great promise of becoming a rather awkward patient," she playfully retorted. "Mr Darcy, has your cousin always been so contrary and I have failed to notice?"

With some effort, Darcy sought to match her raillery like for like.

"Miss Bennet, chances are you have seen nothing yet."

"Just so," Fitzwilliam promptly came to his assistance. "It pains me to own it, but Darcy is right. Chances are you have not seen me at my most cantankerous and headstrong. So you might still change your mind about marrying me— "

Georgiana giggled at the jest and Elizabeth's smile grew wider when her father promptly observed that she was not celebrated for her meekness either. And, in the ensuing affectionate chitchat with Mr Bennet, she forgot to wonder why her betrothed had not laughed at his own sally as he was wont to do, but had cut it short and had exchanged swift troubled glances with his cousin.

Across the sickbed, Mr Darcy stood.

"I should send word for breakfast. And afterwards I might go to Brooks's. Mr Bennet, would you care to join me?"

Mr Bennet did. In fact, over the forthcoming days, mornings at Brooks's became somewhat of a habit. They would leave shortly after breakfast to read the papers at Mr Darcy's club and while away time in gentlemanly fashion, then Darcy would return Mr Bennet to Berkeley Square to seek delights in the well-stocked library and, for his part, endeavour to find other gentlemanly ways to while away the hours. Ways that would take him out of the house where Elizabeth was keeping his cousin company as he continued to recover. Reading to him, Darcy surmised, or taking turns with Georgiana to play cheerful pieces on the smaller pianoforte in his sister's sitting room above-stairs, which was not far from the sick-chamber, so the music would easily reach him, through the open doors.

Darcy's first choice was to go riding, nearly every day. Long rides to Richmond or on Hampstead Heath. Punishing rides that would exhaust him, so that at night he stood some chance to sleep, rather than lie awake vainly attempting to ignore the fact that, five doors down, Elizabeth would be ensconced in bed, in her own chamber.

Encountering her at mealtimes was no better. If he had his way, he would have forgone mealtimes altogether. For every time the party of five congregated in the same intimate parlour where they had dined with Bingley and his wife when they had brought Elizabeth into his home for the first time, much as he sought to – with determined effort, every day – it was impossible to set aside the notion that this was precisely how they might have sat, had the stars been kinder and their circumstances different.

A small family circle gathered around the table.

A constant reminder of what he could not have.

It was a trifle easier when the Bingleys joined them, but not much. The same family circle, just a little wider. The same exquisite lie. But when his friend was there, at least he would invariably lead the conversation and give him a respite from the task that was growing more onerous by the day.

He was inclined to think that, all things considered, he was acquitting himself of it with tolerable credit – until one morning, when Georgiana came to disabuse him of that notion.

She came to see him in his study and he looked up from the stacks of long-neglected papers, to see her fidget in discomfort at his side.

"Yes, dearest? Did you wish to speak of something?"

"Why, I… Am I interrupting?"

"Not at all."

He dropped the paper he was holding and stood to take her hand.

"What is it, Georgiana?"

He could easily see she was reluctant to begin.

Nevertheless, at length she did.

"Brother, might I ask… is there anything troubling you?"

"Nothing whatever," he bristled, heartily sick of being asked. "Why?"

"Well… 'Tis only that you were so grim and silent over breakfast. And I would hate to trouble you further, but I am finding it so very difficult…"

"To do what, sweetling?" he gently coaxed.

"Be a good hostess, keep up a conversation, make our guests feel welcome. Mr Bennet is not one to talk much either and Mrs Annesley does her best, but… I find I need your help."

"Oh. Of course."

"It must be hard for you as well. I know you do not relish company and sometimes I fear that you regard their continued presence as an imposition."

Goodness! He had first led Bingley and now Georgiana to assume this. Did he *ever* learn?

"It is not an imposition. They are very welcome," he hastened to assure her.

"Then… might you not exert yourself at times, to make your welcome clearer? 'Tis just that, as Richard's wife, Elizabeth will be one of our closest cousins, almost a sister, and I would very much like her to feel so. From what Emily said, she will get precious little warmth from our Fitzwilliam relations, and I would not wish for us to seem to side with them."

He stood aghast, forcibly reminded of his own vow – his promise.

'She will be a sister to me, just as Georgiana.'

So he had failed dismally, if even the dear shy child had suddenly seen fit to take him to task.

She must have noticed his distress, for she promptly spoke up to apologise, and thus increase his guilt tenfold.

"Pray forgive me. I did not mean to sound so forceful and speak out of turn."

"Not at all, sweetling. You could not speak out of turn if you tried," he sought to cajole her into a smile. "Besides, you are perfectly right and it is testament to your caring heart that you should feel so. Of course we should provide the welcome the others will not vouchsafe her. I thank you for making me see that I might have unwittingly given the wrong impression. I am… "

"Not at ease with strangers, I know," she finished for him with a smile, although this was not what he was about to say. "But Elizabeth is not a stranger. She will be family ere long."

"Yes," he tiredly acknowledged. "I know, sweetling. I shall try."

She thanked him with a smile and stood on tiptoe to lightly kiss his cheek – and left him to wonder what on earth he might have done, in this life or another, to warrant the endless punishment.

A bitter laugh escaped him at the thought that, unknowingly, they all took turns to cast their stones. Even Georgiana. But she was right. Heaven forfend that Elizabeth should think him unwelcoming or disapproving!

He needed to exert himself, try even harder. How much harder though, for goodness sake? And where exactly was the cursed line between showing too much or not enough?

He tried. To speak at dinner. Engage her in conversation about books, music, even Longbourn. And Mr Bennet too. He tried. And he could see from Elizabeth's surprise at his loquacity and Georgiana's encouraging smile that he was fairly successful.

And they would never know how much it cost him. No mean feat, for one to whom disguise of every sort was his abhorrence, Darcy thought with a derisive snort much later and vented his frustration on his blameless pillows, pummelling them into shape as he settled in for yet another sleepless night, five doors away from Elizabeth's bedchamber.

⋙⋘

He awoke at dawn, to the same thoughts. Surprise that he had slept at all. Dreary disinterest in yet another day. Elizabeth's sleeping form, warm to the touch, and very soft. In her bedchamber, five doors down, no more than thirty paces. A sleepy little smile on lips simply begging to be kissed, as she would stir and stretch under the counterpane with the languid ease of a purring kitten. The sheer perfection of awakening to find her bare arms reaching to wrap around his neck, as he would seek her blindly in his bed, beside him…

With both yearning soul and treacherous body, he responded to the forbidden picture. He swore under his breath as he reminded himself in no uncertain terms that he was going all devils of a wrong way about his vow, and that he would mightily benefit from a cold bath.

The intruding thought of Fitzwilliam stirring from his sleep to blindly seek her and find her arms wrapped around *his* neck cooled him as effectively as being doused in ice-cold water. He sprang out of bed and went to give the bell-pull a sharp tug.

That morning he did forgo breakfast and went for a long ride instead. He returned several hours later, to be greeted by a very flustered Georgiana.

"Brother! Thank goodness, you are here at last."

89

"Why? What happened?"

"Our aunt is here. And she is not best pleased."

"Lady Catherine?"

"Oh, no. Worse. Lady Langthorne."

Foreboding spread through him like lightning.

"What happened?" he repeated.

"She arrived unannounced half an hour ago— "

"Where was everybody?"

"Mrs Annesley, Elizabeth and I were sitting with our needlework when Lady Langthorne stormed in, lost no time with civilities and demanded to see Richard. She was most put out when Elizabeth warned me that he might be asleep and offered to go up to check. And— Oh, Brother! I wish you had been here. No sooner had Elizabeth said as much than our aunt drew herself up to her full height and asked me in her most forbidding manner who was the young woman who was making so free with her comings and goings to her son's bedchamber. But I am sure she knew. She looked very grim when I made the introductions and said she would wait for a *footman* to go and check instead. Thomas went and confirmed that Richard was asleep, so our aunt installed herself in state in the drawing room, refused refreshments and demanded to see you— "

"Where is Miss Bennet?" Darcy interjected.

"In her chambers, I think."

"And her father? Is he with her?"

"No. He is not in. Mr Bennet left right after breakfast to call on Mrs Bingley."

"Blast!" Darcy muttered.

Her father's support might have been welcome, both during and after the uncivil encounter. Why the blazes had he seen fit to tear across the turf in Hampstead Heath this morning? But he knew why, and pointless questions would not make the current situation any better. Just now, he needed to reassure himself that Elizabeth was well and not distressed unduly – but he could not very well seek her in her bedchamber.

Perhaps Georgiana might be sent to ask her if she would see him in the upstairs sitting room?

It was a sensible solution, and it might have been a workable one as well. Sadly, an imperious voice rendered it utterly useless.

"Darcy! I see you have returned. Good. I would speak with you."

His jaw set, he turned to acknowledge his relation with a bow and a terse "Lady Langthorne."

"Pray join me," her ladyship intoned, making him arch a brow at having been peremptorily summoned into his own drawing room.

Besides, he had his own opinions on the matter.

"Might I suggest my study? You would be more comfortable and you might prefer a private setting."

"I am not concerned for my own comfort, Nephew, nor am I seeking to keep my opinions private. But you can have your wish. Let me to your study."

Darcy squared his shoulders and showed her the way.

"Pray, be seated," he said, once they were within and he had closed the door for further safety. "May I offer you refreshments?" he stalled with a civil offer, which was so brusquely rejected that it was beyond uncivil.

"Not now. Tell me about Richard."

"He is alive and well."

"Is that all you can tell me?"

"What would you wish to know?"

"A vast deal. But I should begin by thanking you. My housekeeper has written to inform me that you took the trouble of fetching him from Portsmouth."

"I could have done no less."

"I beg to differ," the lady loftily retorted. "But firstly, is he safe?"

"Dr Graham thinks so."

"Good. Then he is fit to travel."

"Might I ask where?"

"To be with his family."

The lady's crisp retort and her non-existent effort at civility could not fail to provoke him into replying, just as crisply:

"Forgive me, I was under the impression that he was with family already."

"Then perhaps I should say, with those members of his family who are prepared to see to his best interests."

"Pray tell me, how do I fail to qualify?" Darcy spoke up firmly, having determined it was time to bring matters into the open.

He was not surprised when the lady instantly obliged.

"Frankly, Darcy, I am bitterly disappointed that you would contrive to force his hand by allowing the country chit at his bedside. I had every hope that he would conquer his preposterous infatuation, but how can he do so when you allow that person to ingratiate herself with him? Worse still, force him to keep his word, if it becomes known that she enjoys free access into his bedchamber."

Violent anger choked him and goaded him into a sharp retort:

"No man of sense and feeling would need to have his hand forced into marrying Miss Bennet. She is the very best that anyone could hope for."

"Is that so! Do you imagine me ignorant of her connections?"

"Richard does not object."

"Seemingly not. But I do. And it is time I made my feelings known without equivocation. I would never consent to this disgraceful union."

"That would make your ladyship's situation more pitiable, but I doubt it would sway him."

"Even if he finds himself deprived of every material comfort he is accustomed to?"

"Even so. I have it from him that a genteel sufficiency would suit him just as well, or even better."

"I doubt that a colonel's pay can guarantee it. And the war cannot last forever."

"Then those of us who care for him might find a way to secure him advancement."

"You would go this far? Wilfully act to disoblige your own relations?"

"Richard is my relation too. It would be an honour to oblige him."

"And see him shunned, censured and despised in almost every circle that had once welcomed him?"

"Those are heavy misfortunes indeed. But his wife would provide such extraordinary sources of happiness that, upon the whole, he would have no cause to repine."

"I beg your pardon?"

"Surely it does not surprise you that affection would outweigh the loss of any number of fashionable circles. Rest assured, he will be happy. I would have hoped that, as his mother, you would value this above all else."

"Do not presume to lecture me on my feelings and duties as a mother. Affection indeed! Arts, allurements, my son's wilful blindness and a young upstart's wishes for self-aggrandisement do not make for a happy union."

"You have said quite enough, Madam! I perfectly comprehend your feelings. But it would serve you well to comprehend another's. Miss Bennet is deeply attached to my cousin. Her devoted care has brought him from death's door. I should have thought that this alone entitles her to your deepest gratitude— "

"She would have my deepest gratitude if she removed herself from his path. But there is no hope now, is there? Tittle-tattle will oblige him— "

"His sentiments will oblige him! And as for tittle-tattle, I can assure you that no one in my household would spread rumours that might endanger Miss Bennet's good name. If rumour spreads, it could only come from Langthorne House."

"This is uncalled for, Darcy! But I daresay no more so than everything else you said today," Lady Langthorne icily observed, finally expressing a sentiment he could reciprocate in full. It was beneath him though to say as much, so he merely bowed his silent contempt. "I fear our relationship will be irretrievably damaged once your uncle hears of this," the lady resumed. "But be that as it may. You have made your point, and I shall make mine. You might as well know I do not intend to leave this house without my son."

"Then you must excuse me. I should instruct my servants to prepare another guest chamber," Darcy retorted, as icily as she.

"That was not my meaning, and well you know it! I have no wish to lodge under the same roof as the young upstart. My son will be moved to Langthorne House."

"Madam, my cousin is not a child in leading strings. He will leave this house when he sees fit, and not a moment sooner. Besides, if you have any care for his safety, you will forbear from distressing him with open conflict and unsavoury remarks. Dr Graham has expressly forbidden disquiet and strong emotions," he added, painfully aware of his own role in causing plenty of each already.

"If you are seeking to re-enact the parable of the disputed child, you are not presenting yourself to advantage," Lady Langthorne scathingly replied and suddenly Darcy grew terribly weary of the entire business.

"Sadly, there is no King Solomon at hand to settle the matter," he shot back. "Lady Langthorne, you are most welcome to see Richard, come and go as you please – stay with us, even. But you cannot distress my cousin or my guests."

"Of which *she* would remain one."

"Yes. And this is not negotiable."

Lady Langthorne sniffed.

"I wish to see my son."

"Of course. Allow me to escort you."

"I would rather not. Unless it is mandatory that I see him under supervision," her ladyship added with a scornfully arched brow.

"Not at all," Darcy retorted coolly and rang for a footman.

Peter was swift to answer, and was instantly instructed to show her ladyship to the Colonel's chamber and, should he be still asleep, to the adjoining sitting room. And then the lady and the footman left him to a modicum of peace and quiet, at least by comparison.

With a sigh of equal parts relief and exasperation, Darcy went to pour himself a drink. He drained a sizeable proportion of the glass, then ran the back of his finger over his lips.

Strangely, for once anger had served him well. Incensed by Lady Langthorne's intolerable conduct, he had been able to defend Fitzwilliam's position without the dead-weight of personal anguish.

He took another draught, then set his glass down. He could not loiter there, he had matters to attend to – one of greater import than the rest. It was high time to seek Elizabeth.

Chapter 7

Little did Mr Darcy know that she was much, much closer than he thought. When she had ceded the drawing room to Colonel Fitzwilliam's imperious relation, Elizabeth had been reluctant to go to her own chamber above-stairs, lest Lady Langthorne be further provoked by the suspicion that she had wilfully disregarded the express instruction of not going to check on her betrothed.

Elizabeth saw little benefit in seeking to oblige a lady who seemed determined to be disobliged. All she wished was to make the unpleasant circumstance easier on Georgiana by keeping out of sight.

She pondered walking out into the small garden at the back of the house, but rejected the notion soon enough. The many windows overlooking it would make her feel uncomfortable. Exposed. Watched.

She chose the library instead. She settled into a very comfortable chair and closed her eyes, letting her surroundings work their magic and revive her spirits – the pleasant setting, the warm earthy colours, the delightful scent of books. She inhaled it deeply, letting it soothe her, loving it. And suddenly her eyes flashed open, and every trace of comfort left her.

Voices reached her from behind the small side-door that linked the library with Mr Darcy's study. The door was closed, but the very distinctive voices were raised in anger – and angry voices carried.

"Frankly, Darcy, I am bitterly disappointed that you would contrive to force his hand by allowing the country chit at his bedside…"

She gasped, shocked by the sheer venom in Lady Langhorne's tones. Yet what had she expected? The lady's manner earlier in the drawing room should have given enough warning of the welcome – or rather lack thereof – that she would receive from her.

The subsequent snide references to Richard's *'preposterous infatuation'* and her own free access into his bedchamber sickened her, and she gripped the armrests in readiness to stand. She should leave. She would hear no more! But the only way out of the library was along the corridor that ran past the main door into Mr Darcy's study, and if it was open she might be spotted and further pilloried as an impertinent eavesdropper. Yet, were they to walk in here, would that not be a million times worse? Where...? How...?

She cast around in a tumult of confusion, only to be stupefied into frozen inaction by the next words that reached her. Mr Darcy asserting with the greatest firmness that she – *she*, of all people – was the very best that anyone could hope for, and no man of sense and feeling would need to have his hand forced into marrying her!

Regardless of all niceties of ladylike deportment, she could not stir another inch – and indeed who would have had the hypocrisy to blame her? Who, in her place, would have had the strength to walk away from the thoroughly shocking and just as gratifying overhearings?

Thus, she remained fixed to the spot, listening to Mr Darcy defending her more staunchly than anyone had ever done before. Defending her character, her person, the sincerity of her attachment. Declaring that her unremarkable connections mattered not, nor did the disapproval of fashionable circles, in the face of a marriage of affection. Declaring, moreover, his firm intention to become their greatest ally and even go as far as disobliging his uncle and aunt by ensuring Richard's material comfort, were the selfsame relations to withhold it. And lastly declaring that her own welcome as his guest was not negotiable.

By that point, she had tears in her eyes and her hands were shaking. She could barely hear the goings-on in the adjoining chamber. The anger had subsided or was better held in check and the voices had grown much more subdued. She heard another voice that sounded like Peter's, and then the loud scraping of a chair. They must be leaving – and, goodness, so should she! She could not be discovered here! If only there was a way of safely retreating to her chamber. The servants' stairs? No, that was foolish and conspicuous and she did not know the way.

Still overpowered by the shock of the last few minutes, which she had not even begun to make full sense of, she walked to the door and opened it with caution.

There was no one in the corridor, thank heavens, and she ventured out, her heart pounding. Ten silent steps took her past the main door into Mr Darcy's study and she cast a fleeting glance within. With a sigh of relief she noticed it was empty, at least as far as she could see, so she ventured further, only to stand frozen in her tracks when Mr Darcy's voice came from somewhere ahead – somewhere out of sight, but far too close for comfort – instructing a maid to seek her in her chamber and ask if Miss Bennet would kindly spare him a few minutes, as he would like to speak with her.

Instinctively, she darted through an archway to the left, into the small hallway that led towards the garden. She opened the outer door, praying it would not creak and breathed a small sigh of relief when it did not. Quietly and swiftly, she made good her escape and closed the door behind her, then hurriedly stepped away along the gravelled path. She no longer cared one jot about the large windows above-stairs, from which she might be watched, for Mr Darcy was clearly not there. She tightened the shawl around herself with trembling hands and briefly closed her eyes in fervent gratitude for her fortuitous escape. She could not have borne to have him know she had been eavesdropping, and mortify him with the knowledge that she had heard every repulsive word his aunt had uttered.

Her unsteady steps brought her to a wooden bench set against the back wall of the house to face the garden and the wintry sunlight. The warming rays were welcome, since she had walked out without her coat, but the midday glare was not. It was almost too strong for her stinging eyes, yet she sat down because her knees were shaking.

She crumpled the ends of her fringed shawl in nervous hands that would not be stilled, and stared blankly into space as she endeavoured to come to grips with what had happened and what she should do next.

First and foremost, she would have to remove herself from Berkeley Square, there were no two ways about it. Richard was out of danger and her presence was no longer justified. As Lady Langthorne had so vehemently pointed out, it would only give rise to malicious gossip. Jane would welcome her, the dear heart. So, as soon as she was confident that the coast was clear, she would make her way to her bedchamber and pack her trunk. Then she would speak to her papa when he returned. She need not tell him everything and she had no intention to. A bare minimum would suffice. There was nothing to be gained from distressing him with fears for her future and anger him by repeating Lady Langthorne's comments. Their implications would have to be considered later, in private reflection or, at most, in a conversation with her dearest Jane. No one else need know that, if Lady Langthorne and most of her relations had their way, Richard's reviled engagement would be broken.

Elizabeth shivered at the thought, yet she could derive but meagre consolation from knowing that he was too honourable and too attached to jilt her. What would it do to him, this marriage? His ambitious mother's cruel words had spelled it out, so very clearly. Comparative poverty. Disharmony with his relations – a rupture, most likely. The disdain of his peers, their ridicule.

Unwittingly, she gave a bitter laugh. Mr Darcy, in his extreme kindness, had declared that she would compensate for such misfortunes but, deep in her heart, Elizabeth could not fail to doubt it. What did she have to offer, to make amends for depriving him of so very much? Of everything he had been accustomed to for over thirty years? And of nearly everyone whom he held dear?

It was reassuring that he would not lose Mr Darcy's affection and support, and presumably not Georgiana's either, but what of the rest? And how would it sit on him, to find himself reduced to the circumstances of a poor relation, dependent on his cousin's generous promise of a livelihood – and all because of her?

Would it not sour him against her, in the long run? And how could she bear to know she was to blame? Oh, she could weather his family's disapproval, withstand it with her head held high. But knowing she had been instrumental in depriving him of every comfort and foreseeable advantage was a different matter altogether.

She could not think of this just now. It was too much, and far too painful. She would go to Jane, as soon as may be!

She sighed. Richard would wonder why, as would Mr Darcy. She ought to be careful and merely supply the sensible reason: that Richard was much better, and it was time she left.

It served no purpose to hinder his recovery with conflict and strife.

Dr Graham had insisted on tranquillity, and she dearly hoped that both Lady Langthorne and Mr Darcy would have the good sense to refrain for now from needless revelations of blatant acrimony and manifest dislike.

She sighed again at the thought of Mr Darcy and how grievously she had misjudged him, time and again. Mere days ago she had been persuaded that he still saw little or no wisdom in his cousin's proposed union, and tolerated her presence in his house merely for Richard's sake. True, she was not accustomed to deciphering very reserved people. No one in her circle was known to show restraint excepting her father, yet that had never stopped him from making his opinions known.

Unlike her father, Mr Darcy was not liberally dispensing his opinions. Until today, at Lady Langthorne's provocations. Learning that in fact he thought the very best of her was little short of humbling and a stark reminder that she still failed to make allowances for his very private nature.

He was a good man, one of the best she knew, and it would behove her to deal with him more openly and warmly. This might not be his way, but it certainly was hers. And now that she knew beyond a doubt that he welcomed her into his family not merely for Richard's sake but for her own, there was no reason to maintain this cautious, artificial distance. She *would* show him the appreciation and the kindness that were his just deserts.

No sooner had she reached this most desirable conclusion than her resolution towards warmth and openness was promptly to be tested. The ornamented door was opened and the gentleman himself walked out into the garden, only to throw her into instant discomposure with an innocuous question.

"Miss Bennet! I was told you were above-stairs, but Martha could not find you. Have you been here long?"

"For quite some time, Sir," she supplied, blushing. She hated deception but sometimes it was necessary, and this was one of the occasions. "Was anyone seeking me?" she added, although she knew the answer.

He did not hesitate to give it.

"Yes. I was. May I be allowed to join you?"

"Of course, pray do," she invited him, moving to one side.

He sat beside her on the bench and thanked her, then turned towards her and cautiously began:

"Miss Bennet, I must apologise for the unpleasant scene Georgiana told me you have been subjected to."

"Pray, do not be concerned. It was no more than I expected."

"That is as may be, but I wish I had been at home to prevent it."

"Sir, that is most thoughtful. But I cannot keep hiding behind your protective shadow," she airily observed, only to see him frown.

"You are a guest in my house," he replied, quietly but firmly. "It was my duty to offer my protection, especially as the offending party is my own relation."

"None of us have the great fortune of choosing our relations, Mr Darcy," she steadfastly persisted in the same vein of light-hearted repartee. "Let this not trouble you unduly. Besides," she added, seizing the opportunity, "I truly cannot fault her ladyship for pointing out the obvious. Your cousin is much better, so my presence here is hardly necessary now." She paid no heed to his evident desire to protest and finished her thought: "My father and I will remove to Charles Street, so I shall remain close by to call upon him often, if I am allowed."

"That goes without question," he retorted warmly. "But you need not leave."

"I think it would be for the best. I have no wish to provoke your relations."

"They can go hang! This is my house and you are welcome to stay indefinitely," he burst out, then for some reason cleared his voice and looked away. "In any case, you are a great deal more welcome than many of my blood relations," he resumed, with an obvious attempt to lighten the tone of their conversation, and Elizabeth obliged him with a little laugh.

"You have my word that they will never know," she teased, and he smiled at that. A genuine smile that softened his solemn features, for too brief a moment giving him the air of an impish schoolboy.

It suited him, that cheerful air, a vast deal better than the cool reserve. He should smile more often, she thought, and settled that one day, when they would have grown closer, she would tell him.

It might be rather too soon to do so now, so she said nothing, but on impulse she reached to press his hand, eager to put her recent resolutions into practice.

She felt him start at her unprecedented overtures, but she would not be daunted. She sought his glance and earnestly said:

"Words cannot express how deeply I appreciate your kindness, Mr Darcy. I have no reason to expect it of you, and it is testament to your generous nature that you should offer your support." For a moment, it seemed that he would seek to withdraw his hand, yet he did not, and she continued: "I hope that in the fullness of time Lady Langthorne's displeasure will have softened. But for now I do not wish to place you between the devil and the deep blue sea," she finished with a smile and pressed his hand once more, before releasing it.

She leaned back, not expecting an answer – and got none. Somewhere ahead, a sparrow chirped, seemingly more inclined to conversation than a certain gentleman. The notion made her smile. Now that she understood him better, Elizabeth was not about to take offence. So she merely stood and excused herself, privately deciding it was time to leave him to his own devices. And could not guess that, as soon as the door closed behind her, Mr Darcy dropped his head into his hands, with the distinct feeling that a hundred devils had just hounded him into the deep blue sea – and he was drowning.

๏๛ ๛๏

Father and daughter disappeared around the corner into Charles Street, and Darcy made his way back into the house. They could not be persuaded to be taken to Mr and Mrs Bingley's house in the carriage, along with their travelling cases, and both insisted with matching diverted smiles and equal stubbornness that it bordered on the ludicrous to order the carriage for a journey of two hundred yards, cases or no cases. In the end, they had at least agreed to leave without them and allow Darcy to have them conveyed by his own people. At that very moment, his butler was supervising the entire business, instructing Thomas and Simon to gather up the modest pile and be sure not to drop the small but unwieldy box initialled E.B., the only one without a handle.

As the last traces of her presence in his house were taken out of doors, Darcy made his way up the marble staircase, with Georgiana at his side.

"I shall ask Richard if he would care for company," she quietly observed. "I might read to him perhaps. Although I doubt I could make amends for— He will miss her greatly."

"Yes."

And he was not the only one.

"Are you coming with me?"

"In a while."

He would have to go to Richard and provide some carefully worded explanation for Elizabeth's sudden departure, that would not incense his cousin and make him leave his bed for an unprofitable altercation with his mother. It would not be an easy task and would very likely threaten their strange and fragile truce. For when Elizabeth had gone into the sick-chamber to announce her imminent departure and had asked him to join her – presumably as a result of Lady Langthorne's damned impertinent injunction – Richard's instant reaction had been to questioningly glance in his direction, his eyes tinged with reproach and doubt. As though he harboured the suspicion that Elizabeth's departure was somehow *his* fault, or at least his doing.

The upstairs corridor was empty once Georgiana had made her way into Fitzwilliam's bedchamber.

It was exceedingly unwise to follow the foolish impulse. He knew as much, yet the notion would not stop him. He walked down to the furthest room and confidently opened the tantalising door that, for days and nights on end, had been out of bounds.

If anyone should wonder, there was always the excuse of checking that nothing was left behind. A diligent master would not leave every task to servants. Not that it was anybody's place to look for an excuse. It was his house, for heaven's sake, and if it was his pleasure to walk into an empty chamber, whose business was it but his own? And who would dare question?

Nothing was left behind. Not a kerchief, not a single shawl, hairbrush or stray piece of ribbon. There was no trace of her presence in his house, in this room. Just the faintest hint of jasmine and gardenia.

⁓⁕⁖⁕⁓

He could not fathom why the dreams should start that night. Why *then*, when she must have been abed in some unknown chamber in Charles Street rather than tantalising him from thirty paces?

There was no sense to it – no sense at all. Just recurring dreams, achingly vivid in their impossible perfection. And he would awake bereft, half-fearing he was about to lose his reason. But reason was cold comfort as he lay with his arms crossed under his head, staring unseeing into the empty darkness. If this was a slow descent into insanity, then he would take it, and be thankful. So he would close his eyes and breathe slowly and deeply, praying for sleep to come again and bring exquisite dreams of Elizabeth Bennet.

༺ ❀ ༻

She visited often, just as she said she would. Never alone, but with her brother by marriage and her sister. Not Mr Bennet. He had returned to Longbourn, once his presence was no longer needed for moral support or to silence tongues that, unbeknownst to him, would not be silenced.

It was different, now that she was but a visitor in Berkeley Square. He would not meet her over breakfast and at dinner, or simply come across her wandering up and down the stairs. Their encounters were not formal, as morning calls were wont to be. To Darcy's surprise and carefully guarded pleasure, ever since their most affecting meeting in the garden, she sought to engage not only Georgiana but him as well in cheerful and friendly conversation. But the very fact that she was there for scheduled, structured visits, rather than a constant presence in the house, was a change he should have welcomed – yet could not.

Fitzwilliam was different too, sullen and more silent. Not to Elizabeth, Darcy surmised yet could not know, for he never intruded on their time together but left Georgiana or Mrs Bingley to act as unnecessary chaperones. Thus, he could only assume that his cousin's withdrawn manner was reserved for *him*.

They had not spoken further of their pitiful triangle. What on earth was there to say? The only matter that, for Elizabeth's sake, Darcy had felt obliged to bring to his cousin's attention, now that he was virtually out of danger, was Lady Langthorne's unrelenting opposition to the match.

103

"I know," had been Fitzwilliam's sole comment.

"How?"

"She had mentioned it."

"Your mother?"

"Yes. Who else?"

"Indeed," Darcy had retorted, inwardly wondering whether Lady Langthorne had been as forceful to her son as she had been to him, or whether she had reverted to catching flies with honey rather than vinegar.

Presumably the honey had been liberally laced, or Fitzwilliam was astute enough to detect even a subtle poison for, when he was finally recovered and must have had his fill of the insidious tension in Berkeley Square, he did not repair to Langthorne House but to the establishment in Charing Cross where higher-ranking officers would lodge when they were in town.

Again, Darcy could only assume that he called in Charles Street often. He did not ask, and his cousin did not come to tell him. Neither did they run into each other on the days when Darcy unwisely gave in to his own wishes and acceded to Georgiana's warm insistence that they call upon Mrs Bingley and Miss Bennet.

Until one day, when they finally did meet.

Darcy and his sister were received by Bingley and his wife, only to be joined a short while later by the other couple. They came in from a nearby parlour, clearly not aware of the visitors' arrival, and showing every sign of having just concluded a most dissatisfying conversation. Fitzwilliam looked grim. Elizabeth was pale. And both seemed disinclined for company.

They took their seats and accepted cups of tea, but the conversation lagged. The little that there was of it was largely due to Bingley, as had often been the case of late, and it did not take Darcy long to ascertain that himself and Georgiana were, if not unwelcome, then at the very least *de trop*.

The notion could not fail to sadden him, but not nearly as much as the telltale signs of Elizabeth's lack of spirits. Something had distressed her, and it was sheer hell to have no right to offer comfort or assistance.

Upon reflection, he should have known better. Kept his distance. Left them be.

And yet, when the pervading tension forced him to cut the visit short, he could not help settling a steady look upon Fitzwilliam and saying with undue insistence:

"I trust you would be able to drop by in Berkeley Square on your way."

"On my way to where?"

"Wherever you are going when you are leaving here."

"Oh. I see. Then I shall do my utmost to oblige you," Fitzwilliam drawled, clearly resentful.

And much later, when he did do as bid and called in Berkeley Square, his resentment lost every pretence of civil disguise. He had barely been shown into Darcy's study when he spoke, in the same breath as a terse greeting.

"So this is what I am to expect every time I displease her or fall short of the mark? Being summoned into your study for a grilling? Pray speak, Headmaster. What do you wish of me?"

"I wish you would sit," Darcy suggested, striving to contain his own vexation at his cousin's manner.

Pointedly, Fitzwilliam took the offered seat.

"Anything else?" he asked, arching a brow.

"Yes. Would you care to tell me what has got into you?"

"What makes you think you have the right to pry?"

"I do not pry. I care."

"For whom?"

"That is uncalled for!"

"Is it, now!"

"Cousin, this is not helping matters…"

"Oh. Forgive me. Was I supposed to help?"

"Pray, settle down. And have a drink."

"I have no need for your blasted brandy any more than your damned interference! As I just said – I will not be summoned to your study as an errant schoolboy every time you think I put a foot wrong."

"I have not issued a summons."

"Indeed? You could have fooled me."

With a huff of insurmountable vexation, Darcy went to pour a glass of brandy and drained it in one draught.

"There is a limit to what I can bear, you know," he warned without turning.

"Rest assured, Cousin, I have reached my limit long ago."

At that, Darcy spun around in one fluid motion, the sort he made when he was holding a rapier. He did not have one now, so instead he skewered his cousin with a question.

"What have *you* to complain of?"

From his seat, Fitzwilliam snorted.

"I suppose it is too great an effort of imagination for you to understand."

"Understand *what?*"

"Dependence!" the other snapped, then the tirade continued. "It was bad enough in April, when I offered for her knowing that the lot of a soldier's wife was all I had to give. Any man would want to take his wife to a better home than the one she is quitting to follow him, and even then I knew I would fall short. But now I have the joy to know that my esteemed father is determined to withhold whatever advantage might have come my way. And then, lo and behold, there is *you* – one devil of a mark to measure up to!"

"And this is supposed to be my fault?"

"Damned sure it is not mine!" Fitzwilliam shot back, then bent his head to rub his eyes.

He pinched the bridge of his nose between thumb and forefinger and sighed.

"Look, Darcy," he tiredly said at last, "I owe you my life, and this is already more than I can repay. I cannot face owing you even more. Not for every ounce of her future comfort."

Darcy stared nonplussed at the unexpected turn of the conversation, until a flashing recollection came to explain the matter. Further details of his controversy with Lady Langthorne must have finally reached his cousin, he surmised, only to have Fitzwilliam confirm it.

"My mother mentioned your offer of assistance during our latest unpleasant conversation. A clever ploy, I grant you, for needless to say it was not meant as reassurance but as a crafty move to play on my disdain for charity. Little did she know she hit the mark far better than she could have possibly anticipated, and that your charity is the last I would bring myself to take."

In one respect at least, Fitzwilliam was in the right. It did take Darcy some effort of imagination to comprehend how he would have felt, had their situations been reversed.

A well-off cousin's charity would have been hard enough to bear.

A rival's would have been pure poison.

There was nothing Darcy could say to alter that, so he said nothing. In the end, Fitzwilliam resumed, with an air of finality.

"So I shall have to make my own way into the world. And for now there is but one option. I am going back."

To the Peninsula. Without marrying her first. Fitzwilliam did not spell it out, yet there was hardly any need for him to do so. Darcy had already joined the dots.

"And you have gone today to tell her that."

Which was what had distressed her.

"Yes, if you must know," Fitzwilliam resentfully confirmed. "Not that it is *your* concern in any way."

It was not the tone or the obvious truth that raised Darcy's ire, but the thought of how Elizabeth must have felt to hear that her betrothed would rather face French muskets than imminent marriage. Unwisely, he burst out:

"So you would take the coward's way out and leave her to the lions!"

Fitzwilliam sprang to his feet at that, looking very much as though he would have liked to hit him.

He did not. His fists remained clenched at his sides. But there was red-hot fury in his every feature and his narrowed eyes shot daggers.

"Cousin, you can go to hell!" he hissed through gritted teeth and, turning on his heel, he stormed out of the room.

For his own part, Darcy forbore to gracelessly point out he was already there.

"Wait!" he called instead, and moved to follow.

Fitzwilliam stopped halfway along the corridor, but did not turn.

"What do you want?" he asked, too incensed for civil repartee.

Darcy was slow to answer. He wanted them to part on better terms, for one. And also wanted to retract his comment. There was no doubt that Fitzwilliam had to return to his regiment sooner or later, he could not avoid it. If anything, after his departure Elizabeth would be more grievously left to the lions as his wife, rather than still unmarried, in her father's house. And, unlike last spring, Fitzwilliam could not ask *him* to stand beside her and protect her.

He did not put his epiphany into words. Instead, he said simply:

"Forgive me. And… pray come back in."

Fitzwilliam did not ask why. Seemingly as disinclined to part in seething anger, he turned and followed his cousin back into the study. Yet neither sat and neither spoke, until at last Fitzwilliam tiredly said:

"Perhaps I should apologise as well. I thought I could come to accept this. I thought we might survive it and not come to blows. Lately I have begun to doubt we can. And it is probably my failing more than yours."

On impulse, Darcy came forward, hand outstretched, and the other took it. A handshake, a hesitant pat on each other's shoulder – and without really knowing who made the first move, to their utter shock they found themselves embracing like brothers. Something they had not done in over fifteen years.

There was a reason for it, Darcy thought as he awkwardly stepped back and gave a rueful chuckle. His cousin echoed it and ran his fingers through his tousled hair.

"Yes, well. I had better be off. We are turning maudlin," he airily remarked, but he was fooling no one.

Least of all Darcy, who said warmly:

"Godspeed, Cousin. And come back in one piece."

"I shall do my best," was the prompt and casual reply.

Yet, despite the affectionate lightness of the moment, they both knew they still had no answer to their quandary, and the road ahead would be a rocky one.

Chapter 8

Fitzwilliam left a fortnight later, but nobody else did. Unwise as it might have been to remain in town, Darcy could not face the prospect of a Pemberley Christmas. Not just because of Elizabeth. But the tradition of Christmases at Pemberley had died with his father, and ever since his passing Darcy and Georgiana had always spent that time of year in town or with their relations. Of course, there was no question of joining them now. He did not even know where Lord and Lady Langthorne were. A frosty silence had settled between their houses ever since Fitzwilliam's return to the Peninsula. So much the better, to Darcy's way of thinking.

As for the Bingleys, he knew they were in town. Likewise Elizabeth. Bingley had mentioned in passing a fair while ago that she was reluctant to return to Longbourn, which suited Jane very well indeed.

Darcy could not help wondering as to the cause of that reluctance. She wished to be near her sister? Or she missed Fitzwilliam and chose to remain in a place that reminded her of him? Or was loath to bear her mother's lamentations that the foolish man had gone to war leaving her unmarried still?

Regardless, he persistently kept his distance, although Georgiana still called upon them often. By sheer dint of will, he frequently contrived to be away when calls were returned. But he could not avoid her altogether, nor refuse invitations to dine at Bingley's house.

When he felt he could not in all civility delay reciprocating, he made a point of inviting larger parties of carefully selected guests, who would not come determined to either slight or gossip.

The only unavoidable exceptions were Miss Bingley and her sister, and the pair's penchant for snide remarks couched in terms of punctilious civility made Darcy wish he could ask them to be gone and henceforth refrain from darkening his threshold.

Although obliging his mother had never been Fitzwilliam's intention, Lady Langthorne nonetheless had her wish and the engagement was still not public knowledge. Presumably well aware of their sisters' delight in hurtful gossip, Bingley and his wife had not seen fit to take them into confidence either. Thus, Miss Bingley and Mrs Hurst were not able to make malicious remarks regarding the pain caused by the continued absence of a certain officer. However, no further than the previous evening, Miss Bingley had made a point of loudly asking Elizabeth at dinner if she had lately visited in Cheapside.

By now, Darcy had made Mr and Mrs Gardiner's acquaintance. A dinner invitation in Charles Street had brought them together and, to his surprise, Darcy could not fault them. Although a tradesman, Mr Gardiner had all the markings of a gentleman and as for his wife, the revelation that she had spent a large part of her life in Lambton could not fail to serve as a good recommendation.

Truth be told, the evening spent in Charles Street with the Gardiners had been less fraught for him than many. Their presence had helped diffuse some of the tension, to the point that Darcy had found himself talking more than was his wont, at first with the gentleman over drinks, then over coffee with the lady. Elizabeth had joined them to listen to tales of Derbyshire and, when Mrs Gardiner had concluded hers, Darcy had shared some too, along with Georgiana, who had greatly surprised him with her aplomb and readiness for conversation with a lady she had never met before.

That was when Darcy had begun to notice the changes in his sister. Her shyness was not fully conquered, but it no longer held her in its crippling grip. And, with warm gratitude and the same old yearning in his heart, he knew full well whom he ought to thank for the transformation.

As of that day, rather than merely allowing their interaction, Darcy sought to foster it. After all, it was for Georgiana's benefit, not his. The association was clearly advantageous to his sister, and he would fail her most grievously indeed if, for personal reasons, he forbore to seek it.

Or at least that was what he told himself as he penned the letter destined to invite Bingley, his wife and Miss Bennet to his box at the Theatre Royal for a performance of Signor Rossini's much-acclaimed new opera, *The Touchstone*.

The grand auditorium teemed with fashionable people in glittering apparel and the small party took their seats amongst them, but Darcy could not care less who was in attendance. Nor did he care much about the performance either, although he might have found the theme oddly familiar. The man of substance, uncertain of the motives of all who assiduously pursued him, seeking to test their declared affection, only to find himself embroiled in a maze of jealousy, deception and despair.

Tonight however, the haunting similarities and painful differences could not affect him. He sat with Bingley in the second row of red-cushioned chairs, more or less in the shadows – and he had the best seat in the house. For, by careful design, he could command a full view of Elizabeth's profile. The glittering chandeliers suspended on either side of every box cast a warm glow over her cheek and ensured that he would not miss a single play of emotion on her expressive features. He easily identified them, one by one. Enchantment, surprise, sometimes amusement. Familiarity with one of the arias, for he could see her lips move to silently form the words. The magic of another aria rising in crescendo, to bring a sheen of tears to her eyes.

Below, on stage, the performers did their duty. All around, fashionable people chatted and occasionally even deigned to listen. Yet their empty chatter could not reach him through the glowing halo of forbidden joy.

At the entr'acte they all walked out into the grand saloon, restrainedly ornamented with nothing but bright chandeliers and a few allegoric statues. Despite its vastness, it seemed hardly large enough to contain the crowds that had poured out of the boxes to greet their friends, see and be seen, and show their fashionable apparel to advantage. Most of those whom they came across were common and indifferent acquaintances that brought neither satisfaction nor displeasure. But the encounter in the following entr'acte was a wholly different matter.

On this occasion, Darcy walked out on his own to perform the unpalatable duty of calling in Lady Langthorne's box. She had made an appearance with a large party of family and friends towards the end of the first act, as was the habit for many of the patrons.

Her two daughters and her youngest son were in attendance, as well as her son-in-law, Lord Lytham, but thankfully he could not see Morton and, having bowed from a distance, Darcy excused himself and left his own box to pay his respects.

They received him warmly, all except Lady Langthorne. But she refrained from any comment regarding the small party gathered in the Darcy box and for that at least, he was disposed to thank her. His duty done, he bowed and left. But he had barely closed the door and taken a few steps, when he came almost chest to chest with the very man he least wished to meet. He stepped back.

"Darcy! How glad I am to see you," he found himself greeted with unusual warmth.

He did not let his surprise show and merely nodded.

"Morton."

"I see you have come to pay your respects to my mother. I was about to do the same. I came with Lady Grantley's party, and oddly enough they insisted on hearing the first act. But I am positively thrilled they did. I would have been distraught to miss such a peerless occasion."

Out of character as it might have been for his eldest cousin to enthuse over a musical performance, Darcy saw fit to civilly agree.

"The soprano is uncommonly good."

"Oh, nay, nay, you mistake my meaning," the other laughed. "I was not speaking of the opera, although it is pleasant enough, I grant you, for a production of a human composer sung by featherless bipeds, to quote the late Diogenes," he drawled.

Darcy forbore to observe that it was actually Plato who had defined man as a creature with two feet and no feathers. Morton's tenuous grip on the classics was none of his own affair, and he was about to bow and take his leave, when his cousin fixed him with a diverted stare.

"It was you, Darcy, whom I must thank for the best entertainment of the evening."

"I have not the pleasure of understanding you."

"Whereas now I can safely say the opposite. Oh, Darcy, this is priceless! My honourable cousin lusting after my dear brother's woman. You could not take your eyes off her all night!"

Darcy's hands clenched behind his back.

"You are mistaken," he enunciated darkly.

"Oh, spare yourself the trouble to deny it. I saw you clearly. Does Richard know? Is this why he stormed away in such a haste? Oh, I could not have wished for anything grander! Mind, it explains your charming fit of passion when you heard me speaking of what you must have dearly liked to do yourself. But you cannot, now can you? Pray tell me, how does it feel to know that your dearest relation will be the one to enjoy your best-beloved's charms – indeed, that maybe he already had? And under your own roof, no less. Or are you and my brother still so close that you would share everything?"

The savage urge to maim and kill – kill with bare hands – erupted in him with the devastating force of a volcano. Under the thin veneer of civilisation, the primeval instinct of the wounded beast battered to break through – and it was terrifying, because the last vestiges of sanity screamed that this time he *could not* react. Not here. Not in the sight and hearing of so many people, who would delight in vicious gossip that would drag her through the mud. And since he would rather die than let that happen, he *must* find the strength to walk away.

Yet his feet would not obey him. He remained frozen to the spot and could not even stop himself from shaking. The only victory was that his hands were still clenched behind his back rather than strangling the living daylights out of Morton.

Oblivious to the risks, or perhaps perfectly aware of Darcy's reasons for inaction, the other gloated.

"What, no bare-knuckle fights? No more threats of sending seconds? How very sensible of you. Let me assure you, I shall reciprocate. I will keep your entertaining little secret. I do not wish to spark a scandal that might let you have your heart's desire. Nor would I help my brother out of the pit that he has dug himself into. No, let him marry her and starve. I am looking forward to us all gathering together at some time or other. Shall we say at Ashford next year for Christmas?"

With that parting shot and a scant bow, Morton walked past him towards Lady Langthorne's box, leaving Darcy to return in a dark trance to his own.

Belatedly, it came to him that he should have had the sense to stay away until his temper settled. Georgiana's concerned gasp apprised him of his error.

"Brother, what is amiss? Are you unwell?"

She was not sitting in her place at the front of the box but in his seat, and Elizabeth in Bingley's, presumably to make room for the latter, who was just then busily paying court to his own wife.

"Do sit," Georgiana urged and rose to relinquish his place, and Elizabeth followed her example.

Incautiously, Darcy all but snapped.

"Pray keep the seats, ladies. I am well. A sudden headache. Fear not, I am not about to swoon."

Guilt washed over him at Georgiana's look of hurt dismay and, cursing his unguarded tongue, he encompassed both in a prompt apology. His sister nodded timidly, only to make him curse himself once more for good measure. Still standing at his side, Elizabeth laughed softly:

"Do not concern yourself, Mr Darcy. We shall not censure you. My own father has all the patience of a goaded bear when he is plagued by headaches. To everyone's good fortune, he does not get them often. But your sister is right. You should sit," she urged and placed a gloved hand on his arm, as though to add weight to her entreaty.

The bittersweet appreciation of her kind concern was tainted by the notion that even then Morton was very likely watching from Lady Langthorne's box, but Darcy knew better than to glance in that direction.

His first instinct was to withdraw his arm, to avoid adding fuel to Morton's evil fire, yet he did not wish to have her misconstrue it as untoward coldness or rejection. So he took the middle path and sat, only to have her regard him with mild satisfaction and an impish hint of laughter as she walked to take her own seat at the front.

"Well, that was a surprise," she turned towards him to airily remark, once she was seated. "I would not have thought you quite so easily persuaded and I am glad to have been proven wrong. Perhaps one day I should instruct Georgiana on a particular fashion of massaging the head and temples with camphorated spirit of wine. It works wonders for my father, although he is known to complain bitterly of the strong odour."

The picture of a cantankerous Mr Bennet brought a fleeting smile to Darcy's lips and she readily returned it.

"There. That is much better. But if you are dreading the moment when the music is due to recommence, we can always leave," she kindly offered. "I daresay we can dispense with the ballet and the farce. Besides, there will be other evenings."

"I thank you, but there is no need," Darcy replied promptly. "I do not wish to suspend any pleasure of yours."

Nor did he wish to give Morton the satisfaction of thinking he had unsettled him to the point of leaving the theatre. He was still there, in his mother's box, and although Darcy made the greatest effort to avoid looking in that direction, his eyes betrayed him, and he did – only to encounter Morton's malicious glance and see him give a smirk and a mocking bow.

He looked away, towards the stage this time, and fixed his stare on the fancifully attired dancers who had just begun filing in to delight the audience with an elaborate ballet.

Darcy crossed his legs and clasped his hands together on his knee, settling in for the long wait, an ignored performance and the sole delight now left to him: picturing Morton leaving this world in a rich variety of very gruesome ways.

ళ్లe ౨ల

He did not even try to retire for the night at the usual time.

There was no purpose. He knew he could not sleep.

Nor was there any purpose in berating himself for betraying feelings he had steadfastly guarded – and to the very worst of men. Not that he harboured any fears of discovery. Out of fiendish malice, Morton would keep his word. Much as it might have pleased him to besmirch Elizabeth's good name and hurt both him and Richard in the process, he had astutely put his finger on the mark. With his knowing silence and very discreet goading, he had every chance to hurt them even more.

If anybody else had stumbled on the secret they would have had no reason for restraint. So perhaps he should heed the warning. It would have been a step too far to be thankful for it. While a good man with a Christian upbringing, Darcy could just about accept the precepts of loving one's enemy and turning the other cheek in theory. Not so much in practice. So feeling gratitude for Morton's inadvertent warning was out of the question.

115

But the truth remained. He should be far more careful. That she should fall victim to malicious gossip because of his inability to keep his feelings under good regulation, or at least under a very good disguise, was simply unthinkable.

The migraine he had feigned at the theatre had since then turned real. Hammers seemed to pound against his temples, and Darcy thought twice about draining the second glass of brandy that he had just poured.

He leaned his head against the backrest and closed his eyes, in equal measure soothed and pained by the recollection of Elizabeth offering to teach Georgiana to massage his aching temples with camphor or some such.

He sighed. Only a fool would fail to see the signs. Tonight and nearly every time they had been brought together since that day in the garden, when she had held his hand and had spoken to him with all the kindness of a sister, that was precisely what she had uniformly offered him. Sisterly affection. Which was as it should be. In perfect accordance with his vow that, so far, he had failed dismally to keep.

It was time to take her sisterly affection and be thankful. And bring himself to respond in kind. High time to get a grip on treacherous feelings and resume control. Over himself. Over his life. It was time to put his life in order. Do his duty and cease agonising over backward glances.

The migraine notwithstanding, Darcy reached for his glass and drained it.

There were no two ways about it.

It was time to take a wife.

ৎৡৢ ৡৢ৹

"I love you. I love you," she repeated.

Over and over he heard her say the words as she stroked his hair and took him in her arms. Her insubstantial form was real, he could feel it. He could feel the warmth and every soothing touch. And yet he could not see her, it was very dark.

He reached out, seeking, seeking, and knew that he would find her. There. With him. Safe haven. Comfort. Entwined limbs. Entwined bodies. Ultimate fulfilment. Just as it ought to be.

"I am yours. I love you," the disembodied voice whispered again, daring him to believe the perfect lie.

And he believed. He had to.

Seeking. Seeking. In tangled sheets, in the frustrating darkness.

"Elizabeth…"

"I shall not leave you," the shadow lied again, and this time anger stirred.

"You are deceiving me," he accused blindly. Thrashing blindly.

"I am not. I love you. I am here. Touch me. Love me. I shall not leave you."

"Oh, I wish you would! Come. Stay. Or, for God's sake, leave me alone!"

And he awoke to find she had obeyed.

∽⟩℘ ℘⟨∾

The solitary candle left fast-moving shadows as Darcy strode towards his study, his dressing gown flapping at his heels. He marched in and closed the door, then placed the candle on his desk and reached for pen and paper.

He had no control over his blasted dreams but, by God, he still had control over his actions! He flicked the inkwell open, dipped his pen and began to write. Bold lines, in firm strokes. Then he sealed and addressed the letter pertaining to plans for Christmas at Rosings.

∽⟩℘ ℘⟨∾

Lady Catherine must have been versed in reading minds, Darcy determined. She welcomed him and Georgiana with a sort of lofty glee she had never displayed. But then she had never come so close to fulfilling an ambition she had fostered for so many years.

"I have always thought that Christmas is a time to spend with one's nearest relations," she announced at dinner. "I shall not scruple to say that you should have come to us for Christmas several years sooner, but be that as it may. I am pleased to see that your attachment to Rosings is steadily increasing."

She fixed him with an anticipating stare from her seat at the other end of the laden table, as though she fully expected him to declare himself over the roast beef and the saddle of lamb.

He barely suppressed a grimace. Anne was a good sort and they might do reasonably well together, but he was not eager to have Lady Catherine presiding all too often at his table.

"So, Georgiana, tell me of the plans for your coming-out," her ladyship intoned, presumably tired of waiting for a reply from him.

The dear child stammered something, making Darcy think that perhaps it had been unwise of him to bring her. Years of warm encouragement from Elizabeth and Mrs Bingley could not boost her confidence enough to face Lady Catherine.

"Georgiana will be presented in the spring," he intervened, to channel his aunt's overbearing inquiries away from his sister.

"So soon? I thought you would have waited until you had assistance in the matter. But then I daresay you could not wait too long. Georgiana is… What is your age, child?"

"Nearing seventeen, Ma'am," came the subdued reply.

"Well, precisely. Your brother should have foreseen the need of female guidance and acted accordingly a great deal sooner. But this is neither here nor there. Perchance Anne and I might be in town for Easter. I shall consider it my duty to assist as best I can. So, Darcy, who is presenting her?"

"Lady Langthorne had originally offered, but I think it more likely that it would be our cousin."

"Which one?"

"Harriet, of course."

Richard's married sister was the best option by far, and Darcy could only be grateful to her for the offer. The relationship with Lady Langthorne being what it was these days, he would much rather entrust Georgiana's welfare and successful entry into society to another member of the family, one who was disposed towards kindness and affection.

"Well! I hope Lady Lytham is equal to the task. But I daresay you did well to favour her over her mother," Lady Catherine acidly observed, to no one's surprise, as they all knew too well there was no love lost between the two sisters by marriage.

For the remainder of the second and third course, Lady Catherine pontificated, as was her wont. She required little from her listeners, just nods of acquiescence now and then and, well-accustomed to their role, Anne and Mrs Jenkinson readily supplied them.

Georgiana was slower to understand her duty and as for Darcy, he was unwise enough to go as far as contradicting once or twice. But thankfully all things must come to an end, and the same could be said of dinner.

There was no separation of the sexes – one of them was poorly represented. Others might have chosen to imbibe alone, given the alternative, but not Darcy. He had come to Rosings with a purpose, and that purpose had to be fulfilled.

Thus, having accepted the second cup of coffee from the obliging and mousy Mrs Jenkinson, Darcy came to sit on the same sofa as his cousin and, while Lady Catherine was emphatically instructing Georgiana on the only proper way to travel between town and Kent, he lowered his voice to ask discreetly:

"When might I have the chance of a word with you?"

Anne flashed a glance towards him.

"Alone?"

"Preferably, yes."

"My sitting room, before breakfast? Shall we say at eight? Not too early for you, is it?"

"Not at all. I thank you. I shall come to find you."

Not too conspicuously, of course. He would much rather speak to Anne without the song and dance of openly requesting a formal interview. Once they settled the details between them, there would be plenty of time to inform Lady Catherine.

They retired early, which was always the case at Rosings. Darcy had long suspected that the habit was established because Anne sought some respite from her mother, and the too-malleable Mrs Jenkinson could not provide Lady Catherine with sufficient challenge to make her wish for longer *tête-à-têtes*. What a dreary life the three women must have, confined at Rosings with little society but each other's and occasionally the sycophantic parson and his practical wife.

Anne would fare a great deal better at Pemberley. How he would fare was largely a mystery. But when he awoke in the middle of the night from yet another achingly vivid dream, it dawned on him that, once married, he had better hope he was not talking in his sleep.

৩৫ ৩৫

He did not sleep for half the night, which was no surprise. Since he had retired ludicrously early by his standards, once the dream had awakened him there had been no way to fall asleep again. So he had spent the remaining hours until dawn struggling not to reminisce over the last time he had been at Rosings – and failing miserably. Not the sort of night to lift the spirits and coax one into the frame of mind befitting a marriage proposal. Nevertheless, at the appointed hour he made his way towards Anne's sitting room.

He found her already there, ensconced in the window seat with a book, which she set aside at the sound of the opening door.

"You are very punctual," she observed matter-of-factly. "Pray come in and sit."

He did, although not beside her, but on a chair that he moved closer to the window.

"So, Cousin, what did you wish to speak of?" Anne asked with a directness she must have acquired from her mother.

Darcy cleared his voice. He was not versed in this. Offering marriage. And even less in offering marriage as a contract of mutual understanding, rather than affection. In different circumstances he might have spoken of ardent admiration and regard. His features tightened and he refused to let his thoughts wander in that direction. That was precisely why he had come here: to close that avenue once and for all.

"I believe, Anne, that a certain conversation is long overdue," he cautiously began.

"Oh. I suspected this might be brought up, when you asked to speak with me."

"Yes, well. Thank you for giving us the opportunity to speak privately first— "

"Before my mother sees fit to voice our lines for us," she laughed lightly, with a touch of humorous irreverence he had never heard from her.

It was little wonder. Although he had been a regular visitor at Rosings, his direct interactions with his cousin had been few and far between. He knew little of her. Anne's most notable feature was her ability to tolerate her mother's overbearing manner with placid indifference, from behind a screen of complacent remarks interspersed with a great deal of silence.

They would get to know each other better once the betrothal was finally formalised. There would be no particular surprises. Anne was a gentlewoman of good breeding, and anyone who could bear Lady Catherine for six and twenty years must be made of stern enough stuff to undertake the duties of Pemberley's mistress.

It made perfect sense to offer for her. Perhaps the tacit engagement that Lady Catherine had frequently mentioned was her wish more than his own mother's, but that was irrelevant. There was good reason to believe that, over the years, Anne herself might have come to expect it, so he owed her this.

The perceived duty to his cousin would have carried far less weight if he could have had his heart's desire. But as matters stood, it was only natural that he should offer for Anne rather than undertake the dreary task of sorting through the eligible Misses freshly launched on the marriage mart.

Intimacy would be a challenge. A great deal of time would very likely pass until he could see her as his wife, rather than his cousin. But at least there would be companionship. For himself. For Georgiana. And some long-needed structure in a life that had begun to go awry.

So he spoke up with a smile, endeavouring to match Anne's lightness with his own.

"Not to be encouraged. Myself, I would much rather deliver my own lines."

He drew breath to do so but, to his surprise, she interrupted.

"Cousin, I believe that in all common decency and kindness I should stop you now."

"Oh?"

"My dear, dear Darcy! Steadfast, reliable and loyal to a fault. You would do your duty by everyone around you, would you not?"

"Of course."

"I hope you will not take it ill, but I have no intention to abet you. Lady Anne and my mother might have planned our futures in scrupulous detail, but for my part I would much rather steer it my own way. I trust you do not love me," she added with a directness that wholly disconcerted him, not merely because he was not used to finding it in her – but how on earth would a gentleman answer a question such as that?

Thankfully she came to his rescue and resumed, rather contritely:

"Forgive me, that was a very foolish thing to say. Of course you have affection for me as your cousin, but I dearly hope you are merely prepared to offer me your hand because it is expected of you, and not for sentimental reasons. I would hate to give you pain."

So he was not fully rescued from having to provide an answer, Darcy noted in predictable discomfort. He chose his words with care.

"I do have the greatest regard for you, Cousin, but... it would not pain me if you were to take a different path in life."

"I am relieved to hear it. And frankly I am very grateful that you chose to come to us for Christmas and we could finally bring this matter in the open. I wish to marry, Darcy – but not you."

"Oh. Do you have someone in mind?"

"Can you keep a secret? Of course you can, Richard always said you were born poker-faced. Do you remember Thomas Metcalfe? No? I thought you might have, you must have seen him here on occasion. He is Lord Metcalfe's cousin. We became better acquainted last year, when he came to spend some time with his relations and... Well, long story short, we are engaged."

"Goodness! Pray let me offer my congratulations."

"They are a little premature. For obvious reasons, our engagement is a secret one till February, when he will be called to the Bar. And then he will procure a special licence, and we shall marry. In his parish, at All Saints' Church in Margaret Street."

"Goodness!" Darcy said again, and felt like a fool.

"Indeed," Anne laughed with a gayety that should not have surprised him, given their conversation, but he was still taken aback to witness it.

"So your timing is a trifle wrong and I might have to bear Mamma's displeasure for longer than intended, but I daresay I shall weather it quite well."

"You need not say a thing, not yet. You can be assured of my secrecy."

"Honestly, Darcy! Are you not acquainted with my mother? Doubtlessly by now she has been informed we are having a private conversation and is arranging our nuptials as we speak. No, she must learn that you have proposed and I have refused you. I shall withhold the reason until February, or life in this house would become unbearable and poor Lady Metcalfe would fall from her good graces.

It is bound to happen, but there is no need for it to happen yet. The question is, are you ready to play the part of the jilted lover, once I have spoken to my mother?"

"I shall play it with gusto," Darcy assured her with a smile. "But would it not serve you better if instead I played the cad who came to let you know he would soon be engaged to another? And then it would be only natural for you to fall into the consoling arms of Mr Metcalfe."

"It would not be fair on you."

"I live a long way from Rosings."

"She would want to know the lady's name."

"And I might refuse to tell her."

"As I just said, loyal to a fault," Anne smiled warmly. "I thank you, Cousin, but I cannot let you take the blame. Besides, truth be told, I have been looking forward to the confrontation. You know, the lamb becoming lion. I was not expecting to rise up so soon, but I would hate to miss it altogether."

"As you wish. But you need not face her ladyship alone. I would be glad to offer my assistance."

"Would you? That is very kind. Well then, I suppose there is no time like the present…?"

"Quite. But pray give me a moment. I should warn Georgiana not to come down for breakfast yet."

⁕⁂⁕

They walked into the morning room together, to find Lady Catherine glancing up with a look that reminded him forcefully of Mrs Bennet. Darcy's lips twitched and he turned to close the door and thus hide the unholy merriment the comparison engendered.

Valiantly, Anne walked in to take a seat and he leisurely followed. And then the rebellious lamb lost no time in facing the maternal lion.

"Ma'am, I believe there is something you should know," she began, and Lady Catherine beamed. "My cousin Darcy has just done me the great honour to propose – and I have refused him."

The expectant smile withered into shock and disbelieving horror.

"What possible reason have you to do such a thing?" she fulminated, as soon as she caught her breath.

"The plainest. I do not wish to marry him."

"This is disgraceful! You know very well that from your cradles you were destined for each other."

"As I am no longer in my cradle, I saw fit to make my own decision."

"Anne, you ought to know I am not to be trifled with!"

"Let me assure you this was never my intention."

"I will not be interrupted. Hear me in silence. You and Darcy are formed for each other. You are descended on the maternal side from the same noble line. Your fortune on both sides is splendid. You are destined for each other by the voice of every member of your respective houses. What is to divide you? Childish whims and foibles?"

"Pray allow me to remind you, Ma'am, that it is many years since I was a child."

"Yet your conduct proves the very opposite. Very well. I shall know how to act. Do not imagine I shall allow you to cast aside such a sterling offer."

"It is my choice, Ma'am. And no amount of cajoling would serve to make me change it."

"I have no intention to cajole. Let me be rightly understood. If you do not marry Darcy, you forfeit your inheritance."

"I was dearly hoping we would not slide into acrimony, Mamma!"

"You should have considered it when you decided to act against my express wishes."

"That was not my meaning. What I aimed to say was that I was hoping I need not mention that your threats are without substance. You see, I have taken the liberty of consulting my father's last will and testament— "

"You have consulted— !"

"Yes. And I can affirm with certainty that I cannot be disinherited. Moreover, the full control over the estate will revert to me as soon as I am married. So on these grounds, I should have thought you would be pleased to hear it would not happen yet."

"But this is one of the reasons why I wished you to marry Darcy! He would have dealt fairly with you, me, everybody. Nephew, have you nothing to say?"

Darcy was almost glad to be summoned to give his opinion for, despite offering assistance, up to that point he had done nothing.

Not that he needed to. Anne had handled the situation with perfect ease and confidence. What a light she had been hiding for years under a small, drab bushel!

"I fear there is nothing I can say, Lady Catherine," he steadily replied. "It is my cousin's choice and I can only assure her of my full support – assure you both of my continued affection and esteem. We might not become closer related, but we shall lose nothing of our family connection."

"See?" Lady Catherine burst out towards her daughter, her hand shooting palm up in Darcy's direction. "See whom you are rejecting? Can you imagine a more honourable and steadfast character?"

"No, Ma'am," Anne replied quietly. "I cannot."

"Then you should see sense and withdraw your objections!" Lady Catherine commanded and at that Darcy felt compelled to intervene.

"I would beg you do not importune my cousin any further on the subject. I understand her wishes and I withdraw my offer."

"And now he has changed his mind and begins to say he will not have you! Oh, foolish, foolish girl!" Lady Catherine remonstrated, almost choking with vexation.

"Pray have a care for your health, Aunt," Darcy said placatingly. "We would not wish to lose you to a fit of passion."

"At least there is one person in this house who has a care for my comfort."

"We all do, Ma'am," Anne added, only to receive a scowling "Hmph!"

ৡৎ ৡৎ

The matter was very far from over. During the following days – which, for Anne's sake, Darcy felt compelled to spend at Rosings in accordance with the original scheme – Lady Catherine firmly pursued her doomed crusade.

She talked to Anne again and again; coaxed and threatened her by turns. She talked to Darcy too – *"My poor boy, your mother must be turning in her grave to see you so ill-used. But rest assured, I shall not let this rest!"* – until he had to tell her in the strongest terms that the matter was unequivocally at an end, and he *would not* marry his cousin.

Thus, he did get to shoulder some small part of the blame, for Lady Catherine did not take his stern declaration kindly.

In all likelihood, Anne would have another fearsome battle on her hands come February, when she planned to disclose the full truth to her mother. But for now, the fierce storm had no choice but to quieten down and the raging gale to turn into a steady rumble.

Christmas came and went without much goodwill in a certain quarter, but plenty of it in the other three. Their better understanding had made a great deal of difference, and it was thoroughly delightful for the trio – Darcy, Anne and Georgiana – to spend most mornings out of doors together, riding out in the smallest of Lady Catherine's carriages, and returning only when driven in by the cold, to face grim dinners with the lady of the house.

The parson and his wife were often invited, to act as buffers or rather as scapegoats for Lady Catherine's grim displeasure, and civility also compelled Darcy to call at the parsonage twice, despite the painful recollections that the place engendered.

At least Lady Catherine had the kindness or the sense of propriety to refrain from mentioning her major grievance to Mr Collins in her nephew's presence. But after her relations' departure from Rosings, in the end the full truth was out, and she received profuse words of consolation from her shocked and saddened parson.

Unbeknownst to her, the gentleman was in a dreadful quandary. So far, he had never been faced with the awkward circumstance of discord at Rosings. But now he had to do a balancing act between supporting a treasured patron in her grief, without antagonising the prospective patron.

There was just one matter that brought him no difficult choices, just a vast deal of self-satisfied consternation. It seemed that being in possession of one of the most illustrious fortunes in the land did not guarantee acceptance of one's offer of marriage. Thus, a great many philosophical reflections were penned in his letters to his cousin Bennet, on the subject of poor Mr Darcy and his grievous disappointment.

Chapter 9

January in town was cold, wet and dreary, but still preferable to loneliness at Pemberley. At least the town could offer the distraction of plays and social engagements. And then there was the dancing master, calling every week to instruct Georgiana in the intricacies of the quadrille and the other dances a young debutante was expected to excel in, so that she could present herself with credit at Almack's.

As the month progressed, there were also increasingly frequent visits from Lady Lytham, who was clearly disposed to fulfil her task with diligence and care. Darcy would often escort his cousin and his sister to shops and warehouses patronised by people of fashion, for many purchases were needed in preparation for her impending coming-out. Dressmakers were likewise engaged to furnish her with all manner of elaborate creations and of course the requisite court dress.

Truth be told, the entire scheme filled Georgiana with more than a little awe bordering on alarm, and it was quite fortunate that Lady Lytham was kindly and encouraging, a far cry from her mother.

It was not just the fulsome attention that Georgiana dreaded, but the clear notion that her coming-out was to signal her readiness for matrimony. And she would have dreaded the latter even more, were it not for the fact that, during their return journey from Kent, the brother and sister had eventually drifted into an unusually open and, for her, most reassuring conversation.

It had begun with speaking about Anne. Georgiana had already gained a vague understanding of what had come to pass, but there had never been enough privacy at Rosings to cover the details.

They were assured of privacy in the slowly moving carriage so, conquering her reluctance to intrude, Georgiana had cautiously observed:

"When you suggested we spend Christmas with Lady Catherine and Anne, I failed to see you did so with the intention to propose…"

"Forgive me. Perhaps I should have mentioned it."

"No, I did not mean— What I wished to say was that I hope the outcome has not distressed you greatly. I cannot imagine why Anne has refused you."

"Because she is to marry someone else."

"Oh! Truly? Who?"

"A neighbour's cousin. But I was told as much in confidence, and you cannot say a word of this to anybody. Lady Catherine will not be informed till February."

At that, Georgiana could not suppress a giggle.

"I had not thought Anne could be such a dark horse."

"Nor I."

"But... what of you, Brother?"

"What of me?"

"Are you... terribly affected?"

Darcy released a long breath.

"No, sweetling, I am not."

"So you are not in love with Anne?"

"I esteem her."

"And did that suffice for you to offer marriage?"

"Sometimes it does."

The rumbling of the wheels was all that could be heard for a long time, until Georgiana found the courage to continue.

"Is that what you expect of me, Brother? A sensible marriage of convenience?" she whispered, close to tears, and was immensely comforted when Darcy protested warmly as he moved across to sit by her and take her hand.

"Not at all, dearest. I wish you to be happy and marry for affection," he said earnestly, then lightened the tone and added with a smile, "Just take care to fall in love with a man of good fortune."

"Unlike..."

"No, Georgiana," he interrupted firmly. "We shall not let this distress us any longer. It was a youthful error of an inexperienced schoolgirl, and pray believe I do not blame *you*. I could strangle *him* for seeking to take advantage, but we shall dwell on this no more. What I meant is that I hope you will find happiness in the sphere you are accustomed to, with someone of good character and independent fortune. I most certainly do not wish to see you trapped in a marriage of convenience."

"But you would choose it for yourself?" she daringly asked and instantly regretted it, for her brother did not seem best pleased and his voice grew impatient.

"I offered for Anne because I have been told time and again that it was expected of me. Our mother's wish, if Lady Catherine is to be believed."

'*So not convenience but duty…*' Georgiana thought but did not dare press him further. It was a great relief that he was not about to demand anything similar of her, but the prospect of her dear brother not having the joyful life she wished for him saddened her more than she could own.

The sentiment could only deepen over the subsequent weeks in Berkeley Square, once he had made it abundantly clear to herself and to anyone with eyes in their head that he had openly and firmly joined the marriage mart. He, who disdained fashionable gatherings and artificial engagements and would only stir out of doors to ride, go to his club or accept invitations from close and trusted friends, was now out at all hours attending balls, assemblies and soirees – and the Season had not even begun in earnest.

Worse still, they were now beset with callers. *She* was beset with callers. Young ladies and matchmaking matrons, most of whom she barely knew, calling nearly every day to drink tea and make oblique inquiries into her brother's intentions and concerns.

Oh, how she detested these disingenuous encounters with young women who professed great delight in furthering an acquaintance, but could not care less for her other than as a means to put themselves in her brother's path. Was he blind? Did he not see that only one in twenty was worth knowing – if indeed there even were as many as that? Was he truly about to foist one of those vacuous creatures upon her as her sister?

But of course she could not tell him that. What gentleman takes matrimonial advice from a sister more than ten years his junior?

How she missed a genuine friendship! Thanks to Elizabeth and Jane, she could now recognise one when she saw it – and she saw nothing of the sort from the ladies who assiduously courted her favour and her brother's.

Why could he not choose someone like her dearest friends? Elizabeth and Jane had other sisters. Could they not go to Netherfield and get to know the younger Miss Bennets better?

Maybe one of them would catch his eye. Surely they must be a great deal better than the town's simpering Misses, if the two eldest were any indication.

Oh, how she missed them! But the house in Charles Street was firmly closed and shuttered and in all likelihood would remain so for a long time, for Jane must be drawing near her confinement.

Maybe she should stop being such a ninny and suggest to her brother that they call on his friend at Netherfield. But she *was* a ninny, pitiful and hopeless, and she said nothing, daunted by the distance her brother seemed to have put between them. He had never shared his innermost thoughts and feelings, and she had not expected it of him, but these days every trace of openness was gone. He was as affectionate as ever, but they never spoke of anything of consequence, and his deliberate withdrawal was painful to behold.

Yet one day the dear wish she could not even entertain was suddenly granted. Mr and Mrs Bingley came to town, and brought Elizabeth with them. It was a great joy and an even greater surprise, for Jane's condition was advanced and it was a wonder that she should be in town, instead of comfortably settled near her relations.

Some explanation was provided when they came to call in Berkeley Square. Mr Bingley was in a flurry of excitement, expansively telling Georgiana's brother of this place his agent had just brought to his attention, a country house in Staffordshire.

"From what I hear, it would suit us admirably. Ready for immediate occupation, I am told, a good size, a decent manor and in a most desirable location. Close enough to Pemberley and far enough from— "

He stopped short, and his wife finished his sentence for him with a little laugh.

"From Hertfordshire," she supplied, and Mr Bingley looked abashed.

"Forgive me, dearest, that was insensitive of me, and downright uncivil."

Georgiana glanced at her companions in turn, with the distinct impression that everyone else in the room, including her own brother, had a perfect understanding and more than a little sympathy for Mr Bingley's wish to put some distance between himself and Hertfordshire.

His wife had a warm smile for him in response to his obvious contrition and reached to press his hand.

"Think nothing of it. You have every reason, and I am in full agreement."

"In truth, Jane and I are awed and grateful that you have lasted for so long," Elizabeth added with a mischievous little laugh, thus bringing a diverted twitch to all lips but Georgiana's.

"So," Mr Bingley gleefully resumed, once acquitted of any need to feel contrite, "the fact of the matter is, we are here to perpetrate a little deception. We did not wish to share our plans until they were brought to fruition, so we have allegedly chosen to spend a few weeks in town. But I will travel into Staffordshire directly, to visit the place and ascertain its merits."

"Would you like me to join you?" Darcy offered.

"I thank you. That is very kind and I appreciate it. But 'tis high time I cease relying on you for guidance in every step I take. If anything, I would be easier knowing that you are here, at hand. Jane will remain in town, as will Elizabeth, and I would be greatly reassured to know they are not left wholly to their own devices."

"Would you not care to come and stay with us for a few days while Mr Bingley is away?" Georgiana suggested without thinking and belatedly shot a glance towards her brother, to silently ask permission.

As such, she could not fail to detect the fleeting shock, before he carefully removed every trace of it from his countenance and spoke up to second her invitation.

"An excellent notion. You are very welcome."

"Capital. That would put all my concerns to rest, if you are certain there is no inconvenience."

"None at all. Had Georgiana not suggested it, I would have done so myself," Darcy replied promptly, setting his sister's heart at ease – and leaving her blissfully unaware of his real thoughts.

The deuce! Georgiana, you should have asked privately first! Nay, 'tis just as well that she did not, I would have found a reason to refuse. If Morton hears of this, he would— But he is not in town, and I say damn him! This is unwise in every way, but I could not care less. She will come to stay. Not for long. Three days. Maybe four. Enough.'

No. Not enough. Nothing short of forever would be enough.

But she would come to stay.

❧⊛❧

In fact, Bingley estimated he would be absent for a se'nnight rather than just four days, and in due course he set off, while his wife and Elizabeth came for their all too brief sojourn in Berkeley Square, as arranged.

So Darcy would see her at breakfast and at dinner. Find her in the library, when he would wander in there for no reason. Hear her in the music room, where she would sit with Georgiana, taking turns in playing the pianoforte. Or covertly watch her in the drawing room, as she would help his sister entertain the endless horde of females whom he could not but find vexing and unwelcome, devoid of charm and beauty and falling short in everything when measured against *her*.

❧⊛❧

They were still beset with morning callers, but Georgiana found them a great deal easier to bear with Elizabeth at her side, knowing that at all times there was an understanding presence in the room. Someone with whom she could exchange a telling glance, when one could be exchanged with impunity, whenever the assiduous and insincere flattery was pouring in excess.

They had been apportioned more than their fair share of visitors that day as well and, as soon as the last one was finally escorted out by the obliging Simon, Georgiana breathed an obvious sigh of relief.

"Hopefully now we might have our time to ourselves. 'Tis hard to believe sometimes how busy our mornings have become of late," she could not help remarking, then instantly regretted it, for she was loath to have her brother know she felt imposed upon.

She was glad of Elizabeth's assistance when her friend gave a little laugh and airily observed:

"Do you suppose a note might have been put in the paper to let it be known that Mr Darcy is in search of a wife?"

And then she turned to Georgiana's brother to offer with a smile:

"I hope you will also find affection into the bargain, Sir, although if you do not mind my saying, it does not appear very likely with anyone from the last contingent."

Darcy set his teacup down and, to her sadness, Georgiana heard him say matter-of-factly:

"I am not seeking a marriage of affection, Miss Bennet."

Promptly, Elizabeth voiced the question that Georgiana did not dare ask:

"Whyever not?"

At first it seemed that the only answer she would get would be a mere shrug, but in the end he added as somewhat of an afterthought:

"Because the world is misaligned and the quest for a love-match is seldom rewarded."

"Then let us pray the world would mend," Elizabeth exclaimed with feeling. "Forgive me for intruding on such a private matter, Mr Darcy, but I believe you deserve much better than a loveless union."

"I thank you for your kind concern," he retorted crisply. "Ladies, would you excuse me?" he added and stood, and then was gone.

"I fear I have offended your brother yet again with my propensity to speak too freely and go where I am not wanted," Elizabeth said wistfully once they were left alone, but Georgiana hastened to put her mind at ease.

"Pray, do not regard it. He is too good to take your words amiss and I, for one, was very glad to hear you say as much to him. I have long wished I dared make the same plea, for I dread him marrying for sheer duty. To me, to the estate. I wish him to be happy and I fear he would not be, were he to offer for any of those ladies."

"This is my fear also."

"I must sound positively awful, just like a horribly jealous sister," Georgiana exclaimed in clear remorse, and resumed without allowing Elizabeth to intervene and reassure her. "'Tis but my fear that they would be ill-suited. I do not wish to cast aspersions on them all and distrust everybody's motives. Some of these young ladies might be genuine, and pleasant enough," she saw fit to retract the sweeping censure. "Miss Wyatt, for instance. She seems rather sweet and kind, as does the youngest Miss Grantley and her cousin. And perhaps Miss Hewitt too. And Lady Morley's daughter, although... Oh, I do not know! I wish Richard were here, he would know how to advise him," she sighed, then brought her fingers to her mouth in sudden contrition. "Forgive me, Elizabeth. You must wish for his return as well, and for better reasons. Why did he have to throw himself in danger's path again, after everything that happened?" she incautiously voiced the thought that had been with her for months, before she realised what it was that she was saying. "Goodness! Whatever has got into me today to make me say all the wrong things, over and over?"

"Pray, do not fret," Elizabeth entreated as she endeavoured to fight off the turmoil brought by Georgiana's words, for she had asked herself that very question too often to count, and every time she had come to no reassuring answer. "Might there be something in the tea, do you imagine, to make us both say things we wished unsaid?"

"I should imagine not, otherwise it might have affected my brother as well. He too had the tea, if I remember rightly," Georgiana replied in the same jesting vein, and her countenance brightened.

Elizabeth was pleased to see that her attempts at light-hearted repartee had borne fruit. She only wished it would be as easy to gain Mr Darcy's pardon for her untoward interference in his affairs.

An encounter in the downstairs parlour an hour later gave her the chance to try. She was sitting by the fireplace with her book, waiting for Georgiana to return from a conference with her housekeeper and for Jane to emerge from the daily rest her condition required, when the door suddenly opened to admit Mr Darcy. He froze in his tracks, as though he had expected the parlour to be empty.

"Forgive me. I thought..." he hesitantly said.

"That no one was here?" Elizabeth finished for him with a smile.

"Not at all! I did not mean..."

"Nevertheless," she came to his rescue, "this gives me as good an opportunity as any to apologise."

"Whatever for?"

"My earlier comment, in the drawing room."

"Pray do not. I know it was said in kindness and... I do appreciate it," he added with manifest difficulty.

"You are very gracious."

"I am not. I was not. Miss Bennet, I must beg your pardon— "

"Mr Darcy, we simply cannot continue in this manner," she cheerfully interrupted. "We seem to have been apologising to each other more or less constantly for many months now, and I think we ought to have some variety in our conversations. So let me change the subject by saying that perhaps it is time to cease being so very formal. As we are to be cousins, can I not persuade you to address me by my Christian name?"

He bowed, but she still glimpsed his countenance for long enough to see that his lips tightened.

"I would be honoured," Elizabeth heard him say.

"I thank you. And might I be allowed the same liberty? Oh, how foolish of me," she exclaimed with a hint of laughter. "After all this time, I find I do not know your Christian name."

For some reason that she could not fathom, he swallowed hard, and at last he answered.

"Fitzwilliam."

"I beg your pardon?"

"My Christian name, Miss Bennet – Miss Elizabeth – is Fitzwilliam," he quietly elaborated.

Then he excused himself and left the parlour, without taking the time to seek whatever he might have walked in there for.

༄ ༅

Fitzwilliam Darcy. Fitzwilliam.

How strange that she had never known.

Yet perhaps not so. To the best of her knowledge, Georgiana uniformly addressed him as *'Brother'* and spoke of him likewise when he was not there. As for the others – Richard, Charles, his relations and general acquaintances – she had only heard them call him *'Darcy'*.

Fitzwilliam Darcy. There was resonance in the uncommon name, a stately ring to it which, if anything, made addressing him by his Christian name seem even more formal, and not less.

Elizabeth turned under the counterpane in the same comfortable chamber that had been hers before, and closed her eyes. Yet a moment later they flashed open and she turned on the other side, with something of a huff.

She had begun to regret having asked him what his first name was, especially as he had seemed rather displeased about it. Besides, her intended purpose was not served, for she felt she could not possibly address him thus.

Then… what?

Cousin? That was presumptuous. They were not related yet.

William? Wills? Will? Or something in that vein?

135

Of course not, she would never dare! No one of his acquaintance had used such appellations in her hearing, and it would be far too forward of her to be the first. Besides, that would bring the noble-sounding name into the realms of the ordinary, the banal.

Anyone could be a William – even Mr Collins.

There was only one Fitzwilliam Darcy.

And yet – Fitzwilliam? No, he would have to remain Mr Darcy to her, and hopefully he would not think her distant, especially after prompting him to address her by her Christian name. Whatever had possessed her? Now she would have to find creative ways of speaking to him while avoiding the use of his name altogether.

She tossed and turned under the counterpane, dismayed that her attempts at friendliness always seemed to serve her ill where Mr Darcy was concerned.

As yet, she did not begin to wonder why it was so thoroughly unthinkable for her to address him as Fitzwilliam, and so she eventually drifted into peaceful slumber, blissfully ignorant of the storm to come.

♥

Five doors down – the whole of thirty paces – Mr Darcy held no hopes of peaceful slumber. He had not even readied himself for the night, but had dismissed his man before Weston could do as little as come forth to remove his coat.

He removed it himself eventually, along with the waistcoat, and cast them both in a careless heap upon the bed, before walking over to the seat near the fire. As always, Weston had seen to his comfort and had diligently moved the three books found by his bedside to the little oval table now placed at his elbow, along with a fresh glass and the port decanter. The ruby liquid gleamed in the firelight in ever-changing shades of red, but Darcy ignored it and fixed his stare on the leaping flames before him.

Unlike the last time she had been a guest in this house, now he knew precisely where she would be, for each and every second of the night. Fitzwilliam's chamber was closed off and empty and the night-nurse role was at an end, so she would not go to check on him, summon Dr Graham or fetch something from downstairs.

She would be in her room. Before the looking-glass perhaps, brushing her hair? Or walking barefoot to the bed, her shape outlined through the light chemise as she stopped to stoke the fire? Propped up against the pillows, reading – or already asleep, her lips curled into a smile at some pleasant dream or other?

His own lips tightened and Darcy stood to grab the poker and needlessly pester the fire in the grate. If unruly thoughts gained purchase even when he was awake, what chance had he against them while asleep? So doubtlessly he would dream of her again tonight. The near-certainty brought him no pleasure. It was a long time since he had ceased to welcome the wild, futile imaginings, the achingly impossible illusions that only served to leave him yearning and bereft.

He slammed the fire iron in its place and snorted. Perhaps keeping off the port was not enough. Perhaps he should consider locking the door to his bedchamber, before he found that he had also taken to walking in his sleep.

◦◦◐ ◑◦◦

"Are you well, Brother? You look very tired."

"I am quite well," Darcy dissembled, rather dismayed to hear that he looked no better than he felt, so presumably his assurances were fooling no one.

He had not walked in his sleep last night, but had not slept much either. As if on cue, Georgiana asked:

"Did you sleep poorly?"

"Pray, do not concern yourself. What do you plan to do today?" he asked, hoping to distract her and casting a glance around to include the other ladies in the question.

"Something very tame," Mrs Bingley smiled, and Mrs Annesley nodded in assent. "Reading perhaps, or sitting in the garden room."

"If you sit in the library, you might hear the music," Georgiana advised, to Jane's slight confusion.

"The music?"

"Oh, forgive me. Of course you would not know. Monsieur Dupont, my dancing master, is due to call today to instruct me, and he usually brings along some very skilled performers. You are of course welcome to sit and watch the lesson, but I fear you would find it very dreary. I am not as proficient as I would like to be."

137

"When I saw him last, Monsieur Dupont declared himself satisfied with your progress," Darcy encouragingly contradicted.

"He told me I have mastered the basic steps and figures, but that I need to practise a vast deal more. Worse still, practise in larger company," she incautiously imparted the advice that had given her nothing but trepidation.

She did not wish to practise in larger company and have her lack of skill exposed to all and sundry. Especially as there was only one ready source of practising companions, the one she dreaded most, and Mrs Annesley was quick to spot:

"Could you not ask some of the young ladies who come to call? Doubtlessly they would oblige you and be glad of the instruction— "

"I would much rather not," Georgiana swiftly interjected and was extremely glad when Elizabeth, much more attuned to her inner feelings, spoke up to assist her.

"What of a smaller party, to begin with? The exercise might be too much for Jane or Mrs Annesley, but I would be glad to help in any way I can."

"That is a splendid notion," Georgiana clapped in undisguised relief and joy. "Elizabeth, would you? You can dance the quadrille, I gather?"

"Not with the greatest skill, but the little I possess might just about suffice, if your brother would be so kind as to partner me."

And thus the decision was suddenly made for him by the two ladies dearest to his heart, whom Darcy could not bring himself to disappoint. Their childish delight at the impromptu scheme was obvious, and it could not fail to bring the old admixture of pain and pleasure at what might have been, had Elizabeth been by now Georgiana's sister.

Monsieur Dupont, who joined them at the appointed time, also voiced his agreement when applied to.

"At least four couples would 'ave been *ma préférence, mais…* zis iz better zan no ozer couples at all, *non?* We shall place two chairs *ici…* and two *là*, to remind us of where ze ozer couples should 'ave been. And zen we shall take our turn, zen dance again for zeirs. Zis should be good, more *occasion* to practise, as long as you remember, *Mademoiselle*, 'ow ze dance goes when zere are four couples. I shall try to remind you. So I shall partner you, if you *permettez*. Let us stand on zis side. Monsieur d'Arcy and Mademoiselle Bennette, if you would care to take your places, *s'il vous plaît?* "

And then he turned to the musicians with a flourish of his hand.

"Let us begin with *Le Quadrille Français. Un, deux, trois et...* right and left... *balancez...* ladies' chain... *chassez-croissez... petits moulins... et promenade...*"

For Georgiana's benefit, Monsieur Dupont continued to call the figures and instruct on each forthcoming move. Guided by his voice, they launched with gusto into the sprightly dance and bowed and turned and twirled around each other on strains of lively music as, in their seats behind them, Mrs Annesley smiled benignly and Jane clapped the time, seemingly well-pleased with the morning's entertainment.

They were not the only ones. Georgiana beamed, clearly enjoying dancing practice more than ever and, with the warm glow of Elizabeth's smiling countenance before him, Darcy abandoned himself wholeheartedly to the surreal experience.

It was equally surreal to find himself going against his very nature and simply taking the moment as it came. Delight in the joy of it, the glory. *Carpe Diem.* No overburdening reflections, no efforts and no schemes.

She was delightful. Rosy-cheeked, eyes sparkling, she skipped and twirled and reached for his hand to clasp it in her own as they promenaded to change places with the other couple. No gloves and no formality, just the sheer delight of music and light movement, the *'now'* more precious than all the whys and wherefores.

"I am enjoying this a great deal better than our dance at Netherfield, if I may say so," she observed, and not even that reference to the past had the power to distress him.

He smiled and replied truthfully.

"So am I."

Then he released her hand, to receive Georgiana's for another set of figures.

"This reminds me of a pact I have made with myself," Elizabeth resumed when she was returned to him.

"Which pact would that be?"

"To tell you something, as soon as I dared."

"Now that is novel. As soon as you dared? I do not remember you having any qualms about speaking your mind."

Elizabeth laughed.

"That was at the time when I never spoke to you without rather wishing to give you pain than not."

"Was there such a time?"

"You know very well there was."

He did not, in truth, and the intelligence was rather unsettling. But it was unwise to pursue that thought, so he merely asked:

"What did you wish to tell me?"

"That you should smile more often. It suits you," she cast over her shoulder; then, finishing her pirouette, she clasped his hand again for a short promenade.

It was just as well that they were separated by the next figure, for there was no answer he could make to that, but when she returned her glance was almost wistful.

"Or have I overstepped the mark again and spoken too freely?" she asked ever so sweetly, and thus put paid to all his caution, so much so that his reply was frank and prompt.

"No – never. I hope you know you can tell me anything."

The closing bars rang out and they bowed to each other and to the other couple, then turned to the musicians to clap in a well-deserved show of appreciation.

The wisest choice by now might have been to withdraw, but Darcy could not bring himself to do so. Georgiana was enjoying this and the practice seemed eminently useful and—

The deuce! Could he not be truthful, at least for once, at least to himself? *He* was enjoying this. A morning, a few dances. Where was the harm in something as innocent as that?

The harm, the angel at his right shoulder sternly warned, was in the conversation. In the openness she offered, as warmly and artlessly as Georgiana. To her, it must have been a friendly chat between future cousins. To him, it had all the bitter-sweetness of missed chances at courtship.

'And what of it?' the devil on the left shoulder shrugged. He was still harming no one. No one but himself. And he was a grown man, and could surely weather a fleeting spell of sunshine, as well as all the storms past and yet to come.

So when Monsieur Dupont announced the Lancers Quadrille Darcy squared his shoulders and smiled to his sister, then his partner, and offered Elizabeth his hand as the dance began.

They practised the quadrille until exertion got the better of them all, and it was time to clamour for rest and lemonade and tea. Refreshments were duly brought and they partook, still chatting freely; a satisfied review of their achievements. Then afterwards Monsieur Dupont suggested they might try a country dance or two, or perhaps a reel – although Mademoiselle D'Arcy, he added, would not be expected to dance the latter at Almack's.

"I should have danced a reel with you at Netherfield," Elizabeth laughed breathlessly, once they had returned to the floor to act upon Monsieur Dupont's suggestion and were merrily skipping arm in arm to the tune of a very lively Scottish air. "I would have dearly loved to hear Miss Bingley enthuse on such skilful footwork, though I cannot imagine what praise she could have possibly offered that would rank higher than *'a man without fault'.*"

"Elizabeth, surely you are not attempting to make me lose my footing by provoking me into laughter."

"Perish the thought. Such an underhanded ploy would be its own punishment, and I would feel duly mortified should my dancing partner go careering into the other couple."

"Like some clergyman we know."

They snickered like two errant children.

"It was most ungenerous of you to laugh at him."

"I did not."

"Fiddlesticks! I saw you smirking."

"And you glowered at me for good measure."

"If you remember my glowering so clearly, how can you in good conscience claim you did not laugh at him?"

"I did not strictly speaking *laugh.*"

"I never thought I would see the day when you would resort to sophistries."

"And I never thought I would see the day when you would speak in defence of the good vicar."

"How is Mr Collins, by the bye?"

"Truly, Elizabeth? Are we to speak of Mr Collins and his poultry in the middle of a Scottish reel?"

"Perhaps not. I find I have not the breath for such a fulsome conversation. We might return to him a little later."

"Impossible. During the next dance I plan to speak of the size of the room or the number of couples."

Elizabeth smiled widely at that.

"Or perhaps books?" she willingly played the game.

"No, surely not. You can never talk of books in a ballroom."

"Not with tight-lipped near-strangers, I cannot. But I am prepared to make exceptions for a close acquaintance."

"You are very kind. Still, you might have had the right of it the first time. Let us leave talk of books for later, in the library."

"Speaking of which, I have yet to see as impressive a collection."

"I thank you. Needless to say, you are most welcome to peruse it to your heart's content or borrow anything that takes your fancy."

"A much appreciated offer. For now though, I would be quite content with a less sprightly dance."

"Along with the rest of us. Monsieur Dupont, should we not take a moment to draw breath and have another glass of lemonade?"

ঙ৩৩ ৩৩৵

What a day it was – what a phantasmal day!

The dancing practice continued for a little longer, with a few tamer pieces followed by a return to the quadrille. And then Monsieur Dupont declared himself more satisfied than ever, gave thanks and expressed wishes that the arrangement might sometimes be repeated, maybe even with a few more couples, then summoned his musicians and was gone.

That day, the butler was informed that Mr Darcy and his sister were not receiving morning callers. Instead, they took their guests into the garden, to stroll along the narrow gravelled paths, then settled for luncheon in the airy glasshouse – a fair compromise and as close to a luncheon *al fresco* as the wintry season would allow.

They lost track of time as they sat together in blissful informality, reclining in comfortable garden chairs and nibbling at the selection that was laid out for them, as they talked of everything and nothing. Nothing contentious, worrisome or sad – that was deliberately avoided by all four, as though by some tacit agreement. Other than that, they were not in the least selective. Everything was fair game. Books. Music. Plays and operas. Pemberley and Hertfordshire. Georgiana's presentation. The Bingleys' hopes of a new home in Staffordshire. Former travels. School years and of course choice childhood tales, as ludicrous as any, of climbed trees and torn apparel, of adventurous albeit muddy treks ignominiously rewarded with the birch, or successful night-time raids into the pantry.

Elizabeth could not honestly remember having heard Darcy laugh quite so much before, if indeed she had ever heard him laugh at all. She could not fathom what might have caused the transformation – this unaccountable transition to unreserved good-humour – but she dearly hoped that it would last, for his sake as well as Georgiana's. The dear child was verily glowing, and the cheerful, easy-going manner was doing him a few favours too. Still, this time Elizabeth forbore to say as much. To her way of thinking, Mr Darcy must have had enough advice from her already.

So she merely sat back to enjoy the newfound camaraderie which would hopefully brighten family gatherings in the future. Somehow, with Darcy and Georgiana so warmly on her side, the Langthornes' displeasure was less vexing, and certainly less daunting.

The only oppression that even their manifest approval could not ease was her persistent guilt at being instrumental in depriving Richard of every known advantage, and the distressing notion that, caught between herself and his family's opposition, he had found no better answer than going back to war…

But this was not a day for such unsettling thoughts, nor for conundrums without resolution, and it was not her way to increase difficulties by dwelling on them, long before their time.

They would find an answer, once Richard was returned in safety.

When – she knew not. She could only pray it would be soon.

Chapter 10

The unreserved good-humour did not last. But then perhaps it was too much to ask for in the present company, Elizabeth uncharitably thought as she sipped her tea and endeavoured to make civil conversation with Mrs Hurst and Miss Bingley.

They were much surprised to find her and Jane there and far from delighted. In fact, Miss Bingley was sufficiently put out to observe, in her most infuriating mixture of feigned civility and thinly-veiled displeasure:

"I wonder at my brother, Mr Darcy. Why should he task you with looking after dear Jane and Miss Eliza, when he has family in Grosvenor Square?"

Elizabeth looked away to conceal a smile when her host arched a brow at the petulant question.

"Perhaps because you were not in town at the time of his departure?" he smoothly observed.

"Surely he could have made arrangements. He should have sent us word, and we could have easily returned a few days sooner. Not forgetting of course the family in Hertfordshire, whom he might have appealed to, just as easily," Miss Bingley added with a grimace masquerading as a smile.

"Your brother must have had his reasons," came the calm reply.

"He always does! But the imposition…"

"I thank you for your concern, Miss Bingley, but let me assure you, there is no imposition whatsoever."

A venomous glance was shot her way at that, Elizabeth could not fail to notice. A glance that clearly said *This is precisely what I was afraid of!*

She stared in wonder. Surely not! And yet the lady's air and every feature gave weight to the ludicrous suspicion. Miss Bingley was profoundly jealous! *Of her.* Of her very presence in this house.

It required every ounce of self-possession to keep herself in check and not burst into unseemly laughter. Had Miss Bingley deigned to spend more time with her new family in Hertfordshire – and with Mrs Bennet in particular – she would have doubtlessly acquired a deep affection for the latter, Elizabeth all but giggled, for surely her mother would have set Miss Bingley's troubled heart at ease.

For her own part, she saw no purpose in obliging the deeply vexing lady by taking her into a confidence she had done nothing to deserve. If Miss Bingley chose to see her as a threat, then she was free to do so. It would serve her right to taste the bitter medicine she had forced upon Jane over a year ago, when she had sought to persuade her that Mr Bingley would marry Georgiana. Besides, she would soon spot the different and very real danger.

To her good fortune, Miss Bingley could not possibly have known of Mr Darcy offering for his cousin. But should she extend her morning call, she would very likely see the house in Berkeley Square teeming with competition. Ladies markedly younger than she was, more poised, some better looking, and presumably better connected too. To his good fortune, she did not stand a chance, Elizabeth thought with satisfaction, and raised her eyes to meet Miss Bingley's squarely, only to see them narrowing in vexation.

"Jane," the lady suddenly spoke up again, "pray tell me, just how long is Charles planning to absent himself from town?"

๑๑ ๑๑

As Elizabeth had predicted, an hour later the drawing room was full. Georgiana looked mildly harassed, Jane tired and Miss Bingley as though she had begun to see, understand – and panic.

She and Mrs Hurst remained with them for longer than civility required, presumably in an endeavour to emphasise their status as particular and intimate acquaintances. But their extended stay merely served to strengthen the sense of clear and present danger.

From her place, Elizabeth allowed herself the unholy entertainment of surreptitiously watching Miss Bingley coming to grips with her predicament. Considering her unpardonable conduct at Netherfield and afterwards, her comeuppance, truth be told, was long overdue and rather gratifying.

But at what cost?

Did Mr Darcy truly know what he was about? Why was he suddenly intent on rushing into marriage? Why had he even hastened to offer for Miss Anne de Bourgh?

Elizabeth could be nothing but glad to learn from Mr Collins's letter to her father that Mr Darcy had met with a refusal from that quarter. She could not fathom why his hand had been rejected any more than she could sympathise with his reasons for offering in the first place. From the little she knew of Miss de Bourgh, she could surmise it would have been a dutiful marriage of convenience – and he deserved better. Far better than that, and far better than a union with any of the Miss Bingleys of this world as well.

Should he not take the time to form an attachment and find a wife that would make him happy, rather than rush to sift through this plethora of questionable options?

It was enough of a concern to think that he had put himself on the marriage mart for the wrong reasons, whatever they might be. Actually witnessing him doing so was no easy matter.

Involuntarily, her eyes kept drifting towards the far end of the room, where Mr Darcy sat in quiet conversation with Georgiana and Miss Wyatt. Well, not so much in conversation, for he hardly spoke. For most of the time he merely sat listening and watching them as they exchanged their comments. Watching them in a mild, detached, almost paternal manner.

Was he contemplating offering for Miss Wyatt next? Elizabeth dearly hoped that he would not, even though a few days ago Georgiana had spoken well of her. But she seemed so very young. Too young for him. Too tame as well, and far too mousy.

He needed a very different sort. Not just a quiet, acquiescent wife, but someone who would challenge him into giving the best he had to offer. Elizabeth felt she understood him now. Much like herself, he would not be happy unless he could respect his partner in life. He could scarce escape discredit and misery in an unequal marriage. He deserved so much more. He should have sparkle in his life, and laughter.

Miss Wyatt did not suit, and Elizabeth could only hope that he would be wise enough to see it. To give her her due, at least she did not seem to be of Miss Bingley's ilk. But then still waters ran so very deep, and goodness knows what lurked under that placid surface.

Catching herself about to look their way once more, Elizabeth pursed her lips and purposely turned her head in the opposite direction. It surely was no concern of hers for whom he would decide to offer. But she wished him well, she wished him the very best and could only hope that he would have it, although so far she had not seen anyone who could make him happy. Who, of this multitude of simpering nothings, could possibly fit the part? None of them, absolutely no one struck her as good enough for him.

From the other end of the room, she could hear him laugh softly at something that Georgiana might have said, or perhaps it had been Miss Wyatt. She sighed and pursed her lips again, dearly hoping he knew what he was doing. He did not need a substitute for Georgiana, to keep him company when his sister married. He needed a true, worthy companion. A soul mate. A union of hearts and minds. Did he truly imagine he would find it with someone like Miss Wyatt?

Elizabeth folded her fingers tightly in her lap and turned to Miss Bingley, a small smile tugging at the corners of her lips at the realisation that, just like the aforementioned lady, over the last quarter of an hour she had trained her ears on Miss Wyatt's mild and quiet tones, trying to catch what she might have said to Mr Darcy.

Now that would be a fine to do, if she should start following his every move with the same determination as Miss Bingley. Not with the same purpose in mind of course, she thought and giggled, and at that Miss Bingley threw her a suspicious glare.

"You are uncommonly diverted, are you not, Miss Eliza? Would you not share your thoughts with us? At times, we would all dearly love a laugh, though goodness knows what *you* might find amusing at the moment," she venomously added with a sidelong glance towards Miss Wyatt, which only served to entertain Elizabeth anew.

"I was merely thinking of something that my mother might have been inclined to share," she thinly offered to the other.

True to form, and to her detriment, Miss Bingley lost all interest at the reference to Mrs Bennet and her communications, and haughtily looked away. For her part, Elizabeth held her peace.

Thank goodness she and Mrs Hurst would soon be gone, as would the other unwelcome visitors, and leave them to the quiet comfort of sensible conversation, with no bid for attention or disingenuous undertones.

If that should change one day, if Miss Wyatt or some other woman should come to put her stamp on this home, make it hers, it would be Mr Darcy's choice and no one else's.

With a slight frown, Elizabeth squared her shoulders and refused to think about it. For some reason, it was something she did not feel at ease to dwell upon.

⚬ᨣᨢ᠊ᨢ⚬

A noise he could not readily identify reached him in his slumber and Darcy stirred in his seat, not quite awake enough to notice that this time he had fallen asleep before the fireplace in his bedchamber, next to the untouched bottle of port and the small stack of books he could not read.

The noise persisted and he groaned and stirred again, then finally staggered to his feet to walk still half asleep in its direction. The door…? Somebody knocking…? What…?

He rubbed his eyes and shook his head in an attempt to rouse himself as he reached to turn the handle. The door slid open – and he blinked. Once. Twice. Yet the vision did not fade. Not dressed in white, but a vision nonetheless, more beautiful than ever.

So he must be dreaming still. How strange! His dreams had never begun thus. And he could have sworn he was awake. No matter. He would not quibble, not tonight. Not when this picture of perfection stood before him, her eyes shimmering in the candlelight. So glorious. So real. The touch of her hand seemed real too, when he reached to hold it and lightly stroke it with his thumb.

"Elizabeth," he whispered with the same old yearning, and opened the door wider.

Perhaps this time the rest of her would seem real too, when he would take her in his arms and run his fingers through her hair to free it from the haphazardly pinned knot, as he would lead her into his bedchamber. To his bed. Perhaps this time she would stay for longer and the delicious deception of her kisses, her embraces, would make up for the searing reality, when it would return to torment him with her absence.

Or perhaps not.

But he would gladly risk it nonetheless.

"Forgive me for disturbing you," the vision said through trembling lips and her hand turned in his, to clasp it in earnest. "I rang for the maid, but I could wait no longer. Dr Graham, how soon can he be summoned?"

Neither Dr Graham nor Fitzwilliam had played a part in his dreams before, but it was not the bizarre intrusion that shook him from his trance. It might have been the rush of words that did, or the hand that was now gripping his to the point of pain, nails digging into his palm.

"Dr Graham?" he repeated numbly.

"Yes! For Jane. She is— 'Tis her time."

Reality hit at last, with the almighty shock of what he had been about to say – and *do*. What he was contemplating. A moment more, and she would have been in his arms. Heavens above, he would have kissed her! Brought her into his bedchamber! And this time she was not a figment of his imagination. Her hand felt real, *she* felt real because this time she *was*.

The unmitigated horror of having come so close to betraying himself in the worst, most callous manner stunned him for a long moment, until she gripped or shook his hand again, he could not tell which, and called his name in anxious impatience.

He could find no form of expression for the shock he felt, which was a mercy, for there was nothing he could safely say. So he just expressed the other, incomparably milder shock.

"Her time? So soon?"

"Yes. Yes! She thought there was at least another month to go, but she was mistaken, and so was Dr Hughes— "

"Dr Hughes?"

"Our old physician in Meryton. But this is neither here nor there. Dr Graham must be summoned. He might know of a midwife. And Charles – he is not here!"

The panic in her voice finally awoke him to his duties. He was needed. He had to think – and act. As was the case in every time of crisis, sense came to the fore and spurred him into action.

"Return to your sister," he earnestly instructed. "I will send word to Dr Graham and fear not, he will answer promptly. And it might be good to inform your aunt— "

"My aunt! Of course. She would reassure Jane immensely. I should have thought of it."

"No matter. Can you tell me where she can be found?"

"In Gracechurch Street at number 57. Not far from St. Benet's, on the right. Can you send someone to tell her… fetch her?"

"I shall go myself. It would be quicker."

"You would? I thank you!"

"No need, you must know that. Go back to Mrs Bingley and assure her that help is at hand. I will send someone to rouse Mrs Annesley. And Mrs Martin too."

"Mrs Martin?"

"My housekeeper."

"Oh, yes, of course. Forgive me, I am all confusion."

"You have every reason. I will leave you now. Will you manage while I am gone? Pray do not fret, I shall return as soon as possible. There is not much *I* can do, but Mrs Gardiner— "

"You are doing more than enough already," she interjected swiftly, then fervently added, "I thank you! I do not know what I would have done…"

With that, she hastily left him, her candle casting swaying shadows on the walls as it flickered wildly in her hand before she thought of sheltering it with her palm, in her great haste to return to Jane's bedchamber.

Darcy stepped back into his own and closed the door. He allowed himself the briefest moment to run his hands over his face and heave a relieved breath at having been saved from making a horrific blunder, before rushing to find his discarded coat and waistcoat and don them over his crumpled shirt as fast as he could, then haphazardly tie an equally crumpled neckcloth.

There was no time to dwell on what might have happened, or how he could have justified the inexcusable. Time was of the essence. There were urgent matters to attend to now.

֍֎֍

Time seemed to fly, to him at least.

The journey into Cheapside was not long, not at that time of night, and his coachman was apt to find the way without difficulty, although he had never driven the Darcy coach in that particular direction.

Under regular circumstances, showing up unannounced on a relative stranger's doorstep in the middle of the night would have made Darcy feel dreadfully awkward, but there was nothing regular about the present ones.

Thankfully, he had come to the right place, as he knew he would, even on a very superficial acquaintance with Mr Gardiner and his wife. Although dragged from their sleep at an ungodly hour, the pair were quick to rise to the occasion. Capable and swift, the lady was ready to travel to Berkeley Square with Darcy in no time at all, while Mr Gardiner remained behind, charged with several duties – one of which was to send several articles of necessity as soon as the maid found them, such as soft linen and a crib for this new babe who was in a vast hurry to make an entrance in the world.

By the time Mrs Gardiner and Darcy reached Berkeley Square, Dr Graham had already arrived, from his much closer lodgings. Once introductions were performed in the sitting room next to Jane's bedchamber, he showed himself most willing to give his professional opinion.

"I could find no signs of trouble with this birth despite its timing, so there should be no particular reasons for concern. Perhaps there was an error with the date. It happens. I can recommend a very reputable *accoucheur* and a midwife as well. 'Tis early hours yet, but I have no doubt that it is happening. This little fellow is determined to be born today."

He was not wrong. Over the following hours the Darcy townhouse saw a flurry of activity that it had not witnessed since the birth of Darcy's own grandfather, the last of his line to come into the world in town rather than at Pemberley.

Maids trooped up and down the backstairs fetching hot water and fresh linen. The *accoucheur* arrived and was brought up. Soon after him, the midwife. Then footmen came laden with armloads sent from Gracechurch Street to set them in Jane's sitting room, for Mrs Gardiner to determine what was of instant use and what could be left and examined later.

The only one untouched by the commotion was Georgiana, who was still asleep in her bedchamber overlooking the gardens, at a comfortable distance from the guest rooms.

As for Darcy, all that was left for him to do was play the part reserved for gentlemen on such occasions: waiting in the downstairs parlour, although without the port or brandy commonly prescribed to the expectant father. That is, until some hours later, when a new role was assigned to him.

He had walked up, hoping to encounter one of the maids, who might have had some knowledge of Mrs Bingley's progress. Instead, he came across Elizabeth and Mrs Gardiner. They had both come out of the birthing chamber and at first Darcy thought that something was amiss, until Mrs Gardiner's words removed every fear of that nature. It seemed that the difficulty the lady faced was not with Mrs Bingley but her younger sister.

"No, Lizzy, I will not relent. You have done enough, and now you cannot help her. There is a limit to what an unmarried lady ought to see, and for your sake and Jane's, 'tis time for you to keep away. Oh. Mr Darcy. How fortunate that you came up. Would you be so kind as to escort my niece to the downstairs parlour? Or anywhere. Just away from here."

Narrowed eyes and a very stubborn lip told them both that she would not go willingly. With a light frown, Mrs Gardiner pressed her point.

"Do be sensible, dear girl. Pray do as I ask and let me go back in. I cannot stand here debating this with you. I should be with Jane."

"And so should I!"

"No. She frets about you seeing her in pain – seeing everything. Just go downstairs with Mr Darcy. I promise to send word," she added swiftly, clasped her niece's arm in tender reassurance, then hurried away and vanished behind the heavy door.

Even in the poor light of the flickering candles Darcy could see the look of pained confusion overspreading the most beloved countenance. In a few steps, he was beside her and scrupled not to take her hand.

"Come," he urged softly.

"Can I not wait in the sitting room instead?" she pleaded.

"I think your aunt would rather you did not," Darcy ventured an opinion and, with a deep sigh, it seemed she was about to listen.

But just then a long muffled cry was heard from behind the door, and Elizabeth tugged fiercely at the hand that was restraining hers.

"Let me go!" she hissed in anger.

He did not.

Neither of them could tell how it came about, but a moment later she was in his arms, mindlessly struggling for release, despite his every effort to soothe her with disjointed words of comfort.

At last she stilled and he most reluctantly withdrew, but took her hands in his.

"Come away. Come away with me," he urged again. "Let us go to the parlour, as your aunt suggested, and play at chess or something…"

"*Chess?*" she exclaimed in disbelief, and stared at him as though he had utterly lost his senses.

Ruefully, Darcy chuckled.

"A poor suggestion, I agree. But you must see my difficulty. If you were Bingley, I would ply you with a vast quantity of brandy, but Mrs Gardiner might have a thing or two to say if I were to give you the same treatment."

Almost despite herself, Elizabeth chuckled too and half-heartedly allowed herself to be led towards the staircase. They descended, her hand still clasped in his, and slowly made their way into the parlour. Darcy settled her on the small sofa by the fireplace, only to see her shiver and huddle forward, arms tightly wrapped around herself.

It might have been due to anxiety or fatigue and not for cold, but he took no chances. He went to rekindle the fire in the grate, added more coal and poked and prodded it until new flames leapt up, casting an orange glow over their faces. He stood and turned to offer:

"Let me send up for your shawl."

"No, leave them be. They must have enough to do already."

"Then pray excuse me for a moment," he mentioned in passing and, without waiting for her reply, he went to fetch a cloak from the small room they were kept in, just off the entrance hall.

He brought it to the parlour and quietly approached to drape it round her shoulders. She looked up in surprise, which melted into gratitude.

"I thank you. I *was* cold."

"I thought you might be. 'Tis chilly in here. But it will warm up soon enough."

He walked to the marble-topped table where a few decanters glittered in the firelight and cast a smile over his shoulder.

"I will not offer brandy, but can I get you something else?" he asked. "Sherry perhaps?"

"No, I think not. I thank you."

Darcy wandered slowly back, having selected nothing either. Instead, he sat beside her and reached to cover the hands clasped together on her knee.

"Talk to me," he entreated softly.

"About?"

"Anything. Jane. Or your other sisters. Your father's favourite books. Or better still, Mr Collins's poultry," he added with a muted chuckle and she glanced up at that with a faint smile of her own.

"Or perhaps his bees," she offered in her turn. "He keeps bees too, you know, but they do not much like him. Charlotte says they sting him now and then, but he is very sanguine about it. He has it on very good authority that a bee-sting once in a while is good for one's health."

"My aunt's authority perchance?"

She gave another quiet laugh.

"I would not know. But I think it very likely."

She dropped her eyes to stare for a long moment at their fingers, tightly interlaced, and nothing was heard but the crackling of the fire, until at last she looked up again.

"I thank you," she said softly.

"Whatever for?"

"For being here when I need a helping hand. You always are."

A long breath left Darcy's chest, or it might have been a sigh. Fitzwilliam would not like this in the slightest, but it was a truth that would never alter. Without a second thought, he put it into words.

"I will always be. Whenever you need me."

"You are very kind."

'*Aye. Aren't you just!*' the devil on his left shoulder grinned and, with a sudden huff, Darcy stood to poke again at the blameless fire and take some time to steel himself before returning to her side to diligently play the part of the detached kindly relation and coax her into talking of everything and nothing, to take her mind off her sister's plight.

⁂

It was finally over, not long after daybreak, and a beaming maid came in to announce that the babe was born. A tiny girl with a lusty cry despite her size, to the delight of everyone who heard her.

Elizabeth lost no time in hurrying above-stairs to swell their number, but Darcy did not follow until a fair while later, when a tired but glowing Mrs Gardiner came to tell him that her eldest niece was doing well and was now resting peacefully after her ordeal, whereas the new arrival was in the adjoining sitting room, and Darcy was most welcome to come up to greet her.

He did. And, although he surmised that Elizabeth would be there as well, the sight he came across was not what he had expected. The little bundle was not silently rocked in the borrowed cradle, but lovingly wrapped in tender arms. From where she sat holding the baby, Elizabeth looked up at his entrance, her face radiant with a beatific smile.

The achingly maternal picture shook him to the core. A newborn babe in the Darcy house. Not hers – not his. And yet it looked so much as though it could have been that his heart lurched again, twisted and broke afresh, in ways he had not envisaged. A new level of pain, a sharper sense of loss, as if he had not felt her loss so many times already.

Unthinkingly, his legs carried him forth until he found himself bent on one knee beside them.

"So beautiful," he breathed, and his voice caught.

"Is she not?" Elizabeth beamed back, turning the babe just so, that he might see her better, and Darcy's features tightened at the profound intimacy which by rights should not have been forced upon him thus.

By rights?

Nothing was right. It could never be. But Elizabeth was happy, so he brought himself to whisper, although this had not been his meaning.

"She is the most beautiful babe I have ever seen."

"I agree. Yet people are apt to change their minds when they get to hold their firstborn," she whispered back as she reached to stroke the fingers curled into an impossibly tiny fist, so caught in the miracle wrapped in her arms that she failed to notice she did not get an answer.

Chapter 11

Georgiana awoke an hour later to discover that, while she had slept the untroubled sleep of the very young, the number of people in the household had increased by one, and she eagerly joined Jane, Elizabeth and Mrs Gardiner to coo over the new addition.

Mr Gardiner made an appearance that morning as well, for a brief but most affectionate visit. As for Mr Bingley, he arrived in Berkeley Square the following day, to receive the shock of his life, be awed and overjoyed at meeting his daughter and also overwhelmed with guilt for being so far away from his wife at her time of need and peril.

The intelligence he brought paled in comparison, and did not have the power to surprise his lady, who had grown well-accustomed to his impulsive nature. The property he had gone all the way into Staffordshire to see was now legally theirs. The purchase was agreed upon, documents signed, deeds drawn and his father's dearest wish to see his line established as landowners had been fulfilled mere days before that selfsame line had been continued.

There was no question of travelling there yet, of course. At the *accoucheur*'s most particular insistence, Mrs Bingley was not even allowed to leave her bed for at least another fortnight so, with profuse apologies, warmly and eagerly dismissed by their recipient, the Bingleys were obliged to trespass on their friend's hospitality a little longer.

During that time, the new father was busily engaged. Every waking moment that was not spent at his wife's side was employed in preparing a welcoming nest in Charles Street for Jane and their new daughter, and he was endlessly harrowing craftsmen and shopkeepers to achieve the desired result. In that he was helped, they said – although *he* would have said hindered – by his wife's mother and younger sisters who, along with his father-in-law, had descended *in corpore* upon him as soon as news of the birth was incautiously sent rather too soon to Hertfordshire.

The Bennet contingent did not take up residence in Berkeley Square – neither Jane nor Elizabeth would have countenanced such a dreadful imposition – but were quartered just around the corner, to drive Bingley to distraction with fears of what arrangements he might find implemented in his absence. However, they called in Berkeley Square nearly every day, to visit their reluctantly bedridden daughter and increase the commotion to levels which the peaceful Darcy house had never experienced before.

Finally Jane was allowed to move, so the commotion was relocated to the nearby Charles Street. They only emerged twice: firstly for Jane's churching and, soon afterwards, for the small and heart-warming ceremony where Mr Bingley's best friend and Jane's dearest sister stood godparents to little Miss Elizabeth-Rose.

A few days more, and they were truly gone. Away from town, and back to Netherfield.

This time Elizabeth's departure was unbearable to Darcy. It had been bad enough to see her leave his house, but for a while at least she was around the corner and, since Georgiana eagerly insisted they go to visit Jane and her babe nearly every day, he would still see her.

But now the house in Charles Street was empty – and so was his, horribly so, which weighed on him more heavily than ever. And that was for the days. The nights were reserved for the agony of dreams that had become nothing short of torture.

So much so that he was driven to extremes. One day, he went as far as renewing an old acquaintance. He called upon the lady of uncertain age and impeccable discretion whom his father had made known to him some years ago, when he had determined it was time for his son to be initiated into the arts of Venus. She was surprised to see him but welcomed him nevertheless, with comforting arms and the wisdom of silence. And it was then that he finally understood how, for nearly a year now, he had fought a losing battle.

He belonged to one woman, and that woman was Elizabeth. That she would never claim him was simply his misfortune. He would always love *her* and none other. And in the marriage bed or in any casual encounter it would always be Elizabeth that he would seek. It would be her whom he would embrace, whether she was there in reality or not. Hers the lips he kissed, hers the body he would worship and that would welcome him in the ultimate union and fulfilment.

Which was why he would never marry. No wife of his deserved this sort of fate. Certainly not some fresh-faced young woman with a head full of dreams who might marry him because she thought she loved him. Not even the countless Miss Bingleys of the *ton*, who would have him just for his name and fortune – and in any case he did not think that he could bear the added cold misery of such a wife.

So Pemberley would go to Georgiana's children. At least they might be the product of a rightful union. As for himself, he would have a companion in his sister until she married, hopefully well, and hopefully for love. And he would have Pemberley to dedicate his life to, and some other worthy causes, still to be determined.

A waste? Perhaps. But the alternative was something he could no longer bring himself to undertake.

The three candles cast an uncertain light over his study and fashioned moving shadows on the dark-panelled walls when he drew the candelabrum closer, although he did not need it. By now, even without looking, he knew every feature, every brushstroke on the small ivory oval secreted in his drawer. He took it out again and placed it on his desk.

A hollow presence? Maybe. A sad conclusion to his parents' hopes for him, that he would choose a small miniature as the companion of his lonely hours?

All this was true. But he felt truer to himself now than in all the months when he had struggled to forsake her. He ran his thumb over the thin, delicate frame. *She* was his choice. His first and only choice. For him, there could be none other than Elizabeth.

ഇൽ ഇൽ

Eight hundred miles south-eastwards, in Ciudad Rodrigo, the twin of the miniature was brought out from a secret pocket, at almost the same time, and was perused with an equally heavy heart, although for vastly different reasons.

He missed her. Dreadfully.

The aching emptiness was nothing short of physical pain.

What was in store for them? Heaven only knew. His life was not his own and would not be for a fair while yet. Not until Old Boney had lost his appetite for fighting.

Dangers to life and limb aside, if he still struggled with the notion of his failings measured against what his cousin had to offer, Fitzwilliam knew full well that, just as he had told Darcy on their last encounter, the fault lay with himself more than anyone else. But there was more to it than that. It was the dread of a future poisoned by an unthinkable triangle that would not be undone. The only hope was to make their life elsewhere. Far from English shores perhaps. Take her away from everything that she held dear. Could he ask it of her? More to the point, how could he not?

At the discreet knock on the door, Colonel Fitzwilliam wrapped the miniature in its silk kerchief, then returned it to its velvet pouch and then his pocket.

"Come," he called, and his man was quick to show himself.

"'Tis time to dress, Sir," he quietly announced, and Fitzwilliam grudgingly conceded he was in the right.

It was time to dress if he was to be punctual at the dinner offered to a handful of high-ranking officers by the grandees of the town.

There was not a great deal to do in Ciudad Rodrigo until spring settled in earnest and Lord Wellington ordered the campaign to recommence. Just endless drills during the day, and endless cold and dreary evenings, enlivened by the men with sundry amusements, in which the officers would have no part. They had their own amusements. Cards. Countless wagers. Women for some, the bottle for the others, and for the rest a smattering of all of the above. Sometimes there were impromptu assemblies. Other times dinners, such as the one he was expected to attend tonight.

Fitzwilliam stood and grimaced. He dearly hoped that on this occasion Doña Teresa would not be of the party.

In an unguarded moment, when he had incautiously imbibed more port wine than was good for him, he had spoken a great deal more freely than he should have.

It was at some blasted assembly that Henshaw had badgered him into attending. The habitual assortment of redcoats and blushing maidens with jet-black hair and almond-shaped eyes, keenly watched by a number of dueñas and stern-looking fathers.

Doña Teresa Patricia de Mendoza y Aguilar was far too young for a dueña, yet did not have the air of a blushing maiden either. Rather, the quiet confidence of more mature years and the calm security of her noble birth and statuary beauty.

Her departed husband had belonged to an ancient and well-connected family, Fitzwilliam had eventually learned, and in the five years since his premature demise she had not been induced to tie her fortunes with another. Perhaps she was content to be mistress of her own affairs. Or perhaps she had been left disconsolate at her husband's passing.

Fitzwilliam did not feel inclined to pry, nor was he of a mind to bend his ear to gossip. For there *was* gossip, for those who cared to listen, linking her name to that of a British officer. To Major Sir Henry Vernon-Rees, to be precise. Wagging tongues claimed that there had been more to their association than met the careless eye. That she might have considered becoming Lady Vernon-Rees, and indeed making haste about it and acquiring the protection of his name before the passing of too many months showed her in the untenable position of a widow visibly with child.

But the months came and went and brought no such disgrace.

They brought no marriage either, presumably for the very worst of reasons: the Major had fallen at the fifth assault on Burgos, the very one that Fitzwilliam himself had been injured in.

He had no way of knowing how affected the lady was by the Major's loss. If they had been as attached as the gossips claimed, then the blow must have been severe. But Doña Teresa's air of cool detachment did not seem to invite pity. Which made the fact that she pitied *him* so much more galling, and infinitely more grating.

Doubtlessly it was nobody's fault but his. His own loose tongue at that assembly, two months ago nearly to the day, when Doña Teresa had stopped at his side to smilingly observe:

"I see you are not dancing, Colonel Fitzwilliam. Are your injuries still troubling you? Or have you left your heart on English shores, safely out of these young ladies' reach?"

He should have told her that his lungs were not up to the exertion. Instead, like the veriest dolt, he had replied:

"The latter, Ma'am."

"Oh. For your sake, I hope the affection is returned."

"It is. I thank you."

"Then should I offer my best wishes?"

"I beg your pardon?"

"An injured lover makes for the best inducement into matrimony."

"Perhaps it does. But we are not wed yet."

"Whyever not? You should take joy when you find it. Life is too short."

"That it might be. But it is also very tangled."

"What tangle is there, that affection cannot conquer?"

"Sometimes too much affection brings tangles of its own."

"Whose affection would that be?"

"That of two men for the same woman."

"Ah! And are these two men close?"

"As close as brothers."

"*¡Dios mio! ¿Su hermano?* I beg your pardon, Señor, I meant— "

"Pray do not trouble yourself, Doña Teresa. After all the time I have spent in your country, I have acquired some little understanding of the language. As to your question, no, not precisely brothers but very close cousins nonetheless."

"I see. *Muy triste.*"

"*Sí. Nada más triste*," he had instinctively and incautiously retorted.

A fleeting but deep shadow had clouded the lady's handsome features and at that, he had been sufficiently drawn from his self-centred anguish to recognise another's, and had remembered with justified misgivings exactly who he was speaking to. He had attempted to apologise for his ill-chosen comment, but before he could form the words, the lady had spoken.

"I pray you will never find anything worse," she had replied mildly and was gone.

And that was that, the full extent of their exchanges on the matter. But every time they had come across each other since, with mounting vexation he had felt himself watched. And pitied. And it riled him more than he could ever own.

It soon became apparent that tonight would be no different. She *was* of the party. Worse still, when they went in to dinner, he found that she was seated at his right. His features tightened as he endeavoured to be civil and address her equally as often as Captain Henshaw's wife, his other companion. That he was not entirely successful became apparent some time later, when Doña Teresa quietly observed:

"I see you are avoiding me, Señor."

"My deepest regrets for giving that impression. You may be assured this is not the case," Fitzwilliam dissembled, but she would have none of it.

"Perhaps I owe you an apology for disconcerting you with my forthrightness last time we spoke of matters of the heart. But English reserve is something I could never master. Nor do I see much wisdom in seeking to acquire it. I have no patience for it. No more than for your still waters running deep or the proverbial stiff upper lip or every other platitude designed to make a virtue of concealing one's thoughts. For my part, I have always found that still waters turn murky and eventually fester."

He could make no reply to that. Her statement held true with regard to his own murky waters. Yet everything he stood for, every proper feeling, made him recoil from the repulsive notion of exposing his innermost concerns to the scrutiny of others.

"For several weeks now," the lady resumed, "I have meant to speak to you, but I was unsure how to go about it. So perhaps by association I have acquired some smattering of the prized English reserve," she laughed softly, "and now I am anxious to shake it. What I wished to say, Colonel Fitzwilliam, is that I fully understand the hardship of having a heavy burden and no one to speak to. If you need a friendly ear, you only need ask. There. It is said, and nothing more needs to be added on the subject. Now, Señor, what do you think of this delicious trout? I find the sauce complements it admirably."

Despite himself, Fitzwilliam chuckled.

"I must say, Ma'am, that you master the subtleties of English reserve and dinner conversation much better than I could ever hope to emulate."

"I beg to differ. You speak English uncommonly well," the lady retorted with a twinkle in her eye.

This time he laughed in earnest.

"I assume I need not explain I was doubting my proficiency in *your* language."

"You assume rightly."

"May I ask how you acquired yours?"

"I spent several years at Mrs Rossiter's seminary in London."

"How so?"

"My father's wish."

"And is this where you also acquired your disdain for English manners?"

"I do not disdain the manners, Colonel. Just the way they are employed for the purpose of concealment."

"We cannot claim full responsibility in that regard. Monsieur de Talleyrand himself is known to have once said that man was given words so that he could conceal his thoughts."

"I see you are of a mind to join the diplomatic corps, Señor."

"Perish the thought, my lady. With my non-existent talent for dissimulation, that would be a disaster for my country."

"And so you feel the need to practise."

Whether or not this was a hint to their earlier conversation, Fitzwilliam's smile faded.

"Perhaps I do. But the respite is welcome," he added after a short silence and turned to look her in the eye. "I thank you for your kindness, Doña Teresa. I did not see it for what it was at first, and I fear I was ungracious."

"And I held some concern that I was rushing in where angels fear to tread. The best intentions often go awry."

"That they do," he solemnly agreed.

Yet somehow this time they did not.

In due course, before March was out, he had told her everything. In some ways she was in the right. It brought some comfort to speak to a perfect stranger, wholly distanced from the matter and unacquainted with any of the parties, except him.

Not that he expected she would supply the answers. But she listened with kindness and compassion to the grim tale of the love triangle that put such a strain on his connection with his dearest cousin — that is, until the day when he reached the end of his disclosures. That day, her common sense cut straight to the heart of the matter, and she finally gave him the full, unhindered benefit of the female perspective.

"Men! Of all the vexing species!" Doña Teresa exclaimed in exasperation, once he had brought himself to explain the extent of his predicament and pecuniary disadvantage.

They were seated in her elegant and comfortable salon, with nothing but the fire and their wineglasses for company. She set hers on a nearby small table and stood to pace up and down the chamber, as though her tempestuous disapproval made her unable to sit still.

"Must you always know what we should think and feel, and what we need, oh-so-much-better than we know ourselves? Did you not say that the young lady is in love with *you*, and not your cousin? And as such, might she not be a great deal happier to eat bread at your table rather than the fatted calf at his?"

"I believe Darcy's excellent cook might supply a few partridges and a venison pie as well, not to mention some delicious tarts and jellies," Fitzwilliam quipped, rather uneasy with her vehement plain-speaking.

"Oh, do not play the fool! Or if you must, then pray leave me and do so in your quarters. *¡Madre de Dios!* Of all the self-centred, idiotic notions! So you are uncomfortable with the little that you have to give. But what of her wishes? Your selfish disdain for the feelings of others— "

"Doña Teresa— " Fitzwilliam sought to interject, but she was too incensed to let him.

"Oh, I have heard it all before! Difficulties, disparities, not having enough to offer. But what if a French musket puts paid to all this nonsense and one day you are fetched lifeless from the field? Do you imagine that your scruples and misgivings would console her for your loss? That she would deem you noble and selfless for depriving her of the few months of happiness she might have had with you?"

By then, it had become increasingly clearer to Fitzwilliam that Doña Teresa was no longer speaking of Elizabeth – or not only of her. Eyes sparkling in anger flashed towards him as she burst out and confirmed it.

"Oh, I know what is said of me and I do not doubt you know it also. It makes no difference that little of it is true. I wish everything was! I wish I was left with *something!* His child, and better memories than empty wishes and regrets. If you inflict the same on your Miss Bennet, then she ought to curse you! Love you – but curse you nonetheless, as I do him. Oh, go! Just go and leave me! Go and wallow in your ludicrous self-pity. But if you have a heart, bring yourself to think of her as well, before you find 'tis all too late."

He stood and walked to her, vainly racking his mind for the right words of apology and comfort. Yet none came but poor substitutes, and again she bade him leave.

He did, and as of that evening there was an end to visits and confidences. Nothing more was said between them on that subject, other than the briefest but most earnest exchange on one of the occasions when, unfailingly, the social rigmarole in Ciudad Rodrigo brought them again together.

"I will go back to marry her as soon as I am allowed to leave," Fitzwilliam told Doña Teresa, when he was assured of a private moment.

"Good," was all she said but, undeterred by the laconic comment, he reached for her hand.

"How can I thank you?"

"Be happy. And make her happy too."

He nodded without words.

By all that was holy, he *would* do his best!

Chapter 12

March was a month of madness in Berkeley Square, and equally so at Netherfield and Longbourn.

In Berkeley Square the madness had begun with Lady Catherine's unannounced and inopportune arrival. She had just learned, later than originally planned, of Anne's matrimonial intentions. Somehow, as the event drew nearer, Anne lost the courage to address the issue and only did so when it could no longer be avoided and her wedding was a mere se'nnight thence.

They were in town by then. Anne had induced her mother to accept the hospitality of Lord Langthorne's house, for it suited her very well indeed to be as close as possible to her betrothed when the storm would be unleashed at last.

Lord Langthorne and his family were still at Ashford, and thus Lady Catherine was deprived of her brother's support in this contentious matter. Likewise his wife's, for although Lady Langthorne uniformly disagreed with virtually everything that Lady Catherine had to say, the issue of family consequence was the sole topic on which they would see eye to eye.

So Lady Catherine had no recourse but to turn to Darcy; that, and send a frantic express to Ashford. But she knew full well that Lord and Lady Langthorne could not possibly arrive sooner than three days after the express was sent, so in her nephew lay all her hopes of a satisfactory resolution. She came, she badgered, she even came as close to pleading as one of her disposition could ever lower herself to – but to no avail.

Kindly but firmly, Darcy told her there was nothing anyone could do. Anne was of age and, thanks to her father's will, she was mistress of her fortune and her fate. She could not be dictated to, cajoled, threatened or kept under lock and key.

The only assistance that was in his power to give had already been offered and accepted. As agreed with Anne at Christmas, his own attorneys had inspected the marriage settlement to ensure that everything was in order and Anne's interests, as well as her mother's, were as protected as could be. Of course, he did not provoke the lady's ire by disclosing that he had been in the know for so much longer, but confined himself to the comforting facts.

"As soon as I learned of my cousin's plans, I urged her to allow my attorneys to review the settlement. They confirmed that the documents are eminently satisfactory, Lady Catherine, and neither you nor Anne have anything to fear on that score," Darcy sought to reassure her as gently as he could, but his aunt gave a derisive snort.

"Nothing to fear, you say. There is everything to fear! She plans to marry a *professional* man, for goodness sake," she spat the epithet as though it were an invective. "She could have been the mistress of Pemberley and instead she aims to take a barrister!"

"Such is her choice, Aunt, and she would not be thwarted. Moreover, she cannot be, even if you wished it."

"Her choice! Her choice!" Lady Catherine almost choked with indignation, knowing full well that every word he said was true. "What is with young people these days, choosing their own ruin? Look at your cousins, both of them – Anne and Richard too. My brother tells me Richard aims to attach himself to that young outspoken chit, Mr Collins's relation, who came to stay with him last Easter. Had I known it would come to this, I would have forbidden him to ask her. I am speaking of Collins asking the girl to visit, naturally, for I suspect that whatever I might have said to Richard would have fallen on deaf ears, just as it does with Anne. What is the world coming to, Nephew? Pray enlighten me, for I have lost the ability to comprehend it."

Darcy did not even try to answer the rhetorical question, and Lady Catherine shook her head.

"This is not to be borne," she muttered – mostly out of habit, he surmised, for bear it she must, she could not escape it.

She did not. Despite her continuously voiced objections, echoed by Lord and Lady Langthorne – who had indeed answered the plea conveyed in her express and had come to town to work upon their niece – Anne would not be dissuaded.

The marriage took place on the appointed day, with only Darcy, Georgiana and Lady Catherine in attendance on the part of the bride. The groom's side was better represented, and more cheerful too. Mr Metcalfe's relations remained in good humour, despite the scowls Lady Catherine cast in their direction, and descended just as gleefully upon Darcy's house for the wedding breakfast, which was the best present he could make his cousin, on the occasion of her marriage.

And then they left. Anne and her new husband for a sojourn in Margate, Mr Metcalfe's relations to their homes and a sullen Lady Catherine back to Rosings, to vent her ill-humour on her parson, his wife and Mrs Jenkinson, whom she seemed inclined to keep in her employ for that very purpose.

That was not to say that the house in Berkeley Square was left to peace and quiet. Soon after Anne's wedding, it was time for Georgiana's presentation, her coming-out ball and all the other formal gatherings pertaining to her entry into society.

It must be said that both she and Darcy sought to endure them with good grace, but it was a struggle. The elaborate ceremony of the presentation at St. James's, daunting as it might have been, paled in comparison to the subsequent engagements. Just as Darcy had been deluged with invitations and countless morning calls from hopeful Misses and their scheming relations when he had put himself on the marriage mart, now it was Georgiana's turn. Her coming-out had marked her as eligible for matrimony, and the attention she attracted sat ill with her, and also with her brother.

Some of the suitors might have been genuine enough, but they were too many, and it made for an onerous task to receive them all and strive to determine which had come with an eye to the young lady's purse and which her person.

After too long a stretch of such thankless exertions, Georgiana was disheartened and exhausted. When they returned home after yet another elaborate dinner for far too many guests and sought to raise their spirits with a short interlude of peaceful companionship in the parlour before bedtime, Georgiana tentatively asked:

"Brother, would you mind terribly if we were to seek a respite from this incessant bustle?"

Darcy laughed ruefully at that.

"You know me well enough to see that nothing could please me better. So, what do you propose? That for a se'nnight or so we refuse invitations?"

"Frankly, I was considering something very different. Could we...? Brother, could we not return to Pemberley?"

"Now? But the Season has only just begun."

"Which is enough to terrify me. If what we have experienced so far was but a prelude, I have not the strength to face the rest."

"But, Georgiana— "

"Oh, pray do not quote Lady Catherine to warn me that my first Season will be ruined."

"I had no intention to. But you must see that after all your efforts and your preparations— "

"I would be loath to have you think they were for naught. But Brother, I... I need to draw breath. 'Tis too much! I know I shall have to be more sanguine about it and face it for longer if I wish to marry, but surely there is no rush."

"Of course not. I am in no haste to see you go. It will be very lonely at Pemberley without you."

Georgiana smiled.

"Not so, once you marry. And fear not, I am not likely to leave you till you do."

Darcy sipped his brandy, absent-mindedly ran the back of a finger over his upper lip and turned to his sister.

"You will," he said matter-of-factly.

"What makes you so certain?"

"I shall not marry, Georgiana. Your firstborn will inherit Pemberley. Or your second son, if you prefer it."

Georgiana's eyes widened in shock.

"How can you say that?"

"Well, it must go to someone..."

"Not that. About you not marrying. Of course you will! For a while I thought Miss Wyatt— "

"No. Not Miss Wyatt. Nor any of the other Misses."

"I must say, I am rather glad to hear it. None were good enough for you, and your heart did not seem to be in it. But this will change. You will fall in love and— "

She broke off with a sharp intake of breath.

"Unless... But no, this cannot be."

Darcy's features tightened, as he found himself caught between the wish and the dread to hear what exactly she was thinking. He did not dare ask. In the end, it was she who ventured:

"Forgive me. For a moment I had the foolish notion that you *have* fallen in love, but the lady would not have you. This is preposterous, of course. Who would not? You are too good – the very best of men."

Darcy forced a smile.

"You are blinded by sisterly affection, dearest. I am not. Far from it."

But Georgiana would not be distracted.

"I grant you, it was a ludicrous suggestion. But, Brother, if it is not this, what is it? What can possibly make you say you would not marry?"

With a swift flick of his wrist, Darcy drained his glass.

"'Tis late. We should retire," he quietly observed.

"We should not," she protested firmly, then her voice softened with the deepest affection. "Would you not talk to me, let me share your burden?"

"There is no burden, sweetling," he replied, but Georgiana shook her head.

"That is precisely what you have been claiming for the best part of a year, yet all this time I have rarely seen you cheerful. Brother, if I am old enough for us to discuss my firstborn's inheritance I daresay I need no longer be protected as a child. Pray let me share your troubles," she pleaded, close to tears, and reached across the small space between their chairs to hold and clasp his hand.

Darcy raised her fingers to his lips for a brief kiss, then stood.

"Forgive me, dearest. I fear I have spoken out of turn," he said lightly, and promptly changed the subject. "Now, about your wish to leave town for a while, perhaps we should go to Pemberley for Easter and stay for a month or so. Just the pair of us. Mrs Annesley might wish to spend some time with her daughter. There, would that suit?"

Georgiana sighed. It did not suit her, not by a fair margin, to see that he was still intent on shutting her out. She pursed her lips and rose to her feet as well. Yes, they would go to Pemberley together. Just the two of them. And maybe, with time on their hands and with a great deal of loving kindness, she might find a way to help him yet.

◦๑ ๑◦

The trouble at Netherfield and Longbourn was of a very different kind. Strangely, it was jointly caused by Mr Bingley and Mrs Bennet. With the lease of Netherfield due to expire at Easter, Mr Bingley had seen fit not only to inform his Bennet relations of his recent purchase of an estate in Staffordshire but, far more controversially, he had also told them that, under the circumstances, both he and his wife saw no valid reason to extend the lease of Netherfield. He aimed to relocate his family to their new estate – and Mrs Bennet was profoundly shocked and horrified.

"Have you ever heard of such a thing?" she fumed to her sister Phillips. "The babe not two months old, and he would uproot my Jane to the wilds of Staffordshire, to some ruinous estate or other! I said the same to Mr Bennet only yesterday, but he is of no assistance. He only chuckled in that provoking way of his and maintained that a gentleman of five thousand a year would not purchase a ruinous estate for his wife and daughter. But what does he know, and Bingley too, of a mother's heart? Or Jane's, so dutiful and affectionate! How must the poor girl feel, to be dragged away from us and deprived of my help and guidance? I told Mr Bennet this as well, and the vexing man only replied that there can be too much of a good thing. Too much indeed! He has no compassion for me and his poor daughter. With them at Netherfield I can be with Jane from morning till night. But how can I be of any help whatever when they are all the way in Staffordshire, at that dreadful place, Bleakhill Park they call it, or some such?"

"I thought Jane said Blakehill," Mrs Phillips observed, but Mrs Bennet scoffed.

"Whichever one may be, 'twill still be bleak! Thorns and thistles everywhere, I'd wager, not to mention the cold and dreary weather of the north. Now tell me, Sister, is that a place for a newborn babe and her mother? But this is not the last he hears of it. Mark my words, I shall carry my point yet!"

With a sigh, Elizabeth stopped in her tracks and retraced her steps instead of walking to the parlour, as she had intended before learning that her aunt was visiting and her mother was venting her manifold frustrations, just as she had ever since Mr Bingley had announced their plan to leave these parts.

A small smile curled her lips at the thought that their removal into Staffordshire could not come too soon for either him or Jane, and it was easy to see why. Mrs Bennet had been too close for comfort ever since their marriage. Now, with a newborn babe at Netherfield, she was unstoppable.

She sighed again. If only she could be away from all this madness. She could not bring herself to stay at Netherfield, not only for Charles and Jane's sake, but also her father's. The Bingleys deserved whatever little privacy could be had, and her papa had been deprived of her society for far too long, during the time she had spent in town.

The contrast between Longbourn and Bingley's house or Mr Darcy's could not fail to strike her yet again. The peace, the warm companionship, the sensible and stimulating conversations were in very short supply at Longbourn.

Having eventually recovered from the loss of the militia regiment and the missed opportunity to go to Brighton as Mrs Foster's special companion due to Jane's wedding the previous May, Lydia was now fully restored to her vexing self. If anything, she was more boisterous than ever. As usual, Kitty followed wherever her youngest sister led, and it uniformly led to frivolous pursuits and noisy pastimes.

Mary was caught in her books – that was no change – and so was Mr Bennet. As was his wont, he would retire to the library to escape silliness and commotion, and these days, with his wife constantly in a state, he seemed to be virtually living there.

Whenever she was not roaming through the countryside, Elizabeth often sought him in his retreat, but however enjoyable it might have been to sit together with their books rather than listen to their vociferous relations, it was still a poor substitute for the joy of chatting to Jane or Georgiana, even if her time with the latter had been disrupted by the young ladies who had come to Berkeley Square to assiduously court Mr Darcy.

Elizabeth could not but wonder if he was getting any nearer to offering for one of them. Georgiana had not mentioned anything of the sort in her letters. Instead, they were full of engagements that she and her brother were attending, and imagining him dancing with Miss Wyatt or any of the other Misses at all those fashionable assemblies painted a most uncomfortable picture.

There was little doubt that she missed him too, although their conversations had been few and far between, and most of them restrained, except on that delightful day of the dance practice, when he had been as cheerful and light-hearted as she wished he could always be.

The very best of men, Georgiana had once described him as, and she was not far off the mark. As a recipient of his constant kindness, Elizabeth readily agreed. He was as thoughtful and kind as Richard. Even more so, in a way – for it had been he, not Richard, who had come to her assistance every time.

Richard was never there. Mr Darcy always was.

A sobering thought, that, and it gave her pause, but she did not have the leisure to pursue it. Jane's carriage pulling up at the door sent her hastening out of the hallway into the bright spring sunlight.

"Jane! And little Lizzy too! What joy, we were not expecting you."

The footman lowered the step and, with great care, assisted his mistress to emerge with her precious bundle.

"I thought I should spare Mamma the trouble of coming to us today."

'*Or spare Charles the trouble of having to host her,*' Elizabeth assumed with a twinkle in her eye, which Jane promptly mirrored, but neither put the shared sentiment into words. Instead, Elizabeth said brightly:

"Come, let us go in. Our Aunt Phillips is here too this morning. She will be glad to see you both, as am I. How is my darling namesake?" she asked, reaching to take her from her sister's arms.

"Asleep like a little treasure, as you can see," Jane smiled as she carefully allowed her baby to move from one loving embrace into the other. "She needs her rest now, she has kept me and the nurse awake for the best part of last night."

"Oh, dear."

"Troublesome colic, they say, and Dr Hughes agrees."

"Pray do not tell Mamma," Elizabeth smilingly warned, but the caution was in earnest. "She will bemoan your loss of her guiding wisdom with even more gusto than she is otherwise bound to."

"Poor Mamma! Has it been so very bad, Lizzy?"

"Nothing out of the common way. How are your preparations progressing, by the bye?"

"Very well indeed. Nearly half the household is to leave us in a se'nnight, with the greatest part of our trunks and possessions.

They will have the house readied by early April. I am so thrilled that Mrs Nicholls is to come with us! Did I tell you?"

"Not yet, no. I am glad to hear it."

"She has been in charge of Netherfield for very long but, despite her attachment to the family who owns it, she is ready to come with us to Staffordshire."

"Lizzy must be the lure."

"I do not doubt she is. It will be a great relief to have so trustworthy a housekeeper."

"What of your other people?"

"Most of them are coming too. 'Tis but a few maids and stable lads who have a strong attachment to Meryton."

"You must be so pleased that everything is falling into place. And Charles as well."

"He is delighted, but rushed off his feet. All the arrangements have fallen on him: exchanges of letters, commissioning repairs and improvements at a distance. There was little I could do to assist him, and it troubles me to see him drawn in all directions. And now this business with Caroline— "

"What business?"

"Lizzy! Whatever are you thinking, keeping them on the doorstep? Come in, Jane, come in! And you, Lizzy. Come, bring the babe indoors!"

With a little smile, they both obliged and the hubbub led by Mrs Bennet made its way into the parlour. It could not fail to wake little Miss Elizabeth-Rose, who lost no time in voicing her intense displeasure. A flurry of suggestions came her way, or rather her mother's, followed by the predictable stream of complaints regarding the reviled Staffordshire scheme and its architect, so it was the best part of an hour before Elizabeth had a chance to ask about the *'business with Caroline'* that Jane had begun to speak of.

"She wrote to announce she is engaged to be married. We got the letter yesterday."

"Engaged? My word! To whom?"

"Lord Hambledon."

"Do you know him?"

"Not very well. I have only met him once. But Charles knows him better. Apparently he lost his wife last year and is now ready to wed again."

"And he would marry Caroline?"

"Yes, well… Therein lies the rub. The story goes that he has also lost a sizeable proportion of his fortune on… I cannot be certain. An unwise investment? Or at the gaming tables? Something of that nature."

"So Caroline's portion is destined to cover his losses?"

"We fear so. And now Charles is forced to go to town by the end of the month to meet with his attorneys and draw a marriage settlement that would protect her interests. Needless to say, this is a complication he could have done without."

"Goodness! Well, that is a surprise. I have always thought her matrimonial intentions veered in a very different direction."

"I believe she has finally seen sense and realised there is no hope in that quarter. Besides, the chance to style herself as Lady Hambledon must have provided sufficient inducement."

"Who is this Lady Hambledon?" Mrs Bennet asked, finally able to spare some attention from the babe in her arms and her sister's conversation.

"Miss Bingley is engaged to Lord Hambledon, Mamma," Jane supplied. "We have just learned yesterday from her letter."

"Well! I assume the wedding will be held in town, which is another good reason for you to delay your departure."

"The date is not yet fixed, nor is the location, but Lord Hambledon's seat is in Cheshire, so I imagine Miss Bingley can just as easily be married from Blakehill."

"You see, Frances? It *is* Blakehill. Just as I thought," Mrs Phillips remarked with satisfaction and bent to stroke the baby's chin, oblivious to her younger sister's glare.

⁂

Mr Bingley did go to town as Jane had mentioned and, when he returned, he brought his sister with him. He had met with Lord Hambledon's attorneys, but there was a great deal still to be arranged, and he could not remain in town for the duration.

With some difficulty, he had persuaded Caroline to join him at Netherfield for a few days. Which was why one morning, when her amble through the countryside turned without conscious thought into a walk to Netherfield, Elizabeth found none other than Miss Bingley in the breakfast parlour.

"Why, Miss Eliza," the lady greeted her as soon as she was shown in. "This takes me back. I see you came on foot again and the local lanes are just as mired as they were when your dear sister was taken ill at Netherfield," she remarked with a pointed look at the hem of her guest's dress, then added, "Louisa always said you were an excellent walker."

Elizabeth arched a brow and, unlike the last time, she made no effort to conceal the traces the muddy walk had left on her petticoat, for Miss Bingley's disapproval mattered not one jot. She cast a glance around her. Also unlike the last time, nobody else was in the parlour. Not Mr Hurst, who had been so intent on his pork pie. Not his wife either. Not Mr Darcy, who had been watching from the far end, by the window, with what she had taken for disdainful disapproval, but had long since come to see it might have been nothing but inborn reserve. Strangely, not Charles or Jane either, and before she could greet Miss Bingley and inquire of her relations' whereabouts, the lady spoke up:

"You find me all alone this morning, Miss Eliza. My brother has ordered a tray in his study and your sister has just been summoned up. Her insistent little girl seems to require her presence. As for the rest of the party you came across last time you walked to Netherfield to find us at breakfast, I am distraught to disappoint, but none of them are here. Would you care to join me for a cup of tea? Or breakfast perhaps, if you left home too early to have yours at Longbourn?"

Rather reluctantly, Elizabeth took the seat the other had indicated.

"I thank you, Miss Bingley. May I take this opportunity to offer my congratulations."

"Oh, you have heard?"

"Of course. Jane told me."

"Fosset, some tea for Miss Bennet. And warm rolls," Miss Bingley instructed her brother's footman, then turned to Elizabeth again. "I daresay you were surprised."

"A little, I must own. I was not aware of your interest in Lord Hambledon," Elizabeth replied as she began to butter the roll she had chosen from the plate the footman had offered with a bow.

"Some of us have the ability to conceal our interest," Miss Bingley retorted with a dainty shrug.

With some difficulty, Elizabeth suppressed a snort, but the deliberate if misplaced barb still provoked her into retaliating.

"At times, perhaps. Though certainly not always."

Miss Bingley laughed. It was not a pretty sound.

"What an ungenerous remark, Miss Eliza! I would have liked to say that I am shocked, but I cannot. You and I have been acquainted for too long. Well, let me say instead that some of us know when to walk away from a lost cause. I suggest you follow my example," she smoothly observed and reached for her teacup, but did not drink. Instead, she paused to stare over the rim, before pointedly adding, "By the bye, rumour has it that Miss Wyatt has just become engaged."

So it had happened! Although Elizabeth had long feared it might, the finality of the intelligence still shocked her. With a vast deal of effort, she schooled her features into nonchalance and retorted, like for like.

"I see. Is this the reason for your own engagement?"

Miss Bingley smirked.

"Not at all. But I am excessively diverted by your assumption and your line of thought. I am content with my own lot, Miss Eliza, and I wish you equal felicity in marriage. But perhaps my good wishes are for naught. We cannot all expect to attract a titled husband."

"Indeed not," Elizabeth airily replied. "Some of us might choose to marry for affection."

"A laudable principle, I grant you. Though it might serve you well to bear in mind that it is the gentlemen who are endowed with the power to choose. Ours is merely the privilege of acceptance or refusal."

"I thank you for the kind advice, Miss Bingley," Elizabeth seethed and reached for her own cup to take a sip of the scalding brew.

Thankfully, Jane's entrance rescued her from the most provoking *tête-à-tête*. Her sister came to her with a smile.

"Lizzy! I was just told you were here. Would you like to come up once you had your breakfast? The little miss is bathed and ready to receive."

"Yes, let us go to her. I have just finished," Elizabeth said swiftly and stood.

"Do join us, Caroline, if you wish," Jane civilly offered and was not in the least surprised when her sister by marriage hastened to decline and assured her with a thin smile that she would come to see the youngest Miss Bingley once she had finished some pressing correspondence.

Thus, it was just the sisters by blood who made their way above-stairs to the nursery. Miss Elizabeth-Rose was as adorable as ever and her godmother embraced her tenderly, yet this time tiny hands and rosy little cheeks could not quite banish the heaviness of heart and, in the end, Elizabeth could not stop herself from asking:

"Is it true, Jane? Has Mr Darcy just become engaged?"

Her sister looked up in surprise.

"Oh. That is news to me. How did you hear of it?"

"Miss Bingley dropped a hint. I thought Charles might have also been told when he saw him."

"He did not call on Mr Darcy. He only spent a day in town, to meet with Lord Hambledon and an assortment of attorneys, then drove back at first light. He is much engaged here, he could not afford to lose a minute. Well, I hope Mr Darcy will be happy. And Georgiana too. She and Miss Wyatt seem to be on good terms and very close in age, so the young lady might make her a very pleasant sister. She will tell us more in her next letter. Come, Lizzy-Rose, come to Mamma. She has outgrown her first set of caps already, did I tell you? No wonder, there are days when she will not stop feeding. Who has ever seen such a greedy little thing?" Jane cooed and laughed in sheer delight when she was answered with a squeal and tiny fists were waved in vigorous agreement.

From her own seat, Elizabeth could only manage a faint and absent smile.

Chapter 13

So Georgiana's next letter would bring an announcement. Probably. Unless they were not ready to announce it yet. A summer wedding then? Perhaps. Perhaps even a spring one. If he had been in such a haste to offer, perhaps he was also in a haste to wed. Miss Wyatt. He had offered for Miss Wyatt, the mousy little thing!

Mud squelched under her boots, vexingly liquid, as Elizabeth walked to Longbourn at uncommon speed, having refused her sister's kind offer of a carriage. She could not sit still. She *had* to walk. The fast pace born of agitation carried her forth over stiles and meadows and along hedges of blooming hawthorn interspersed with gnarled old trees. Though why she should hurry to return to madness and commotion, she truly could not fathom. Was there not enough commotion ruling in her head?

Having finally grasped the error of rushing like a mad thing, her footsteps slowed until she drew to a halt and leaned against the trunk of a leafless tree. She snatched her bonnet off and looked up towards the bare branches stretching like pleading arms into the bluest sky.

It was done. He had done it. Anger choked her at the mere thought. Anger at him, for making the worst mistake of his life. Miss Wyatt! What had he been thinking? Goodness knows! But it was done now. He had offered for her!

Had he been solemn and reserved, proposing a union of convenience? Or had he held her hands – kissed her – held her in his arms?

There was much comfort to be found in his arms, as she knew full well. Great comfort, even in a passionless embrace. It would be very different for Miss Wyatt. She would be held with passion.

No, she would not! He did not love her – did he?

Then why, oh, why would he settle for a loveless union?

179

Yet love might grow. She would be in his house. Every day. Share his life. Bear his children. Someone as honourable, as warm-hearted as Mr Darcy could not fail to grow attached in time. So he would find passion with Miss Wyatt. So much the better…

The bonnet fell in the grass and her face into her upturned palms.

So much the better?

No. No. No!

So much the worse!

The truth hit her with staggering force. She loved him! And until this very moment she never knew herself.

She gasped and raised her face into the sky again, seeing nothing.

He was her betrothed's cousin – and she loved him!

The thought she had barely acknowledged a few days ago returned, dreadfully disloyal but nevertheless true. Richard was never there. Mr Darcy always was. And she had warmed to him as she had grown to know him, mistaking that warmth for cousinly affection.

The selfsame error had a vast deal to answer for. It had misled her into finding nothing improper in spending more time with him, and more informally, than any young woman had ever spent with someone who was neither her brother nor her husband. Nothing improper in turning to him in every hour of need. Nothing improper in being held and comforted. And now she knew precisely how it felt to be held in arms so strong that they could preserve the one he loved from every evil. And her heart broke to know that henceforth it would be Miss Wyatt who belonged in that embrace.

She loved him. She was in the middle before she even knew she had begun. All those days, weeks, months of seeing him in his own home, of getting to know him if not at his most intimate, then certainly at his least formal – a kind and loyal man, an affectionate brother, a considerate master – had wrought something that could not be undone.

She slowly slid onto the grass into a pool of crumpled muslin, into a pool of misery, too shocked for words or coherent thought. Save one: she loved him.

It was nothing short of dreadful.

❦

Twelve dreadful days followed – and twelve sleepless nights.

The days were spent in wrenching thought and desultory rambles through the countryside. The nights, in vain attempts to formulate a most difficult letter. To Richard – to break their engagement. A great many sheets of hot-pressed paper had been covered in feverish writing, crossed out, re-written, then crossed out again and cautiously burned when, unable to continue, she had retreated exhausted under the bedcovers.

It was not finished yet, that letter. But it had to be. She could not marry him. It would be unthinkable to proceed as though nothing had happened. Give herself to Richard when her heart went unbidden to another. His cousin, no less! His dearest, closest cousin!

How had it come to this? She hardly knew. Her broken heart did not know half the answers. And now she had to break Richard's heart as well. It felt horribly callous to do so in a letter, but what other option had she? He was not there, and it might be many months until they came face to face again. She could not have him believe all this time in an impossible engagement.

And now it *was* impossible.

She once thought she loved him. An error, born of youthful inexperience? It might have been. Or maybe she did love him. In some way, perhaps she loved him still. But that warm interest in his welfare, that calm affection was colourless and placid compared to the yearning that had begun to rule her soul of late.

Her newly-discovered sentiments for Mr Darcy had taught her the full meaning of love. And that meaning was need, measured in the pain of loss, as intense as it was hopeless. No, she could not do it. She could not become Mr Darcy's cousin and witness him at close quarters making a life with his Miss Wyatt. And even if she could force herself to do so, even if in some unimaginable selfless act she would seek to at least make Richard happy, how could she let him face a rupture with his family for something which she knew to be a lie?

On the thirteenth day since that most revealing conversation in Jane's breakfast parlour, Elizabeth went for yet another of her long, restless rambles.

She could not bear to be at Longbourn. She could scarce bear to be at Netherfield either, although Miss Bingley had hastened back to town shortly after concluding her business with her brother.

Nevertheless, in view of Jane's imminent departure from these parts, Elizabeth had sought to spend time with her and assist her with the necessary preparations, but it was the greatest struggle to conceal her heaviness of heart.

The only place where she need not hide her turmoil was out over the fields – alone. Everybody's company was wearying. Certainly her mother's and her youngest sisters', but even her father's, even Jane's, even her own. Yet she could not go into the woods to live like a hermit, more was the pity, so after several long hours, Elizabeth bent her steps back to her rowdy house.

She needed no confirmation of the epiphany triggered by Miss Bingley's revelations. Nevertheless, she got it when her path joined the lane to Longbourn and she suddenly came across two riders approaching at a leisurely pace.

One of them was Georgiana. The other was her brother.

Her heart leapt in her chest. Her eyes leapt to his face. He had not seen her yet and was smiling to his sister – that adorable half-smile that made him look so handsome. Impossibly handsome. He looked well. He seemed happy. Betrothal became him, she bitterly thought and bit her lip as she desperately sought to ward off tears.

Dizzy with the racing of her unruly heart, Elizabeth instinctively reached to the stone wall beside her for support. For the briefest moment she considered stepping swiftly back and hiding. Vanishing somewhere out of sight. But it was a foolish notion. There was nowhere to go, not enough time. They only had to advance a little further and they would have a full view of the path behind the wall. Would see her scurrying away. A ludicrous and pointless scheme, Elizabeth determined, so she brought her hand up to her chest to at least steady her breathing, if her heart would not obey, and took the last few steps into the lane.

Darcy was still not looking ahead, so Georgiana saw her first and her countenance brightened into the warmest smile.

"Elizabeth! We were just coming to call upon you and your family. You are returning to Longbourn, I assume. What a stroke of luck to come upon you, it would have been a dreadful shame to find you had gone out. Brother, would you be so kind as to help me down?" Georgiana asked in an eager rush, and it was only when she said the last that Elizabeth summoned the courage to glance at the gentleman in question.

By then, the warm smile for his sister had given way to his habitual reserve, and Elizabeth saw him touch his hat with a "Good morning, Miss Bennet" – a bland counterpart to Georgiana's enthusiastic greeting.

So it was *'Miss Bennet'* yet again…

Whatever had happened to *'Elizabeth'*?

She suppressed a sigh, cast her eyes down and dropped a curtsy, then finally looked up to see him dismount with easy grace and walk to assist his sister in doing the same. Once safely on the ground, Georgiana gathered the train of her riding habit, cast it carelessly over her arm and hurried to Elizabeth to greet her with a warm embrace, then fell into step beside her while Mr Darcy took it upon himself to act as groom and follow them at a slight distance, leading both horses. Thus, Elizabeth found it a little easier to converse with Georgiana, despite the building tension in her shoulders, growing tighter by the moment with the effort of not turning to look back.

"'Tis very good to see you. And such a surprise! What brings you into Hertfordshire?"

"We thought we might see our friends, on our way to Pemberley."

"You are leaving town just as the Season has begun?"

"I fear I must. The excitement has become rather too difficult to handle," Georgiana smiled consciously, and Elizabeth pressed her hand. She had found enough in the young girl's letters abounding with details of her coming-out to understand why she should need a respite from the bustle.

"I wish you could have stayed for my coming-out ball," Georgiana voiced a sentiment she had often put in the selfsame letters.

Despite her young friend's earnest entreaties, Elizabeth had chosen not to, at the time. Not because she could not prolong her stay in town once Jane and Charles had made plans to return to Netherfield after their baby's christening. She might have stayed with her uncle and aunt Gardiner instead. But Elizabeth had doubted the wisdom of provoking an unpleasant scene with Lord and Lady Langthorne by showing herself at their niece's ball and, in view of everything that had come to pass since then, she determined with a sigh that avoiding them had been the wisest choice.

"I understand it was a great success," was all that she could bring herself to say.

"It was… tolerable. And largely thanks to my dearest brother," Georgiana replied casting him a tender smile over her shoulder, and Elizabeth felt compelled to glance his way as well.

"Not at all. I have done nothing," he protested, but Georgiana would have none of it.

"You stood beside me when I needed you," she warmly retorted.

With another sigh, Elizabeth fixed her stare on the road ahead. Yes. He would have. It was in his nature. He had stood by her as well in her time of need. But not in this. It was the hardest trial – and she would have to face it all alone. She pursed her lips and frowned at the maudlin thought. It would not do! If she did not cease this instant, she would burst into a flood of tears like a fool.

She struggled for something to say, but Georgiana was there before her.

"We have determined to go to Pemberley for Easter and stay till May or thereabouts. We shall return to town then, both of us feeling better for the respite, I imagine."

A May wedding in town, then? Or at Miss Wyatt's country home, wherever that might be? Elizabeth knew that by rights now would be a good moment to offer her congratulations, but words caught in her throat. Instead, she brought herself to ask:

"How long are you staying in Hertfordshire?"

"For the next four days, until your brother and sister quit Netherfield. Mr Bingley kindly suggested we extend our stay until their own departure and then travel north together and perhaps stop with them for a little while. Their new home is not thirty miles from Pemberley," Georgiana answered brightly, unwittingly throwing her friend into an unbearable mix of elation and distress.

So he would be at Netherfield. They might come across each other every day. Just now, when she could scarce bear it. Just now, when she needed all her strength to overcome the worst turmoil she had ever faced.

Removing herself from his circle by severing her ties to Richard would not afford complete protection, Elizabeth knew it well. She fully expected that his connection with her brother would bring them together in the future. But she thought she would have warning. Plenty of time to manufacture an excuse. Flee elsewhere. Feign illness. Or anything that might suit the part.

Short of confining herself to her own bedchamber, victim to some contrived sudden ailment, there was nothing she could do to shield herself from the pain and pleasure of his company.

Confined between four walls at Longbourn.

There was no surer way to lose her mind!

Caught in her dark reflections, Elizabeth failed to express the joy her friend's communications should have caused under normal circumstances but, when they reached the house and made their way within after entrusting Mr Bingley's horses to a stable lad, Mrs Bennet was prompt to express all the glee that her second daughter had not felt.

"What a sterling notion, Mr Darcy!" the lady exclaimed as soon as she was informed of the travel arrangements. "Well, if *you* are going to Bleakhill, then surely Mr Bingley cannot object to his wife's relations joining him as well. How I long to see Jane's new establishment! We shall all go, it will be such a merry party," she enthused, to Elizabeth's unmitigated horror.

She suppressed a gasp, but her fortitude was ill rewarded.

Mrs Bennet had a vast deal more to say.

"Let me order refreshments, and we can lay our plans. Then I will write to Jane and perhaps you would be so kind as to carry that letter. I will call on the morrow so that we can settle the details. Of course, Bingley and Jane will travel in their carriage with the little lamb and her nurse. May I impose upon your kindness, Sir, to ask if you would allow Lizzy and Mary to follow in yours? Then the rest of us can squeeze into the landau and we need not bring another carriage. Surely Mr Bingley can let us have the use of his spare one, or his chaise perhaps, on the journey back. I should have thought about this scheme much sooner and asked him to hold another carriage back, rather than sending them all up to Bleakhill. Well, no matter. My sister Phillips will be disappointed not to come with us, but surely she must see that dear Jane cannot be expected to host the pair of them as well. So, what say you, Sir? Can I rely on your assistance?"

"But of course," Darcy was heard to offer, and Elizabeth could not fail to detect his shock under the thin veneer of civil reserve.

This time she winced in earnest and stood to busy herself with pouring another cup of tea. She was not left for long to school her features into a convincing mask. In a trice, Georgiana was beside her.

"What a delightful notion, your mother's! Then I will not lose you quite so soon. And if you come to Staffordshire, perhaps you can be persuaded to travel the last thirty miles and visit us at Pemberley. I would so love to show you that dear place, Elizabeth! 'Tis at its best in the spring and summer."

There was only so much time that one could occupy with pouring a cup of tea so in the end Elizabeth was obliged to return to her sofa. She sat, dreadfully aware of Mr Darcy's stare, firmly fixed upon her. Or perhaps his sister, she could not be certain without purposely looking – and she did not dare look. At her side, Georgiana was merrily chatting about Pemberley and Derbyshire and all the wondrous sights she would like her dear friend to see, and Elizabeth could only try to smile at the young girl's excitement, and not scald herself with her fresh cup of tea.

ৡৣ ৡৣ

Detestable as such a step might make her in her mother's eyes, should she be informed about it, Elizabeth could not help making her way into her father's study later on that day, once their guests had left them, and secretly advise against Mrs Bennet's scheme. She represented to him all the inconveniences and the dreadful imposition on Jane's comfort and Mr Bingley's kind nature – but to no avail. He heard her attentively, and then said:

"We shall have no peace at Longbourn if your mother does not have her wish. As to Bingley, I feel for the young man, but he has brought this on himself. Did no one tell him that when he marries a woman, he marries her family? Besides, once your mother is fully satisfied that Jane is well-settled, there will be an end to her complaints about the much-reviled Bleakhill. She will leave them to it and Bingley will have his peace at last."

"But why must we all impose upon them? Cannot Mamma go by herself?"

"And leave us in charge of Lydia and Kitty? Lizzy, you are made of sterner stuff than I," the old gentleman quipped, to his daughter's vexation.

"I cannot see much sign of Mamma curbing their excesses," she replied in frustration. "Besides, they can go if they wish. We can remain behind with Mary."

186

"I should have thought you eager to see Jane's establishment, my child. What makes you shy away from this arrangement?"

"Merely the notion of such a dreadful imposition," Elizabeth replied swiftly, all too wary of her father's most perceptive eye.

"It would be no lesser for the absence of the sensible members of the party. You would be pleased to see how Jane is settled, and frankly so would I. This is an opportunity to do so, without the inconvenience of making our own travelling arrangements or struggling to find our way. Come, let us hear no more about it, Lizzy. I believe all will be well."

Effectively silenced and with a heavy heart, Elizabeth left her father's study. She had no expectations of the kind.

Neither did Mr Bingley, when his friend returned to Netherfield with a letter for his wife and an apology to him for not handling the situation better.

"You lack the opportunity to practise," Bingley retorted with a grimace and went to pour himself an unusually generous measure of brandy. "In the face of my wily mother-in-law you must have been as defenceless as the rabbit to the fox. Well, what is done is done. I hope she will not stay long enough to drive us to distraction. Poor Jane was at her wits' end when she read that letter. No, pray do not apologise again! Fear not, I do not hold you responsible. The blame rests in a very different quarter. Besides, I should have seen it coming. I shall have to send word to the coaching inns, to be ready to accommodate a larger party. Come, Darcy. Drink that brandy, pour yourself another and give thanks that having Mrs Bennet for a mother falls to my lot rather than yours!"

✿ ❧ ✿

Mr Darcy's lot was in Elizabeth's thoughts every waking moment, as was the gentleman himself, but she found no opportunity to speak of either during the few days left until the dreaded incursion north.

Georgiana came to call with Jane and her baby, but he did not, to Elizabeth's partial relief mingled with the severest disappointment. The April rain that drummed steadily on the windows only increased the latter, for it put paid to every hope of a private conversation in the garden, when she might have found a way to extract further intelligence from Georgiana, much as she dreaded it.

As for Mr Darcy, Elizabeth only saw him once, on the night before the planned departure, when the Netherfield party was asked to come and dine at Longbourn rather than in a house that was all but closed. Mr and Mrs Phillips had also been invited, as had Sir William, Lady Lucas and Maria, so the Longbourn dining room was stretched beyond capacity and ringing with the din of several simultaneous conversations and with Mrs Bennet's voice, loudly carrying over everybody's.

There was just one quiet spot at the large table: the one where Elizabeth sat, with Mr Darcy at her right. She had no knowledge as to how he came to be her dinner companion. Mrs Bennet would frequently choose the informality of not assigning places – and this Longbourn dinner certainly was more informal than most.

The same could not be said of his demeanour. He hardly spoke, and when he did it was with restrained civility, to ask her if she wished to be served with some dish or other or if he could refill her glass of wine.

She made the profound error of accepting the latter offer only once. She would not run the risk again, after the one disturbing instance of raising her hand to move the glass closer to him, only to find their fingers touching as they both reached for the fragile stem.

She withdrew her hand as though it had been burned, and so did he. It was a wonder that neither happened to unsettle their plates or the wine carafe with their too sudden movements.

She swallowed and pointedly crossed her shaking hands into her lap, to signal that he could handle her glass in safety. Yet he chose not to, and poured the dark-red liquid halfway up without touching the glass at all, then returned the carafe to its place and retrieved his cutlery, but it was merely to aimlessly push his food about the plate.

She did not retrieve hers, but thanked him quietly for his assistance as she surreptitiously rubbed her thumb over fingers that still tingled from the touch.

Had she not felt like crying, she surely would have laughed at her own response, so unaccountable and Missish. Had he not held her hands before? Had she not sought his of her own accord, pressed them in reassurance, without the slightest qualm, the slightest tremor?

Yet that was in another life.

At a time of blissful ignorance of her own feelings.

Her mouth went dry at the very thought, leaving her longing for a sip of water, but she would not trust her shaking hands to handle the tall glass without spilling its contents all over the table. She ran the tip of her tongue over her lips instead. At her right, Mr Darcy sighed, for no reason she could fathom.

Eventually she returned to her veal and he to his roast lamb with glazed roots and vegetables. And still neither spoke, their silence unnoticed in their loquacious surroundings, until at last Elizabeth found herself quietly addressed:

"Are you looking forward to visiting Blakehill, Miss Bennet?"

Miss Bennet' still! She put her knife down without the slightest clatter and dabbed the napkin to her lips before answering simply:

"Not quite."

"How so?"

Elizabeth looked up towards him then, drawn despite herself by the concern she thought she had detected in the question. She regretted her intrepidity at once and glanced away. It was unwise to meet those eyes at such close quarters.

"I fear it would be an imposition on Mr Bingley and my sister to host us all so soon, before they are even established in their home. And I regret that my mother has imposed upon *you* as well with her request," she added.

His reply was earnest and prompt.

"Pray let that be the least of your concerns. It would be my pleasure to convey you to Blakehill."

"I thank you."

"You are very welcome."

He took a sip from his glass and added:

"Georgiana and I will arrive at Longbourn at seven in the morning. I hope that would be convenient."

"Of course. Anything that suits you."

"'Tis Bingley who has set the time. He is hoping to arrive at the *Black Swan* at Alconbury by the evening and fully expects it will be a slow progress."

Elizabeth could not fail to smile at that.

"I daresay it will be. Young Miss Elizabeth-Rose can be a very demanding little person."

"Unlike her godmother," he smiled back and the unexpected flash of dimples left her at a loss for a sensible answer.

At last, she choked out a laugh.

"Indeed. 'Tis a very long time since I was that little."

"In fact, I was speaking of demanding."

She blushed profusely and, vexed for doing so, she forced herself to answer lightly, just as she might have done several months ago.

"You are very kind, but sadly misinformed. For a more accurate opinion you should refer to my relations. They have the doubtful privilege of living with me everyday."

He did not smile again, as she had hoped he would. Instead, he reached for his glass of wine, leaving her to fret in the ensuing silence over the ways in which her words might have been misconstrued.

⁂

There was no comfort for her for the remainder of the evening, nor for the night that followed. Sarah, her mother's maid, woke her after a too short and restless slumber, to the taxing experience of the Bennet household preparing for imminent departure.

Her mother's voice, raised sometimes in excitement and sometimes in sheer panic, but uniformly louder than it ought to be, punctuated every moment of the preparations. Not even the closed door could offer a good shield, and in the end Elizabeth resigned herself to no longer seeking one.

She stood from the bed and, gathering her satchel, she opened the door into the hallway. She stopped for a parting glance over her chamber, dreading the days until she would return to the familiar surroundings. A sudden shiver of foreboding ran along her spine and a sinking feeling gripped her heart – that, one way or another, nothing would ever be the same.

Chapter 14

They were not to breakfast in their home before departure, but at the *Roebuck* in Baldock, where they would stop to bate the horses, so the family was not assembled in the breakfast room but in the morning parlour, in a confusion of people, cloaks and bonnets. Hill's voice could barely be heard when she came in to announce that Mr Darcy's carriage had pulled up at the door.

"Lizzy, Mary, come, make haste! Do not keep Mr Darcy waiting. No, Lydia, we simply cannot wait till you go back to your bedchamber to choose another bonnet. This one is very handsome. No, green does not make you look sallow. With a complexion such as yours, you can wear anything you wish. Make haste, make haste! Your father has gone to order the carriage and you know he detests it when we dawdle. For heaven's sake, Kitty, have some compassion for my poor nerves! Let Lydia have that shawl, you have half-a-dozen. The pair of you would tear my nerves to shreds!"

Elizabeth's own nerves were not faring any better when, with Mary in tow, she made her way out of the house and towards Mr Darcy's carriage. The door was open and he stood beside it, waiting – and could not possibly have missed a syllable of her mother's ceaseless admonitions. His countenance gave no indication of it though. He merely bowed in greeting to herself and Mary, bade them good morning and offered to hand them in. By the time he had done so, Mr Bennet joined them.

"Good morning to you, Miss Darcy – Mr Darcy. And my thanks for looking after my daughters, Sir."

"A pleasure, Mr Bennet."

"It might have been a trial with the other set, but no man of feeling could have inflicted the pair of them upon you in good conscience," the older gentleman quipped, to Elizabeth's discomfort at her father's propensity to mockingly emphasise her youngest sisters' failings, rather than exercise his right and duty to correct them. "Well then, time to go. We are to *rendezvous* with the others in Meryton at the *Red Lion*, are we not?"

"We are. Mr and Mrs Bingley will be there in no time at all. They were to set off shortly after my sister and myself."

"Then we should not keep them waiting. You will excuse me, I must harass the rest of my family into our carriage. Safe travels. Mary, pray restrain yourself from pontificating for the entire duration of the journey. Lizzy, farewell and think of me with some compassion. Right, then. We shall see you in Meryton."

∽᎒ஓ᎒ஓ

Meryton was far behind now. Likewise Baldock, as the swaying carriages proceeded at a stately pace along the Great North Road.

In the first there was silence. Fed and content, Miss Elizabeth-Rose was sleeping in her mother's arms, and the three other occupants were keen to prolong that desirable state of affairs for as long as they could.

In the second there was a mayhem of Mrs Bennet's, Lydia's and Kitty's making, which would cease for some ten minutes or so whenever Mr Bennet determined he could not tolerate it any longer and threatened with bidding the coachman make an about-turn and head back home to Longbourn.

In the third there was no mayhem but, despite appearances, there was precious little peace. One of the seats was taken by the readers – Mary and Mr Darcy. Presumably mortified by her father's injunction, Mary took it to heart and forbore to say a word, devoting her full attention to Mr Gibbon's *History of the Roman Empire*. Mr Darcy's reading matter, although less ponderous, still lacked the power to engross him fully, for now and then he would close his book and leave it in his lap, his finger holding his place between the pages, until he would tire of staring out of the carriage window and take up reading again, with infrequent glances at the seat before him, where Elizabeth and Georgiana were maintaining a cheerful conversation.

Truth be told, the cheer was all on Georgiana's side. Elizabeth's sole contribution was to skilfully drop the necessary words here and there, that would encourage her young friend to share more tales of town and Derbyshire.

No one could doubt Georgiana's excitement and her delight with the company and the travel plans – she was chattier than ever, which was a surprise but no less of a blessing, for otherwise the carriage ride would have been mostly spent in awkward silence.

Elizabeth clasped her gloved fingers in her lap and smiled to Georgiana as she declared her intention of visiting the Lakes in the near future, thus providing the young girl with another topic that would bear lengthy and elaborate descriptions, and giving *her* leisure to cast a surreptitious glance towards her friend's brother. She longed to speak to him – she did not dare – and her own unprecedented shyness vexed her beyond endurance.

He was intent upon his book, so she allowed her glance to linger. Dark tousled hair, a few long, wavy forelocks falling over the wide brow. Eyes cast down, lidded as though closed, with only the flicker of dark lashes to prove it was not so. Lips pressed together, presumably in concentration, making the chin jut ever so slightly forward. Strong jaw above the neckcloth and the pointed corners of the collar, no longer perfectly aligned as they had been this morning. Cheeks vaguely shadowed. A very straight nose, the nostrils widening all of a sudden with a deep intake of air. And then the lips again. Perfectly formed. Still tightened.

Did he kiss Miss Wyatt when he offered for her?

She had no answer to that question. Likewise to another: what alerted people when they were being watched?

A sixth sense, or whatever else it might have been, prompted Mr Darcy to glance up so suddenly that he caught her staring. Someone who had nothing to hide might have met his eyes squarely. Those who still had their wits about them would have looked away casually and slowly, as if their mind was elsewhere and they were simply staring blankly into space. Sadly, the sensible alternatives occurred to her when it was all too late. When her cheeks were already flaming as though set on fire, and her eyes had darted in panic from his face.

She did not look his way again, not for a long time, and Georgiana was surprised to note that she was getting monosyllabic or rather odd answers to her questions. Across from them, Mr Darcy turned to stare at the Bedfordshire countryside again.

There was at least another hour and a half till their next stop.

And to Blakehill – one hundred and twenty-two gruelling miles.

When they finally stopped to bate the horses, Georgiana suggested a short walk.

"Would you care to join us?" Mr Darcy asked with an uncertain glance from herself to Mary, and Elizabeth could not miss the hesitation.

"I thank you, no. Jane might need me," she dissembled, perfectly aware that between her mother and three sisters, not to mention the maids at the inn, Jane would be assured of all the help she needed.

It was clear from Georgiana's countenance that she thought the same. Mr Darcy's remained closed and solemn. At the next stop he did not ask again, and Elizabeth wistfully watched the brother and sister strolling together arm in arm out of the busy courtyard of the coaching inn, while she followed her relations indoors, to listen to her mother complaining of dark hallways and the likelihood of very draughty parlours.

Once the horses had been watered, fed and rested, they resumed their journey, for Elizabeth to feign great interest in Mrs Edgeworth's *Belinda* and pretend not to notice that, now and again, at more pronounced jolts of the moving carriage, Mr Darcy's knee would touch her own.

They reached Alconbury in good time and were treated to a very decent dinner, then the ladies eventually withdrew in small groups to their chambers, Georgiana and Elizabeth among the first to go.

It became apparent to the latter that leaving the dining parlour at the same time as Mr Darcy's sister was the wrong choice, as soon as she saw him take two sets of candles with the obvious intention of escorting them above-stairs.

They made their way in silence up the creaking steps and then along the narrow corridor to the bedchambers. Georgiana's was the nearest and, with a light kiss on his sister's cheek, he gave her one of the candles and bade her good night.

The room that Elizabeth would share with Mary was only three doors down – a very short distance, covered in no time at all.

When he offered her the other candle, Elizabeth shook her head.

"I would not wish to leave you in darkness," she whispered. "I can light my own from this, and you can keep it."

"No need. I can find my way."

"Are you certain?"

"Quite."

"Then I thank you and good night."

The hand that reached for the door handle was stopped midway and clasped in his.

"Pray wait. Miss Bennet, may I ask, are you well? You have been uncommonly quiet lately. And… you seem distressed."

'I am. By you calling me Miss Bennet, among other things,' she thought, but could not say it. Instead, she replied:

"No, not distressed. Just tired."

"Then I should leave you to your rest."

Yet he did not release her hand, but raised it to send it tingling wildly with the touch of his lips on her cold fingers, with the warm breath of his whispered "Good night."

She hurried in and closed the door to lean against it, head tilted back, and finally release the flood of silent tears, not knowing that, a mere inch of solid wood away, a wide brow covered in a host of dark unruly forelocks was leant against the other side, in the temporary privacy of the deserted pitch-black hallway.

လ၉ ၄ၕ

It was not pitch-black in Mr Darcy's carriage when it took to the road the following morning, but the low-lying clouds gathered above with an ominous threat of rain made the hour seem a great deal earlier than it was.

Despite the predictable delays caused by travelling with a young babe and with Mrs Bennet, they had left the coaching inn as early as may be, in the hope of reaching Leicester by nightfall.

Few words were spoken by the four occupants of Mr Darcy's conveyance once they were on their way – and after a while, none. Eyes closed and heads lightly rocking from side to side with the sway of the moving carriage, Mary and Georgiana seemed asleep, or at least seeking to rest and compensate for the discomfort of having left their beds much sooner than they would have chosen.

Elizabeth's eyes were closed as well but, despite the overwhelming tiredness caused by yet another troubled night, she was not lured into slumber, but into wretched thoughts.

The low light and the silence broken only by the rumbling of the wheels brought to mind another journey in the selfsame carriage, when she had travelled in the dead of night with Mr Darcy and her father to reach her betrothed's bedside.

She sighed, burdened by the pain she had to cause him, and no less by the fact that she had not finished that most difficult letter.

She must. She would.

And henceforth they would all go their separate ways.

Hopefully Richard would find another to share his life with. Someone who would love *him* and be worthy of his affections.

Her own sole option was to hide. At Longbourn for a while, and then maybe as a spinster at Blakehill, to teach Lizzy-Rose and her unborn sisters to play their instruments very ill indeed.

And Mr Darcy would return to town to marry. Next time this carriage travelled from town to Pemberley, it would convey Miss Wyatt thence – by then Mrs Darcy. The ever so happy Mrs Darcy…

She did not even notice that she sighed again, a heavier sigh and much more audible, until she heard a low whisper coming from the other corner.

"You are not well. Is there anything I could get you?"

"No, nothing. I am well. Quite well."

"You were sighing."

"Was I? I had not noticed."

"Twice. In rather quick succession," Darcy observed, the light tone suggesting he was attempting to cajole her into a smile.

Elizabeth obliged, but since she was not certain he could see it clearly, she sought to match his lightness with her own.

"Some would count sheep rather than sighs to fall asleep, Sir."

"Some would," he casually conceded. "You are not cold, I hope."

"Perhaps a very little."

"Would you care for another travelling rug?"

"Not yours. You might need it."

"I am not using it."

"Then yes, I thank you."

He leaned forward to drape the rug over her knees and she could see him clearly now, but only for a moment, until he leaned back into his darkened corner.

"Is that better?"

"Yes. I am much warmer now."

"Good. Once again, I thought it less than proper to offer you brandy," he teased softly, and the recollection of the warm intimacy on the night when Lizzy-Rose was born made her draw a shaky breath. Yet this time she was careful and she released it slowly, inconspicuously, so that he would not hear a third sigh.

⋅ೕ⅁ ⅁ೕ⋅

They reached Leicester sooner than expected, which brought a change in their travelling arrangements. Mr Bingley decided to hire a horse at the last coaching inn and ride ahead of the rest of the party for the remaining thirty miles or so, make it to Blakehill that very night and personally ensure that everything was in readiness for his wife and daughter's arrival on the morrow.

And Mr Darcy chose to ride with him.

Thus, when they retired for the night, Georgiana and Elizabeth fetched their own candles and made their way to their bedchambers at the back of a procession led by a giggling Lydia, rather than in a quiet and – for some – deeply unsettling group of three.

In the morning, when the convoy resumed its careful progress, they were the sole occupants of the Darcy carriage, for Mrs Bennet had insisted that Mary take Mr Bingley's place and travel with Jane to be of assistance. And so it came to pass that Elizabeth was finally presented with the opportunity for that private conversation she had long been impatient for, and equally long dreaded.

She began promptly, almost as soon as they left the inn, lest she lose her courage.

"This is most remiss of me. I have neglected to give your brother my best wishes on his recent engagement."

Georgiana flashed a surprised glance towards her.

"But he is not engaged," she instantly replied, and it took Elizabeth all the restraint she still possessed to keep an even mien and a placid tone.

He was *not* engaged!

"Oh? Miss Bingley mentioned Miss Wyatt has become engaged and I assumed…"

"Now I see. She has, two or three weeks ago, but to a Mr Lewis, not my brother."

Elizabeth released a little choking laugh.

197

"Pray pardon my assumption. Miss Bingley's communication was not very clear."

Undoubtedly on purpose, Elizabeth saw it now. A gratuitous unkindness, a sly comment, deliberately and maliciously incomplete, to hurt a supposed rival however briefly, until the truth would be revealed at last.

A rival. How extraordinary that Miss Bingley should have seen it rightly, even before *she* did. Astuteness or plain spite? No matter. He was not engaged! As for Miss Bingley's spiteful comment, if anything, she should be almost glad of it. It did not bear thinking that she might have discovered her true feelings when she was already bound in matrimony to Richard.

The sobering thought cut through her elation. Mr Darcy was not betrothed to Miss Wyatt. But someday he would marry another, and it could not be herself. Her engagement would be broken, but he would never offer for someone of her station. Someone his own cousin had once wished to marry. And even if he were to offer, woefully unlikely as it was, how could she accept him and knowingly hurt Richard twice? And in the worst possible manner. How could she come between them, the cruellest of Jezebels?

From the other seat, Georgiana's low, hesitant voice broke her painful chain of thought.

"Before we left town, my brother told me he would not offer for Miss Wyatt or anybody else. He said he would not marry, and that Pemberley would go to one of my children."

Elizabeth fixed her eyes on her friend's wistful countenance with a start.

"He did?"

"Yes. Perhaps I should not speak of this, not even to you, but it distresses me so very greatly. He must be... He must have his reasons, but he would not share them, much as I have begged him to let me help shoulder his burden. He claims there is none, but how can I believe it?"

She got no answer.

In the ensuing silence, she continued:

"There was a time last spring when he was in a dreadfully bad way. Downcast – nay, positively grim. Withdrawn. Painfully silent but for a few short-tempered outbursts, so out of character for him. Upon reflection, I thought perhaps something had happened then.

That he might have proposed and was refused. But this is foolish, no one would refuse him. And then it came to me. I did not dare ask, and I still do not. I fear it would hurt him even more if I asked whether there was any truth in my suspicion that perhaps he loves someone he cannot have. Heaven forfend, someone who passed away. Or someone married to another."

'Or someone promised to another.'

Elizabeth barely suppressed a gasp as the thought shot and splintered through her like forked lightning, casting a stark light over every darkened corner. Bringing every disregarded instance into the sharpest focus. Every misapprehended instance. His deep reserve around her, always holding back, yet always coming to her aid whenever she would find herself in need of assistance. His promise to continue doing so in the future. His violent reaction to Lord Morton's vile remarks. His staggering defence of her to Lady Langthorne.

'No man of sense and feeling would need to have his hand forced into marrying Miss Bennet. She is the very best that anyone could hope for.'

Had she been alone, she would have buried her face into her hands. Such blindness! Such dreadful, wilful blindness, to have assumed he was defending Richard's interests.

It was not his cousin he had championed. It was her!

The splintering forked lightning spread into her heart, and her heart broke for him, for what he had endured over such a length of time. If he loved her, what hell it must have been to see her promised to another! To the one man for whom he cared the most.

She cared not one jot for Miss Wyatt, so she had experienced an incomparably paler version of that hell for a few days only, and still had found she could not bear it. He had faced worse for months. The very best of men condemned to the worst torture. By her own hand unknowingly inflicted.

This was wicked – monstrous! Why had she not seen it? Then at least she might have had the kindness to avoid him, rather than agree to spend so many days under his roof and force herself into his life, unbidden. Then perhaps none of this would have happened. She might have still believed herself in love with Richard...

Oh, aye! And discovered her true sentiments years later, when she would have been a matron raising Richard's children.

The bitter laugh the thought engendered sounded so much like a broken sigh that Georgiana glanced at her and whispered mournfully:

"And now I have distressed you too. But you care for him as well. You understand."

"I do..."

She understood. So very clearly. Much better than her friend did, thankfully. Yet that minor blessing weighed virtually nothing against the dreadful heartache with no possible cure.

Chapter 15

The remainder of the journey was a waking nightmare, as was their arrival at Blakehill. She could not even trust herself to glance in his direction and keep herself in check. Keep the anguish hidden.

The habitual commotion caused by her mother and her youngest sisters was of vague assistance, something to hide behind. It also helped somewhat that Mr Darcy did not join them on their tour, but withdrew to the gardens, claiming he had seen the house already. And so they walked without him, as soon as Jane had settled Elizabeth-Rose into her new bedchamber. They wandered from the drawing room to the music room, and then through the dining room, the library, the morning room, the mistress's sitting room and the master's study, through sundry parlours and bedchambers.

At last, they were shown to their quarters and Elizabeth learned that again she was to share with Mary for, although there was a plentiful number of bedchambers, not all had been readied as yet for occupation. The notion did not trouble her, only the lack of privacy. She desperately needed time alone. Time to think and feel, without the exhausting effort of keeping up a crumbling *façade*.

She would not have that luxury in the chamber that she shared with Mary, nor elsewhere in the house, and she did not dare go into the gardens and risk coming upon him with her composure shattered and in a flood of tears.

Mercifully, at last she found a quiet spot in the orangery, on a small bench sheltered by two overgrown bushes dotted with wilting pink camellias. These were not the only ones showing signs of mild neglect. Most of the plants in the orangery seemed to have been allowed to run a little wild, too tall and some untrimmed, with an excess of foliage. Which suited her well enough as she sat down, fairly concealed in her secluded corner, the murmur of water in a distant fountain a soothing antidote to her wrenching thoughts.

She wished to see him. Not a wish, a need. But first she must regain a measure of control, at least over the tears that were now flowing freely. Flowing as though they would never cease. She let them have their way. Likewise the choking sobs that followed, deep and racking, shaking her hunched shoulders as she sat face in hands, the very picture of the deepest misery.

Thus she appeared to Darcy when he aimlessly wandered in from the gardens, least expecting to come upon a scene that tore at his heart. It was not a choice to come forth and bend down on one knee beside her. It was a compulsion that defied every reason for restraint.

She did not hear his footsteps on the moss-covered path and violently jumped, dropping her hands, when she heard his urgent whisper:

"Elizabeth, what is it? What has distressed you so? You must let me know. Pray let me help!"

The stilted formality of address he had employed in their recent exchanges was instantly discarded. It had been born of caution and necessity, then fostered by her newfound reserve since their encounter on the lane to Longbourn, but had no place in a moment such as this, when he could barely stop himself from gathering her into his arms to kiss her tear-stained face and vow to set everything to rights.

She shook her head and would not speak, but brought her hands back up to hurriedly wipe her cheeks, and then to hide them.

"You cannot," a muffled answer came at last, but he was not asked to leave, not that he would have.

Nor was he willing to allow that barrier to remain between them. His hands encircled her wrists and his thumbs came up to brush against them as he gently drew her palms off her face and the barrier was gone. He kept her hands in his and urged again.

"Tell me."

And, unknowingly, she did. Not in so many words. She would not have found them, had she tried. The truth was in her eyes – wide-open windows into her very soul – and the unspoken message he had despaired of ever finding there changed everything in one stunning instant.

It was not a choice to reach and cup her face into his hands, but a necessity. And run his thumbs over her cheeks to brush away fresh tears. Lean forward until his lips touched hers in a light caress at first, a mere flutter that in a heartbeat turned into a blaze. Into open-mouthed hungry exploration, born of too long a self-denial and a need so deep that it bordered pain.

It was beyond his wildest dreams to find her joining him avidly in that, but join him she did. Her hands went about his neck, then came to tangle in his hair as she brought him closer, responding to his kisses with a fervour that mirrored desperation. As though she had longed for this as much as he. As though she could not bring him close enough, and could not bear an instant's separation.

He willingly obliged and wrapped his arms around her, his wide-spread hands roaming over her back in sweeping caresses before they stopped, fastened in place to bring her closer still. And still they kissed, the need of air forgotten, both finding that shallow breaths served just as well or even better than deep ones that would require separation. Which they both dreaded, and rightly so, for it would bring this exquisite madness to a stop, and also bring countless wrenching questions that would not be silenced for much longer. Yet still they sought to silence them, the hungry exploration sliding into abandon. Reckless. Splendid.

They both allowed it gladly, for a length of time neither stood to measure until, ill-advisedly – as he would berate himself a moment later – his lips left hers to seek her cheeks, her eyes, taste tears on her damp eyelashes, thus making it possible for her to burst out in a ragged whisper:

"I must go."

"Go?" Darcy exclaimed in shock, drawing back to stare into her eyes. "After *this?* Do not, I beg you! We must talk!"

"I know," she said brokenly. "But I cannot, not now. I need to think. I need a moment."

Darcy clasped her hands in his.

"Do not take too long," he earnestly pleaded and bent to press his lips into her upturned palm.

With a choking sigh, she spread her free hand into his hair and, as though this was all the encouragement he needed, Darcy sought her lips again.

The kiss was different this time. No elated urgency in it, but no misgivings either. Just deep need, and no little dread of what must come.

Too soon for both, Elizabeth broke away and stood, her hand still clasped in his till the last moment, when it was tugged out of his grasp and she hurried off almost at a run back into the house, leaving him to drop onto the bench, head in hands, more exultant and more terrified than he had ever been in his entire life.

ೲഉ ൦ൢ

What chance had she to think? What private moment and, for that matter, *where?* With any luck, by now Mary will have found the library so it might be safe enough to go to their bedchamber. But to what purpose, though? To think? This could not be tackled with cold reason. Not with raw feeling either – therein lay madness, luring her into hope.

And there it was – the conflict between head and heart.

One warned they could not be together.

The other bled at the mere thought of living their lives apart.

She had cowardly run from the orangery, chased by the selfsame conflict that had tugged to and fro ever since Georgiana's revelations in the carriage. But what answers did she expect to find alone in her bedchamber? He was in the right. They had to talk.

She stopped at the bottom of the stairs to draw a steadying breath and find the wherewithal to return to the orangery. Far from assured she had, she slowly retraced her steps nevertheless.

She saw him from a distance, in the spot that had been hers – on the wooden bench, leaning against the backrest, eyes closed – and her heart went out to him, urging her forward.

Slightly more attuned to his surroundings than she had been, his eyes flashed open and a devastating smile brightened his countenance. Her hand shot instinctively to her chest and she released an uneven breath, quite certain that he had never looked so handsome.

Darcy was beside her before she had taken two more steps, his hands on her elbows, and his eyes spoke volumes. For one, they assured her he would like nothing better than to take her in his arms again and kiss away every shred of reason.

And yet he seemed to have retained at least *some* sense, for all he did was run his hands over the thin muslin sleeves until he found hers, and clasped them both in his.

"Thank you," he whispered fervently. "I did not dare hope you would return so soon."

He bent his head, but did not kiss her. He pressed his lips on her fingers instead, then entreated:

"Come. We cannot be assured of privacy here."

Her spirits rising to effervescence at his touch and the glow in his eyes, Elizabeth shot him an arch glance, as though to suggest they had been favoured with a fair share of privacy already, on that very same disparaged spot. Sense seemed to fly to the four winds at that particular reminder, along with all his caution and, with a sharp intake of breath, he captured her lips again. A wild, reckless indulgence, cut short with the greatest effort lest they be found thus by some dreadfully shocked relation.

"Come," Darcy urged again and tucked her hand into the crook of his arm, their fingers still tightly interlaced – a poor substitute for the much greater closeness they both craved.

He led her out into the garden, then down the gravelled path that sneaked away from the house beneath tall pines and barren trees, through the wide expanse of fresh green dotted with daffodils.

They did not stop to sit on any of the benches found along the way – there was no hope of privacy there either. Elizabeth could not care less where they were headed, nor that they soon must have their heart-wrenching conversation. She firmly pushed aside all thoughts of the dreaded future to savour this. The intimacy. The closeness. The certainty that he loved her. The feel of his warm hand clasping hers as though afraid that, should his hold slacken, she would vanish into thin air.

Which was precisely what he felt: the most unsettling admixture of wild joy, tainted with the deepest fear that it might not last. She loved him – otherwise she would not be there, would not have kissed him as she had. The miracle of it took his breath away and tampered with his senses. She loved him!

How? Since when? How was it even possible? Yet all these questions could be set aside for now. All but one. And he could not refrain from voicing it any longer.

"Where do we go from here, Elizabeth?" he asked, ever so softly.

For a long time – the whole of eighteen footsteps – he got no answer. Nothing was heard but the twittering of birds and the crunching of gravel underfoot, until at last she whispered brokenly:

"I do not know. Oh, how I wish I did!"

She sighed. The wrenching conversation was upon them. Too soon, much too soon, breaking the spell of the glorious *'here and now'* with all the heartache of the dreaded conflict between what the soul craved and what reason commanded. They could not be apart. They could not be together.

The words caught in her throat, yet she forced them out.

"I can see no option but to return— "

"To Richard?" Darcy exclaimed in horror, and there was horror in his eyes as well when he stopped walking and spun round to face her.

"To Longbourn," she finished the interrupted sentence. "Of course I cannot marry Richard now. I have struggled for days to find a way to tell him."

His eyes came to bore into hers as he forcefully said, in a voice so uneven that the words sounded almost harsh:

"Elizabeth, marry *me!*"

"How can I?" she burst out in the deepest anguish. "We cannot hurt him so! Can you not see it? His best friend and his betrothed!"

"I cannot lose you," he said simply, before his voice grew ragged again, and pleading. "Elizabeth, *I cannot!* Not now. Not when I know you love me. And you do. You love *me* – do you not?"

The touching insecurity in his earnest plea broke her heart anew.

"Yes. *Yes,*" she fervently replied, unable and unwilling to deny him the reassurance he was seeking. "I love you."

"You do!" he whispered back, overwhelmed to hear it spoken in so many words, the sheer wonder of it all making him forget to berate himself for not saying it first. Belatedly, his own deepest truth came out in a rush: "And I love *you*. More than anything!"

"I know. You have shown it for so many months, and I have been too blind to see it," she bitterly reproached herself, and the tears she had so far suppressed with great difficulty welled in her eyes and spilled over her cheeks. "Forgive me…"

"There is nothing to forgive, my love," he said with the utmost gentleness.

Yet she would not be soothed. Instead, the novelty of the tender appellation only served to bring fresh tears and self-recriminations.

"The pain I have caused you! Naught but pain…"

"Not so," Darcy protested, barely able to restrain himself from cupping her face into his hands again and leaning to kiss away her tears – there, in the open. He took a deep breath and clasped her hands tighter as they resumed their walk. "The pain was of my own infliction. I should have proposed months ahead of Richard— "

"And I would have refused you," she interjected, her voice full of self-loathing.

He stared in shock.

"You would have?"

"Yes. I cannot think of my prejudice without abhorrence. I had taken you into a firm dislike based on an unguarded comment and Mr Wickham's lies."

Darcy inhaled sharply, not needing to inquire of what she was speaking. His cousin had acquainted him with the rumours Wickham had not scrupled to spread once assured that he could safely do so, for the Netherfield party had already quitted that part of the country. As to the unguarded comment she had mentioned, it could only be his monumentally uncivil remark at the Meryton assembly.

"You cannot know how I regretted it!" he burst out forcefully, with the deepest contrition. "Long before I came to see that in fact you were the handsomest woman of my acquaintance."

Her brimming eyes softened at the obvious exaggeration, excusable from a besotted man, and she wistfully resumed.

"I should have had more sense than letting mistaken pride blind me to the impropriety of Mr Wickham's communications to a perfect stranger. Ever since I learned the truth from— Ever since I learned the truth," she instinctively avoided the direct reference to Richard, "I have longed to apologise for misjudging you so grievously. Yet I could find no way to do so without causing us both further mortification."

"Pray do not speak of pride," Darcy sighed. "This is *my* sin. For too long I thought of no one but myself. In my arrogant conceit, I was certain of your good opinion even though I did nothing to gain it. I should have courted you when I had the chance. I should have told you every day that your smile made my life worth living!"

Elizabeth swallowed hard at the depth of feeling in his voice and the declaration overwhelmed her, coming as it did from a man of few words.

She thought she had grown to know him well, yet even now he had the power to surprise her with this proof that reserve was but a mask he wore for strangers. A mask he had worn for her at a time when he had not been at liberty to show his feelings.

It was dropped now, even more so than earlier, when he had kissed her, and this glimpse into what he would be to the woman he loved – to *her* – only served to show how blissful their life together might have been, were it not for their abysmal errors.

She looked down at her swishing skirts, blurred by yet another film of tears. She heard him sigh, and still would not turn to meet his eyes, dreading the anguish she knew she would find there. Instead, she fixed her stare on the winding path ahead. It was now branching into another, a narrower one weaving its way through evergreens that made room here and there for leafless magnolias seemingly poised to burst into flower.

He led her down the new path and their further progress eventually revealed a garden folly shaped as a small Greek temple, which might well have been his intended destination. Doubtlessly they would be assured of privacy there, far from the house and screened by the curtain of greenery that was only opened on one side, into a little glade overgrown with daffodils.

A bench stood in the deep recess of the temple, yet neither chose to sit. Instead, in wordless accord, they turned to face each other and Elizabeth raised her eyes to his at last, to find not anguish, but a warm glow that was infinitely more affecting.

They came together without haste this time, without the rush of feeling that had pervaded their earlier kisses, but in joint recognition that this was where they had to be. In each other's arms, his lips slowly exploring her face, inch by soft inch. The wide brow, smooth and cool under trailing ringlets. A closed eye. A cheekbone. A cheek growing steadily warmer with a creeping blush. The other cheek, where his lips lingered whispering endearments, before descending at an exquisitely unhurried pace to find her own. The corner of her mouth first, and he lingered there too as she waited, eyes closed and breathless, until she could wait no longer and turned her head a fraction, to fully yield her lips to his.

To do otherwise was unthinkable, unbearable. An almost painful longing rose and built in her, urging her to raise her arms from around his waist to clasp at his shoulder blades, anchor herself to him as though in fear of being wrenched apart. She wished, she *needed* the kiss to grow much deeper, as forceful as the whirlwind of emotion that swept every shred of sanity away. With wild joy, she found he understood her and crushed his lips on hers. Crushed her to his chest, gloriously close. A low moan rose in his throat, sending shivers through her and compelling her lips to part in hungry welcome. The moan turned into a deep throaty groan and she thrilled at the sound and the bewildering sensations it triggered in her. Alien sensations, unlike anything she had ever felt before.

She clung to him with all her might, wishing he would clasp her even tighter as his mouth claimed hers possessively, branding her as his own in defiance of any precept that might have opposed it. And she responded eagerly, giving herself over to his demanding kisses and the deliciously intolerable ache they built in her. Incomprehensible and strong, the ache peaked and rose, then peaked again into an unbearable yearning, although she could not tell precisely what she was yearning for.

The sense of loss might have been overpowering when his lips finally left hers, had they not moved to drop feathery kisses along her jaw line and tease her earlobe as he raggedly whispered that he loved her, needed her – had he not held her very close, one arm still wrapped around her waist and the other around her shoulders, his hand reaching to cradle her head and bring it to rest on his lapel.

Elizabeth felt his kisses in her hair, then the warm pressure of his cheek when it came to lean atop her head, and she stood there, floating, floating… Hazily floating back to earth from the dizzying splendour of the seventh heaven, as she listened to his thundering heartbeats gradually slowing to a steady rhythm she found as soothing as the movement of his thumb lightly stroking the sensitive skin in the small hollow underneath her ear.

And without warning she was brought straight down from her floating by a sudden thought: this was exquisite and marvellously new – it had *never* been thus with Richard!

She barely suppressed a gasp of shock, not merely at the intruding recollection of other kisses and the untoward comparison – unintentional as it might have been – but at the sharp realisation that it was most unseemly to compare them so. Unmaidenly, even.

A gently-bred lady should not be able to compare!

Well, perhaps Lydia might be, but that was no excuse, nor was it lessening the impropriety one iota.

Her cheeks flamed at her own brazen thoughts, yet a sense of relief came to soften her mortification. Brazen, aye, but also reassuring to have one further proof that her engagement to Richard had been a youthful error born of inexperience. She admired him, she felt comfortable with him – how could she not, when their natures were so very similar? – but the regard she had been so quick to mistake for love bore no resemblance to the feelings that now rocked her very soul.

Brought into sharp focus by the discovery of what it truly meant, being in love, the affection she had felt for Richard – that she still felt – was finally revealed for what it was: fondness for a kindred spirit, esteem, warm understanding and attraction to a handsome man. Enough to base a marriage on, of course – most women entered matrimony with less – but woefully insufficient now that she could compare one set of feelings with another.

And then she sighed.

It brought relief, that revelation, but it could not fail to bring pain as well, for what hope was there for each of them to be happy?

Darcy must have heard her sigh, or perhaps he understood, just as she did, that they could not deny the existence of the outer world forever. His hand dropped from the side of her head to find her chin and turn her face to him, but not to kiss her this time. Warm with love yet clouded with her own unspoken fears, his eyes met hers and he repeated softly:

"We must talk."

She nodded wretchedly and drew back from his embrace with an unnecessary explanation.

"I cannot think when you hold me so."

A rueful chuckle, rife with feeling, was his first answer, and then Darcy said:

"Neither can I. Come, let us sit," he sensibly suggested and, holding hands, they walked to the wooden bench together.

They sat very close, knees touching, her hand still clasped in both of his, a thumb tracing a tingling line over her skin. Elizabeth pressed her lips together. This simple motion was just as apt to prevent her from thinking straight as his embrace.

And then every trace of forced composure left her when he reached to raise her chin again – and her eyes to his – and she heard him whisper, not raggedly this time, but with an intensity that reverberated into her very soul:

"Marry me."

Predictably, her eyes filled with tears.

"There is nothing I want more! But you know I cannot."

His hand dropped from her chin to grip his knee. Then, exhaling sharply, he forcefully ran his fingers through his hair.

"You must leave me some hope, or I shall lose my mind," he said very quietly, each anguished word painfully distinct.

"What hope can I give?" she brokenly exclaimed. "You know as well as I do that we cannot hurt your cousin so!"

Darcy's jaw tightened and he enunciated darkly:

"I stepped aside when you chose him. It is his turn now to return the favour."

The grim tone made her mouth twist into a remorseful grimace.

"My fault! My own wretched error. I thought myself in love. And discovered all too late I was mistaken," she tearfully whispered, only to find his tone and mien softening at once.

He shook his head.

"No, Elizabeth," he said, gently but firmly. "We shall not do this now. We shall think of the past only when its remembrance brings pleasure. One day, when we are together, free of all this and blissfully happy, I shall beg you to remember and share every instance that worked to change your mind. For now, I just thank heavens that you have. And all I need is for us to settle the future."

The picture his words painted, of a rose-tinted life, could not fail to bring fresh tears to her eyes. She could not force herself to play the devil's advocate again. Instead, she continued as though he had not spoken.

"All the time we have spent together showed me the kind of man you were – you *are*. And still I failed to understand my feelings until I thought you betrothed to another."

Despite his own declared wish to look to the future first, the temptation was too strong.

"To whom?" he asked.

"Miss Wyatt."

"Miss Wyatt! Why would you think so?"

Elizabeth had no wish to mention Miss Bingley's role in the affair, so she ignored the question, but wistfully said:

"When Miss Wyatt called in Berkeley Square and you seemed to half-heartedly pay court to her, it troubled me. Fool that I was, I thought it felt unsettling and wrong merely because you deserved better…"

Darcy smiled, clearly touched by her revelations, and earnestly replied:

"I dread to think what I deserve, in truth. I know I do not deserve *you*. But I would make it my life's work to alter this. Elizabeth, marry me, I beg you!"

She could no longer bear it. With a broken sob, she wrenched her hand from his grasp to put her arm around his waist and bury her face into his shoulder.

"If we could leave the world behind, I would!" Elizabeth burst out in anguish, only to hear him exhale in something that, strangely, sounded like incommensurate relief.

He wrapped his arms around her and pressed his cheek against her brow.

"God bless you for this," he whispered and forcefully added, "Aye! Leave the world behind. We can. And so we shall."

Still ensconced in his tight embrace, Elizabeth glanced up to meet his eyes. She could not, not quite, he was too close, but she asked nevertheless:

"What are you saying?"

"How would you like to live in Cornwall, my love? Or Wales? Or perhaps Ireland?" Darcy asked, a warm smile tugging at the corner of his lips. "We might even consider Sardinia or Malta, but they are a tad too close for comfort to the trouble on the Continent. Or the New World, although I would be loath to take you quite so far away from your relations. Italy would have served a vast deal better. Florence or Naples, or a villa by Lake Como. Perhaps after the war, it cannot last forever. Unfortunately, anywhere in France might be out of the question even then. A pity, for Brittany is delightful. Very much like Cornwall, I am told, but for that incomprehensible dialect of theirs," he added, a hint of laughter in his gentle tones, which only served to confuse her further.

"Surely you are not in earnest!" she exclaimed, still trying to draw away so that she could see him better.

He would not allow it. He kept her close and bent his head to drop kisses on her furrowed brow, only desisting from his ministrations for long enough to whisper:

"I have never been more so."

"But what of Pemberley? What of your life here?"

By then his lips had trailed all the way down to hers and he silenced the shocked questions with a forceful kiss. He drew back by a fraction to say "*You* are my life", before returning to claim her lips again. Insistently. Compelling her to accept this madness.

She had not the slightest intention to comply. Her hands came up to push against his chest until she gained sufficient distance to stare at him as though he had lost his mind. In truth, she half-suspected that, if not lost, his mind must have been addled by their closeness. By the wild kisses that forced sanity aside to the point of him declaring that he would leave Pemberley for her!

She had not the slightest intention of allowing that either. She had found it very hard to countenance depriving Richard of the advantages he was born to, and they were nothing to what Darcy stood to lose, were she so callous as to accept his sacrifice.

She would not. Not in this lifetime!

"This cannot be. You know not what you are saying," Elizabeth observed sensibly, willing him back to *compos mentis*. "You cannot forsake your heritage, nor that of your unborn son."

He gave no sign of listening to reason.

He was still smiling when he said:

"Then let us pray for daughters. Elizabeth-Rose would have been a perfect name for one of them. A pity that your niece claimed it first. Do you imagine your sister would object if we chose the same?"

"Desist, I beg you!" Elizabeth admonished sternly. "I shall not say it is a cruel jest, for I know you are not jesting. But you cannot possibly consider such extreme measures either."

His countenance lost all gentle merriment and every hint of teasing as he replied calmly:

"This extreme measure I have already settled for, Elizabeth, when I determined I would never marry if I could not have you. So there would have been no direct heirs, and Pemberley would have been entrusted to Georgiana's children."

"I know," she sighed, to his vast surprise.

"You do?"

"Yes. Georgiana told me, earlier this morning."

"Oh. You see then that little is changed – in that respect, that is. Everything is miraculously changed for *me*, but those other plans need not be altered. Before long, Georgiana will marry, and hopefully she would go to a worthy man. They would have the guardianship of Pemberley together. The only difference is that they would not have to wait until my death – that is all."

"*All* ? " Elizabeth exclaimed, in equal measure horrified by what she was hearing and humbled by the depth of his love for her.

Horror prevailed, aided by the casual reference to his own death. A world without him would be barren, empty, devoid of all its purpose. As his life would be if he relinquished Pemberley. A sob broke through. She *had* to make him see it!

"You are not thinking straight. Today's events have tampered with your judgement."

"Elizabeth, pray let my judgement be my concern alone. From the very first days of our acquaintance I sat in judgement instead of courting you, and I paid a terrible price for it. After a year such as I had, there is nothing – *nothing*, do you hear? – that I would not do to be with you!"

"And how do you imagine I could live with myself, were you to take this dreadful step for me?" she burst out in excruciating guilt, only to find her hand raised from his chest and brought to rest with her palm against his cheek.

For all her inner turmoil over the enormity of his suggestion, she could not fail to respond to the exquisite sensation of clean-shaven skin, smooth and soft over the hard jaw, the tingling in her fingertips building into a quiver when he pressed his lips on her wrist, to warm her flesh and her blood with his intense whisper:

"I can only beg you would be willing to, my love. Because I cannot face living without *you*."

Before her own treacherous response to his affecting touch could lure her further into outright madness, she drew her hand from his grasp and wrenched herself from his embrace. She stood, putting distance between them, yet her efforts were for naught. He instantly followed to gather her into his arms again as he entreated fervently, persuasively.

"It need not be so. You can have anything you wish. We can seclude ourselves at Pemberley instead. See no one but our tenants. Live in our little world – together. There or elsewhere. Elizabeth, this is all I ask for. All I need is you!"

He kissed her with a passion bordering on desperation, then burst out, more fiercely than ever:

"You *must* leave me room to hope! Or, as God is my witness, by this time tomorrow I will have carried you off to Gretna Green and damn the consequences!"

She could never tell whether it was the accent of sheer agony in his tortured plea that finally broke through her defences, few that she had left. Scruples and twinges of her conscience – what chance had they to prevail over her deepest feelings, over his?

Perhaps she had instinctively known she would relent from the moment he had kissed her in the orangery. Even then, deep in her heart, she might have known that she would finish by following him wherever he would choose to lead her. In truth, there had never been another option, and resisting the utmost need of both their souls was a futile effort, doomed to failure from the very start.

As soon as she had regained enough sense to speak – or rather as soon as her lips could be employed for that ever so dull purpose – she shared this, her second epiphany, and her vow unconsciously echoed his:

"I *will* marry you. Follow you anywhere. And live with any consequences."

Not many words could have done justice to his explosive joy.

Not for a moment did Darcy stop to seek them.

Chapter 16

They were late for dinner. Not very late, but noticeably so. More mortifying still, Elizabeth feared everyone would notice her near-constant blushes – and her lips. She had no time to change, so she could not find reassurance in her mirror that they were not as visibly bruised and swollen as they felt. She sought it in the pier glasses that adorned the hall, but the fleeting glimpses were of no use at all, and she did not dare linger. The fact that Darcy understood her purpose and quietly whispered "Do not fret, you look lovely," as soon as he found the opportunity to safely do so, was of no use either. Quite the contrary, for it made her blush so fiercely that her father was moved to ask if she was unwell.

Upon reflection, she should have gratefully taken that excuse and retired to her chamber, but it would have been most unkind to Jane and Charles should she miss this, the first family dinner at Blakehill, nor could she bear the thought of secluding herself above-stairs, deprived of every chance of seeing *him*.

She could see him now across the dinner table, which brought its own difficulties. Doubtlessly Darcy was more skilled in the subtle art of dissimulation, given the full year he had had to practise. She could claim no such questionable advantage for herself, and her heart thumped so forcefully in her chest every time their eyes met that she thought her nearest companions would be apt to hear it.

The hours after dinner were a challenge in themselves. Her father, Charles and Mr Darcy did not linger over port and brandy, but joined the ladies a great deal sooner than Elizabeth expected, thus forcing her to seek a quicker resolution to an impossible conundrum: *how* was she to sit with him as though nothing had happened, pour his tea and speak of commonplaces, when all that she could think of was the too-short time she had spent in his arms?

His cool composure was a source of wonder and, truth be told, vexation and no little envy. How could he sit and placidly listen to Charles talking of pastures, sundry crops and coveys of partridges?

That he was not truly listening became clear to her only a little later, when her brother-in-law remained poised for an answer to his query regarding the deer park – and the answer never came.

"So Darcy, what is your opinion?" Mr Bingley impatiently prompted, and it was only then that his friend opened his lips to say, commendably smoothly:

"I fear I cannot say as yet. Perhaps we could discuss this on the morrow?"

"I daresay we could," Mr Bingley conceded with little satisfaction and went to offer his father-in-law another drink, leaving Darcy at his leisure to sit on the sofa, stare blankly into space and toy with his signet ring.

His countenance could only be described as stern, even when he glanced in her direction, but instead of wondering at it, Elizabeth was suddenly jolted into recognition. She had seen that mien oftentimes before. At Netherfield. At Hunsford. Dozens of times in Berkeley Square and in Charles Street. And it was only now, when she knew what she knew, that she could see it for what it truly was: a determined effort at caution and restraint.

Her heart went out to him at this stark reminder of what he had endured, and still did, for her sake. She all but winced, distraught at her blindness in assuming that the all too familiar reserve reflected his true nature.

His true nature had been revealed to her in the Greek temple earlier that day, and a shiver coursed through her at the delicious recollections. She shook her head in response to the unmitigated folly of having thought she knew how he would behave in his own home, on the misleading basis of the time spent with him in Berkeley Square. Another shiver followed, to grow into a strange quivering sensation building deep within her at the clear knowledge that a life with him would not be one of tame exchanges in a quiet parlour, but something on the par with the wild feverish craving in the temple.

"You are cold. Should you not sit closer to the fire?" she heard him say, and the mere sound of his deep voice worked on the strange quivering to turn it into the beginnings of a veritable tremor.

She was not cold. Not in the slightest. Nevertheless, she followed his suggestion and moved to the sofa he had indicated, to sit and watch him build up the fire for her. Large hands, with very long fingers, going about their business steadily, expertly, until the flames rose higher to cast a vivid glow over his handsome features and send his eyes sparkling, not unlike that very afternoon, when she was rendered breathless with his kisses. When the same hands had caressed her. Clung to her.

Lydia's loud laughter coming from somewhere behind broke the exquisite spell, but Elizabeth did not turn to look towards the table where her youngest sister was sitting with Kitty and Georgiana, whom she had cajoled into a game of cards. Instead, her steady gaze remained fixed on Darcy's crouched form until, alerted to her scrutiny, he turned to her.

The stern reserve was gone. His eyes burned quite as brightly as the nearby fire, kindling a matching one in her. His lips curled into the smile that she adored and had not seen often. She returned it, half-wondering if the wild beatings of her heart were about to bounce her garnet cross clear off her chest, but would not look away when she saw him coming to sit beside her.

The privacy was illusory, as she knew full well, and she dearly hoped the little that they were allowed would not be too soon interrupted. She cast a surreptitious glance over her shoulder and reassured herself that her relations were otherwise engaged: the youngest ones with their game of cards; Mary teasing a rather mournful tune out of the pianoforte; her father in conversation with his son-in-law and her mamma instructing Jane on the finer points of motherhood.

Elizabeth smiled in silent gratitude and turned back in her seat, only to notice his hand coming to rest in the narrow space between them, palm up – a clear invitation. On rash impulse, she did not resist it. She placed her hand in his, thrilling at the touch – reckless and deliciously forbidden – and could not even think of trying to suppress the gasp when his thumb came to draw tight circles into her tingling palm.

"Perhaps I should commend you on your talent for dissimulation," she whispered, and was shocked to hear how uneven her voice sounded. Regardless, she continued: "You seem to master that skill far better than I."

His low throaty chuckle raised another thrill.

"You are mistaken. I envy your composure."

"And I yours."

"*Mine?* Mine is in tatters. Even Bingley, the most unobservant man I know, noticed that I was distracted. Thankfully he cannot be so much of a mind-reader to know that while he was talking of his pheasants I could only think of kissing you."

"Partridges," she corrected, in a vain effort to resort to archness as the sole means to temper her wild reaction to his voice – and his words.

"Pardon?"

"He was talking of partridges, I think. Or perhaps deer."

Darcy's smile widened.

"Seeing as they are so easily confused, I daresay we are both doing rather well to tell the difference," he teased, then sobered. "Would you like me to leave tomorrow?"

Shocked by the suggestion as well as by the sudden transition from one thing to another, she shot him a glance of disbelief.

"Why would you say that?"

"I thought it might be easier for you if I did," he quietly remarked, but Elizabeth vehemently shook her head.

"Not easier. Never that!"

It might be wiser and doubtlessly safer, but not easier, not by a fair margin. As though he had read her mind, he spoke again, only to shock her further.

"Then I should speak to your father."

"Goodness, no!" Elizabeth shot back, almost forgetting about the need to whisper.

"And why not?"

"First I must write… to Richard," she finished with difficulty.

Darcy sighed.

"It would be several weeks at least until a letter reaches him. Surely you do not suggest we keep your father in the dark for as long as that."

"No. But in any case, it is *my* place to inform him."

"Whereas I think 'tis mine."

"Why?"

"Because it will be me that his ire will and should be directed at."

"Ire?"

"I should imagine so. Elizabeth," he added, interrupting what would have been a protest, "your father will be concerned for you. He must be reassured that you will be protected from every hint of scandal."

She shrugged.

"Society has seen worse. Men, married or otherwise, eloping with other gentlemen's wives. Lord Paget and Lady Charlotte Wellesley, or his younger brother and Lady Boringdon, for instance. Your cousin's hurt feelings are my sole concern. Compared to *that*, do you imagine that the malicious tongues of busybodies matter one jot to me?"

"Malice would matter to your father. As it should. As it does to me on your behalf."

"I thought we were to seclude ourselves at Pemberley and see no one but your tenants."

"Our tenants, by then," he corrected with a smile. "But aye, this is one of the possibilities that should be presented to your father."

She arched a brow.

"It is the only one worthy of consideration. The other is sheer insanity, and my father could hardly countenance my marrying a man who is out of his wits."

Yet again, he chuckled softly.

"I fear he must find a way to reconcile himself to that. My wits are beyond redemption, and I would not wish them otherwise," he said in a low feeling voice, which grew solemn when he added, "Write your letter, Elizabeth, and then let us deal honestly with your father."

She released a long sigh.

"I shall write it tonight."

Her hand was clasped in gratitude, or perhaps tender reassurance, then to her disappointment it was hastily released. Elizabeth could not fathom why, until she understood that his hearing must have been sharper than hers and his disparaged wits more focused, so he must have already caught the sound of approaching footsteps.

Vexed with her inability to control her blushes, she drew her hand back from its very conspicuous place on the sofa to return it to her lap before they were joined by whoever was coming. She did not turn to look, but the sound of voices told her it was Mr Bingley and her father, when she heard the latter say:

"Nothing like a roaring fire on a nippy night, eh, Bingley? I should be happy to retire to the fireside with your excellent brandy and perhaps a game of chess, if you would indulge me."

But his son-in-law laughed in response.

"From what Jane said of your prowess, I fear I shall disappoint. You would find a much worthier opponent in Darcy here. What say you, Darcy? Would you pit your skills against Mr Bennet?"

"It will be my pleasure," his friend replied and stood, ceding his place to Elizabeth's father.

Bingley rubbed his hands.

"Let me fetch the chess set," he offered and walked off to do so, while Darcy drew another chair and reached to place a small oval table between himself and the older gentleman.

The set was duly brought, the pieces laid out and, with a blissful smile Elizabeth leaned back in her seat to watch them. God willing, she would see them thus in many years to come. It was a very happy thought, and her warm glance moved back and forth from one beloved man to the other. Her father's white hair glowing in the firelight, his dear heavily-lined face showing his enjoyment of the challenge. And then the other, treasured in a very different way, on whom her gaze lingered at leisure. Dark eyes fixed on the chessboard. Dark hair, as ever adorably unruly. One elbow on his knee, his chin resting on his thumb and his fingers curled before his mouth – all but his forefinger, that reached up to the bridge of his nose, absent-mindedly tapping as he pondered his next move.

Her father's satisfied "Ha!" when he took the unwisely placed rook with his bishop forcefully reminded her that, even when they were looking elsewhere, some people were intensely aware that they were being watched. So, for Mr Darcy's sake and to preserve his reputation as a worthy opponent, Elizabeth smoothed her skirts and said lightly as she stood:

"I should leave you to your game."

"No need, Lizzy," her father protested. "I enjoy having you near."

Mr Darcy was not at liberty to say the same but she could not fail to read it in his eyes, along with a diverted twinkle showing he had fully understood her reasons, when he rose from his seat to offer a deep bow.

The letter was written, after three long hours spent in the sitting room adjoining her bedchamber. She had retired there without even changing for the night, as soon as she and Mary, along with many of the others, had made their way above-stairs to their quarters. Mary was surprised but, unlike their younger sisters, she was not given to querying and pestering, so Elizabeth was left to her dreadfully painful task.

It was done now, tearfully and with a heavy heart. Inadequately perhaps, but there never was a way to convey such a message adequately. The uneven lines would have to do, and before she could change her mind and strive to alter them for the sixth time, Elizabeth folded and sealed the letter.

She shivered, and not just for cold, although the room had grown quite chilly. She stood and, wrapping her shawl closer, she reached for the letter and the solitary candle.

The house was dark and still as she made her way down the wide staircase to the great hall where, on a large veneered cabinet, she had previously espied the salver which Jane and Charles had used at Netherfield for letters waiting to be sent.

The faint glow of the candle revealed it was still employed for the same purpose, for several letters lay there, the uppermost in Mr Bingley's unmistakable hand. Gingerly, with one last rueful stroke of her fingers over the cream-coloured paper, Elizabeth added her small wretched offering to the pile.

Her eyes stinging, she turned to retrace her steps, but did not get far. Arrested in her tracks by the strip of light that suddenly appeared and widened at her feet, Elizabeth glanced towards the bright rectangle that now stood in place of the library door, framing a silhouette that was most familiar.

She could not see his face, light shone from behind him, but Elizabeth reasonably assumed him as affected as herself by the encounter, unsought and unexpected as it was. The very air between them grew charged, across the vast dark hallway, and even more so when he slowly walked towards her.

"I wrote the letter," Elizabeth brought herself to say, with a conscious gesture towards the salver on the cabinet behind her, and she saw him nod.

He was already at her side by the time he spoke to quietly offer:

"Would you like me to ride out and post it on the morrow?"

"I... Would you?"

"Of course."

"I thank you. Yes, pray do."

Nothing else was said as they went together to retrieve the letter. Elizabeth did so and placed it in his hand, her eyes drawn to his face, so near. His fingers curled over the paper and over her own, yet he did not bend his head to kiss her, and this time she was glad. Not just for fear of being seen by some servant or sleepless relation, but because it would have felt uncomfortable and profoundly wrong, with the letter to Richard in their joined hands – between them.

Uncannily attuned to her feelings, Darcy let her fingers slip from under his and stepped aside to let her pass. She did, with a soft "Good night," and hurried above-stairs, her senses reeling with the astounding changes a mere day had wrought, his parting words treasured all the way – a promise of the joy to come and soothing comfort against all guilt and sorrow.

"Good night, my love. Sleep well, and God bless you."

❧❧ ❧❧

Long before the new family at Blakehill gathered to sit down for breakfast the following morning, a lone rider left the stables to follow directions into the nearby village, whence a letter would travel to the Peninsula. The second one in Elizabeth's hand that he had been entrusted to send in that particular direction. Doubtlessly – and thankfully – very different from the first.

The letter began its very long journey later on that day, at the lightning speed of the London mail coach. And, unbeknownst to all concerned, it would rush past its addressee on the very busy Great North Road a few miles beyond Highgate.

Chapter 17

"You were going to propose the very next day?" Elizabeth exclaimed, overcome with compassion.

The opportunity to return in safety to their little sanctuary had been long in coming – an entire day – but on the second morning after their arrival to Blakehill their relations had declared their wish to drive to Ashbourne, the nearest market town. Even Mr Bennet had allowed himself to be persuaded and it was only Jane who chose to stay at home rather than spend the day fifteen miles away from her baby daughter.

Mr Bingley was eager to explore the area and his mother-in-law scarcely less so. As for Georgiana, she was rather disappointed that neither her brother nor her two closest friends would be of the party, but was enticed to go nevertheless. Lately she had begun to find enjoyment in chats with Mary about music and, truth be told, Kitty's society was rather pleasing too – whenever Lydia was not around to shock her with some unguarded comment – so if Elizabeth and Jane chose to remain behind, then at least she might be able to find amusement in an outing with the others.

Now that she knew the younger Miss Bennets better, she could only laugh at herself for thinking that her brother might find happiness with one of them. They were pleasant girls – well, at least two of them were – but clearly not the sort that would attract his interest. She dearly hoped that one day someone would, regardless of his firmly declared intention not to marry. She did not quite regret her impulse of sharing that private conversation with Elizabeth, although goodness knows what her brother might say if he ever learned of it.

Little did she know that he already had – nor that, at the same point in time, her brother and Elizabeth were having their own private conversation.

They had retraced their steps to their Greek temple, leaving Jane happily engaged with her little daughter and, in the exquisite privacy of a leisurely morning, when they would not be needed back at the house for a fair while, a vast deal more than feverish kisses was finally shared.

The revelation that he was intending to propose and Richard beat him to it by mere hours saddened and perplexed her with the implications. She would have refused him, fool that she was! Would they still have found their way to each other? Who knows? But one thing was certain: he had been through hell and back since then.

A bitter laugh cut her ruminations short.

"Aye. I was busily building castles in Spain, when Richard came in to tell me that you were engaged."

His hand, tightly clasped between both of hers, was brought to rest against her cheek, then to her lips. She said nothing. Her wistful gaze conveyed everything.

He lightly brushed his thumb over her chin.

"I deserve none of your compassion, my love," he whispered. "Indeed I would have received none if I had the opportunity to address you. You said you would have refused me," he explained, in response to her puzzled glance, and before she could interrupt with more self-recriminations, Darcy silenced her with a kiss. "Perhaps I should tell you now what I would have said, and then you will reproach yourself no longer on that score, and find that a refusal would have been fully justified," he added, his current happiness enabling him to look back complacently at former sorrows and even go as far as laughing at himself.

"Surely you could not have said anything so very bad."

"Oh, aye. The most ungentlemanlike offer in history – past, present or future."

"This is most intriguing. Perhaps I should hear it," Elizabeth teased, thoroughly enchanted with his strange good-humour.

Darcy put an arm around her and drew her very close.

"Perhaps you will, but only if you promise to marry me regardless," he smiled, then sobered. "And also to kindly bear in mind the only reason why I am willing to share this."

She reached to drop a light kiss on his cheek.

"You have my word. On both these counts."

"I shall hold you to it. Very well. A gentlemanlike man would have expressed his ardent admiration and regard and concluded promptly with asking for the honour of the lady's hand. He most certainly would not have dwelt on his lengthy struggles to conquer his attachment because of family obligations and the disparity in their respective stations," Darcy said tentatively and fell silent, waiting for her response.

He was not kept waiting long.

"Perhaps the second part would have done little to recommend his suit, especially given the lady's ill-supported prejudices, but truth be told, his scruples were natural and just. There *is* a great disparity in their respective stations. Of which the headstrong lady is well aware now. More than she ever was in the early days of their acquaintance."

"Elizabeth, this is nothing," he felt compelled to interrupt. "Nothing but shallow trappings."

She shook her head.

"Not so. And there is more, of course. Some of the lady's relations have little understanding of propriety and would very likely be a source of deep mortification to both, oftentimes in the future."

"No more than mine," Darcy replied promptly. "Mine add malice to the mix."

"And you defended me against their malice more staunchly than anyone," she exclaimed, forgetting or disdaining to continue playing the little game of speaking as though of a third party. "*No man of sense and feeling would need to have his hand forced into marrying Miss Bennet. She is the very best that anyone could hope for,*" she quoted, very quietly.

His first response was a shocked intake of breath.

"You heard?"

"Every word. Eavesdropping is dreadfully unladylike. What must you think of me?" she teased, but the playfulness was gone when she earnestly added, "Or indeed of my obtuseness in thinking that it was Richard you were championing, to both Lady Langthorne and Lord Morton."

"Morton!" Darcy exclaimed in horror. "Good Lord! What else have you heard?"

"His slander," she owned, with a conscious blush.

"When? Where?"

"At Netherfield."

"Ah…"

"Why? Was there more?"

"There was…" he brought himself to say, knowing that he had to, lest she hear it later from the man himself. "At the theatre. He noticed I was staring at you throughout the performance. Taunted me with it. And on that occasion I could not even have the satisfaction of planting him another facer. For your sake, I could not make our conflict public. I could not retaliate. Not then."

The livid anger in his voice and the underlying threat in the last two words filled her with the greatest terror.

"You must promise me you never will!" Elizabeth urged breathlessly, her hands coming up to clasp his shoulders. "Promise me there will be no more talk of sending seconds!"

"Elizabeth, insults to me I might let pass, but I will not allow insults to *you*."

"And I will not lose you at the hands of that repulsive man!"

"He does not stand a chance," Darcy scoffed.

"Even so, you *must* promise me."

"Elizabeth— "

"No! You said there is nothing you would not do to be with me."

Darcy sighed.

"Are you planning to make a habit of using my own words against me?"

She smiled to see him mellowing.

"Indeed I am. You should consider yourself warned."

"Duly noted," he smiled back.

If he was sufficiently unwise to hope that a long kiss might put an end to this discussion, she was quick to disabuse him of that notion as soon as she could speak again.

"Your word?" she pleaded, reaching to hold his face between her palms.

He leaned to rest his brow on hers.

"You have it," he finally gave in, knowing full well that one day he might come to regret this promise but, judging by her warm response, it would not be today.

⋙⋘

The lengthening shadows of the pine trees gave stern warning of the advancing hours, and Darcy reluctantly reached to consult his pocket watch.

"We should return. Your sister must be wondering what has become of us and the others will not be out for a great deal longer."

Ensconced in his arms with her head on his shoulder, Elizabeth gave a murmur of assent, but did not stir. Neither did he. A rather uncomfortable wooden bench in a temple-shaped garden folly had unsurprisingly become his favourite place in the entire world. Perhaps he should have a matching one built beyond the lake at Pemberley, he thought with a smile. Elizabeth would like that.

He dropped a light kiss on her brow.

"When can I speak to your father?" he asked, idly stroking the nape of her neck.

"Pray let me be the one to tell him."

"When?"

"Soon."

"When?"

She raised her head to glare at him and it was difficult to tell whether or not she was in earnest.

"You can be quite vexing when you set your mind to it."

"So I have been told," Darcy smiled, but soon his voice became urgent and persuasive. "My love, it would not do for him to learn of it in some roundabout manner."

"I know," she said dejectedly. "But once everything is brought into the open there would be an end to… this," she added with a small gesture around them. "Not to mention that the mere thought of seeing you exposed to my mother's raptures— "

"It matters not, Elizabeth," Darcy interjected. "Besides, I am quite certain that, for a while at least, we can rely on your father's discretion."

"It is not merely he who ought to know. Once he does, I would very much like to confide in Jane. And what of your own sister? Goodness, what will she think of me! She will be shocked and grieved on Richard's behalf— "

"And thrilled on mine."

"Yes. But it would pain her deeply, as it does me and doubtlessly you as well, to think that we might never see him once he learns that the man whom he values most is in love with his betrothed."

An uncomfortable silence followed, until Darcy brought himself to voice the truth.

"He knows that already," he said quietly.

Elizabeth gasped.

"Good Lord! How?"

"It… came out while he was recovering in Berkeley Square. By sheer accident," he added swiftly in response to her look of horror mingled with reproach. "Of course I would not have told him while he was— Not *then*. Not ever. I made every effort to keep it from him – from you. I did not know he was awake when— "

"When?" she gently prompted and, with great difficulty, Darcy told her of his bedside promise and the wrenching and unwise adieu that his cousin had witnessed.

Her heart broke anew for the two men she cared for, in very different ways – the worthiest men of her acquaintance – as she wished for the hundredth time that she was not forced to deal one the most dreadful blow in order to be happy with the other. Who could have known what misery would spring from a casual slight at a small country-town assembly?

"We must return," Darcy reluctantly advised once more and this time she obeyed, but not before reaching to press her lips on his again, for one last sweet indulgence that would have to sustain them both for a long time to come.

It did not subdue the yearning. Quite the opposite, in fact. Nevertheless, they finally drew apart and stood to walk back to the house arm in arm, to face the world – together.

⁂

"What a glorious day!" Jane exclaimed over the breakfast table the following morning. "So warm and sunny. I could think myself in June. I believe today we should have a picnic," she declared, to be met with warm approbation from most quarters, although not a vast deal from Mrs Bennet.

"The ground will be damp," the lady observed, but Jane's enthusiasm would not be curbed.

"Not so much now. It has not rained in days. And besides we can lay down several layers of rugs and sit on cushions. Or a chair can be brought for you, Mamma. I know just the spot. That lovely stretch of lawn by the garden entrance— ”

“I could suggest another,” Georgiana intervened, “but it is much further from the house, so you might find it a long way to take Lizzy-Rose— ”

“Surely you do not aim to keep the babe out of doors for the duration!” Mrs Bennet admonished, making her son-in-law discreetly roll his eyes.

He did not intervene, for Jane was quick to do so.

“The sun will do her good. What spot were you thinking of, Georgiana?”

“There is this lovely glade full of daffodils, down that path yonder. By a small Greek temple. Has anyone seen it?”

“Yes,” said Darcy.

“No,” Elizabeth said at the same time, blushing for a reason Georgiana could not fathom.

“Is it not delightful?” she enthused. “Elizabeth, you would love it. I wonder that you did not show her it, Brother. I saw you walking together from that very direction.”

Darcy did not answer, but settled a long meaningful look on Elizabeth, before pointedly glancing at her father. She sighed and squared her shoulders.

“Yes. I believe I shall. Perhaps tomorrow?” she hesitantly said.

Darcy gave a reluctant nod, and it was only Georgiana who spoke up to answer the question she thought was for herself alone.

“Of course. It is a very pleasant walk. I cannot tell how long exactly, but I believe the other day it took Kitty, Lydia and myself about an hour to stroll to the temple and back,” she added, not noticing her brother’s eyes widening in something very much like horror. “Perhaps next time the pair of you would care to join us.”

“Yes. Tomorrow!” came Elizabeth’s oddly firm reply.

༺ ༻

The last ten miles were the very worst. Even more frustrating than arriving at Longbourn after long days of travel, to find it shuttered and learn from dear old Hill that the entire family had joined the Netherfield party on their journey to their new abode in Staffordshire.

Thankfully she was able to give him clear directions and even offered to put him up for the night, bless her kind soul. But the warm welcoming house felt barren and empty without Elizabeth within its walls, so he put up at the *Red Lion* in Meryton instead and began his journey at first light.

Upon reflection, he would have been better advised to board the *Stamford Regent* or any of the other coaches heading north, rather than ride all the way to Staffordshire. Or maybe not. Much as the ride exhausted and perhaps delayed him, it was better than sitting in some godforsaken carriage and battling for hours with his impatience to see her.

Ever since Doña Teresa's eye-opening admonitions, waiting for leave to return to England had been sheer torture. Likewise the seemingly endless journey back, when it was finally granted.

Not long now. Ten more blasted miles, and he would be at Blakehill. See her. And beg her forgiveness for the self-centred blindness of putting his views above her own. Of not being prepared to accept that she *would* be happy to share whatever he had to offer – eat bread at his table rather than the fatted calf at Darcy's, as Doña Teresa had so aptly put it.

His tired and dusty countenance softening into a smile, Colonel Fitzwilliam dug his heels into the horse's flanks, spurring him on to cover the last ten wretched miles.

♣ ♣

"The family is picnicking on the lawn, Sir," Bingley's butler advised as soon as he had taken his hat and gloves. "Pray let me fetch my master."

"Do not trouble him. I should be pleased to join them."

"Of course. This way, Colonel," the butler indicated and Fitzwilliam followed him through the silent house.

The sound of merry voices reached him as soon as they gained the corridor that led to the garden door, and it hastened his steps until he easily overtook the ageing butler.

"I thank you, I can announce myself," he cast over his shoulder, not stopping to see the man halting in his tracks to bow in acquiescence, then make an about-turn to let him have his way.

The gleeful voices, he soon came to see, were Kitty's, Lydia's and Georgiana's, merrily engaged in a game of sticks-and-quoits. His searching glance swept eagerly over the others. Mr Bennet and Mary in garden chairs, reading. Mrs Bennet in another, talking to Jane who was sitting on a cushion, Bingley's head in her lap. And at last he found her, sitting on a rug, a bundle of creamy lace and linen in her arms. Bingley's new daughter, he assumed, whose arrival Elizabeth had announced in her last letter to reach him.

Fitzwilliam stopped in the doorway under garlands of climbing rose and honeysuckle to take in the glorious picture she presented. Rosy-cheeked and more beautiful than ever. More enchanting than ever, in that maternal pose. Glowing with love and laughter, she bent her head into the bundle of lace to kiss a chubby little face.

A delighted squeal emerged from her wriggling burden, as did an arm, to wave with energy and reach out until the tiny fingers got hold of the curls above her ear and pulled this way and that, with no sign of ever aiming to let go.

"Lizzy-Rose, that simply will not do. You are hurting your aunt," came a mild admonition, in a voice which he easily recognised as Darcy's.

A further step revealed him, beyond some shrub or other, that had previously narrowed Fitzwilliam's field of vision. Free of such encumbrance, he had no difficulty in seeing Darcy now, as he reached to disentangle the determined little fist from Elizabeth's hair, to be thanked with a blush, a long gaze and the warmest smile.

"Here. Let me hold her. She cannot do quite as much damage in my hair," he said and Elizabeth laughingly complied, edging closer to pass the squirming bundle into her companion's waiting arms.

"I daresay your hair is safe, but she will wreak havoc with your neckcloth," Elizabeth cheerfully warned.

As though on cue, the little fingers shot unerringly in the very direction she had mentioned and, with a soft chuckle, Elizabeth reached for them before they could take a firmer hold. Unthinkingly, she smoothed the disturbed folds with the back of her hand and leaned in to delight her niece with the age-old game of playfully catching and kissing each tiny fingertip, her head and Darcy's almost touching over the babe he held between them.

"Nay, let her have her fun," Darcy replied in unconcern – his fastidious cousin Darcy, never before known to be at ease with children of any parentage or age, let alone bounce babies on his knee or let them have their way with his impeccable cravat.

Fitzwilliam's eyes narrowed and a knot formed in his jaw at the profoundly domestic picture – wrong in every way, yet horribly easy to mistake for a family scene.

That was bad enough and his chest tightened at the sight, and no less at their laughing ease in each other's presence. There was worse to come. Georgiana spotted him in the doorway and dropped her sticks and the beribboned circle to run to him, calling excitedly:

"Richard! Elizabeth, 'tis *Richard!*"

Whatever the last few seconds might have led him to fearfully expect, the response he witnessed was staggeringly worse. Instead of an outburst of joy, his betrothed gave a violent start at the intelligence of his sudden arrival. Under his very eyes, the countenance he had come all the way from the Peninsula to see instantly altered from delighted laughter into blanching confusion. She swiftly exchanged a glance with Darcy and, with the best will in the world, that glance could only be described as shock. Most certainly *not* relief or pleasure. Then, with great difficulty, her lips curled into a dreadfully conscious smile. And *that* was not the sort of welcome he had travelled nine hundred and forty-three miles for!

♦♦♦

So the tables had turned. How? When? He suppressed a snort. There must have been plenty of time for Darcy to find a way to carry the day, as he always did. Somehow or other, sooner or later, matters *always* had a way of settling to his advantage.

Doubtlessly before too long he would receive a confirmation, but the drastic change in Elizabeth's countenance when she had been alerted to his presence told its own story. As did the other swift glance passing between her and Darcy, when Mr Bennet cast his book aside and stood to greet him with a cheerfully spoken "Welcome, Son! Come. Come and join us."

Naturally, he declined.

"Forgive me. I have had a dusty ride. I should change first. I am not fit to be seen."

"And we care nothing for it," Bingley retorted brightly, springing to his feet to greet him too.

The others followed suit. Darcy long-faced and looking as guilty as the very devil – to someone who knew him well, at least. As for Elizabeth, she sought to meet his eyes for longer than three seconds, only to blush and fail abysmally.

It was this more than anything that made him insist on retiring to change. He had his way and that eminently decent chap, Bingley, took him up himself and sent for his man to come and assist him.

He did not need assistance and certainly not company, so as soon as Bingley's valet had removed his coat and finished brushing it, Fitzwilliam told him that he required nothing more than a pitcher of cold water and his belongings brought from his saddlebags.

They were duly fetched and Bingley's man was too well trained to show surprise at finding that his master's visitor travelled light, with just the bare necessities and a limited wardrobe.

The valet offered to lay out fresh garments for him, but he was thanked and sent away. With a bow he obliged, leaving the self-sufficient guest to remove his own apparel, strip to his waist and go to the washstand to throw fistfuls of cold water on himself, then stand there, gripping the edges of the marble top, to stare unseeing beyond his own reflection in the looking glass. That is, until a determined knock made him straighten with an oath.

"Come!" he called, grabbing a towel to furiously rub at his face and hair.

He had a very strong suspicion just who the visitor might be, and he was not mistaken. Darcy walked in and closed the door.

Fitzwilliam eyed him briefly over the crumpled cloth, then resumed drying himself with renewed energy. Neither spoke and Fitzwilliam went about his business, rightly assuming that his cousin was at pains to choose his words.

He scowled. Let him stew!

He would be damned before he opened his lips and made it easier for him, Fitzwilliam fumed and balled the towel to throw it on a chair in a petulant manner he might have regretted, if he could have brought himself to care.

He reached for a fresh shirt and shook it to unfold it. He thrust an arm in, then the other, and pulled it forcefully over his head, only to emerge from folds of rather crumpled linen to discover that Darcy's eyes were fixed on him. And then his cousin found some words at last – not many.

"Richard, I am truly sorry."

"Are you! What for?" Fitzwilliam retorted crisply as he tucked his shirt into his breeches and brought the braces to fall on his shoulders with a snap.

The other drew a deep breath and said simply.

"She had a change of heart."

"About what?"

"About which one of us she wishes to marry."

"How frightfully convenient for you."

"Cousin, this is not— "

"Not what you wanted? Pray do not make me laugh! I might split my sides and this is the only clean shirt I have with me at present. Unless of course you were about to say this is not fair, in which case I can only wonder at your having the gall to talk."

Darcy made no answer. With a frustrated oath, Fitzwilliam began tightening his cuffs.

"Let me help," Darcy offered, only to be fixed with a withering stare, before his cousin returned to his cuffs again.

"She had a change of heart, you say," he burst out eventually. "How?"

"I know not. Time… Circumstances…"

"Your earnest endeavours…" Fitzwilliam sarcastically continued the hesitant enumeration.

"No! I thought you knew me better than that."

"Aye. I thought so too."

From his own side of the room, Darcy sighed.

"I shall not say you are being unfair. I can imagine why you would not wish to hear it. Think of me what you will. I only beg you would be kind to her. She is waiting in the sitting room across the hall to speak to you and… she is dreadfully distressed already."

"I do not doubt you will be happy to supply the shoulder she can cry on," Fitzwilliam was compelled to acidly observe.

"Cousin, if throwing punches might give you a modicum of satisfaction then… here I am," Darcy said, spreading his arms out in a gesture of both defeat and invitation. "Just do not make Elizabeth the target for your anger."

As though he had not spoken, Fitzwilliam turned his back and began fastening the collar of his shirt, so that he could tie his neckcloth. In the corner of the looking glass, he saw Darcy walking slowly to the door.

"Wait," he called and their eyes met, first in the glass and then across the wide bedchamber, when Fitzwilliam spun around to face his cousin. "So this is it, then? A slight change of bridegroom? Of which I was to learn from – what? A wedding invitation?" he burst out, his distemper fuelled by the reproachful glance Darcy had the audacity to cast him.

"She wrote you. She struggled with that letter ever since she understood how her sentiments have changed. It was posted last Friday."

Fitzwilliam gave a bitter laugh.

"A very recent change! Is this why you are here now? Because you fear it might still go the other way?"

Under Fitzwilliam's wary eyes, the reproachful glance twisted into compassion, before Darcy sought to rearrange his features into cautious blankness. But it was too late. Quite clearly, there was no fear in him in that regard. By fair means or foul, he was assured he had won.

Darcy must have read his comprehension, for he spoke again.

"She refused my hand. Repeatedly. On account of... what it would do to you. Her honourable choice would have been to stay away from both of us— "

"But you would not accept no for an answer."

"In my place, would *you?* "

"So what do you want now? My goddamned blessing?"

"Your understanding. Your kindness to her."

Unreasonable anger gripped him at Darcy's second intimation that he would be anything but kind to the woman he loved. Of course he would be! He did not blame *her.*

No, that was false. An empty claim at sainthood which was fooling no one, for at this point he felt anything but saintly, he inwardly scoffed. He did feel ill-used – how could he not? – and did blame her for it. But nowhere near as much as he blamed his cousin. For not offering first. For offering now.

And...

Beneath the anger, something stirred – and it was much harder to bear than the hurt and the overwhelming jealousy. His features tightening, Fitzwilliam bowed his head to the truth that could no longer be avoided. He could not blame her or anyone else anywhere near as much as he blamed himself.

He had walked right past his chance. Just as Darcy had, by not offering for her long before her visit into Kent. How frightfully ironic to find himself taking his cousin's place in the wretched, sinking boat! How galling to know that Darcy would not have had another chance had *he* grabbed his. Had he not wrestled for so long with his twisted scruples, by now Elizabeth would have been his wife. They might have been married for several months. Might have been married for a year. Happily married.

Until Elizabeth discovered she loved Darcy instead, a poisonous thought came to add fresh gall to the vile mix.

By rights, he should have derived some small measure of comfort from finding that at least they had not sunk into *that* circle of hell. Instead, the hideous image of Elizabeth married to him and longing for his cousin only served to fuel every violent distemper. Eyes glinting like cold steel, he ordered Darcy out.

Chapter 18

Fitzwilliam could not tell how long he took to brace himself for the encounter and smooth his countenance into a placidity he did not feel. It must have been a while. But when he finally brought himself to leave his chamber and cross the hallway to walk into the sitting room that Darcy had previously mentioned, he found them waiting there still. Pointedly apart – Elizabeth on a sofa, his cousin at the far end, by the window – yet their carefully maintained distance gave no satisfaction. Quite the contrary. It merely emphasised the issue.

His antagonism to Darcy thus rekindled, Fitzwilliam indicated the door with a dark glare and a raised brow and, with a sigh, the other most reluctantly complied. Another pleading look was sent his way as Darcy walked past him to the door, but Fitzwilliam pointedly ignored it.

His cousin put his pleading into words.

"Richard…"

"Just go!" he hissed and, thankfully for everyone concerned, Darcy had the good sense to cease goading him further and finally obeyed.

The door was closed from the other side, but Fitzwilliam stopped to assure himself of it. Unnecessarily. Just to gain another moment before confronting the excruciating task at hand.

With a steadying breath, he squared his shoulders and turned around, a smile pasted on his lips.

⋅ঙ৹ ৹৹⋅

He could do naught but walk up and down the deserted corridor, on the other side of the blasted door. Never too many steps away, striving to catch any sound of voices – and agonising when he detected none.

Fitzwilliam *would* be kind, or at the very least he would not be cruel. It was not his way. He might reasonably wish to skin *him* alive and would not grant a shred of reassurance, but he would not be cruel to *her*. Not purposely.

Yet, with extreme provocation, the very best men might struggle to act on the generous impulses that guided them under normal circumstances – and this was the worst of provocations. Likely too much, even for a good man's best nature.

Not that his own presence in the room would have improved matters, reason urged Darcy to acknowledge. On the contrary. But it was sheer torture to stand there – wait – do nothing. It was sheer hell to let her face this trial alone.

"Mr Darcy," a smooth voice broke through his distressing ruminations, and he spun around to find himself under the scrutiny of Mr Bennet's wary eyes.

Above them a brow arched, in an uncanny copy of Elizabeth's own look of cautious displeasure which, at a better time, might have brought amusement and perhaps even comfort. Not so now. With a gesture of authority, Mr Bennet indicated towards the other end of the long corridor, beyond the grand staircase.

"I would appreciate a word, Sir," he said, and it was a request rather than a civil invitation.

Darcy bowed.

"Of course. If I might be allowed a moment to wait for my cousin— "

"I would much rather you obliged me now," came the prompt retort and, his arm still outstretched, Mr Bennet stood there, waiting – an unyielding embodiment of the old adage warning it never rains but it pours.

Darcy had no option but to resignedly comply.

⁂

With the unconsciously firm step of an officer trained to do his duty, Fitzwilliam walked forth to claim a seat beside Elizabeth on the sofa. The forced smile in place, he fought against the devastating tide of recollections from earlier, happier days. From times of tender glances and bright, cheerful welcome.

There was no brightness in her now, just all-pervasive sadness. Worse still, she recoiled slightly, as though she fully expected he would choose to embrace her, as oftentimes before – and sought to avoid it. And pierced his heart in doing so.

Yet she was the one to bridge the gap he had left between them and reach to take his hands in hers. She did not speak and would not look up, which made it easier somehow for Fitzwilliam to raise her hands and bow his head to press them to his lips. Eyes closed, he remained thus. One last indulgence, one last moment of pretending all was as it should be – or one long effort to tug the steel out of a wound, before he could rise and fight again.

"Richard, there is something I must say," he heard her whisper brokenly.

And there it was. The signal he had dreaded, as clear as the bugle call. His head came up and he did not falter, despite the closeness and the mesmerising depth of large brown eyes.

"Pray allow me to speak first," Fitzwilliam said, quietly but firmly. "I have come to beg your forgiveness, Elizabeth," the lie rolled off his lips, more necessary than the deepest truth, "and ask you to release me from an engagement I can no longer honour. I must confess I have formed an attachment— "

He was not permitted to continue. Cold fingers were laid on his lips, and withdrawn just as swiftly, in what must have been sudden mortification at an intimate gesture that could no longer be allowed. Still, she would not let him speak but interjected, her cheeks awash with tears.

"Do not, I beg you!" a dejected plea burst forth. "I do not deserve this."

The words – strangely fitting to a legitimate reproach for what he had just said, had she believed him – left him in no misapprehension of her real meaning. Likewise she fully understood his purpose, as her further plea confirmed.

"I must take the blame for all my errors. I do not deserve— "

"Sh-sh," Fitzwilliam cut her painful self-recriminations short.

He clasped her hand, aching to hold her.

She deserved the world. He had always thought so. Still did. And the last, possibly the *only* gift that was in his power to give was this: an absolution.

He gently ran his thumb over her knuckles, one by one.

"I should not have left," he said simply, for better or for worse relinquishing every disguise, every pretence. "Not as I did. Not when I did. But in truth, I was the only one of us who was at liberty to just stand up and go. And I still am the only one who can."

⁓༄ ༄⁓

"So, Mr Darcy," Mr Bennet began as soon as they were assured of some privacy and the door was firmly closed behind them. "I came above-stairs to find my daughter – Elizabeth, that is," he archly and unnecessarily clarified, "and discover, amongst other things, just why she looked so stricken when she made her way into the house. Not the habitual response to the arrival of one's intended, I must say. But seeing as you seemed so eager to escort her in and offer reassurance, I am inclined to think you might be able to enlighten me in her absence," he prompted, a stern look in his eyes.

Darcy met it squarely – and plunged in.

"I am, Sir. The reason for E— Miss Bennet's discomfort is that she feels she must break her engagement to my cousin. I can only assume she is doing so as we speak."

"Is she, by Jove!" the older gentleman replied with little surprise and a hint of displeasure.

"Yes, Sir. She has agreed to marry me."

The displeasure clearly manifest now, Mr Bennet queried:

"And what makes you believe I would entrust my daughter's happiness to a man who would deal so dishonestly with his own cousin? His *favourite* cousin, I might add," he emphasised, with no little sarcasm.

Pointing out that Elizabeth would soon be of age, if she was not already, was not the way to mend his bridges with her father, so Darcy forbore to say anything of the sort. Instead, he replied wistfully:

"I can see why it would appear so. Yet I assure you there was no dishonesty. Just my misfortune that my cousin happened to propose a day before I would have."

Mr Bennet's eyes widened in shock.

"Are you telling me that my daughter had spent days – weeks – under your roof while you were so far from an indifferent third party?"

"As you are well aware, it could not be helped," Darcy interjected, then added firmly, "And I am hoping your sense of justice will allow that I have kept my distance."

The only answer was a muted "Hm!", before the searching eyes came to bore again into Darcy's.

"Did Lizzy know of this?"

"Not then. Fitzwilliam and I agreed this cross was for us to bear, not her."

The reply only served to confound his companion further.

"Your cousin *knew?* "

"Ever since November. But your daughter was only told three days ago, when I learned that her sentiments have changed."

"How?"

His cheeks suddenly hot, Darcy surmised that he was blushing. Vexingly, there was nothing he could do about it, other than pretend he had misunderstood the question.

"Only your daughter can explain it, Sir. I bless my fortunes for the change, but as yet I do not understand it."

"And your cousin? Is he blessing his fortunes too?"

The ill-tempered query clearly came without the expectation of an answer, and Darcy gave none. But a few moments later he felt compelled to add, in an endeavour to break the awkward silence:

"Miss Bennet intended to confide in you on the morrow— "

"But matters got out of hand," Mr Bennet impatiently interjected. "And now what is to be done about the other matters?"

"Sir?"

"Broken promises, Mr Darcy! And malicious gossip. Or do you imagine it will not be said of my daughter that she has transferred her affections to the highest bidder?"

The blunt remark stung, for there was a strong risk of meeting with such crass assumptions in the future. This, more than anything, made Darcy sound harsher than intended.

"Dogs would bark, Sir, and only fools would deign to listen. We are no fools, Elizabeth and I."

"Elizabeth, is it?" Mr Bennet was swift to censure the ill-timed informality.

"Miss Bennet," Darcy conceded him the point.

"What of your family's opinion?"

Rightly assuming that the conversation would not be served by a full disclosure as to why his most vocal relations would be pleased rather than disappointed, Darcy abridged his reply accordingly.

"They are in no position to complain."

"Except your cousin," Mr Bennet observed sternly, and Darcy nodded.

"Except him."

"And what is your solution for that thorny issue?"

"Frankly, Mr Bennet, I have none," Darcy replied, steadily looking the other in the eye. "But between the three of us, one will be found. In time."

"You seem overly confident," Mr Bennet grumbled.

"I have to be. Your daughter is my prime concern. If she is happy, then everything will fall into place."

"And if she is not?"

"She will be. And I give you my word that I shall do all I can to ensure it."

From their heavily-lined sockets, dark eyes – the very same shade as Elizabeth's – assessed him in silence. After a long time, uncomfortably long, Mr Bennet cleared his voice.

"Mr Darcy, until this very morning you have given me no reason to think ill of you or doubt your word. Quite the opposite, if I may say so. I would be pleased to return to that frame of mind. I hope you will give me no cause to regret it."

"I thank you for your goodwill and trust, Sir."

"Yes, well. If you are Lizzy's choice, you may have both. Tread with care and see you do not lose them. I do not form a good opinion lightly, nor am I hasty to withdraw it, but you should be warned that once lost, 'tis lost forever."

A brief smile fluttered on Darcy's lips. Seemingly himself and Mr Bennet might get on much better than the older gentleman had reason to expect.

"I assume you are eager to return to your outpost," his companion shrewdly observed soon afterwards, fixing him with a not unfriendly stare.

"Aye, Sir. Very much so."

"Then be off with you. Send Lizzy to me when— Nay, leave her be," Mr Bennet reconsidered. "I will see her later. And when the dust settles, I shall have to ask you to join us too, so that we can determine just how we are to spring your news upon the others."

With a nod of thanks, Darcy hastened out.

কৈ ঙ্কু

"There is so much I wish to say," Elizabeth whispered.

She *had* tried, as they sat shoulder to shoulder, hands still clasped between them. Tried to find fitting words to explain the change – the horrible betrayal. Yet how could she speak of the gradual shift in her feelings and convey how she had grown to understand and love one man, without needlessly hurting the other even more?

It was a great deal easier to simply take the blame for the twist of fate, but Richard would not allow it, and his gentleness only served to increase her guilt a hundredfold, just like the subterfuge he had employed when he had claimed a different attachment.

Unbeknownst to her, Fitzwilliam almost wished he had clung to that claim tooth and nail, for anything was better than seeking to find out just *how* he had been replaced in her affections. Part of him rejected the very thought of that pernicious poison. But the other part needed to know – the smallest part, the self-deluding one hoping against all reason that this was nothing but confusion and mistake. That whatever might have taken root in the space left empty by his absence could be seen as spurious and shaken out at his return. So he let her speak, nay, urged her, until everything that could be said was out into the open, and neither of them could bear any more.

"I should go," Fitzwilliam said quietly.

Red-rimmed and wistful, her eyes darted towards him.

"Now?"

"Yes. I must. I hope your relations will forgive me— "

He did not finish, and there was no need to. Her hand gave an impatient flourish, as though to say that niceties concerned her no more than they did him, then came to rest on his lapel.

"Stay safe," she pleaded, her eyes brimming with tears, and at that he was suddenly torn between harshly asking what on earth did she care if he stayed safe or not, and sweeping down to crush her lips with his, until this madness of thinking herself in love with Darcy lost its hold on her.

He did neither, but merely offered a perfunctory "I shall."

She sighed and her hand dropped from his chest. Her eyes downcast, she bowed her head. Fitzwilliam did not reach to tilt her chin up for one last aching kiss – desperate, forbidden and so dreadfully tempting – but it was beyond him to draw back as yet.

He did not. Instead, he drew closer still, the familiar fragrance of jasmine and gardenia filling his senses, tormenting him with recollections from a life that was not meant to be.

He leaned forward by another fraction – to have done otherwise was equally beyond him – and the last indulgence he allowed, and hoped she would allow it too, without self-consciousness or mortification, was to press his lips on her brow. She started, but made no other move – neither withdrawal, nor further acquiescence – and they remained thus. For a long, harrowing moment. Until the words built in his throat, and he drew back by a hair's breadth to utter them.

'Farewell, my love. Be happy.'

With something of a groan, he choked them back at the intrusive, stabbing recollection of having emerged from delirium and hell to hear those selfsame words brokenly whispered by another.

He hastily stood and only said, "Adieu."

⁓⊙ ⊙⁓

The door that Darcy had been guarding was opened forcefully at last, and the two men found each other face to face. The pain on Fitzwilliam's – raw and exposed for a flicker of a second, until he became aware of his presence – was something Darcy had never seen in his cousin's countenance before, and prayed he would never get to see again.

His wish was instantly granted. The pain twisted into acute vexation – at finding him there or finding his pain witnessed or very likely both – and a brow came up, to match the scornful drawl:

"There. The coast is clear. Off you go."

Instinctively, Darcy's eyes followed the direction of the mockingly inviting gesture that had accompanied the drawl and found Elizabeth standing by the fireplace, her face averted as she sought to compose herself or dry her tears.

He did not walk into the parlour, much as he wished to.

Not only to give her some time to herself, which she doubtlessly needed, but also because he felt compelled to follow his cousin, who was already striding towards the staircase.

"What is it?" Fitzwilliam asked brusquely when Darcy caught up with him.

"Are you leaving?"

"What do you think?" the other cast over his shoulder.

"Let me ride with you," Darcy offered quietly.

His cousin snorted.

"Why? To assure yourself that I am truly gone? Or are you in such a haste to ride to Lambeth for a special licence?"

The defensive sarcasm neither fooled, nor deterred him.

"I do not wish for you to ride alone."

At that, Fitzwilliam stopped abruptly and spun round. He ran his fingers through his hair, the earlier antagonism replaced by understanding sadness. He sighed.

"Darcy, I know you well. You want everything packaged and neatly bound. But you must see that some things cannot be fixed as prettily as you might wish them."

"I know that. Still… What of you?"

His cousin shrugged, his glance drifting out of the tall windows.

"I shall weather it."

"What will you do?"

Fitzwilliam shrugged again.

"Old Boney will provide amusement for a while. And then… I might travel. Or settle abroad. Or something of that nature."

The words trailed off, and then there was silence.

Tentatively, Darcy reached to press his cousin's arm.

"Write, when you can bear to," he urged, and the other nodded absently. And still neither moved. But when Darcy cleared his voice to speak again, Fitzwilliam raised his chin and turned his head to face him.

"Go, Cousin! Live your life. Let me go back to mine. This is the only kindness I will ask for," he said impatiently, out of humour with the overlong exchange, and it was Darcy's turn to nod in understanding.

Everything along the lines of *'Treat her well'* remained unsaid.

Presumably his cousin could not bear to say it.

Or perhaps he already knew he would.

Unlike the last time, there was no brotherly embrace and the handshake was brief, almost cursory. But at least there was neither antagonism nor icy distance in Fitzwilliam's parting words, spoken without turning as he took to the stairs at a fast, steady pace:

"And if you are thinking of following me to the stables like some deuced lost pup then think again, by Jingo! You can send someone down with my belongings if you are at a loss for something to do."

⦿⦿⦿

After Fitzwilliam's abrupt departure, as unexpected as his arrival and greatly puzzling to most, for the remaining hours until dinner Blakehill Park was a theatre for several private conversations which were bound to shock every recipient of the startling disclosures.

The first was between Elizabeth and her father and later involved Darcy, as the older gentleman already said it would. This was the only one which was not about disclosures, but rather assurances, clarifications and, above all, plans.

Once nothing was left to settle between them, the three parted. Darcy went in search of Georgiana. Elizabeth found Jane. And as for Mr Bennet, he asked for a private interview with his own wife, to leave her so astounded by the intelligence he had to impart that, on first hearing it, Mrs Bennet sat quite still, unable to utter a single syllable. But great miracles are seldom known to last and at length she began to recover, fidget about in her chair, get up, sit down again, wonder and bless herself.

"Good gracious! Lord bless me! Only think! Dear me! Mr Darcy! Who would have thought it? Oh, my sweetest Lizzy, how rich and how great she will be – what pin-money, what jewels, what carriages she will have! What a fortunate change of plans! The poor Colonel is nothing to it, nothing at all. What a clever, clever girl! I am so pleased – so happy. Such a charming man. So handsome, so tall. Dear, dear Lizzy! A house in town. Everything that is charming. Ten thousand a year! Oh, Lord, what will become of me? I shall go distracted."

Her raptures were precisely what her husband had expected, hence the private interview in a remote part of the house, carefully chosen for the purpose. But what the lady herself did not expect, over and above the said communication, was a stern admonition, together with the firmest promise of no more pin-money, no new dresses and most decidedly no visits to town, if any further mention of Mr Darcy's possessions – including but not limited to the words *'ten thousand a year'* – or any reference whatsoever to Colonel Fitzwilliam should henceforth pass Mrs Bennet's lips in company. And by that he meant Mr Darcy's company as well.

"Evil tongues might mark Lizzy for a fortune hunter," he concluded darkly, "but I will not tolerate any encouragement from her own mother! I hope I have made myself perfectly clear, Mrs Bennet, and I trust you will not forget this conversation. Otherwise you are bound to discover I do have a will of iron."

Never in her life had Mrs Bennet been spoken to in such a manner, and finding grim determination where, for fifteen years at least, there had been nothing but vexing jests and baffling nonsense was highly disconcerting, and not a little worrisome.

It was a great hardship, what he asked of her – what, not bask in her own daughter's good fortune and much wiser second choice? – but the penalties Mr Bennet threatened to impose were very harsh indeed. He might not exert himself to carry them through, but what if he did? Pin-money and dresses – well, with careful management, those could be contrived. But no visits to town, to Jane's new home, to Lizzy's? That was beyond the pale. It did not bear thinking!

Thus, a promise was eventually extracted. More encouragingly still Mrs Bennet began pondering what item she could always carry about her person – a piece of jewellery perhaps, some ribbon or some sort of trinket? – that would remind her of the need to hold her tongue.

Pleased with his success, Mr Bennet was about to mention that the only item sure to never leave her hand was her wedding ring. But seeing that it stood for many other promises which had finished by being disregarded or forgotten – and, truth be told, not only by her – he smiled benignly and offered a different suggestion:

"What about looking-glasses, Madam? Shall we say that every time you see one and seek to meet your handsome face in it, you should consider yourself reminded of your promise?"

His wife beamed. Not so much at the unexpected compliment – experience had taught her that sometimes they were double-edged – as at the eminently practical solution from one who was notoriously impractical. Looking-glasses, what a splendid notion! No modern house was ever short of them. Aye. Looking-glasses would serve very well indeed.

Chapter 19

The journey from Oporto was long and wearying. Imprudent too, for he would have undoubtedly been better advised to travel with the reinforcements he had sailed with from Portsmouth and were heading the same way, rather than ride alone through foreign countryside at war. But the slow pace of marching men and rolling supply carts was not something he could countenance at present.

He might grow wiser later, and forbear exposing himself to danger in such a stupid manner. Perhaps. Perhaps not. The Lady Fortune had a way of compensating those whom she had already wronged and often found the means of keeping them from further harm.

Or so they say.

On this occasion, such tales were proven right. Colonel Fitzwilliam arrived unscathed in Ciudad Rodrigo, to a strangely comforting sense of homecoming. It was understandably familiar, the sight of the encampment preparing for the night. Red tunics milling hither and thither between canvas tents. The sounds – metal scraping upon metal, voices, harsh orders, the odd bark of laughter. The smells – of horse and trampled hay and smoke and meat griddled on the bivouac fires, reminding him that he was ravenously hungry. Familiar and welcome, they brought a sense of purpose.

The stark surprise of his comrades and his commanding officer at his arrival, weeks sooner than expected, brought nothing of the sort, nor was it welcome. No more than the intelligence his man had hastened to convey as soon as he had reached his quarters, that there was a letter for him, delivered in his absence.

Fitzwilliam had no need to open it to know what it contained. Perhaps one day he might bring himself to read it, but not tonight. Or perhaps it would be burned unopened. The latter choice was doubtlessly the wisest. And yet the letter was neither burnt nor read.

Instead, it was carefully folded into a very small rectangle – small enough to fit alongside a miniature into the folds of a well-worn velvet pouch.

❧

Drills and duties were resumed the following day and they provided occupation, as Fitzwilliam knew they would. They also gave him a very good excuse for eschewing a particular encounter. But once three days had gone by and the excuse had begun to smack of deliberate avoidance, Fitzwilliam found the time, or rather the energy, to call at a particular residence up the hill from the main square.

The avowed purpose was to bid his adieus, since orders had just begun to trickle down that the regiments would soon march across the mountains to outflank Marechal Jourdan's troops, strung out between the Douro and the Tagus. Yet he was not so foolish as to assume that nothing else would be discussed.

His expectations were confirmed. He had not been there above a quarter-hour when, with the now familiar forthrightness he had come to associate with a Latin temperament, or perhaps just with her, Doña Teresa remarked:

"I take it that you had a wasted journey."

"Indeed."

"How so?"

Fitzwilliam shrugged.

"The best-laid schemes of mice and men."

"Mice, Señor?" the lady arched a well-shaped brow in surprise.

Clearly the years spent in an English seminary had not made her familiar with the writings of a Scottish poet. Fitzwilliam felt obliged to clarify.

"I beg your pardon. I meant that matters have changed."

"And dining on the fatted calf had become more palatable?"

Incensed by the intimation that Elizabeth's motives could ever touch on the mercenary, Fitzwilliam frowned and retorted sharply:

"No! Not that."

"What, then?"

'Time. Circumstances' was what Darcy said, but Fitzwilliam forbore to use his cousin's words.

"He was there. I was not," he chose to say instead.

"Then she never loved you," Doña Teresa evenly observed.

Fitzwilliam had no wish to hear this either, so he stood.

"I fear I shall have to leave you now. I am wanted at the regiment to prepare for departure."

"Of course," Doña Teresa conceded and rose to her feet as well. "*Vaya con Dios, Señor*. I pray He will give you peace and keep you safe."

He bowed.

"*Que será, será.*"

Instead of being pleased at being answered in her own tongue, Doña Teresa cast him a severe glance.

"True. But only a fool would squander the gifts he was given, and the gift of life is the most precious of them all."

Fitzwilliam forced a smile.

"Fear not, Madam. I am not aiming to leave my bones on the field of honour. If I can help it."

"See that you keep your word, Señor, to the best of your abilities. These hills have seen far too much waste already."

"Aye. So they have."

"Will you return?"

"To England? No!" Fitzwilliam instinctively shot back.

"Then I wish you safe travels, wherever you go," the lady calmly said and saw him to the door.

It was a long time until he understood that, were it not for his fierce bitterness – stark proof of a broken heart – she might have made it clearer she was not asking of his return to England.

⁂

The large oak doors of the church stood wide open and the early May sun streamed through the arched windows to bathe the congregation in a golden light. The pews and wooden posts were adorned with cheerful clusters of evergreens, daffodils, bluebells and small branches covered in spring blooms – bright spots of colour that marked Elizabeth's path to the altar and to the man she loved.

Her heart brimming with joy, she saw him standing there, waiting, his eyes fixed on her with nothing short of adoration, his handsome face a glorious mirror of the overwhelming happiness she felt.

She walked to him, her hand clasped tightly on her father's arm. To her left and right, friendly faces beamed, unfamiliar for the most part, yet all turned to her in smiling welcome. His tenants, his people, gathered there to witness their master's joy and see him united in matrimony with their future mistress. And among them, in the front pews, her own dearest Jane, and Charles, and Georgiana. Her mother and younger sisters. Her uncle Gardiner and her dear aunt, who had travelled all the way from town to share in this very special moment.

It might have been the strangest feeling for Elizabeth to be married here, in the tiny Kympton Church, and not from Longbourn, as tradition claimed. But nothing was traditional about their courtship and no feeling other than elation could find its way into her heart as she took the last steps down the aisle to arrive at Darcy's side.

Her dearest Papa reached to press her hand, then gathered it in his and raised it to his lips before placing it in the waiting, upturned palm of the man she was about to marry – the age-old gesture laden with age-old meaning. Consent to the union. Authority relinquished. Her happiness entrusted into another's hands.

"Bless you, my Lizzy," he tenderly whispered, his eyes misting, as did hers, when he leaned to kiss her cheek.

Then the father stepped back. Smiling at each other, the couple stepped forward. The young reverend took his cue and spread his arms wide.

"Dearly beloved, we are gathered here in the sight of God and in the face of this congregation to join together this man and this woman in holy matrimony…"

The soothing words fell in gentle cadence, undisrupted, and no voice was raised to give just cause why they might not be lawfully joined together. Instead, the small church rang with harmonious rejoicing, once the young vicar pronounced that they be man and wife together, in the name of the Father, the Son, and the Holy Ghost.

❦❦❦

With a jolt, the beribboned open carriage rolled away from the church at last, to convey the newlyweds to Pemberley. Behind it three others followed and, at a slower, human pace, so did most of the congregation along with the vicar, to arrive at a wedding breakfast held on the wide stretch of lawn to the left of the great house, with all the cheerful informality of a village fête.

A wedding breakfast held at the groom's home rather than the bride's was as uncommon as the ceremony being solemnised in his parish, instead of the church where the young lady had worshipped in her unmarried years.

Yet the lengthy journey back to Longbourn appealed to no one and would have made no sense at all. Jane and Mr Bingley had barely settled at Blakehill with their young daughter, their cumbersome removal from Hertfordshire an operation of military proportions. Mrs Bennet, although greatly disappointed to forgo happy days spent in warehouses or with milliners and dressmakers, was of the firm opinion that the bird in hand was worth a dozen in the bush. Mr Bennet was compliant. Mary had no opinion. The youngest Miss Bennets were giddy with excitement. Georgiana was moved to tears at the changes in her brother's disposition and could not find it in her heart to frown over anything that would compound his joy. As for the two most interested parties, neither could countenance a separation a moment longer than strictly necessary. Even the days Darcy had been obliged to spend away from Blakehill in order to prepare the marriage settlement and procure the special licence had been a trial and an imposition.

And now they were behind them, along with the heartache.

A most notable absence from their cheerful gathering could not go unnoticed, by three of them at least, but that sole cloud – persistent and inwardly acknowledged – was forced deep down, and not encouraged to dim the brightness of the day.

The singular wedding breakfast continued in good cheer until Mr Bennet gave the signal for departure, and it was just as singular for the guests to be the ones to leave, instead of the bride and groom. Singular and utterly delightful for Darcy to find himself standing at the door to see his new relations off, with Elizabeth on one side and Georgiana on the other.

The dear girl had been inclined to accept Jane's invitation to return to Blakehill and stay with the Bingleys for a fortnight or so and Darcy would have been disposed to allow it, but a few days ago Elizabeth had gently protested at the notion.

"Pemberley is your home, Georgiana. There is no need at all for you to leave."

So she did not, but she became exceedingly uneasy once the carriages had vanished down the road and she was left with her brother and Elizabeth, not knowing what to say, nor where to look, and feeling most decidedly in the way.

"I think I shall go to the music room, if you would excuse me," she faltered, instinctively choosing her habitual refuge, and made her way into the house without waiting for their answer.

Her acute discomfort was readily apparent to her brother, not least because he felt more than a little conscious too. Overjoyed, of course, and barely containing his anticipation, yet at a total loss as to precisely where to go from there.

'Metaphorically speaking, naturally,' he thought with somewhat of a mischievous flicker of amusement in his eyes. He was in no doubt whatever as to where he would wish to go. But how to get there – and, more to the point, *when* – was a different matter altogether.

Unthinkingly, his hand went to his pocket watch. Quarter to six, it claimed, and Darcy scowled, inwardly cursing every remaining daylight hour – only to put his watch back and seek to smooth his features into a casual smile when he found that Elizabeth's eyes were fixed on him. Her cheeks glowing a soft pink that soon deepened into scarlet, she returned his smile.

It was intolerable that a grown man nearing his thirties should blush like a schoolboy, Darcy thought and forced a cough.

"Shall we go in?"

She nodded, and they did. But it was no easier indoors than out and he still struggled for the appropriate thing to say. Had the wedding been held in Longbourn Church, self-consciousness might still have been the order of the day at first, once they left for town together. But, for her, the journey would have been a natural progression. A gradual transition from one place to another – from one state to another.

Of course he could not have wished for anything better than spending their wedding night at Pemberley. But there were two hours at least until she would reasonably expect them to retire. She might be disconcerted and possibly alarmed if he suggested otherwise. Yet seeking neutral ways to while away the hours felt futile and bordering on the absurd.

"Would you wish to sit with Georgiana?" Darcy said at last. "Or change for dinner? Or… perhaps take a turn around the lake?"

"Dinner?" Elizabeth exclaimed with a shaky little laugh and shook her head. "I do not think I could eat another morsel."

Neither could he, but that was not the issue.

Releasing a long breath, he reached for her hand.

"What would you care to do?" Darcy asked softly, running his thumb in light strokes over her wrist.

She did not reply. Not for a long moment.

Her eyes downcast, she seemed absorbed by the slow motions of his thumb, until she suddenly looked up and her gaze fastened onto his, thoroughly robbing him of breath.

"Whatever you wish," she whispered back.

"Oh…"

Her eyelids fluttered nervously – once; twice – and still she did not glance away. The telltale blush crept into her cheeks again, and the corner of her lips curled up in an uncertain smile. Fresh tenderness welled in his heart at the touching mixture of maidenly daring and anxious innocence, sparking protective instincts that tempered and reshaped the passion, yet – predictably – sent it spiralling as well.

His hand came up to stroke her cheek and he leaned to kiss her. A lingering kiss, neither fierce nor insidiously persuasive, but rather a cautious, carefully restrained promise and grateful acceptance of her treasured gift.

"Come," he breathed against her lips, and he felt her shiver, but there was no fear in her eyes.

From the music room, a poignant tune rose to reach them, filling the great hall with haunting harmonies as they made their way up the great staircase, hand in hand.

They encountered no one – every member of the household was conspicuously out of sight. By the time they were halfway along the upstairs corridor, she was in his arms, and their kisses swiftly left the plane of tentative exploration to flare into smouldering abandon, urgent and compelling. It was only at the door into her chambers that Darcy saw fit to draw back, a very little. Eyes closed and breathless, he leaned his brow on hers.

"I should leave you now," he said, as evenly as he could. "Your lady's maid will be at hand, as soon as you summon her— "

He did not get to finish. Her hand came up to cover his lips, ever so briefly, before she stood on tiptoe to do so far more effectively with hers.

"No lady's maid. Not today," she whispered between kisses.

With a ragged breath, Darcy reached to blindly seek the handle and open the door. He swept her up into his arms to carry her into the bedchamber, brightly lit by the sunlight streaming through the windows, and leaned back to press the oak door shut.

Her hands were in his hair, fingers twisting themselves in it, and as soon as he set her down, his own hands took their cue from hers and found their way into her auburn tresses to take their chances with the elaborate hairstyle.

The little white flowers fell noiselessly to the floor.

Not so the hairpins. They dropped onto the naked floorboards and audibly bounced off, like the muted tick-tock of some unseen clock, ticking away the last remaining seconds until every wish would be fulfilled.

Darcy removed his coat — no mean feat with such a tight-fitting garment, when one was supremely unwilling to withdraw and avail oneself of the offices of a helpful valet. Even breaking the kiss was inconceivable. Her hands came up to offer tentative assistance and ease it off his shoulders, then help free his arms, until the coat fell in a graceless heap onto the floor. The waistcoat, hastily unbuttoned, had the same fate, and then the neckcloth.

Reluctantly, Darcy had to draw back for that, and struggle mightily to suppress an oath when the intricate knot stubbornly refused to oblige him and give way.

With a soft chuckle that broke the exquisite tension, Elizabeth reached to tackle the starched cloth with a great deal more success than he, leaving his hands free to roam into her tresses, knead small circles into her scalp and half-heartedly seek forgotten hairpins, then spread his fingers wide to comb through her hair and loosen it, until it fell in glorious splendour to her waist.

The tension, earlier broken by the offending neckcloth and Elizabeth's conscious chuckle, easily built again as her hands slipped under the collar of his shirt to send a shiver of anticipation through him with their lingering touch.

His mouth crushed down on hers again, as he reached under the cascade of glossy auburn hair to blindly seek and do battle with an unreasonable number of impossibly tiny silk-clad buttons. A low, impatient groan left his lips, to rumble against hers.

The next one rumbled deeper, into her open mouth, and all thoughts of frustration over tiny buttons left him as Darcy angled his head to better avail himself of the warm welcome.

By then, there was no just cause for frustration anyway.

The tiny buttons had already complied – well, most of them had – and his hands could slip unencumbered between the layer of shimmering silk and the ever so thin muslin, moulded to the perfect form it covered without the vexing interposition of unyielding stays. Sparing a thankful thought for their gratifying absence, Darcy nudged a wavy lock out of the way, to trail lingering kisses along the soft curve of her neck and come to rest in the small hollow above her collarbone, mindlessly whispering endearments as his hands roamed over her back, from slim waist covered in thin muslin to silky skin, warm and exposed above the lace border of the low-cut chemise.

Now opened widely at the back, the bridal dress did not require a great deal of coaxing to slip off her shoulders when her arms dropped from around his neck to stroke his chest through the remaining barrier of the linen shirt, but his hands traced along her bare arms to aid it in its progress nonetheless. It fell away, fold brushing against fold in a long whisper of crumpling silk, to shape itself into a creamy puddle at her feet.

Had the chemise followed suit, frothy and almost insubstantial, Darcy might have had his own representation of Aphrodite emerging from the waves of some distant sea, but downcast eyes and a fierce blush came to forcibly impress him with the need to tread slowly, at *her* pace rather than his.

He did not reach to hold her but took her hands instead, to place them back on his chest, covered with his own, until the dark-fringed eyelids fluttered and she looked up again. Her lips formed a barely audible "I love you" and Darcy swallowed hard, moved beyond words at the shyly offered trust and the implied consent. And still he did not stir, other than to lightly stroke her fingers. Waiting. Waiting for her to come to him – and finally she did. She stepped out of the crumpled dress, now left behind like an open flower as she willingly walked into his embrace to reach and press her lips on his bare chest, where the folds of his shirt had come apart. Darcy gingerly put his arms around her, hands still keeping to safe places – spine, shoulders – his lips slowly trailing a line from her temple to her cheek, until her quivering breath came to brush against his ear.

"I fear there are more vexing little buttons for you to contend with," she said, a hint of conscious laughter in her whisper.

His senses reeling with the intoxicating fragrance of warm skin scented with jasmine and gardenia, Darcy diligently applied himself to the appointed task, before sweeping her into his arms to exultantly carry her to the bed.

ༀ෧෧ஓ

Beyond the tall windows, the sky was aflame with the bright orange glow of the setting sun, interspersed with the pink-purplish shadows of a few harmless clouds.

Bright orange tinted the bedchamber, altering the shade of the bedclothes heaped around them in careless disarray, and likewise that of her wedding dress, still on the floor along with Darcy's own discarded apparel. Which was precisely where they ought to be. He could envisage no use for garments anytime soon. In fact, if he had his way, he would not need them for at least another fortnight!

A low chuckle rumbled in his chest, and he reached to drop a kiss on the unruly curls, still close enough to tickle his nose at every breath.

If he thought her slumbering, he was mistaken. Her head came up and she turned to rest her chin on his bare chest, eyes sparkling under thick dark lashes.

"What amuses you so?" Elizabeth asked and Darcy saw no reason why he should not tell her.

"A fair assumption," she grinned back. "Even a tad too soon, in my opinion," she teasingly added, letting her head drop back on his chest. "Poor Georgiana. I should not have dissuaded her from visiting Jane. Chances are she will get rather lonely."

"I suspect she might," Darcy conceded, with a show of nonchalance that might have been tolerably convincing had his voice not caught when she nudged up to kiss his neck.

He sought her lips again at such enticing provocation and only stopped from tender ministrations to tentatively say:

"Elizabeth…? I feel I should ask again…"

"Ask what, my love?"

"If you are… well?"

Her laughter brushed against his lips.

"I thought you need not ask. But since you did," she added between kisses, "no, not exactly…"

When he made a move to sit up in concern, she stroked his face with a rueful little chuckle.

"Forgive me. I should not tease you so. All I wished to say was that I am not merely *well*, my love. I am happy. Blissfully so. As I hope are you."

There was but one answer a red-blooded and thoroughly besotted man could make to the woman he had married that very day, after dreaming of her and despairing for a twelvemonth complete.

And much later, long into the night, when he lay awake cradling her in his arms, their limbs entwined, he gave humbly grateful thanks that this magic they shared was gloriously real and not a host of tortured imaginings any longer.

He also wondered how long it might be until she would address him by his Christian name – and indeed how long until he would even wish her to.

But, as he ran his fingers over the smooth skin, ever so lightly so as not to wake her, he knew beyond a shadow of a doubt that for now *'my love'* suited him very well indeed.

Epilogue

Whoever might have cast a glance over the wide stretch of lawn outside Pemberley House would have encountered a heart-warming and thoroughly domestic scene.

A rug was laid out, far from the water's edge, and upon it sat Elizabeth, her husband lounging alongside, propped up on one arm. A stack of cushions was between them, to support a round-faced babe in a frilly white cap, but since sitting up was a skill but recently acquired, the precarious balance was frequently lost, to their gentle merriment, whenever the little one sought to reach one of the toys or silver rattles scattered carelessly about.

Another youngster, the best part of eighteen months older, was tottering barefoot on the grass, occasionally munching on an apple, only to drop it in a while and cast around for other amusements, such as the flight of a brown and orange butterfly or the greater attraction of the wooden toys strewn within easy reach upon the rug.

The long white dress and the host of unruly curls framing the soft features might have misled the uninformed onlooker into thinking the Darcys had been blessed with two beautiful daughters, just as their father had once hoped they would be.

It was not so.

A firm admonition from the latter soon came to clarify the issue.

"Frederick, this is no way to treat your sister. You should not have snatched that cube from her. Pray give it back. *Now*, if you please. Well done. Thank you. Now sit with us and eat your apple."

"No. No apple. Throw."

"If you wish to throw something, this ball will serve much better."

"You catch, Papa!"

"I shall. In a little while."

"Throw the ball to me, Master Frederick," the nurse obligingly suggested, to receive smiles of appreciation from both her mistress and her master, but the youngster pouted, hastening to make full use of the first word he had ever learned.

"No! Papa catch."

"Perhaps later. Would you like to walk to the lake to feed the fish instead?"

The second suggestion was deemed far more acceptable, so the future master of Pemberley took the generous lump of bread his nurse offered, and also her hand, to scamper to the water's edge and throw large chunks into the lake, with squeals of delight when the fish came up for them, thus leaving his sister to her toys and his parents to their peaceable enjoyment.

Darcy leaned back on the rug with a diverted smile.

"I wonder where he gets his wilfulness from," he teased.

"Not from his parents, surely. They are both models of patient compliance," Elizabeth archly replied in kind and reached to run her fingers through her husband's hair. "I hope he learns to be a little more accommodating by the time his cousins come to visit," she smilingly added with a glance towards their son, and at that Darcy propped himself up again.

"Chance would be a fine thing. But I hope he does. Especially as by then there might be a new addition to our party."

Elizabeth beamed.

"Have you had any news from Georgiana?"

"Not yet. But I did receive a letter. I think you should read it."

He reached into his pocket to produce a folded piece of paper. A short missive, in a hand Elizabeth easily recognised.

"Richard?" she needlessly asked and Darcy nodded.

"What does he say?"

"See for yourself."

Elizabeth took the letter and unfolded it at once.

It was not the first they had received from Richard. Far from it. He had first written when the regiment had marched upon Vitoria, a month after their marriage. He had written to say that he wished them well, which had brought grateful tears to their eyes, but also great heaviness of heart, for the letter read as though he did not wish to leave any bad blood between them, should anything befall him.

The Lord be praised, nothing did.

He came away unscathed from the campaign in northern Spain, from the assault on the Pyrenees, from the battle that Lord Wellington had lost at Dresden and the great allied victory at Leipzig, and lived to tell the stirring and gruesome tale of Waterloo with nothing but a flesh wound to his arm.

Then he kept writing from his exploits abroad, from his lengthy exotic travels and lastly from Spain, where it had pleased him to settle for a while.

One day he wrote to say that he would soon be married. To a lady with a most musical name – Doña Teresa Patricia de Mendoza y Aguilar – whose fortune, as they had later learned, was as impressive as her pedigree.

The tidings brought great joy at Pemberley, along with the hope that their dear cousin had finally found his peace, and all the happiness that he deserved.

The hope was nourished by subsequent letters. They spoke of a cheerful, busy and comfortable life, and eventually brought the even happier intelligence of a son born to the couple, which made the Darcys' joy almost complete.

There was but one wish left and, at her husband's intimation that it might finally be granted, Elizabeth lost no time in learning the contents of the letter.

As was Richard's way, it was brief and to the point.

Darcy, it read

I shall not sport with your patience with a long missive this time.

I am only writing to say that we might see you before long.

Teresa feels that Arthur should take his first steps on English soil and get to know his family. My wife has none left. I have. And I am grateful for her understanding and her wisdom.

She is in the right, of course. 'Tis time to return, and I find I am ready. So chances are we shall see you in July. I have no further news for now, so I will conclude with my best love for you and yours.

Keep well until we meet again.

Yours ever,
Richard Fitzwilliam

Tears welled in Elizabeth's eyes as she folded the note and returned it to her husband. Tears of joy and gratitude that every cloud was seemingly gone, every heartache was over. And each of them had found their way to where they belonged.

Had found their way home.

...for now ...

BY THE SAME AUTHOR

FROM THIS DAY FORWARD
~ THE DARCYS OF PEMBERLEY ~

"A thoughtful and discerning sequel about the Darcys"
(Austenesque Reviews, September 2013)

On a crisp winter morning in a small country church, Miss Elizabeth Bennet married Mr Darcy, and her quiet, tame existence abruptly changed. The second daughter of a country gentleman is now many different things, to different people. Beloved wife. Mistress of a dauntingly great estate. Reluctant socialite. Daughter. Sister. Cousin. Friend. And as the days of her married life go by, bringing both joy and turmoil, the man who stands beside her is her shelter and comfort in the face of family opposition, peril and heartbreak.

Three very different Christmas seasons come to serve as landmarks to their lives, and there are blissful days and times of sorrow at the old English country house. And before too long, a time would come when Darcy must decide if he is prepared to risk everything for the sake of a full life together – or succumb to the collection of his fears.

"Quiet footsteps, eerily quiet, drew him from his trance. He looked up – and followed. The ghostly sound faded as he reached the eastern staircase and he took the steps two at a time, down to the very bottom. A madman's quest for he knew not what drove him to the gallery. In the light of the moon, from her portrait, his grandfather's first wife looked down upon him with the deepest compassion.
He dug his fingers in his hair.
A long, dry sob racked his chest as he pounded the frame of the unfortunate woman's likeness, and broken gilt plaster fell to the floor. He covered his mouth with his fist, stifling the groan. And ran out of the deathly silent room, chased by his demons."

THE SUBSEQUENT PROPOSAL
~ A TALE OF PRIDE, PREJUDICE AND PERSUASION ~

"Achingly romantic and exquisitely expressive"
(Austenesque Reviews, December 2013)

A number of broken-hearted characters from Jane Austen's most romantic novels are thrown together by the vagaries of fate, and all manner of unwise decisions are taken at this vulnerable time. But then their past creeps up on them – and what is there to do but face it, and hope that their convoluted paths will finally lead them to their proper place?

"Elizabeth," he murmured against her lips, her skin, her hair, and then her lips again. "I cannot forsake you! I cannot! I cannot lose you! I cannot bear to think of a life without you – 'tis not worth living, 'tis but a slow death! I cannot lose you! I beg you, do not send me away again! I love you! Elizabeth, I love you!"

Friends, rivals, foes, wrong choices and a duel – Fitzwilliam Darcy's life is never dull. *'The Subsequent Proposal'* follows him in his struggles to decipher the troubling enigma of Elizabeth Bennet's feelings, and correct the worst misjudgement of his life…

꧁ ꧂

THE SECOND CHANCE
~ A PRIDE & PREJUDICE – SENSE & SENSIBILITY VARIATION ~

"A Sensible & Sensitive Variation of Pride & Prejudice!
The expressive tone, the thoughtful and reverent approach to Jane Austen's characters and plots, the playful narratives, the winks at social commentary – Joana Starnes is a brilliant writer." (Austenesque Reviews, July 2014)

Soon after the Netherfield Ball, a troubled Mr Darcy decides to walk away from a most unsuitable fascination. But heartache is in store for more than just him, and his misguided attempts to ensure the comfort of the woman he loves backfire in ways he had not expected.

"Well, Mr Darcy, what will it be? The joy of music or of the printed word?" she asked, in a manner so highly reminiscent of their past interactions as to make him almost giddy with renewed hope.
The joy of you, he thought. My greatest folly was to ever walk away from it!

THE FALMOUTH CONNECTION
~ A PRIDE & PREJUDICE VARIATION ~

"Exquisitely and expressively written and certainly not to be missed."
(Austenesque Reviews, November 2014)

Just as Mr Darcy finally decides to propose to the enticing Miss Elizabeth Bennet, she is summoned to Falmouth, to meet a relation she never knew she had.

Thus, the ill-starred Hunsford proposal is avoided, but before he could even begin to understand his luck, adverse circumstances hasten to conspire against him, and Fitzwilliam Darcy is compelled to follow the woman he loves to the far reaches of Cornwall, into a world of deceit and peril, where few – *if any* – are what they seem to be…

Hammers pounded in his temples and Darcy bit his lip, endeavouring to set aside the pain of his own crushed hopes. Nothing mattered now more than her safety! What vile deeds was Trevellyan contemplating? Justice of Peace, was he – or a wolf left to guard the town? What was Trevellyan's game? Why did he pursue her? For her inheritance, rather than the God-given blessing that she was? Or for some other reasons of his own?

A wave of nausea threatened and dread gripped him, icy, terrifying – and worse, a thousand times worse than the searing notion of Elizabeth married to another. Was she about to fall into a trap of Trevellyan's making? Had she, her great-aunt and her entire family put their trust in a dangerous man?

MISS DARCY'S COMPANION
~ A PRIDE & PREJUDICE VARIATION ~

"Sensitive, poignant, and gloriously impassioned – skilled storyteller Joana Starnes gifts readers another stellar P&P variation that will once again inspire them to fall deeply and irrevocably in love with Mr. Darcy!" (Austenesque Reviews, August 2016)

Miss Georgiana Darcy is need of a companion, and she would much rather not have Mrs Younge. The recently bereaved Miss Elizabeth Bennet is in need of a position. When she accepts the one Mr Darcy offers, she finds herself in his near-constant company and gets to know him at his best. Not as he would present himself to strangers in some remote corner of Hertfordshire, but as his nearest and dearest know him. An excellent brother, landlord, master. A wonderful man, noble, kind – and impossibly handsome.

So who falls in love first? What of Mr Wickham and his dastardly ploys? And how is a lady's companion ever to have a future with one who could marry into the best houses in the land?

Staggering yet indisputable, the truth sunk in, and every fibre of his being accepted it as absolute. He loved her. This was why everything about her touched a chord. He ran his hands over his face, shocked by the revelation as much as by his own former blindness. How had he not seen it? How had he not known? When had she ceased to be a mere appendage to Georgiana, and had become part of his very soul?

When had she become so deeply attached to Mr Darcy? How had she been so senseless to allow him to take such a firm hold over her heart? Insidiously, treacherously, her feelings had grown without notice, until one day she had found herself thoroughly caught in this wretched mire of yearning and despair. For she had no hope. No hope whatsoever. Even as Miss Elizabeth of Longbourn she could have scarce hoped to capture the interest of one who could make an alliance with the most illustrious houses in the land. What hope could she possibly nurture now, when she was nothing to him but yet another name in the wages ledger – one of the many souls in his employ?

☙ ❧

MR BENNET'S DUTIFUL DAUGHTER
~ A PRIDE & PREJUDICE VARIATION ~

"…the rug was ripped out from beneath me, the complex emotions depicted in both characters were eminently sublime… a most magnificent and praiseworthy work and I entreat you to read it immediately if you haven't done so already!" (Austenesque Reviews, February 2017)

When Colonel Fitzwilliam's disclosures are interrupted by the bearer of distressing news from Longbourn, Miss Elizabeth Bennet is compelled to accept an offer she would have otherwise dismissed out of hand. An offer of marriage from the all-too-proud Mr Darcy. Yet how is she to live with a husband she hardly knows and does not love? Will she continue to feel trapped in a marriage of convenience while events conspire to divide them? Or would love grow as, day by day and hour after hour, she learns to understand the man she married, before she loses his trust and his heart?

༄༅ ༄༅

"For all the poor timing, you must allow me to tell you how ardently I admire and love you, Elizabeth. Marry me. As soon as it can be arranged. If we are wed before— That is, if the worst should happen…" He broke off again and released one of her hands to nervously run his fingers through his hair. "Damnation! How can this be said? I hate giving you pain in the midst of my proposal, but if we were to marry before you have to go into mourning, then you would not be left unprotected for goodness knows how long and I would have the right to keep Collins at bay. He might still stake his claims as soon as he could, the wretched scoundrel, but you would not be at the mercy of strangers until I am allowed to ensure your welfare. Can you see my meaning and not judge me for importuning you at such a trying time?" Then there was silence and he stood there, waiting. Waiting for an answer to something that made no sense to her. No sense at all. Ardent love. Marriage. Mr Darcy. Mr Collins. Mourning.

"I must go home," was all she could choke out.

"Yes. There is no time to lose. Let us take the shortest way back." A strong arm was wrapped around her waist. "Come, my love. We can speak further on the way."

The steadying support was withdrawn before she could protest at it or at the appellation, and the arm was placed under hers instead. She could not object to that. At least not until she found her feet, her balance and a fast and sure step that would take her back to the personage in haste and silence. Yet nothing could silence the unforgiving thoughts that whirled furiously in her head, leading to nothing but pain and confusion. Her father. Apoplexy. Mr Collins. Mr Darcy. Marriage. Mourning. Over and over. The surest way to lose her mind.

༄༅ ༄༅

All are available at Amazon in Kindle format and in print.

ABOUT THE AUTHOR

*Joana Starnes lives in the south of England with her family.
A medical graduate, over the years she has developed
an unrelated but enduring fascination
with Georgian Britain in general
and the works of Jane Austen in particular.*

*You can find Joana Starnes
on Facebook at www.facebook.com/joana.a.starnes
on Twitter at www.twitter.com/Joana_Starnes
or on her website at www.joanastarnes.co.uk/*

*Or visit her Facebook page
www.facebook.com/AllRoadsLeadToPemberley.JoanaStarnes
for places and details that have inspired her novels.*

CPSIA information can be obtained
at www.ICGtesting.com
Printed in the USA
FSHW011307051118
53562FS

9 781514 337554